Finding James Herriot

Michael J. Suit, DVM

Happy Trails and Best Wishes!

Printed in the United States of America
First edition

ISBN-10: 1530320887
ISBN-13: 978-1530320882

http://www.findingjamesherriot.com

To Kyla
A magical wife who let me go on an adventure

It's a long way back home.
It's a long way back home again.

Chapter 1

The large manila envelope consumed the small mailbox. With nervous anticipation, he attempted to pry the envelope free. His pace quickened down the path to his apartment as his anxiety tightened its grip on his fragile composure. As he entered the apartment, he tore the envelope open, revealing a familiar packet of neatly typed documents, thick and heavy. He threw his keys on the coffee table and quickly thumbed through the packet page by page, looking for the confirmation he was after — the one word that would fix everything: California. Each paragraph was lengthy, dry, and full of stipulations and expectations.

He had spent the last two breaks from veterinary college in Colorado working and volunteering at the prestigious Rio Vista Equine Center in Southern California, hoping the doctors would be impressed. In the end, they had assured him that he would be their top pick. The "matching" for externships created highly competitive, behind-the-scenes cutthroat competition.

But none of this had dissuaded him. He could almost taste the salty ocean breeze and feel the warm sand under his bare feet. The lure of the West Coast was invigorating, and he knew it was the key to solidifying his increasingly fragile relationship with Becca. His acceptance to Rio Vista would give Becca the beach house and the lifestyle she'd always dreamed of.

Papers, more papers, and finally...

"NVMSA Recipient – Dr. Jason Davies – is hereby requested to report to:
   Birdie Veterinary Clinic
   Dr. John Keating
   Birdie, Oklahoma
   Please Report no later than June 15th."

His eyes blurred, rereading what he thought was an obvious mistake; there had to be a mistake. He slumped onto the couch, letting out an exhausted, heart-broken sigh.

What? No.... There was some mistake. They must have mixed him up with someone else; this wasn't right. He launched out of his seat and immediately dialed the number at the bottom of the paperwork. The recording, prepared for his call, stated that the paperwork was double-checked prior to release and that further questions should be forwarded to another number. When he dialed the second number, the busy signal undermined his resolve as the deafening beeping taunted him.

"To hell with this! No way am I going to Okla-flippin-homa!"

This wasn't how it was supposed to go. What about the beach, the water, and all his California dreams? Surely he could contest this decision; there had to be some way out. He called the one friend he knew could fix this.

"Hey, Brother! Did you get your letter?" Tommy shouted above the voices and the sounds of clicking glassware in the background; it never took Tommy long to find a way to celebrate.

"Uh, well, not exactly. I...," replied Jason.

"What do you mean 'Not exactly'? I got mine just a bit ago and already called Rio Vista. What's the holdup?"

Jason's stomach tightened. "Something's wrong. They must have made a mistake with the paperwork, I guess."

"C'mon, quit jerkin' my chain, already."

"Seriously, Tommy; I don't know, but the way my letter reads they have me heading to Oklahoma."

"What the...? Where? Damn right there's a mistake. Let me make some calls and this will all get sorted out ASAP." Tommy grumbled, "Someone has their head up their ass! I'll get it figured out; don't worry, my friend. We'll be sipping margaritas with our toes in the sand in no time, trust me. Sit tight and I'll call you back." Before Jason could reply, Tommy hung up.

Jason dropped back onto the couch, wondering if it would all be that simple. Tommy always had a way of blowing through adversity, most of the time unscathed. If anyone could figure it out, it was him.

Jason grabbed his laptop and typed in *Birdie, Oklahoma*. As he hit the "Enter" button, his fears were realized.

Right smack dab in the middle of nowhere...Nowhere, Oklahoma.... Birdie appeared as a fly speck on the map, with State Highway 64 and County Road 14 converging over the top of it.

Jason got up and opened the freezer door. He stared at the selection of bland, taste-bud numbing microwaveable dinners, as the cold air blasted his perspiring face.

Tonight was going to be takeout....

The doorbell rang. He figured it was a delivery person from Canton Palace, but instead Jason found Becca in her sweats outfit, holding two brown paper bags.

He forced a smile. "You're not the regular delivery girl."

"Well, I figured no one else in this rat-hole apartment complex was ordering takeout from Canton Palace," she said, handing him the bags as she entered.

"Why's it so dark in here? It feels like doom and gloom. I thought we were going to celebrate?"

As Jason closed the door, he felt the lump in his throat growing. He set the food down and handed her the letter.

With a questioning look, she asked, "What's this?" Reading the letter, she looked up at him with a confused expression. "What's this mean? I've never even heard of 'Birdie!' I thought...."

Jason sat down, shaking his head. "I don't know; I

don't know. I talked to Tommy and he's going to make some calls...."

"Calls, my ass! You've got to be kidding me if you think I'm moving to Oklahoma!" She reached for her phone and began dialing.

"Who are you calling?"

"I'm calling my cousin in San Diego. She's an attorney and will know how to resolve this, quickly. Where's the rest of the paperwork? Hello? Hey, Angie, it's Becca." She disappeared into the bedroom, closing the door.

Jason stayed on the couch, with the smell of the food wafting around his head but now offering little temptation.

Chapter 2

After patient rounds the next morning, Jason found a quiet spot in a deserted office space on the second floor of the veterinary school. Although Becca's cousin had offered to review the paperwork, he realized the urgency of the situation and decided to call the number listed at the bottom of the information packet.

"Have questions?" it read. Relieved, he welcomed the idea that someone was there to help...or so he thought.

"Dr. Davies, as you should have already been aware, as stated on page 67 of the information provided to you, it is the duty of the applicant, in this case you, to relocate to any community within the continental United States, Alaska, or Hawaii that is designated within the NVMSA guidelines as a community in veterinary need. Dr. Davies, it is also your responsibility to report to the veterinary clinic listed in your paperwork on or before June 15th. Should you fail to report by this date, then legal proceedings could potentially be initiated, and we surely would not want that, would we, Dr. Davies?"

"No, uh, no, of course not; it's just that..."

"Dr. Davies, what you and many of your peers fail to understand is that the agreement you made was with the federal government, the United States of America. This contract represents a legally binding venture between you and the people of this country. Your unwillingness to complete your duties per this contract essentially results in a breach of contract with the United States federal government. I surely do not want to have to further discuss what proceedings would ensue should this unfortunate action take place, do you, Dr. Davies?"

"What? No, no, of course not; it's just..."

"Dr. Davies, I hope this information has been helpful, and that you will give serious consideration as you move forward with your obligations in this matter. Thank you, and good day." The phone line went dead.

What just happened? The woman had barely even taken a breath. His mind reeled. How the hell had he gotten himself into this mess, and more importantly, how was he going to get the hell out of it? He had tried to ask about requesting alternative locations, such as California, but it fell on deaf ears. The woman had stated that after four months, documentation could be submitted, as explained on page 127, to relocate based on a handful of criteria: "hostile work environment, deployed for active duty, death of spouse, mentally incompetent, felony charges."

Jason hung up the phone with that feeling that arrives in your stomach at 4:00 A.M. after a night of heavy drinking: the feeling that the toilet is going to be your new best friend.

Chapter 3

Becoming a veterinarian had sure sounded like a great idea. Images conjured from reading James Herriot had been the spark: images of driving along the countryside, helping man and beast. Jason reveled in the Scottish veterinarian's exploits and was quickly drawn into the enchanting, magical world of animal antics. The colorful world that Herriot painted had resonated with Jason at a young age.

However, the choice to pursue veterinary medicine hadn't been an easy one. Jason's family, while moderately supportive, failed to completely understand his motivation. His father and brothers were all in construction. Their large, tanned, muscular builds, jet black hair, and dark brown eyes were always in stark contrast to Jason's average height and slight, thin frame, hazel eyes, and sandy blond hair. As a teenager, Jason had overheard an elder in their church commenting that his parents had been wonderful to adopt Jason; the problem was, he wasn't adopted.

A week went by with no word from Tommy or Becca's cousin, but Jason tried to remain hopeful about his California future. However, finishing final exams while everyone celebrated their externships and associate positions became increasingly unbearable. Endless questioning from classmates drove Jason to the point of seclusion; he sought refuge in the few patients he had left as graduation day quickly approached.

He finally broke down and called his parents with the news. His mother remained positive, reassuring him that the good Lord worked in mysterious ways and that the move to Birdie was most likely a blessing in disguise.

"Your father and I are very excited about your graduation next week, and we hope we can be there; I mean, that is, if the project here gets completed on schedule."

"Mom, it's not that big of a deal. I understand if it doesn't work out."

"What? It most certainly is. It's just that sometimes your father's work has to take priority; I mean, it's just all-consuming sometimes. Well, I'm sure Becca must be interested in where you're headed; I've never pictured her as a small-town girl. Well, I'd better run, but keep us posted and I'll let you know when we'll be out there once I've had a chance to discuss it with your father."

Hanging up the phone, Jason already knew that his parents wouldn't make it to his graduation. Their intentions were sincere, but his father's work would take priority in the end. They would send a nice gift and card; his father might even call him. And the world would move on.

His phone rang. It was Tommy.

"Hey, Brother! What's shakin'? Hey, uh, well, I've run into a bit of a snag with this whole externship thing, I mean at least for now. I've still got some irons in the fire; I'm sorry, Brother. Don't worry; I'll have you out of 'Okieland' in no time."

But Jason knew better than to get his hopes up; moving to Oklahoma was quickly becoming his reality. In a matter of weeks, his life was headed in an entirely new direction of uncertainty, and he seemed to have no control over any of it.

Later in the day, word came from Becca's cousin that sealed the deal. "According to the documents that you signed, Jason, you're required to work in a community in any region of the United States that's deemed to be in need of veterinary services. Therefore, you are required to report to the town of Birdie, Oklahoma. I'm sorry, but you signed a deal with the federal government, and these types of contracts aren't breached, if you get my drift. The best you can hope for is an official transfer based on work environment, etc., that they might consider, but that could take months. Good luck."

Chapter 4

Graduation day arrived, bringing feelings of both excitement and dread. It signified the end: the end of school, studies, exams, and Fort Collins, Colorado. But while everyone else was celebrating, the thought of moving to the middle of nowhere hit Jason like a punch to the stomach.

Becca's incessant fury only further added to the drama. "No way in hell am I moving to some God-forsaken two-bit shit-kickin' redneck village in Oklahoma," had been one of her early rants. She had cooled with the vulgarities; however, the sentiment remained unchanged. Jason tried to call her, but got no answer. She wouldn't miss his graduation, would she?

He wanted to disappear.

His mother called the night before the graduation ceremonies. "You know your father and I are thinking of you, and we're so proud. It's just unfortunate that he's still buried with this job at Denali. I'll have him call you soon. We love you!"

As Jason made his way in line to receive his diploma, he was numb. No one was there to celebrate this moment he had worked so hard to achieve, and the one person he truly wanted to be there was MIA. It wasn't until after the ceremony, as other students' families gathered them around for photo opportunities and hugs, that he saw

Becca walking toward him.

"Congratulations, Dr. Davies," she whispered with an embrace.

"Thanks...I didn't think you made it."

"Well, there was a moment when I wasn't coming. But then I realized this isn't something I can blame you for. Are your parents here?"

He felt a rush of emotion welling up. Fighting back the lump rising in his throat, he whispered, "My dad has some work conflicts...."

"Are you kidding me? They can't even climb out of their own selfishness for two damn seconds!" She paused, then blurted out, "This is going from bad to worse. I'm living a nightmare! I cannot believe this is happening, after all I've been through with you. I don't know Jason, this is getting to be more than...."

"Stop! I know it's not what either of us wants, but I'm sure there has to be some way to fix it, right?"

She turned away, "I don't know. I wanted us in California before the holidays, and now that clearly isn't happening."

He put his arms around her, and as they stood there together, he longed for an easy solution. He loved her, and he wanted to make their relationship work, even if it had to be in Oklahoma.

Throughout the night of celebration, Jason was alternately melancholy and numb; this was the end of yet another chapter in his life. His friends were moving on to new jobs, locations, and lives, exciting adventures and opportunities they had all dreamed about. Veterinary school, a reality he never thought would end, was over. And in the blink of an eye, with a few speeches and some cake, it was gone.

Jason spent the next two weeks cleaning his apartment and boxing up his life. The past four years had seemed to flash by so quickly in the end. During those countless late nights in the anatomy lab, he had wondered if he would ever see the light at the end of the tunnel. He had made it through, but the darkness he now felt seemed to snuff out any light that was there. The highly anticipated race to the finish line of graduation left him empty and alone in his now vacant apartment.

On Jason's last night in Fort Collins, Becca became increasingly distant as the evening progressed. Complaining of an early morning meeting at work, she hugged him half-heartedly. "Call me tomorrow." She turned and disappeared out into the dark, cool evening. He didn't want her to go, knowing that this would be the last time they would see each other before he left. He stood in the doorway briefly and wished for a different, happier ending.

"Becca! Wait!" Jason raced after her. She stopped and turned. He gently grabbed her arms. "Maybe, maybe we could just disappear.... Maybe we could just make this all go away and take off to Europe, or the islands, or something...."

Confusion spread across her face and he watched it collide with frustration and annoyance. "What the hell are you talking about? This isn't some romantic comedy; we can't just disappear! Are you fucking crazy? I have a job! I have a life here, friends, and I don't want to live like a wanted fugitive gypsy!" She paused and took a breath, trying to temper her emotional throttle. "You and I know what we want, what we've dreamed about, and it isn't going to be fixed by running away to some distant land, and that sure as hell includes Oklahoma!" She kissed his cheek, got into her car, and drove away.

Jason stood on the sidewalk, watching the taillights of her car disappear as any remaining hope slowly drained from his body.

On Monday morning, Jason loaded the last of the boxes into his truck, took a final look around the apartment, and locked the door. Standing outside, he smelled the familiar scent of pipe tobacco. As he made his way down the concrete walkway, he gave a slight nod to the old man in the brown cardigan whom he passed almost every day but whose name he had never learned.

"Good luck to you, and take care of yourself," the man

said.

Startled, Jason turned and smiled. "Thank you; I will."

As he made his way to the interstate, the sky grew ominous and dark and the wind started to whistle through the truck doors. Jason rode the steering wheel, trying to steady the truck in its lane. As he made his way south, rain began to fall, working to further lower his melancholic mood. Entering the heavy Denver traffic, he wondered if he should just turn around; maybe all of this was a grand mistake. He could figure something out, couldn't he? It wasn't like they were going to send armed guards or military police out after him if he never showed up, would they?

Rain continued off and on throughout the morning, following him east all the way to the Kansas State line. In all the dreariness, Jason became lost in thoughts of his childhood, homesick for his family, and angry that he wanted to be home. But where was home? His family's transient lifestyle had never allowed him to feel much a part of any community for very long. His father's work as a construction contractor required moving the family every few years, and even every few months at times, always dependent on the next job. Making friends became something to resist undertaking for fear that he would have to say goodbye in the next week or month. Fort Collins had been as much of a home these past several years as any home he had experienced growing up.

He had decided that he would spend the night in

Garden City, Kansas, arriving there in the middle of the afternoon. Most people would have continued on, but Jason, for the first time in his life, didn't feel compelled to rush on to his final destination. Dr. Keating wasn't expecting him until Wednesday, and Jason had no desire to get to this gig any earlier than he was required to. The attendant at the motel's front desk seemed mildly surprised to have a guest wanting to check into his room at 3:30 in the afternoon.

Jason dropped onto the bed and closed his eyes. "What the hell have I done?" he mumbled. The cool air from the window air conditioner felt good upon his skin, numbing his senses as he drifted off to sleep.

He panicked as he jolted awake, worried that he was late. But then remembering where he was, he laid his head back on the pillow. No one was looking for him, and he had nowhere to go. He looked at the clock on the nightstand: 5:17 P.M. He made his way back to the lobby in hopes of finding food somewhere nearby. The front desk attendant directed him to the "Wagon Wheel Inn," within walking distance of the motel.

The expansive and deserted restaurant exuded a smell and décor of bygone Saturday nights. Standing in the red Naugahyde landscape, he imagined wild nights of dancing and drink, raucous and carefree. The deserted hostess stand hinted that this wasn't the hotspot of Garden City anymore. He waited patiently, and then, from out of nowhere a diminutive, elderly Asian man appeared from behind a swinging door.

"Goooood eeeeevening," he said. Jason was taken aback by the man's smile, which displayed only one upper incisor. The menu he handed Jason felt heavy in his hand; was there really that much to choose from? The man made no offer to seat Jason, but patiently waited, smiling, as Jason reviewed the menu items.

"Okay, well, it all looks good. I think I'll have the enchiladas," said Jason.

The man's smile disappeared. "Uhhh, noooo enchiladas tonight, all gone."

"Then may I please have the lasagna?"

"So sorry again, no lasagna tonight."

Jason scoured the menu, looking to avoid a strike three, and then paused. "How about the roast beef sandwich?"

The man hung his head briefly, staring at the floor before replying, "Again, please excuse, but no roast beef tonight."

Jason slowly closed the menu. "What *do* you have to eat?"

The man's one-toothed smile reappeared. "I recommend the chicken fried steak; very good, yes, very popular menu item!"

Jason nodded in agreement as the man bowed slightly and disappeared.

He found a nearby table and sat down; he forgot to tell the man that he wanted it to go. Looking at his phone, he hoped Becca had tried to reach him, but "No missed calls" displayed across the screen. She was still at work, and she wouldn't be home until late, especially on a Monday.

The man reappeared. "You would like to eat here or take to go?"

"To go, please," replied Jason.

The man bowed again and disappeared. Jason wondered if the man was also the cook.

Minutes later, the man reappeared, but this time carrying a large paper sack. Jason paid, thanked him, and made his way back to the motel.

Had he eaten chicken fried steak before? It was surprisingly tasty for small town fare. Turning on the television, he wondered how there could be so many channels, and yet nothing worth watching. He turned off the TV and lay on the bed, staring at the stained popcorn ceiling. He heard voices in the room next door, and he found some comfort in knowing that he wasn't totally alone here.

Tears welled and burned as they rolled down his face. Loneliness was an all too familiar old friend with impeccable timing. He recalled the struggles of his childhood, with countless moves across country. But now, after completing his veterinary program and landing a new job, loneliness had returned rather than excitement.

Wiping his face, he couldn't look at himself in the mirror as he brushed his teeth. He could hear his father's voice: "Men don't cry." He crawled into bed and turned out the light. Tomorrow would be better.

Chapter 5

Jason was up early on Tuesday and on the road before dawn. The quiet stillness in the early morning hours only gave him more time to think; was he prepared for all this?

The sun rose quickly as the heat of the day began to take hold; this humidity and stifling heat wasn't anything he'd had to contend with in the Rocky Mountains. The A/C in the truck needed work and only moderately cooled the truck's interior as the heat continued to rise across the barren, flat wasteland.

Thirsty and in search of a restroom, he stopped at a nondescript faded metal building along the lonely stretch of two-lane highway. The place looked deserted, and Jason paused as he approached, wondering if it was even open. The clerk behind the counter remained fixed on the small electronic game in his hand, nodding toward the rear of the store when Jason asked for the men's room. A bottle of water and small bag of candy later, Jason climbed back into the truck. He sat staring out the windshield, frozen in thought; a flash of Willy Wonka surfaced in his head: "Never back up, always go forward!" Jason smirked and started the truck. The sun and the heat continued to intensify and as the poor truck struggled to keep up, Jason finally turned off the A/C and rolled down the window. "Where the hell is this place?"

Just then he caught a glimpse of a small green sign:

"Birdie, Population 3325." He continued on, passing a small café and gas station, but the landscape quickly returned to pastures and cropland. "Was that it?" Jason pulled the truck to a stop, puzzled. If you've ever been to Birdie, Oklahoma, you probably drove right past it before realizing that the café and gas station on State Highway 64 are the only indicators to turn off; the actual town itself is a half mile east. The desolate landscape gave no invitation as Jason slowly made his way back to the junction. The dry, bleak grassland was pockmarked with deserted vehicles and dilapidated structures one good windstorm away from falling down. "What the hell had he done?" he wondered. This was no place for him.

Off the main highway, the narrow, rough road became difficult to navigate, as Jason attempted to maneuver through a series of potholes and dead animals. Couldn't he just turn around right now, as if he hadn't even been there? Who was going to miss someone they hadn't ever met? He slowed the truck, pulling it onto a small dirt patch at the end of a row of large purple-colored trees, and shut off the engine. The overwhelming feeling of homesickness consumed him. This wasn't how it was supposed to be; this wasn't part of the life he'd dreamed of. He had to get the hell out of here; what would they do if he didn't show up? The worst that could happen would be that he'd just have to pay back his federal school loans, right? Suddenly he heard the sound of cow bells, and seemingly from nowhere, cows surrounded the truck from

21

all sides, lazily making their way along the road as if they had all the time in the world.

"Ya lost, feller?" rattled a voice from outside the truck window. Jason turned with a jump, startled to see a thin, stubbled, gray-haired older man peering into the cab. "You lookin' for Birdie, well, almost there, just up ahead where those houses start, up there," rambled the man. "But maybe you ain't lost, and then maybe you're out of gas. You out of gas? If you need gas, surely I can get the girls back to the house, and come back with some gas. But...maybe you ain't out of gas, and maybe you just lookin' at these trees. They sure are pretty this time of year; these trees are genuine Muskogee Crape Myrtles. You don't look like you're from around these parts, and, well, I'm guessin' you ain't never seen Muskogee Crapes."

Jason, waiting for the man to take a breath, interjected, "No, I'm alright, just on my way to Birdie and...."

"You got business in Birdie?"

"Well, yes, I suppose, I'm going to meet with Dr. Keating...."

"You know old Doc Keating? Well then, right good feller, Doc is; hey, come to think of it, I think I heard he's getting himself a new helper vet over there at the clinic, least that's what he's tellin' me the other day when I stopped in." Just then the man's facial expression changed to a look of recognition. "Well, hey now, maybe that's you, maybe you the new doc over there with Keating." The man extended his hand. "Name's Lefty, Lefty Putnam, at your service."

Jason didn't know what to say; he was speechless. What was happening?

"Say, if you'd be going in to the clinic, maybe I could catch a ride with you, that'd be alright? I mean, I could show you around the town if you need, too."

In a split second, Jason went from the burden of carrying his own homesickness to carrying an unwanted hitchhiker. As the old man slowly made his way through the cows and around the front of the truck, Jason could hear his mother's voice in his head: "Promise me you'll never pick up a hitchhiker; they will take you out in the desert, stab you, and then leave you for dead!" A second later, the old man seated himself in the passenger side of the truck, grinning from ear to ear.

As Lefty waved him on, Jason paused, looking at all the cows still surrounding the truck. "What about your cows? Shouldn't we move them somewhere?"

"Oh, they'll be fine, they know the way home," Lefty quipped, shouting at the Brown Swiss standing in front of them. "Louise, you take these girls on home, hear me? You get them back to the house and no messin' around, I mean it!"

Jason was unsure of what the hell was going on; maybe he had landed in a parallel universe or stumbled onto some redneck reality TV show. They drove in silence as the edge of town became apparent. Lefty jumped into tour guide mode as the downtown shops and courthouse came into view.

Traffic slowed to a crawl as an elderly man in an antique-looking Buick attempted to parallel park. Jason felt his anxiety level accelerate. He wanted to hurry up and get to the clinic, and yet at the same time he didn't want to.

Downtown Birdie was centered on a massive granite courthouse. Large oak trees provided a hundred-plus years of shade to the surrounding grounds and park. Storefronts outlined the courthouse square, in perfect small-town harmony. Jason didn't believe that towns like this still existed; Birdie seemed to be a town that time forgot about in 1955. A gray-haired store clerk in a pressed white shirt stood in front of the corner grocery, placing varieties of apples onto a wheeled cart. The adjacent hardware store displayed its impressive assortment of shiny new lawn mowers on the sidewalk in front. Women in colorful wide-brimmed hats exited the coffee shop on the next corner, as children chased each other out of "Neisner's Five and Dime."

"Now if you ever git a hankerin' for a good cheeseburger, you got to go there, 'Johnny's.' The best burger joint this side of Tulsa, not lying, not lying," Lefty smirked, crossing his heart with his finger. And over there is 'Fred's Shoe Repair,' oh he does good work, but you got to watch him with his resoles. Thinks pretty high of those damn resoles...."

Jason stopped at the light as Lefty rambled on, and at

that exact moment a black BMW pulled up next to him. The woman behind the wheel in her dark sunglasses caught his eye. She turned and smiled as the light turned green. She quickly disappeared up ahead, as Jason remained stopped at the intersection. Who was she, where had she come from, and what was she doing here? Horns honked behind him as Lefty chuckled, "Hey, you going to fit right in around here."

Jason regained his focus, deciding to cut the tour short. "Lefty, which way to Doctor Keating's?"

"Oh, sure thing, well, I 'spose the best way is down 10th to the next stop sign and turn east, but why don't you let me out at the next corner. I need to pick up some nails and glue."

"But how will you get back home?" Jason asked, only slightly concerned.

"Oh, like always, just walk until somebody stops and gives me a hop, and don't worry about me Doc, you got bigger problems with old Doc Keating...."

Jason pulled to the curb at the next corner, thanking Lefty for his help.

"Oh, surely was my pleasure, and sure hope it all works out with Doc, but...if it don't, you always got a milking job at my place, cross my heart." With a short whistle and a wink of an eye, Lefty turned and walked away.

Jason had spoken with the veterinarian at the Birdie Veterinary Clinic; the conversation had been brief, and his potential new boss sounded grumpy and old.

Keating, looking to slow his caseload by bringing a young veterinarian into his practice, had applied to the Department of Agriculture for assistance through the program. Jason was not encouraged when he found out that Dr. Keating's clinic had had a revolving door of veterinarians. In recent years, Keating had three veterinarians leave the clinic.

Jason scoured the street signs, trying to remember Lefty's directions. Had he missed the street? He continued to drive around the courthouse, wondering how he could be so lost in such a small town. Finally, he spotted 10th Street, and shortly afterward he spied the Birdie Veterinary Clinic sign.

Jason pulled into the clinic parking lot and shut off the truck's engine. He sat quietly for a moment, wondering if his stomach would ever feel right again. The building did not exude fresh and new like he'd dreamed, but instead the stale, pale green exterior and cinderblock construction reminded him of something the National Forest Service might have built in the early 1960s. He took a deep breath and headed toward the front door.

As he entered, a woman seated at the front desk jumped to her feet with a smile.

"Good morning, I'm Jason Davies, here to see Dr. Keating," Jason said quietly.

"Oh, Dr. Davies, what a pleasure to have you here!" The woman scurried from behind the counter. "Welcome to Birdie; I'm Mary." She was tall and slender, with short gray hair; Jason sensed almost immediately her worldly air. The kindness in her eyes told Jason that she had to be the wife of a tough-talking, crusty old veterinarian. Through a doorway a young woman appeared, beaming and energetic.

"Dr. Davies, I would like to introduce Shelly Martin; she is our most amazing veterinary assistant here at the clinic."

"It's a pleasure to meet you, Dr. Davies." Shelly extended her hand.

"Thank you; it's nice to meet you." Shelly's firm handshake and cowboy boots indicated she was no wallflower.

"Dr. Davies, let me introduce you to my husband; please follow me." Mary guided Jason down the narrow hallway to Keating's office. "Please have a seat and John will be right in. We are so glad you are here." Mary gently patted Jason's shoulder before exiting the room. As the door clicked shut, a bolt of panic raced through him. He was instantly returned to tenth grade, alone in the assistant principal's office after skipping school one day. During a particularly rough move to a new town and new school, the assistant principal had been hell bent on squeezing Jason as to his whereabouts that day. Jason had been unwilling to share his harmless trip to a wooded area outside of town where he simply sat and grieved his situation of moving to yet another school. The silence had cost him two weeks of in-school suspension.

Suddenly the door flew open with a sudden jerk, and a tall, lean figure entered with a tired confidence. Slowly removing his low-slung cowboy hat, an aged Clint Eastwood with leathered and tanned skin turned and stared at Jason with his steel blue eyes. He removed a small white handkerchief from his back pocket and wiped his brow before dropping into the leather chair behind the cluttered desk. Jason felt the sweat beading up on his face; his gut screamed to run, far and fast. Keating looked like a force to be reckoned with, and Jason immediately knew that this was a bad idea.

Jason read Keating's face, sensing he was a man of few words.

Keating finally broke the silence. "It's sure the hell hot out there today. You made the trip okay I take it?"

Jason nodded, swallowing hard because his throat felt tight and dry. "Uh, yes, it was long, but everything went fine, thank you."

"Good. Well, I suppose we need to get down to some housekeeping details, and then get on with it." Keating quickly ran through a list of duties and expectations. Jason's mind raced, wondering how this was ever going to work. He was not the toughened cowboy equine vet, but the city kid who liked horses.

"Bottom line here, Son, is that you keep your nose clean and stay out of my way, and we will get along just fine. The patients that come through here need to be seen timely and no monkeying around, got it?" Jason nodded, swallowing hard, his mouth still dry.

Keating glared at him, and then without a word got up and walked out of the room. What was Jason supposed to do now?

"Davies!" boomed Keating's voice from down the hallway. "Let's go, Bud, we've got a busy afternoon."

Jason followed Keating through his afternoon appointments, and as the last horse was loaded onto the trailer, Jason quietly grabbed his things to go. Dr. Keating appeared in the doorway. "You look like you could use a drink."

Jason paused nervously, wondering if he was being tested. Looking into Dr. Keating's discerning eyes, he realized it was a simple yes or no question; nothing more.

Keating revealed a small dark bottle, poured two glasses, and handed one across the desk. "Hope you drink Scotch, and if you don't yet, you will soon." Keating sipped in silence, staring out the small corner window.

Jason placed the glass to his lips and could feel his nose hairs burning. This stuff was toxic. Who could drink it? He paused, and then resolving himself to the situation, chased the drink in one swallow. His throat was on fire and he choked back a cough, not wanting to draw attention.

"It's been warm here," said Keating. "Not normally this warm."

Jason nodded, unsure of what to say.

"Not sure we've had heat this long for a while now, but makes that corn come in nice and ripe though," said Keating.

"Really, they grow a lot of corn around here?"

Keating nodded between sips of the Scotch. "Oh, not so much anymore, but I tell you, nothing better than fresh sweet corn from these parts, absolutely nothing better."

Keating poured a second round and refilled Jason's glass.

"Anyone shown you your place?"

"No," Jason replied.

Keating's rugged and worn face revealed a spark of a grin as he said, "Well then, let's you and me take a ride." Keating grabbed his glass and stood. He waved for Jason to follow. At the back of the clinic's property stood a small green metal garage. Keating opened the door, revealing an historic Army green motorcycle, complete with sidecar. The smell of oil and gasoline rushed Jason's olfactory senses, as his eyes laid witness to the weather- and war-beaten machine. It appeared to be an original, as if it had just been driven from enemy lines during World War II; Jason wondered if it even ran.

Keating replied in his deep, throaty voice, "Yes...it runs. It runs well, actually. I know it doesn't look like much, but she still has some life in her. Get in."

Jason tentatively crawled into the sidecar. Realizing that he still had the drink in his hand, he began climbing back out, when Keating grumbled, "Where are you going?"

Jason froze. "Well, I realized I still had my drink, and..."

"Awww." Keating waved him off. "Keep it, we're not going that far; you're in Birdie now."

Keating fumbled for a switch under the seat before kicking the pedal.

Pffft...Pffft....

He kicked the pedal again and then once more before he grumbled some words that Jason didn't understand. Gruffly, he turned to Jason and handed him his Scotch. "Here, hold this, and don't spill it."

Keating made more adjustments and then kicked the pedal once more. The engine came to life with a long, slow moan, and then quickly rumbled to a deafening, unbridled roar. Smoke filled the garage as Keating geared the motorcycle in reverse.

Without saying a word, Keating grabbed his glass back as the motorcycle lunged forward. With no regard to the traffic on the main road, Keating shifted the motorcycle through its gears. He paid no attention to their speed, while Jason gripped the side of the car, hoping this night wouldn't be his last.

Keating slid them tightly through the neighborhood streets, around several tight corners, nearly missing a woman and her small, portly pug. The woman smiled and waved.

Seconds later, they stopped suddenly in front of a one-story 1960s ranch-style house. Jason was immediately intrigued as he looked at the well-manicured lawn with the large oak trees providing a shaded canopy to the lush, green, freshly mowed yard. The house had been cared for and even looked like it had recently been painted. A smile came across his face as he thought, "This might not be so bad."

Keating shut off the motor and headed up the main walkway. Jason followed with anticipation of what he would find inside: a spacious two-bedroom house suitable for the newest doctor in Birdie? Keating unlocked the front door. The house's interior was warm and inviting, with large leather couches and a gigantic flat screen TV in the living room.

Jason's smile grew as he realized that the job in Birdie might not be as dismal as he had previously envisioned. Jason marveled at his luck, while Keating ducked into the kitchen. As Keating returned from the kitchen, he handed Jason a set of keys. "Well, are you ready to see your new home?" he asked.

Jason was confused. "Well, isn't...?"

"This is Pauline's place. She's a great gal; used to work for me at the clinic. She offered to give you a place to stay."

Dazed and confused, Jason followed Keating

hesitantly out of the house, across the gravel drive, to the barn. The building before them was the antithesis to the freshly manicured and painted house, and at first glance he wasn't sure they were in the right place at all. The combination of rusted metal and weathered wood indicated that the entire structure had been someone's idea of a "weekend work in progress." A small door and window at the end of the barn looked deserted and uninviting. The peeling red paint on the old weathered barn gave Jason little hope about what he would find inside. Whoever had cared for the main house hadn't had the same vision for the barn out back. The smell added to the ambience as Jason walked by a pen of large sows wallowing in the mud. "Humidity, flies, and animal feces seem like a great living environment," he thought to himself as they walked toward the small, paint-peeled door.

Jason fumbled with the key in the lock. Finally, with a hard turn and a push, the small door creaked open and Jason tumbled into a small, dark room.

Looking around, Jason wondered if this was it, or where the rest of the apartment was. The room smelled of mothballs and dusty drapes. It didn't appear as if anyone had lived in the space for years. "Well, it sure as hell isn't much, but it should work," Keating said as he cleared a cobweb from around the overhead light and a family of spiders scurried across the ceiling to safety.

Jason felt his face flush, as sweat began to build on his

forehead. What the hell had he done? This was a mistake.

He turned to Keating, but before he could object to his new accommodations, Keating turned to the door, saying, "Well, let's get you back to the clinic to gather your things; got a busy day tomorrow."

Jason was quiet as the motorcycle roared through town. The apartment in the barn was a disappointing dump—something Becca would never step foot into. What had he done?

And so began life in the barn....

Chapter 6

Jason moved his few belongings into his new home. Cobwebs and dust covered the small, stale studio apartment. Jason felt helpless as to where to begin. Everything was foreign and unwelcoming in this small, dark space. It reminded him of his bunk bed at summer camp; how lonely he had felt that summer as his parents drove away.

The room included few furnishings: a double bed, a chest of drawers, a small plaid chair, and a nightstand with a lamp. The walls were a drab pale blue and the even less inviting industrial pea-green carpet swirled in a pattern of casino-esque chaos that made Jason slightly nauseous. Two small windows were covered by dusty metal blinds, layered in tell-tale signs of fly deposits and spiderwebs that only further illustrated the squalid accommodations.

Looking for something to clean with, Jason found a small spray bottle of what smelled like ammonia under the kitchen sink. He made an attempt at cleaning the necessary areas: toilet, shower, sink, in that order.

He then found his sheets and made the bed. He crawled onto the bed, seeking something familiar and comforting amidst his swirling reality. He laid his head on his pillow and wondered how long it would take the smell of this place to infiltrate all of his belongings.

He tried to call Becca, but she didn't pick up, probably still at work. Distance made the heart grow fonder, right? He worried that this move and their work schedules would set a course for a long-distance drift apart.

The phone rang. She was finally calling.

"Hey! How are you?" Jason exclaimed.

"You made it," she replied.

"Yeah, finally; the drive took longer than I anticipated, but I met the vet and found the place I'm staying. It's not exactly what I had in mind, but it should work, at least until we can find something else. So when do you think you can come out? I already miss you."

"I don't know, Jason.... We're gearing up for some things at work, and the weekends are going to be tight. I guess I can check the schedule and see, but not guaranteeing anything. Where is this place you're staying? I thought you told me it was supposed to be furnished...and nice."

"Well," he said, glancing at the threadbare, dusty chair, "it's furnished, but it definitely needs a woman's touch."

"So...it's a dump; is that what you're saying?" she groaned with a sigh.

"Well, I wouldn't say that, but it's only temporary. I mean until we figure out how to get you here and find something."

There was a long pause.

"Yeah...well...I need to get back to a meeting..."

"K...thanks for calling back...wish you were here."

"Yeah...talk to you later," she replied.

"Love you," he said.

"You too," she replied flatly as she hung up.

Chapter 7

Jason lay on the bed, staring at the stained, discolored ceiling. The smell of mothballs and dusty carpet irritated him. He could feel his skin itching, reminding him of a recent hotel bedbug outbreak in Denver. This place was disgusting. Tomorrow he would be on the search for air fresheners, a candle, something....

He readied himself for bed and climbed under the sheets. He lay in the darkness, staring at the water-stained ceiling tiles and thinking about his situation. What the hell had he done? Had he made a mistake in signing on for this? It would help with student loans, and it would reduce the financial rope around his neck, but it also created the potential for losing Becca. He rolled over and tried to close his eyes; the truth was it might already be too late. Their relationship had struggled from the beginning, but since Becca's promotion at work, and then Jason's increasingly difficult schedule at school, the conflict had only worsened.

BOOM! BOOM! BOOM! The wall shook.

"What the...?" he exclaimed, leaping from the bed.

He paused and listened. Another bang made him jump once more. He slowly unlocked the small door in the kitchen that connected the apartment to the rest of the barn.

He opened the door. Staring back at him were two

glowing eyes. The largest red and white Hereford bull he'd ever laid witness to stared back at him. Its eyes were molten red in the darkness, encased between the animal's gnarled and twisted horns. A large nose ring protruded through both nostrils, and a thick, purulent layer of mucous dangled in midair.

The bull stood motionless, glaring at him. Jason tried to remember from vet school the proper method for handling bulls. Should he move slowly? Look larger? Look him in the eye? He warily closed the door and quickly locked it, as the door suddenly shook with another thud. It was going to be a long night.

Morning brought the sound of pigeons cooing above him in the recesses of the ceiling. His eyes opened in an instant, panicked that birds were in his room. He climbed out of bed and nervously approached the bathroom. The fact that he had failed to give the shower a test run before his first big day of work only served to increase his anxiety level.

"Please work, please work," he chanted, running the hot tap. The pipes groaned and then rattled through a short series of clanks, and then, the sputtering of rusty, red water began to trickle from the faucet. He frantically turned both faucet handles, as a weak spray of cold, rusty water dribbled from the shower head; he had a feeling this was going to be a long day.

Arriving for his first full day, he could feel his nervousness building. Dr. Keating had taken off early that morning and wouldn't be back until later; nonetheless, Jason mentally prepared himself for the barrage of clients and quickly scrambled through a textbook minutes before the first appointment.

At 9:00 A.M., Sarah Thatcher arrived with her horse for a lameness exam. The 70-year-old woman, recently a widow, had a line of divorced and deceased husbands. Men had failed her; horses had not. She remained active, not only in the show circuits of Oklahoma and Texas, but also in keeping Birdie up-to-date with the latest gossip, and this visit had an agenda.

As he walked toward her, Sarah glared over her dark Greta Garbo-style sunglasses. Jason introduced himself and extended his hand. She folded her arms and with a blank stare pointed to the horse. "Well, alright, anyway, my horse is lame."

"Okay, now which leg does he appear to be lame on?" Jason looked at the horse's feet for a clue.

She turned slowly, as a slight, devious smile spread across her face. "Well doctor, that's what I want to see if you can figure out. I know which one it is, but you tell me." At that moment, Jason realized an interview was underway. Sarah Thatcher had made an appointment to meet the newest topic of Birdie gossip, and she intended to be the first to get the scoop. Jason smiled and took a deep breath, determined not to let an eccentric old woman get the best of him; he didn't want to screw this up.

Jason's day seemed endless, but with the exit of the last trailer, he felt a flood of relief; he had made it through his first full day, no thanks to Keating, who had never shown back up at the clinic. He collapsed into his new desk chair and set to work completing patient records, staying well past Shelly's departure. When he finally finished and looked at his watch, he couldn't believe that it was already 7:30 P.M. He struggled with the keys as he locked up for the first time, hoping he hadn't forgotten something.

He took his time driving back to his apartment, hoping to familiarize himself with his new hometown. Rounding the courthouse square in the little town, he noticed that the heat and humidity were still relentless, despite the evening hour. "How did anyone get used to this type of weather?" he wondered. Regardless of his own grumblings, people continued to gather in the town square. Young mothers watched their children play on the shade-covered grass, old men attempted to solve the latest national crisis over a game of checkers, and a lone

41

adolescent skateboarder tried daring stunts on the courthouse steps while dodging unsuspecting pedestrians.

He was struck by the town's quiet tone; the high-speed traffic and the hustle and bustle of Fort Collins starkly contrasted with the meandering pickup trucks and the half-asleep traffic lights of Birdie. How did a town like this survive when the rest of the planet was spinning at a breakneck pace?

He stopped at the grocery store and made his way through the narrow aisles, looking for something interesting to eat. The strangers in the aisles smiled and nodded with a sense of neighborliness he hadn't experienced before. As he made his way through the store, he could feel the day starting to catch up with him.

He remembered how it used to be with Becca; they were inseparable during the newlywed years of dating. Even mundane grocery shopping had been fun and special. It had been so easy then; no time constraints or work commitments. But time and career aspirations changed that. Becca was now driven to the point of almost becoming someone Jason didn't recognize. Career, status, and money had become her driving forces. Her childhood poverty had deeply affected her, and she had no intention of returning to that life. Her parents had done the best they could, but her father's medical problems and then his subsequent drinking had taken their toll. Becca's family had become an embarrassment to who and what she wanted to be. California promised happiness, money, the good life, and no one was going to get in the way of making that a reality.

Driving back to the barn, Jason wondered if he would see the cute girl in the BMW again. Did she have a story, a mysterious past? Why the hell was she driving around Birdie? Maybe she occasionally visited an elderly aunt in town, or better yet, had she married an oil tycoon, and was now enjoying the trophy wife lifestyle? He slowly drove the streets, wondering if he might see the car parked in a driveway. As he hunted for the mystery girl, he soon realized he was lost in the world's smallest town.

Finally, he found his way back to the barn. Struggling to bring in the groceries, he wondered why his room smelled like horse. As he made his way into the kitchen, he looked at the floor and discovered the source of the foul smell.

"How the hell did an animal get in here?" he yelled.

He checked the door to the barn, finding it unlocked but closed; who or what had let itself in? He cleaned up the manure; from the looks of it, a donkey was the culprit. As he carried in the remaining bags of groceries, he wondered what other surprises he would find.

He put away the items and then opened what was becoming an all-too-familiar microwave dinner; how many of these had he eaten in his lifetime? There were only so many ways to prepare pasta with sauce.

His head swam with the day's cases, questioning everything he'd done, or didn't do, or should have done.

As he sat down, he felt the weight of his exhaustion. Sitting alone on his bed, he ate in silence, wondering if this reality would ever border on feeling normal. This room, foreign, dirty, and uninviting, would make his mother's skin crawl. If she were here, she would have already scoured every square inch of the place. Had this carpet ever been vacuumed, the blinds ever dusted? The lonesome oil painting on the wall, with its dustbowl scene of a drab gray farmhouse surrounded by tumbleweeds and one desperate tree in the yard, further reminded him of his grand mistake.

He called Becca, but she didn't answer, and her surprisingly cheerful voice message reminded him of how happy they had once been. He threw the remainder of his dinner away and brushed his teeth. The clock read 8:15 P.M., but he didn't care. He got into bed and hoped sleep would allow him some temporary escape.

His phone rang.

"Jason, this is Keating. Where the hell are you?"

"What? What do you mean?" he stammered.

"Well, I got back to the clinic and you were gone. You need to get back here; you up for some sushi?"

Jason sat up. Had Keating just said "sushi"? Where the hell do you get sushi in Birdie? How does anyone in this town even know what sushi is?

"Uh, sure, yes, that sounds good," he said with curious disbelief.

"Okay, good; be ready in about 15 minutes and we'll

be by," said Keating.

Before Jason could reply, Keating hung up.

He quickly threw on clean clothes and found his clean pair of boots. "Sushi?!?" he thought.

Moments later, a large black SUV pulled into the drive, with Keating in the passenger seat. Keating raised a glass and smiled as Jason climbed in. Jason recognized Keating's wife, Mary, seated in the back with another woman. Closing the door, Jason was introduced to Keating's friend, Don, and his wife, Joyce. Don waved from the driver's seat as they pulled away.

"We didn't wake you, I hope," quipped Keating.

"John, stop now," said Mary kindly. "Dr. Davies, are you getting settled in okay here, in this little apartment?" she asked. "If there is anything you need, just ask."

"Thank you," Jason replied. "It's going to take some time, but I think it will be alright."

"So Doc, everything go alright today? How did the appointment with Sarah go?" Keating asked.

"Oh John, you didn't make poor Dr. Davies deal with Sarah Thatcher? You told me she wasn't coming in until tomorrow," groaned Mary. "I am so sorry," she said, gently patting his arm. "John, I told you to get her to come in when you would be there, so Dr. Davies wouldn't have to deal with her antics."

"Oh, now, please; Jason is fully capable of handling Sarah," replied Keating, sipping his drink.

The SUV slowed and turned into a small gravel

parking lot. Jason attempted to get his bearings as to where they were. A small, narrow, unassuming restaurant was squeezed between a vacuum cleaner repair shop and the "Hair Affair." A large fish tank consumed one wall in the entry. Keating walked over to the tank and pointed to a large ornate purple and blue colored fish, saying, "Okay, I'll take that one!"

"John!" scolded Mary. Looking at Jason, she said, "This is what happens when he has a day away from the clinic."

"Yeah, and a couple rounds of Glenlivet doesn't hurt either," said Don.

As they were being seated, Don and Keating were having a heated discussion about country music.

Keating turned to Jason. "So what kind of music do you listen to? This beat-bop, boom-boom crap...."

"John!" grumbled Mary. "Now you behave, or you're going back to the car."

"Hey now, I'm just asking. It's okay if you do. Well, as long as you don't play that crap around me," he said with a smirk.

"No," replied Jason, feeling his cheeks blush. "I listen to a lot of different music."

"Country?" Keating asked, "Not the bubble-gum-popping radio stuff of today, but real country music?"

"Like Hank Williams country?" Jason replied.

Keating smiled at Don, saying, "Well now, that's a start. How about Ray Price? Buck Owens? Hank Cochran,

Lefty Frizzell, or maybe Merle Haggard?"

"Sure, a lot good stuff with them for sure," Jason replied nervously. He wasn't sure where this was headed; on the job only a day, his gut told him this evening had the potential of being a make-or-break event.

"Don, tell him your story," laughed Keating.

"I don't know if it's all that entertaining, but alright," he replied. "I used to go out on the road with some guys back in the day, playing some places around here, and some down in the panhandle. I quit the road after Joyce and I got married, but my buddies kept out there. Well anyways, I get this call from one of them the other day and he leaves this message that he's out touring with Merle Haggard. I got home late that night, so I didn't call him back until this morning. It was strange because when I called, some guy answers. I asked him if Jerry was there, but he says Jerry's sleeping. I asked this guy who I'm speakin' with, and he replies, 'Merle.' Well...I about fall over, but then I ask, 'Merle, as in Merle Haggard?' He said, 'Yes, Merle Haggard.' So I couldn't believe it, but I asked him what he was doing answering Jerry's phone, and he says that Jerry had driven all night, so he was sleeping. So I ask him what he's doing right now, and he says, 'Driving the bus.' I couldn't believe it; I am on the phone with Merle Haggard as he's driving the tour bus, and then he says, 'It's not glamorous out here. People think that doing this is all about fame and celebrity.... It's about 30 years on a bus.' So anyways, Merle Haggard is leaving tickets for

47

all of us for his concert in Tulsa next month. Can you believe it?"

The sushi arrived. The conversation turned to politics, guns, and then wild boar hunting, which Jason had never heard of. It alarmed him to hear that these beasts were known to run through Birdie on occasion.

The hour became late, and they decided to call it a night. As the SUV pulled in front of the barn Jason now called home, he said his goodbyes and thanked them before making his way inside.

He quickly readied himself for bed, crawled under the sheets, and closed his eyes. Oh, how he enjoyed the silence, after all the raucous conversation of the evening.

Scratch, schliiiiiik, scratch, scratch, schliik, schliiik. A chill electrified up his spine as the tiny scratching feet of a creature scrabbled along the wood trim. He froze, calculating his next move.

He felt the blanket of his bed move, and then a flurry of fur across his face and chest. Jason leapt out of the bed, as if on fire, scrambling for the light switch.

Thrashing and screaming, he found the switch. He surveyed the room for the onslaught of thousands of tiny creatures overtaking him, but the room was still.

He thought, "I'm a veterinarian; I should love and appreciate all animals, right?" He wondered what James Herriot would do at a moment like this. He saw nothing moving. What the hell was he supposed to do now? He'd remembered a story his father told him of his own college days, and the problems with rodents. He and his roommates had placed pans of water under each bed post to prevent mice from crawling up the sides of the beds. It was worth a shot.

Jason scrambled through the pots and pans in the kitchen. He filled four pans and placed one under each of the four bed legs. Satisfied with his work, he surveyed the room a final time before again climbing back into bed and finally falling into a peaceful sleep.

The following morning, Jason relayed his evening's excitement to Keating, who offered an old, rusted and worn "humane" mouse trap to capture the varmint. "Of course, a good boot or shovel might work better," Keating quipped, taking Jason by surprise. "No, a veterinarian should work to preserve even the smallest creature's life, with the hope of releasing it back into the wild," he thought, as he gathered the trap up and put it in his truck.

That night he turned the light out and climbed into bed. Lying in the darkness, he stared at the ceiling, waiting and listening for the sounds of tiny, scratching feet.

SNAP!

"Gotcha," he whispered. He smiled with a sense of accomplishment and joy; at least he possessed some level of control over his life. He rolled over and closed his eyes.

The next morning, Jason was anxious to lay eyes on

the beast but was immediately disappointed to find only a tiny, fuzzy brown field mouse, frozen with fear. This was the "monster" responsible for the previous night's drama? "Things always appear bigger in the dark," he thought. Jason carried the trap out to the pasture behind the barn and opened the door. The mouse hesitated, then disappeared into the tall grass. Jason returned to the barn, pleased that he had preserved life, while rendering his own home rodent-free.

Throughout the next several evenings, the same pattern of mouse mayhem continued. Each morning Jason would find a new little mouse in the trap and would then release it into the pasture.

Days later, Jason relayed the story to the veterinary assistant, Shelly. Keating quietly came into the lab during the story, and when Jason finished, Keating asked with a grin, "Did you ever consider that you might be catching the same mouse each night, over and over again?"

Jason replied, "No, I guess not, but do you think it's possible?"

"I don't know, just a thought," he said. Grinning as he left the room, he turned and said, "Maybe you should try hiking a little farther away from the barn next time."

Several nights later, Jason heard the familiar snap of the trap; his little nemesis had returned. This time he took action. As Jason walked a good ways down the side of the dirt road, he paused and wondered, "Surely this isn't the same mouse...." He opened the cage door and watched the tiny mouse bounce into the tall mixed grass. "See you again tomorrow night," he called.

Chapter 8

As the afternoon sun took residence high overhead on another steamy June day, Keating took Jason to visit a childhood friend, Carl Tomlinson. Tomlinson's mule was non-weight bearing on a front foot and Carl had asked Keating to come take a look.

Tomlinson had been an agent with the Secret Service for over 30 years and had seen a colorful world of service and danger, including the fateful day in Dallas riding in President Kennedy's motorcade through Dealey Plaza. He forever carried the burden of that day, and the nation's sorrow with it. He continued to serve under Presidents Johnson through Carter, finally taking early retirement and returning to Birdie to work the family farm.

The scorching afternoon sun reminded Jason of how much he missed the Rocky Mountain summers. As they pulled into the driveway, Jason remarked to Keating how much he was looking forward to a cool drink.

"Uh oh," said Keating.

"What?" asked Jason.

"Well, I hope you like coffee," he replied.

"What? On a day like today?"

"C'mon, he's got the air on; you won't even notice it's 100 degrees out here," Keating said with a smile as they walked up the winding limestone stairway to the front door.

As Keating knocked on the door, Jason took in the immaculate landscaping of the yard, pristine and precise; a weed wouldn't dare to grow in this yard. A short, gruff-looking man answered the door, but his expression quickly changed to joy as he recognized Keating. He grasped them both in well-muscled forearm handshakes as he pulled them into the house. Carl represented a powerhouse of retirement, with his blocky muscled build and steel gray hair. He reminded Jason of his eighth-grade gym teacher, and he wondered if Carl, at any moment, might suddenly ask him to "drop and give me twenty." As introductions were made, he motioned them further inside to a small kitchen table.

"Have a seat, men; can I pour you a cup?" Carl reached for several tall mugs. Jason was quickly adjusting to the small town ways of drinking black coffee, anytime of day, and in any degree of temperature. As they sat down, Carl and Keating discussed the upcoming hunting trip they were planning. "Well, speaking of hunting, I had me a bit of a 'man' hunt down here yesterday."

"Now Carl, what are you saying? *Man* hunt?" Keating exclaimed.

"You know that old rail bed that runs along the backside of the property down there. No train been on it in years, but I like to keep the weeds and grass down back there, so I was on my riding mower down there yesterday morning. I see this fella running down the rail bed like he is running from the devil himself, and I know something

53

was up because he wasn't wearing no joggin' outfit, you know. He's got one of those bright orange jumpsuits on, if you know what I mean."

"You mean from the prison?" asked Keating?

"Yeah, that old boy was runnin' 9-0 down the train bed back there," said Carl. "He was moving all right, about 5'7" with a beard, and a pretty fluffy fella."

Jason gave Keating a questioning glance. "Fluffy?"

"Oh, you know," Carl said, motioning with his arms, "got some muscle to him."

"What did you do then?" Jason asked.

"I took on after him with my mower. That old boy was pretty quick though," replied Carl. "I tried to keep up with him, but that fluffy sombitch had his track shoes on, for sure. I radioed it in to the sheriff's office. A while later some of them black SUVs showed up, and they found him in Earl and Laverne's carport just down the way there."

Jason sat sipping his coffee, not sure what to make of it all. This town contained a menagerie of characters, reminding him of an *Andy Griffith Show* episode.

Keating drank the last remains of his coffee and stood up. "Well, I suppose we better get this critter of yours looked at before we need to be getting along." Jason followed the two men outside and down the path to the barn.

One of Carl's mules presented with lameness in his left front foot. Keating turned Jason loose on diagnosing the problem, as he and Carl sat by the fence debating politics and gun control. Jason soon found an abscess on the mule's foot. Excited about his quick success, he set to work opening the abscess and draining the purulent material from the foot. He then packed the foot with a poultice and bandaged it with textbook accuracy.

After the mule was treated, they all said their goodbyes and Keating and Jason climbed into the truck. They drove quietly for several minutes and Jason stared out along the grazing pastures and neatly rowed-planted crops, until Keating looked over at him and said, "Did Carl really say he took after that guy on his riding mower?"

Jason turned with a smile and nodded.

Chapter 9

Jason awoke to the sound of water. Drip......drip......drip.

He lay in bed, waiting to hit the snooze button for a third time, when he realized that water was dripping onto his bed. Water was finding its way in around the window panes, through the ceiling tiles, and directly down into the ceiling light. This new development at first gave Jason pause and then panic when he considered the effect of water and electricity on his health and well-being.

He jumped out of bed and scoured the kitchen cabinetry, looking for bowls and other items to aid in the containment. He readied himself for the day, wondering how quickly the bowls would fill if the rain continued. What the hell was he supposed to do while at work? It hardly seemed appropriate to call in sick because your roof was leaking. He looked through the barn and found several five-gallon buckets that might buy more time. He would make a point of stopping back by to empty the buckets mid-morning, hoping that they wouldn't overflow before then.

When he got to the clinic, he was secretly relieved to find out that his first appointment had cancelled due to the rain. Wet horses standing in mud made for a long day.

Shelly appeared from around the corner. "You ready to go to work?"

"Sure, what's up? Do we need to go out, or are they coming here?"

Shelly looked out the window and nodded without saying a word. "Uh oh," Jason replied, standing up and walking toward the window. "Not looking real good out there; it actually looks worse than it did a little while ago. Do you know where we're going?"

"Yes, but that's the good news." She pulled her hair back into a ponytail.

"Well, what's the bad news?" Jason was confused.

"Where they live is pretty remote, and in this weather it's going to be an adventure...." Shelly turned and walked out of the room.

"You mean a nightmare?" he called after her.

"No, an adventure! C'mon, where's your sense of adventure? Isn't that why you became a veterinarian to begin with, Dr. Davies?" her voice boomed from the other room.

"Yeah, yeah, well, I'll grab my stuff; you ready?" Jason grabbed his jacket and headed toward the garage.

They slowly made their way out of town as Jason stared at the ominous darkness ahead. "This doesn't look good. What's wrong with the horse? I hope this is worth it," Jason said, attempting to turn on the windshield wipers.

"Tammy Gibson's mares always colic when the weather gets wound up like this. During the last storm, one of them nearly tore down the barn before we got there.

Doc usually has them put the horses on medication before a storm, but they must have forgotten this time." Shelly played with the end of her ponytail, staring out into the wet landscape. They turned off the main road onto a saturated mess of muddy clay.

"This is hideous!" Jason braced the steering wheel with both hands, trying to keep the truck centered in the high spot of the road.

"When these storms come in like this there's no telling when the rain is going to end. I remember when I was a little girl, it rained for a week solid. My folks had a small boat that they used to go get my grandma from her house when everything started to flood. Gosh, I even think a couple of people died in that flood." The road narrowed and the truck's tires spun frantically as Jason maintained his focus on keeping the vehicle from losing control.

Jason turned to Shelly, smiling. "Well, at least it's not as bad as that." Moments later, his mood changed when they approached a Buick sedan abandoned in the ditch. Jason slowed the truck, wondering if they should turn around and head back. He was a veterinarian on his way to help an animal in need; a little mud wasn't going to stop him, was it? This horse's life was hanging in the balance, right? He must forge ahead.... At that moment he felt the truck slipping and sinking into the road. He shifted into a lower gear, but the vehicle, not being four-wheel drive, groaned and came to a stop. He remembered Keating's justification for not owning a four-wheel drive vehicle: "If the weather is that damn bad, then I'm not going!" Jason thought, "Right; you don't need four-wheel drive when you can send the new guy out in it...damn!"

"Maybe if I got out and pushed?" Shelly grabbed the door handle, ready to jump out into the downpour.

"No, I don't want you getting wet. Let me take a look and see if there's something I can find for traction." Jason jumped out of the truck and into the pouring rain, scanning the area for anything to place under the tires. He found several large rocks, but unable to move any of them, he searched for something else. He found several small limbs and dragged them in front of the rear tires. He jumped back into the truck and pressed the accelerator. The tires spun, then momentarily took hold of the branches before the truck slipped even further into the mud.

"Damn!" he shouted.

"Dr. Davies, what can I do?" Shelly pleaded.

"Well, you get behind the wheel and I'll find something for some more traction." Jason climbed back into ankle-deep muck. The rain's increasing intensity added to Jason's anxiety; he needed to get the truck out of this mess fast, or the weather would keep them stranded until help arrived. Finding yet another large fallen branch in a cluster of trees, he attempted to drag it toward the truck's tire. Struggling to loosen its muddy hold, he strained to keep his footing. Suddenly his right foot gave way, sending his body sideways into the drenched, clay mess.

"Dr. Davies! Are you okay?" Shelly yelled over the roar of water now pouring down. She ran to Jason and helped him to his feet; his clothes were covered in the thick, greasy clay.

"I think there are some large towels under the back seat. Let me run and get one." Shelly raced back to the truck.

"Could this really get any worse?" he wondered, trying to wipe the mud from his face. Shelly returned with the towels. "I can't get a signal and the phone won't go through. Dr. Davies, this is only getting worse out here and I think we should get you back to the truck and wait it out." He looked at her concerned face and knew she was right. This was no use.

As they slowly made their way back through the trees, he stopped. He heard something: the welcome sound of a truck. He looked at Shelly, and she heard it too; maybe they were rescued after all.

"Let's go!" Jason yelled, as they began to run back to truck. They arrived just as an over-sized four-wheel-drive pickup slowed and stopped.

"You stuck?" the driver asked.

"Yes," Jason said, with a smile and a sigh of relief.

The man looked over Jason's shoulder to the buried truck, his eyes surveying the mess. "Well...I think I'll try to stick to the right shoulder up ahead. It looks pretty soft up there. You folks stay safe; good luck."

Jason, confused, not sure what to say, stumbled for a reply as the man rolled up his window and began to drive away.

"Wait!" Jason screamed, but the cacophony of rain and the diesel engine drowned out his cry. It was too late. Jason watched the taillights of the truck slowly make their way up and over the hill.

This wasn't happening; surely the man was joking and wouldn't leave them there, stranded.

He turned to Shelly, who looked at him with questioning eyes. She motioned for him to follow as they made their way back to the truck. Inside, they sat quietly, staring out the windshield. He wondered how quickly he could get the hell out this two-bit hee-haw town; these people were nuts.

"I think that jerk dated my cousin!" Shelly bristled, taking a sip from her water bottle.

The rain began to slow as Jason prayed for a break. What the hell were they going to do?

"Do you hear that?" Shelly exclaimed, looking toward the road. Jason listened and scowled. "So help me, if that's the moron in the pickup, I'm going to kill him!" They jumped out as a truck slowed to a stop on the road.

"Well, hey, y'all!" A man stepped out of the truck, waving wildly as he slowly made his way through the now calf-high mud. The rain had stopped, and the sun now slowly tried to take a stand through the cloud cover.

"Tammy and I was gettin' nervous about y'all not

showin' up at the house. Figured somethin' musta happened down here, so's I come down this way thinkin' I might get lucky and find y'all. Well sure 'nuff I did!" Donny Ray Gibson began curiously inspecting the truck mud pie. Scratching his chin methodically, he walked around the truck as if deeply contemplating the situation. Jason followed him with interest, in hopes that a solution would be forthcoming. Suddenly Donny Ray stopped at the hood of the truck, where the mud had buried the truck to its axle.

"Y'all are stuck."

Jason waited for more. "Uhhh, yes, sir, we can't seem to find anything that will work to get it out of this mess."

"Hmmmm. Well, let's give a try with my truck and see's if we can't getcha out."

Donny Ray returned to his truck and removed a large nylon tow rope, which he attached to the truck's bumper. Jason stepped toward the driver's door, intending to put the truck in neutral, but Shelly was already ahead of him. Grinning from behind the steering wheel, she gave a thumbs up as Donny Ray waved and put his truck into gear. Donny Ray's truck lurched forward and the rope took hold, but the truck remained fixed in its muddy grave. Several more attempts only proved to worsen the truck's position. When Donny Ray's truck no longer progressed forward, and threatened to also become stuck, his smile dissipated.

"So's I'm thinkin' the only way to get y'all out is to go

get my tractor. It'll take a bit, but I'll be back."

Exhausted, Jason leaned on the hood of the truck and looked up at the sky. The clouds continued to dwindle and the sun had arrived in full force.

"Dr. Davies, you should really drink something. I have some water in the truck. Are you hungry? I found some crackers in the glove box."

"Thank you, Shelly, but I'll be fine."

"Okay, so's you two don't go nowhere, and I'll be back." Donny Ray unhooked the tow rope and slowly pulled his truck forward. The truck disappearing over the hill made Jason wonder if Donny Ray truly would return. Jason climbed back into the truck and leaned back in the seat. Closing his eyes, he felt like crying. He sure as hell hadn't gone to veterinary school to be stuck out on a muddy road in the middle of a rain storm in some hillbilly backwoods of God-forsaken Oklahoma.

Without opening his eyes, he said, "Do they really own a tractor?"

"I only remember a large riding mower." Shelly bit into a cracker.

Jason drifted off to sleep. The sound of a tractor approaching stirred him awake. He and Shelly stared anxiously, waiting as it crested the hill. Jason's heart sank; the machine headed toward them was barely larger than a household, garden-variety riding lawn mower.

The man was all smiles as he once again set to work attaching the tow ropes. Jason watched nervously as the tractor dug into the mud, straining to gain any inch of improvement in the truck's current location...and then...nothing. Jason shook his head, realizing this was going to take a while. On the fourth attempt, the tractor moved to the side of the truck, and as the tractor's tires began to spin, the truck slowly began to slide to the side. Any improvement was celebrated, as the truck slid inch by inch closer to dry ground. Finally, the left wheel grabbed hold of the firmer ground and Jason pressed the accelerator. The truck spun to the left and was free; the oversized lawn mower had saved the day.

As they slowly made their way to the ranch, Jason wished he'd thought more about going to dental school. "Inside work and no heavy lifting," his father always advised.

When they pulled up in front of the barn, Tammy ran toward the truck waving. "Good news," she exclaimed. "Sassy just passed some stool, and she's feeling great!"

Jason's smile froze, as a sense of both joy and anguish bubbled over within him. He followed Tammy into the barn and listened to the horse, concluding that in truth Sassy the horse seemed fine. He sighed deeply as he returned to the truck, clenching his fists as he walked. Climbing back into the truck, he pounded his fist on the steering wheel.

"Crap!" he yelled.

"Yes, yes, she did," Shelly giggled. He turned with a quick glance. He scowled, but then took a deep breath and smiled at her.

"Yes, I guess that's right." He started the truck.

Slowly heading back down the hill, Jason further slowed as they passed the site of their earlier fiasco. Shelly turned on the radio as they traveled back to the main road. He caught Shelly smiling, looking out the window as if their harrowing experience hadn't remotely affected her.

"What are you smiling about?"

"Oh, I was just thinking how great this job is." Shelly handed him a cracker from the glove box. "It beats sitting behind a desk all day."

Chapter 10

The month of June was flying by. Late afternoon storms each day reminded Jason of his childhood summers, running in the rain with friends. These thoughts only served to increase his loneliness.

Lost in his thoughts at the clinic one afternoon, he tried to assuage a rush of homesickness. He missed Becca. He tried to call her office over his lunch break, but the secretary said that she was out on an audit and wouldn't be back until late. She asked if he would like to leave a message, but with a polite "No thank you," he hung up the phone. He attempted to reach Tommy on his cell phone in hopes that he might have some new encouraging leads on getting out of Birdie.

"Hey, Brother, let me call you back. We're just wheeling in a horse for the table. Man, I'm telling you, the amount of amazing things we're doing out here...Gotta dash!" Tommy's phone went dead.

Jason sat in deep contemplation, eating the sandwich he had prepared for lunch. Keating came through the door, looked down at him sternly, and asked, "Everything going okay?"

"You bet," replied Jason, trying to cover his loneliness. Jason quickly finished eating before heading back to a full load of afternoon appointments.

Jason tried to find distraction in his patients, diving

into textbooks, reviewing countless diseases and treatments. No matter how much he learned in school, it didn't seem to be nearly enough for the head scratching that went on day after day. Later that afternoon, as Jason finished up paperwork at his desk, Keating breezed through the door. "Jason, if you don't have plans here in a bit, I wondered if you might want to have a drink back at the house."

"Sure, that sounds great," replied Jason.

"Good. Come on over when you're done," Keating said.

Jason completed the last of the day's accumulated medical records and locked the doors before being the last one out of the clinic. He headed out the back door and through the grove of trees that separated the clinic grounds from Keating's property. Jason approached the back of the house and found Keating seated on the enclosed patio with a glass of Scotch in his hand. As Jason sat down at the table he could feel cool air blowing on him from the ceiling fan, a refreshing escape from the humid Oklahoma heat. "Do you ever get to a point where you feel like you know everything? I mean, where you feel confident about how you're diagnosing and treating cases?" Jason asked.

Keating set his drink down. "Yes, I suppose so."

Jason took a sip of his drink, waiting for Keating's golden words of wisdom to flow. Keating took another sip of his drink, staring off into the distance.

Jason finally asked, "Well, when did you know that you had a handle on all of it?"

Keating looked at him, and then taking another sip he said, "I don't know...I haven't gotten there yet." He stared off into the distance again and said, "Years ago when I was in the Army, this old staff sergeant veterinarian told me that the key to being successful as a veterinarian was to remember three things. Number one: Always be on time. Number two: Always be courteous. And number three: Always get paid before you leave. Now, I'll be honest, I haven't always been successful in any or all of these words of wisdom, but at the end of the day, the key to this job is to take care of the client, and get paid. I mean, hell, it's what every other son-of-a-bitch is out there trying to do, make some money and take care of his family."

Jason stared out into the shadowed yard, stunned at Keating's words. He hadn't made even the slightest mention of the care for animals or preserving life.

"Dr. Keating, with all due respect, don't we have an obligation to help the animals? I mean, isn't that why we do what we do?" he asked.

Keating turned with a smirk, taking another sip, and as he set his glass on the table, he replied, "Son, that's the dream that got us all there, to the front door of that university, but I tell you, you learn real quick that this job will break just about every bone in your body at some point in your career. Your body will ache and your bank account will too. These animals will get better or they won't, and the sad truth of the fact is that most times, we may or may not make a damn bit of difference in the equation. You're right; you work for that horse and nobody else. You always, always, remain true to that animal and make decisions that are in the best interests of that animal. But the truth of the matter is, it's about taking care of the owners, pure and simple."

They sat in silence, listening to the katydids and watching the sun's last few moments on the horizon. The back door opened as Mary appeared with a colorful plate of fruits, cheeses, and crackers.

"Would you gentlemen care for a snack?" she asked. Keating had grown up in Birdie, meeting Mary in fourth grade after her family moved to town.

"I knew she was the one for me," Keating said.

"In fourth grade?" Jason asked.

"No, in high school when she saved me from failing algebra," he replied.

Chapter 11

Keeping one arm locked as he drove home later, Jason was grateful that the drive was short and the roads were deserted. He dropped into bed as the room spun around him. He made a mental note: "No more Scotch."

His phone rang. "Helllloooo?" he answered, his head swimming off the mattress.

"Jason?" Becca asked, "What are you doing? Are you in bed?"

"Uhhh, no, well, sort of. How are you?" His words slurred together.

"What are you doing? You sound like you've been drinking.... I called to tell you that I'm coming out there over the 4th of July weekend.... I'll rent a car at the airport, and be there Friday night."

"No, you don't need to rent a..., I mean, I'll come get you," he stammered.

"No, it's fine. I don't mind, plus I have an early flight back on Sunday, so it just makes sense."

"Oh...okay, well, great...I'm excited to see you," he said.

"Well, me too; do we need to get a hotel room or something while I'm there?"

"No, we can stay here. It will be good. I mean, it's not fancy, but it's cozy," he slurred.

Silence followed. "K...," she replied.

"It will be great to see you; the town has a lot going on over the 4th. They have a big festival downtown, and then there's a fireworks show, and we could also try this little restaurant over by the courthouse...." The silence persisted.

"Well, I need to go, but I wanted to call." Becca's voice sounded weary and indifferent.

"It's great; you made my night." His mind was straining to pull free of the three double Scotches he'd consumed earlier in the evening.

"Okay...so I'll call you when I land."

"I love you."

"Love you," her voice drifted off.

Chapter 12

Jason couldn't take it anymore; the nausea finally forced him to the bathroom. He stumbled into the wall on his way. "Shit!" he cursed as his toes jammed the corner of the wall. He braced himself over the toilet, his stomach wrenching as his body tried to relieve itself of the liquid toxin. He lay on the floor, sweating profusely and wondering why he couldn't die right then and there. He had sworn in college he would never do this again. Staggering back to bed, he wondered what time it was.

His watch said 4:30 A.M. He badly wanted more sleep, but his throbbing head made sleep unlikely. His mind raced back to the conversation with Becca; was she really coming to visit? Had they really talked, or was it a Scotch-induced hallucination? He stumbled back out into the room and stood in the musty darkness of his reality. This placed sucked, and there was no way Becca would agree to staying here. Furthermore, it would lend nothing to his efforts to make Birdie appealing in any way. He needed a plan to make this place livable before she arrived, or he was a dead man. He scanned the room in the early morning light, staring at the discolored, drab walls. It definitely needed some paint, and the dust-covered picture on the wall needed to be thrown away. And the furniture; surely Birdie had a furniture store where he could pick up a couch and chair? He glanced down at his bare feet on the carpet, and despair set in; Becca wouldn't even dare set foot on this disgusting floor. His fell back onto the bed, his hands covering his face. "What an unbelievable mess," he thought, as he slipped back into sleep.

"Pork bellies up two and seven eighths this week, and feeders drop to three and a half. Corn rose again this week...!" Jason rolled over and hit the snooze button on his alarm. "Nothing like the farm report first thing in the morning," he thought. "Crap!" he screamed, as the sun grazed his eyes through the window. He leapt out of bed and looked at his watch: 7:57 A.M.

"Damn it!" he shouted, running for the bathroom. He showered and was out the door in record time, worried about how much Keating would grumble over his tardiness.

He pulled into the parking lot to find Keating climbing into the truck. Keating paused as he watched Jason pull in, then waved for him to get in. Seconds later they were headed down Main Street, toward the edge of town. They arrived at a small white farmhouse that was shrouded, almost trapped, by a large perimeter of ancient, gnarled oak trees laying claim to the house.

As they followed the client through a jungle of high weeds and vegetation down a narrow stone pathway, she explained that she was concerned with her Paso Fino gelding's ongoing hair loss. She stopped suddenly, crying out as she pulled a thorn from her foot. Her colorfully painted toenails and flip-flops hardly seemed appropriate for the setting. Keating shook his head in dismay before again following her down the path toward the decrepit barn at the far end of the property.

The robust dark bay gelding normally had a beautifully luxurious, flowing mane and tail, but now its tail was severely shortened and its mane was dry and thinning. Jason looked confused as he watched Keating further exam the horse's mane, looking for an indication of the source of the problem. Keating took a sample of the hair and two vials of blood for lab submission. "This sure looks like some type of metabolic issue that may need to be addressed, but we'll know more once the lab results are back," Keating stated before turning for the door. Suddenly, the woman cried out in pain once again, "'Ooouuuugh!"

The horse had stepped squarely on the woman's foot. Jason quickly rushed to move the horse. He watched the blood rush to the woman's toes as they began to immediately turn purple.

"You need to get yourself on over to the hospital and have them x-ray that," said Keating, unsympathetically.

Driving back to the clinic, Keating chuckled to himself.

"What?" Jason asked.

"I just got to thinking about that little gal back there, and her foot getting stepped on."

"Okay," Jason thought to himself, "what's funny about getting your foot stepped on?"

"I think it's a little ironic she got stepped on wearing those sandals."

"Why's that?" Jason asked.

"Well, because she owns the cowboy western wear and *boot* shop in town," Keating said, with a smile.

Chapter 13

Jason hurried through his final case notes for the day and slipped out the door in hopes of finally making preparations for Becca's arrival. As he drove to the courthouse square he remembered that the hardware store sold furniture from its basement showroom. Hopefully a new couch or chair would improve the sad state of the little apartment. The selection was sparse, but settling on a small loveseat and matching chair, he watched the two men load the items into the back of his truck. Jason placed two cans of fresh white paint, tape, and brushes on the passenger seat floorboard and raced toward home.

As he entered the apartment, the all-too-familiar smell of Jasper had returned. He paused and set down his bags of items, ready to track down the mischievous donkey, but then he thought better of it. In his current state of joy, nothing, not even the poop-spewing bastard donkey, would dampen his spirits. He quickly and without incident removed the fecal pile and set straight to work with painting the walls. The small room took no time at all, and he decided the little galley kitchen could also use a facelift.

He dropped into bed later that evening, exhausted but elated that the space he currently called home already looked more inviting that he'd ever imagined it could. As he lay in bed he suddenly realized he'd forgotten the furniture still in the back of his truck. Maybe it could wait until morning....

He finally flipped back the sheets and climbed out of bed, slipped on his shoes, and headed outside. He stood at the back of the truck, wondering exactly how he was going to move the furniture into the apartment. He glanced around, hoping by some fate of good fortune a random kind neighbor would be walking by and offer to help. The locust and the crickets responded with a resounding No.

He took a deep breath and began working the loveseat slowly toward the tailgate of the pickup. He lifted one end off and strained to lift the other end off the edge of the tailgate, but he suddenly lost his grip and the loveseat dropped with a thud into the dirt of the driveway. "Ugghhhhh," Jason moaned. "I haven't even barely paid for it yet!" He slowly walked the loveseat step by step toward the door of the barn. The poor couch would be broken in before he even had a chance to sit on it. He finally worked the couch into the room and dropped onto it, exhausted. He hoped the chair would be a little easier.

At last, both pieces of furniture were inside the apartment. Jason stood back and admired the room. He was impressed with how much the paint and furniture had improved the atmosphere and ambiance of the place.

Before heading back to bed, he made a list of items he would still need. Number one on the list would be a carpet cleaning, and then a new lock for the door. Jasper would not be ruining his world any more.

The next day, Jason was loading the last of several Boer goats into a trailer when Mary appeared outside. "Dr. Davies, the carpet cleaner says he will be by your place at 4:00 P.M." She looked puzzled as she reread the sticky note hanging on the end of her finger. "Is everything okay at your place? If you need something, you know John or I would be happy to help...."

"Oh, no, everything is fine; the carpet just needs a little help."

"Your afternoon is free after the cat vaccinations if you needed to leave a little early."

Jason hurried to clean up before the cats arrived. A short visit later, Jason was back in his truck and headed for the apartment. The carpet cleaning truck was already parked outside the door and two scruffy and disheveled men were unloading a large metal machine and several feet of hose.

Jason was all smiles as he approached the men. The taller of the two approached Jason. "This yer place here?"

"Well, yes, I mean I don't own it, but I'm living...."

"We're gonna do the best we can.... Truth is, that carpet really ain't worth cleanin', but we aim to give it a shot."

Jason paused and smiled. The excitement of Becca visiting overpowered any concerns for the disastrous carpet, and anything these two men could do to improve it would be just that, an improvement.

After they were done, Jason paid the men and waved

goodbye. He stood in the apartment doorway, admiring the freshly painted walls, cleaned carpet, and new furniture, wondering if it would do the trick. Did it have a fighting chance at impressing Becca? He smirked; well, maybe not impress...tolerate? He slipped quietly onto the new couch and closed his eyes. It was all coming together....

The phone in his pocket began to vibrate and startled him from his twilight slumber. It was Becca. "Well, hey there!" he answered. The other end of the line was quiet. "Hello? Becca? Hello?" He heard sniffling. "Becca, what happened, what's wrong?" He listened quietly on the phone.

"It's not working anymore," she moaned.

"What's not working?"

"Us..."

"Becca, what are you talking about?" Jason struggled to understand.

"US!" she screamed. "Us, it's not working...."

"Becca, wait.... What do you mean? I thought we were figuring it out, and you're coming to visit...I've been killing myself to get everything all set down here and...."

"Jason, I'm tired; tired of waiting for you, tired of wasting my life, and tired of all this shit! I've just spent way too much time thinking, hoping it would work...I'm done...."

"Becca, but...."

"I know, Jason, I know, I just can't do it this time. I just can't; it's too much and I need some space. This whole thing and wherever the hell you are is not going to work."

"It's only temporary, right? I thought we were working on this together? It's going to get better, I promise."

"I need time for myself, to figure out some things." She broke off as her voice struggled. "I'm sorry."

"Becca, wait. Wait!" The line went dead. She was gone. Jason threw the phone across the room. It hit the wall and landed on the bed, as the sound of tiny claws scurried for safety behind the wall.

"Damn it!" He paced the small room. "This isn't how it's supposed to be! I'm done with this town!"

"Do you hear me, Birdie?" Without thinking, he opened the door to the barn. Jasper stared at him. Jason jumped back. "Dumb ass donkey! I'm done! And I won't have to see your big-eared mess anymore!" He slammed the door and opened the refrigerator, reaching for the bottle of Becca's favorite wine he'd purchased earlier in the week. He ripped open a drawer and grabbed the cork screw.

He slumped on the bed and drank from the bottle. He wanted to call her back, but what more could be said? She was not about to allow her dreams to be doused by his realities. Could it really be over between them? They'd been down this road before, more than once. He could count on two hands the number of times she'd left him in a cloud of dust in a movie parking lot, at the mall, or at a party after countless arguments that ended badly. Her level of drama rivaled some teen movies, and yet the two of them always worked their way back to each other in the end.

He tried calling Tommy, but it went straight to voice mail. Exhausted and more than a little drunk after finishing most of the bottle of wine, he closed his eyes and fell asleep.

Chapter 14

The next day, Keating rushed into the office in the late afternoon, a sense of urgency in his voice. "You got time to go for a ride?" he asked. Jason nodded as Keating handed him a beer and motioned for him to follow. The site of the beer after the night of wine caused his stomach to flip flop, but he popped the top and followed Keating outside.

Out among the trees sat an ancient red oxidized 1940s farm truck. Jason climbed into the cab, wondering if the vehicle actually ran. The rusted machine had seen better years. The smell of oil and grease overwhelmed his senses and hints of daylight peeked unapologetically through the floorboards. The rusted springs of the seat groaned and creaked beneath the well-worn faded red Naugahyde upholstery. The door handles had long since disappeared, leaving Jason to wonder how the hell they were going to get back out of the truck. The floorboard displayed a dizzying array of rusted pedals and levers, which Keating began orchestrating in a series of fluid motions. The truck slowly, painfully grumbled to a start and lurched forward. Jason tossed Keating a nervous glance as Keating confidently put the truck into reverse. The truck jerked and groaned as it slowly began to back up. Keating threw open the driver's door and scrambled onto the running board, while simultaneously commanding the steering wheel like the captain of a ship.

Bam! The truck jolted to a stop.

Keating jumped back into the cab, smiling. "We backed into a tree." Gears grinding, the truck lunged forward, and back out onto the running board Keating went.

As they passed the front of the house, Keating's wife, Mary, was planting flowers. Looking up, she yelled, "Be careful with Dr. Davies, I don't think the insurance covers him in that thing!"

Keating yelled back, "Not to worry, Mary, that's what the beer is for!"

Keating yelled at Jason over the grumbling engine, "We need to roll off a load of debris." He pointed through the small cracked oval rear window. A large load of brush swayed and bounced in the bed of the truck. Keating enjoyed spending time out on his pasture, removing dead tree limbs and overgrown brush, especially after finding out that his homeowner's insurance discounted owners who mitigated their properties for fire.

The isolated ravine dumpsite was located several miles down a gravel road on a neighbor's property, where once a year, when the weather cooperated, Keating and his cohorts set fire to the debris and made an evening out of it. The exceptionally dry summer had caused the pile to grow considerably in recent months. As they approached, Keating yelled over the rattle of the truck, "Okay, so I'm going to back this thing up to the edge of the ravine, but there's something I haven't told you about this truck."

"What's that?" Jason asked.

"Well, the brakes don't work very well. Actually, only one of them works. The good news is that it will stop...eventually...."

Jason looked nervously in Keating's direction, trying to discern the level of seriousness in the situation.

"Hey, don't look so worried, it won't be that bad, as long as you tell me to stop in time."

"What?"

"I need you to tell me how far I am away from the ravine, but I need enough time to stop the truck. We need to be close enough to dump the bed; about a foot or so from the edge of the ravine."

Jason could feel the lower lid of his left eye begin to twitch as it always did when his nerves got the best of him. He was supposed to blindly guide Keating and his truck backwards, giving him enough time to stop before it careened over the side of the ravine, with Keating inside; no problem.

They arrived at the dump site and Jason hopped out of the cab. Walking over to the ravine and looking down, Jason was reminded of an old Western movie in which a runaway covered wagon dives off the side of a ravine into an explosive cloud of destruction.

"So when the back tires get to about three feet away from the edge, you yell, alright?"

"Yes sir," he stammered.

The truck slowly moaned in reverse toward him.

"How much is three feet? Oh God, what if I tell him to stop too soon, or not soon enough?" he thought. Three feet quickly approached, and then..."That's it, STOP!" The brakes groaned. The truck was still moving too quickly toward the edge; it wasn't going to stop in time. Two feet, and still rolling. One foot...six inches...and then...it stopped.

Keating yelled from the cab, "How'd we do?"

Looking down at the tires and the edge of the ravine, Jason replied nervously, "Uh, about four inches."

"Good," yelled Keating.

Jason remained quiet on the drive home; the roar of the engine consumed the cab of the truck. Yelling over the engine, Keating asked, "Do you hunt, or play golf, or anything?"

Jason's gave him a confused look, unsure if he had misunderstood the question. Keating asked again, "What do you do for fun, anything? Do you hunt, fish...golf?"

"Oh, not really, maybe a little fishing when I was a kid," he replied.

"Well, I suppose we need to change that one of these days, and get you lined out for a turkey permit this fall," Keating replied. "Turkey's pretty harmless and won't get you killed, and then we can work you up into the boar hunting."

Jason turned with a jerk. "Boar hunting?"

"Yeah, you know, pig hunts, wild pigs, boars, running all over this county; quite a hoot if you've never been. The pigs are fearless, but nothing better than taking one of those critters down," replied Keating, as they pulled back into the clinic's parking lot. Reading Jason's questioning expression, he replied, "Oh, trust me, you make it back from one of those hunts, and you have a whole new appreciation for man and beast."

Chapter 15

Jason hated his world and everything in it, compounded by the fact that his prison work term was less than two months underway. June had flown by, but now July seemed to smolder like the ever-increasing temperature and humidity. He kept to himself throughout the day, attempting to avoid an appearance on Keating's radar. He wanted to disappear, wondering how he would ever move forward. Becca consumed his thoughts; they had shared everything, including what he thought was their mutual dream.

The minute the last patient left, Jason snuck out. He felt sick to his stomach, and if anyone asked, he would tell them he had the flu. He drove aimlessly around town, wondering how his life ended up here.

He didn't want to go back to that awful, dusty, lonely barn; he pulled into the Buckaroo Mini-Mart parking lot, hoping for anything to distract him from his current state. It seemed to be the only place in town that remained open past 6:00 P.M. With its mish-mash of merchandise, it was a treasure trove of cheap crap; it was Birdie's version of Walmart.

The aisles were narrow and stacked high with decades-old assorted items. He paused to look through a hanging rack of 8-track tapes, before catching himself and wondering why. "When Armageddon strikes," he thought, "this place might keep you alive." The back corner of the store displayed a variety of CB radios and self-sustaining items from water purification pumps to kerosene generators. Jason walked aimlessly up and down the aisles, in awe that such a little store packed so much crap.

He stopped suddenly at a bin of VHS tapes. Television reception in the barn was spotty, but remembering that the television contained a VHS player, he began sorting through the bin. With a copy of Chevy Chase's *Fletch* and a James Bond movie, he made his way to the cashier. The tall, thin man behind the counter eyed Jason carefully as he laid the tapes on the counter.

"You know that you can't play these in your DVD player; these are VHS tapes," he said.

"Yes, thanks, I know."

"K, just checkin'."

When he got back to the apartment, Jason had just microwaved his dinner and sat down to watch his new purchases when his cell phone rang with a call about a sick horse. Cursing under his breath, he took two quick bites of his dinner and headed for the truck.

The down horse lay in the middle of a large, open, dark corral; there weren't any lights, and in the dark Jason tripped over the rough, clumped dirt. A small group of shadowy figures stood motionless, surrounding the horse as Jason approached. The owner reported that "the vet" had been out at noon, but the horse remained unchanged. As she continued with her explanation, Jason wondered where this vet was now. Word of the down horse had spread, and more and more people continued to arrive. Apparently no one had anything else better to do in Birdie that night.

Of course, each of the neighbors had an opinion on what ailed the horse. Jason listened to the horse's abdominal sounds and vital signs before beginning his treatment. He returned to the truck, remembering Keating's advice that a shot of dexamethasone seemed to be a touch of magic for a down horse. Jason hoped it would work tonight.

Minutes later, he heard yelling. He peeked from behind the truck, worried about what he might see; the horse was now standing. The owner ran over to him.

"Doc, you saved Rocky! You know, 'the vet' couldn't even get this horse up, but you did!"

Jason proceeded with a rectal examination, which revealed a significant abdominal impaction and a lot of gas distension. The 30-year-old horse wasn't a candidate for surgery, so he treated the impaction and explained to the owner that it would take time for the horse to heal fully. As the owner walked Jason back to his truck, she asked, "How much is this gonna cost me, Doc?"

When Jason told her the figure, her voice became

shaky, and she relayed the story of her recent divorce and other financial woes, red flagging the conclusion, which was that Jason wasn't going to get paid. In the darkness of the late hour, Jason, tired and hungry, just stared blankly at the ground. "I could pay you $100 cash tonight," she said, as she pulled a small wad of bills from her pocket. He took a deep breath, thanked her, and headed home.

The next day, Jason received various reports of Rocky's condition. The ever-helpful, and sometimes misguided, residents of Birdie were always willing and able to nose into others' business. Many of them who had been witness to the previous night's veterinary care phoned the clinic with hourly updates of the horse's condition. One woman even began radioing on the police scanner before local officials asked her to stop.

Later that day, the owner called to report that Rocky was no longer showing signs of improvement. Jason loaded up and returned to the farm for a recheck exam. His heart sank as he felt several loops of distended small intestine upon rectal palpation; he knew this would end badly. The horse was crashing quickly, forcing Jason to recommend humane euthanasia. Although the cost concerned the owner, Jason comforted her and explained that they could work out a financial agreement later but that he owed it to this horse to end his suffering.

After it was over, Jason returned to the truck and discounted as many charges as he could, in an attempt to help the struggling client; at least the horse was no longer suffering. "Doc, will you take payments?" she asked as Jason handed her the invoice. He paused, wondering what lecture Keating would give him later. "Yes, I'm sure we can work something out." As he closed the doors on the truck to leave, she approached and asked, "I was wondering; if you come across any good horses for sale, would you be sure and give me a call?"

Chapter 16

Tommy was no longer returning Jason's calls. The isolation of Jason's reality had set in over the past two weeks, and he longed for Becca to call; maybe the breakup was just another big misunderstanding, or she'd had a change of heart. Why couldn't he have something that didn't seem to be spinning out of control? The reality of each passing day proved that this time was different.

Keating returned from a weekend getaway with his veterinary cronies on the Great Salt Plains Lake. Refreshed, and seemingly less grumpy than normal, he'd asked Jason to help him with some young colts that hadn't been handled much. Tom Hansen had been enlisted to start the colts. Tom was a 73-year-old cowboy who had spent his life training horses, and Keating's brief summary of Tom told Jason that the man knew a few things about handling horses, both the good and bad; if Tom was asking for help, then it must be bad. Many of these colts had been treated like cattle prior to their arrival, worked in squeeze chutes and wearing ear tags that were normally placed only in the ears of cattle for identification. The ear tags needed to be removed. The local farrier had also been enlisted to properly trim their feet.

Tom greeted them when Keating and Jason arrived and quickly voiced his concerns as they stepped from the truck. "These buggers are some of the bronciest sonsabitches I've ever been around. They'll hurt ya if you give 'em a chance."

Jason, nervous and anxious, wanted to show Keating that he was able to handle these horses. Returning to the truck, he drew several syringes of sedative. Keating pulled him aside and in a cautioning tone said, "Now, no sense in getting yourself broken for these worthless dinks; I damn well mean it. Take your time, and if we have to walk away, then there's no shame in that; live to go another day, the way I look at it."

Jason took a deep breath as he approached the colts, feeling a knot forming in his gut. The horses were part Percheron and part Quarter Horse. They each stood at least five feet at their withers, and their heads towered over Jason's own. He moved cautiously, hoping not to make any sudden movements or startle any of them. Each colt pawed the ground anxiously, with the wide-eyed look of a caged, wild animal. As he nervously tried to set the needle into the first horse's vein, the horse jerked back and threw its head. Jason jumped back momentarily but quickly regained his confidence. Without losing his focus, he took another step forward. This time his needle hit the vein and the sedative took effect; seconds later, the giant colt licked its lips and slowly dropped its head.

The second horse stood without incident while Jason struggled to find the vein. After several attempts, he began to feel the eyes of all the men at the fence staring through the back of this head. He was making yet another attempt when the farrier jumped down from the fence and made his way toward him.

"I'll take it from here, 'Doc,' or we'll be here all damn afternoon at this rate," he shouted in a disgusted tone.

Derrick McKanney was a cowboy shoer with no formal training who had honed his skills following ranch horse herds, hopping from ranch to ranch wherever he could find work. McKanney had a big mouth, a short temper, and no time for anyone getting in his way, especially the academic, veterinarian types who meddled in his work. From the moment of their arrival at the farm, he was less than thrilled about Keating and Jason being there. He believed he could trim the horses without the aid of a veterinarian, and as Jason was taking his time with each one, McKanney had become increasingly agitated and loose lipped.

Mumbling to himself, McKanney stepped up behind the horse. He grabbed the horse's leg and crouched down as he brought the foot to rest in his lap. Grinning a tobacco-stained smile, he sneered, "Hell, boys, you don't need no sedative for this one. I got it all under control!"

At that moment, the horse pinned its ears and thrust both legs skyward. McKanney was sent sailing, kicked not once, but twice in the process. Tom rushed to pick him up, but McKanney brushed off the assistance and hobbled back to his truck without a word.

In the end, all the horses' tags were removed and most of their feet were trimmed. Tom thanked them for coming, and they headed off to another call.

Early the next afternoon, Shelly came into Jason's office. Tom had called and was stopping by. Jason told her that Dr. Keating had left for Tulsa that morning and would be out of the office until the following morning.

"I know, that's what I told him, but he said he wants to talk to you."

"Me?" he exclaimed. "That can't be good," he groaned.

Jason waited anxiously, periodically peering through the shades of the office window and looking for any sign of Tom's truck. He briefly entertained the idea of having a last-minute errand to run, but Birdie didn't really lend itself to running errands. He dropped back into his chair, wishing to be anywhere but there.

Minutes later, Tom's truck pulled up in front of the clinic. Tom slowly made his way to the door, entered quietly, and asked to see Jason. Shelly poked her head around the corner and motioned for Jason to follow her to the front desk. As Jason made his way to the front of the office, he replayed the events of the previous day. What had he done to upset Tom? The sickness in his stomach told him he was going to be set straight by this old cowboy. As Jason entered, Tom removed his hat and slowly extended his hand. A small smile grew across his

95

wrinkled, weathered face.

"I wanted to come by and tell you what a downright good job you did around those horses yesterday. They will as sure as anything hurt somebody...but you got around them fine. I know they teach you a lot at that school, but you can't teach someone how to handle horses the way you did. That's something you learn by taking the time to watch others and knowin' how to be quiet. You did real good, Doc, and, well...I just thought a guy ought like to know sometimes when he's doing good." Jason was stunned. He tried to swallow, but his mouth had gone dry. He finally stammered out a soft "Thank you.... That means a lot coming from you."

"You're going to make a great veterinarian. I want you to know that. I was impressed with you, Dr. Davies." And as quickly as he had arrived, Tom nodded to Shelly and was gone.

As the door closed, Jason was frozen to the spot, trying to grasp what had just transpired. He turned to Shelly, who smiled and winked. He went back to his desk and sat for quite a while, staring at his diploma on the wall.

Chapter 17

Dr. Keating's practice was originally established to focus on and treat strictly large animals, such as horses and cattle. Over the years, he added several small animal exam rooms to care for dogs and cats in the clinic, but that's where it ended. He made his intentions clear that caring for birds was for the birds, and snakes were cared for with a shovel. Jason needed no further explanation.

The only coffee shop in Birdie that offered anything other than Folger's was Flossie's. It certainly wasn't Starbucks, or anything close to it, but Flossie's did provide a small town Starbucks-esque experience. Although many people grumbled that high-priced, high-brow cappuccinos and lattes only spelled trouble with a capital T, Flossie's had become an official morning checkpoint in Birdie. As Jason stood in line for his coffee one morning, two women approached.

"Dr. Davies? We are sorry to bother you, but we wondered if you could help us with some animals at our place. My name is Alice and this is my sister, Jenny Mae."

"Nice to meet you," he said, trying to generate a smile.

"Well, we wondered if you could take a look at our alpacas. We've been raising them for a while now in these parts, but Doc Keating refuses to work with them. We were hoping that with all your professional training at the university, you might be able to help."

Jason dropped a dollar in the tip jar and turned around, finding the entire room quiet and all eyes on him. He tried to remain focused on what the women were asking. "Well, of course, sure, I'd be, uh, happy to help, but I don't claim to be an expert on alpacas by any means...."

"We understand. It's like that for all of us with these critters. There just aren't any vets willing to help. Oh, there was a vet over by Ponca City a while back, but he moved on to Tulsa. We're desperate! We're going to the wool market down in Argyle and need blood tests for some of the animals; we would greatly appreciate your help."

Jason scheduled to meet them the next morning. Returning to the truck, he was torn. Keating wouldn't be happy, but wasn't Jason ultimately making him money by bringing more business to the clinic? Maybe all that talk of snakes and birds had just been idle banter; surely Keating would see the positive cash flow of alpacas.

"If you're crazy enough to work on those damn things, fine; but don't have those folks calling me," Keating grumped after Jason shared the news. "You just better be prepared for the rest of them that start calling; word around here spreads fast."

"Oh, I'm sure this is a one-shot deal, and I already told them I don't know anything about alpacas," he responded.

"We'll see." Keating looked disgusted as he sat down to read over the notes posted on his desk.

The next morning Jason arrived at the sisters' farm. He

filled out the necessary health information and drew two aliquots of blood. As he finished, they asked, "Would you mind following us over to a friend's house? She has some alpacas too, and we just have some questions for you." Following them in the truck to their friend's house down the road made Jason a little nervous. "What were these women up to, and how exactly did I get myself into this?" he wondered. When they arrived, he saw several women standing around an old Ford truck in the driveway.

Introductions were made as Alice looked around at the women's faces. "We all have alpacas and goats and would like to see if you'd consider helping us with them from time to time." Looking at the smiling group of middle-aged women, how could he say No? He felt his stomach ache; there would be hell to pay back at the clinic....

Later, Jason was attempting to catch up on work at his desk when Keating walked in and sat down.

"So, how did it go this morning?"

Jason told him what he had discussed with the women earlier that morning, again hoping that Keating might see the economic potential of the untapped alpaca market in Birdie. Keating didn't see it with quite the same level of enthusiasm. His stare at Jason lasted only seconds, but it felt like an eternity. "Just so long as they don't call me."

The next morning Jason arrived at the clinic to find his desk covered with notes.

"For Dr. Davies: Alpaca question."

"Note for Dr. Davies: A quick question about my alpaca, please call."

"Dr. Davies: Can alpacas be crossed with horses? Please call."

Digging through the pile, Jason felt momentarily terrified. What had he done? A simple cup of coffee had turned into this? Minutes later the back door opened as Keating entered; Jason hoped he hadn't seen the messages.

Keating walked around the desk and set his cup down. "Dr. Davies, you apparently are the new authority on alpacas in these parts; I hope you found the messages on your desk from yesterday, and here are two more that called me at the house last night. There are several others who hung up when I answered, so I don't have any numbers for them...." He gave Jason another look of disbelief before heading outside.

Jason sat back in his chair; it was going to be a long day. He texted Becca, hoping for some sign, even a single emoji, signifying that their relationship might still be intact, or even better, that she might have reconsidered Birdie. Given their rollercoaster relationship, it wouldn't surprise him if she'd met someone at her new job. A therapist Jason had seen back in college during yet another rough patch with Becca had advised Jason to "mind his own mind" in these situations, but this was proving to be exceedingly difficult. Further adding to his personal drama, there was still no word on when or how he was getting out of Birdie.

###

As Jason tried to resolve himself to the fact that he wasn't going anywhere anytime soon, the days slowed almost to a crawl at times, further driving his depression. He wanted to be alone today and had inadvertently achieved that, as everyone else had left him at the clinic alone over the lunch hour.

The phone rang with a frantic client with an injured goat. She loved it like her own child and was devastated that a strange dog had jumped the back fence and attacked it. Jason found the goat traumatized, with severe lacerations of its hind end. He spent the afternoon and early evening cleaning and suturing the wounds, but as the sun began to set, light quickly became an issue. His portable camping headlamp helped illuminate the wound, but to get the right angle he had to lie flat on his chest with the goat's backside less than six inches from his face. Jason chuckled to himself, thinking of Keating's niece's recommendation that they take some "action photographs while working" so they could add them to the clinic's website for its upcoming debut.

When Jason went back to recheck the goat four days later, the animal proved difficult to catch, indicating her resolve and recovery. Jason had spoken with the owner earlier in the day, who had stated that she wouldn't be home but said that Jason should go ahead and look at the goat in the yard.

Finally cornering the animal by himself, Jason went to work changing the bandage and evaluating his surgical goat skills; the wounds were healing well. Just then Jason heard the back screen door slam. Looking up, he saw the owner's thirty-something son standing on the back porch watching him. He wore a hooded sweatshirt and flannel pajama bottoms, which immediately struck Jason as odd since the average temperature in Birdie was reaching the mid-90s.

"Hello," Jason said. The man nodded slightly, taking a drag of his cigarette; his eyes were fixed on the goat's wounds. Jason went back to work on the leg. Several minutes passed, and the man finally spoke.

"What do you think about the honeybees?"

Jason thought he'd misunderstood the man; had he said "honeybees?" "You mean around here?" he asked. "Do you folks raise bees?"

"No...," he slowly replied, taking another drag. "I was listening to talk radio last night, and they said thousands of honeybees have left their hives...not returned."

"Wow," Jason replied. "Does anyone know why?"

"Well, they're saying it has somethin' to do with car exhaust and global warming...but maybe they're just full of shit."

"Well, global warming does seem to be the topic these days," replied Jason with a smile.

The man remained silent for a few seconds, as he

continued to smoke his cigarette. "You know, Einstein said once the bees leave we only have four good years left." Einstein and bees; now there was a connection Jason hadn't ever made. The man seemed distracted, wandering around the yard.

"Did you lose something?" Jason stood up from the goat, looking for anything unusual in the yard.

"I was checking to see if the grass is growing at all."

Jason, unsure if he had heard the man correctly, felt awkward; yet he found himself wandering around the yard, inspecting the blades of grass.

When he finished with the goat, he returned to his truck, thinking, "Just when I thought this town couldn't get any weirder...."

He had just about omitted the honeybees from his memory when he arrived back at his apartment. As he unlocked the door to the apartment, the smell of feces rushed his senses. "That damn donkey!" He bristled, turning the light on to witness the full extent of the animal's handiwork. The floor was covered with a nauseating mess that would be a nightmare to clean up.

He raced to the kitchen and found the barn door ajar. He stormed into the barn, his fury throttled into donkey rage. "Jasper, where the hell are you?" It was dark save for a small bulb in the corner that emitted just enough light for Jason to see Jasper quietly eating in the stall at the far end. He stood at the door, watching the small donkey eating without a care in the world. Jason took a deep breath and counted to ten, holding back a physical urge to beat the short, big-eared mammal.

"Damn you, you sorry sack of donkey misery!" He wondered why anyone would want a donkey. What purpose did they serve except to eat all your food and poop on your floor? But how did he keep getting into the apartment? Hadn't the door had been locked?

Finally cleaning up the manure, he readied himself for bed. The overwhelming smell still filled the small space, and Jason struggled to open one of the windows. Hadn't anyone ever opened a window in this place? He finally resorted to propping the door ajar, hoping no other creature would venture in during the night.

Chapter 18

Jason's cell phone rang. He grumbled, looking for his glasses on the table next to his bed. He hoped it would be Becca, but the frantic woman's voice on the other end of the phone wasn't hers. The woman rambled erratically about a down horse. Jason knew his sleep for the night was over, as he quickly dressed and headed to the clinic for his bags.

Pulling into the parking lot, he froze. The lights were on in the clinic. He looked at his watch: 10:37 P.M.

"What the...?" he mumbled. During his last year at vet school he'd heard of veterinary clinic burglaries on the rise. Crooks would break in and steal cash, ketamine, valium, or anything else that could be pawned for money.

What should he do, call the police? He decided to begin with the obvious and dialed Keating but got no answer. He saw a shadowy figure through the office window. "Son-of-a-bitch!" Jason hissed. He wished he could reconcile himself to owning a gun, but did he really think he would march through the door and take on a meth addict? Best to stay in the truck and call the police. He dialed 911 and explained the situation. The operator told him to remain in his vehicle until officers arrived. Minutes later, two sheriff's vehicles slowly pulled into the parking lot with only their parking lights on. Jason quietly slid out of the truck and scrambled over toward the officers, attempting to stay low. They watched him with curiosity as he approached their vehicle.

"Are you the new doc in with old Doc Keating? You called this in?"

Jason squatted by the passenger side car door. "Yes, I'm on my way to a horse emergency, but when I showed up the lights were on, and I can see at least one person walking around in there." The officers appeared almost identical in appearance: crew cut hair and bulging bicep muscles. Jason felt inadequate next to them; he wondered if he should be working out at a gym. Did Birdie even have a gym?

"So what do you want me to do?" Jason's nervous voice cracked.

"Well, Doc, let me and Caleb hit the door first, and when we're clear, then I want you to follow, so we can make a positive ID and arrest. But we don't need you getting in the line of fire, so we'll motion for you when it's time, got it?"

Jason gave a thumbs up. Following their instructions, he held back as they approached the front door with guns drawn. The first officer tried the door and it opened easily. The men disappeared through the doorway. Jason slid down the wall and crouched outside. He braced himself; hearing the officers' shouts, he feared what would come next. He plugged his ears to avoid hearing the gun shots, and then even worse, the awful cries of someone injured and dying.

Crouched on the ground, scared out of his wits, and plugging his ears, Jason jumped sky high when the second officer tapped him on the shoulder. He waved for Jason to follow him into the clinic. What had happened? He hadn't heard any shots or screams. Had the officers taken the criminals down without incident? Jason felt a surge of heroism as he realized how proud Keating would be. He'd saved the clinic from being burglarized; he might even make the front page of the paper!

However, at that moment he heard a voice that changed everything. The familiar voice sent a pang of terror through him, and his stomach clenched; that voice belonged to Keating. Jason rushed in unprepared for what he saw, and his heart sank as he realized what he'd done. Seated on the exam table, pant leg rolled up just above his knee, was Dr. Keating, with a glass of Scotch next to him and a syringe and needle in his hand.

"What in God's green earth are you doing?" Keating shouted with a fiery gaze.

The officers turned to Jason with looks of confusion.

"I...I...thought that someone was in the clinic, and I...I couldn't reach you, so I called...." Jason glanced between both officers.

"Well, son-of-a-bitch anyway," shouted Keating, "You morons about gave me a heart attack, running in here ready to shoot up the place."

"Dr. Keating, I'm so sorry, it's just that I was worried and didn't want to...."

"Oh, hell, you need to use your damn head once in a while. Ain't nobody ever broke into my clinic, and they ain't about to start!" Keating slid off the table.

"Well, Doc, if all's good here, we'll be on our way," said the first officer, holstering his gun.

"Okay then, and thanks, Adam. Sorry for the confusion and all." Keating turned and glared at Jason with a look of disgust.

Both men nodded to Jason as they left. His heart jumped into his throat; he was bound to make the paper alright....

Jason caught his breath and looked at Keating with one pant leg still rolled.

"Well, you busted me alright," Keating barked, taking a sip of Scotch. "I was trying to inject this knee of mine with a little steroid; it's due."

"Shouldn't you be leaving that to an orthopedist or something?" Jason stared at the needle and syringe.

"Oh, that moron couldn't inject a ripe tomato," scoffed Keating. "He's not even in Birdie but once a month, and the jackass is so full of himself you can't even fit in the same room with him. No, I trust myself a whole hell of a lot more than I do that creep."

"I'm really sorry about all of this. It surely wasn't my intention to...."

"Ah Jason, quit your squabbling and leave me to my business. Just use some damn common sense next time, got it?"

"Yes, sir." Jason could feel the embarrassment of his actions as his face flushed. Keating returned to his work as Jason turned to go. Jason quickly grabbed his bag, hoping it had been restocked with supplies

Driving to the call, he felt numb; nothing seemed to be going right for him. To make matters worse, the back country roads presented a challenge at this hour when trying to find an address on a dilapidated roadside mailbox. He passed the farm, realizing it too late. Trying to find a suitable turnaround only added to his bad mood.

When he finally arrived, he could see a shadowy figure leading a horse in circles around the yard. The person appeared to be anxiously talking on a cell phone. "Why is it so bloody pitch black out tonight," Jason mumbled, reaching under the seat in search of a flashlight.

"I'll call you right back." The woman with the horse hung up the phone, nervously handling her cigarette in the other hand.

They made introductions and Jason set to work assessing the mare's condition.

The owner, Janice Troutman, had recently relocated to Birdie from California. "San Francisco, to be exact," she had clarified. After the horse's arrival the day before, from a lengthy cross-country transport, it hadn't been interested in drinking or eating.

Jason examined the horse and noted that she had decreased gut sounds, and although her heart rate was normal, she hadn't been drinking, and she was showing signs of dehydration.

Jason told Janice, "I think we should 'tube' her. She's dehydrated, and giving her some fluids through a tube might just do the trick."

"Hold on a second." Janice pulled out her phone and redialed, mumbling quietly to the person on the line. "Do you mind if my friend speaks with Tipsy a moment before you proceed with this business?"

"Uh...no...I'll go grab a few things." Confused, Jason returned to the truck. Glancing quickly over his shoulder, he could see Janice place the phone next to the horse's ear. He shook his head; this night was getting stranger and stranger by the minute. He returned to the horse, bracing himself for what he feared would be the fallout of the horse's phone conversation. As he approached, Janice looked curiously at the bucket of fluids, tube, and hand pump.

"My friend in San Francisco is a pet psychic, and she can speak directly with animals. I don't know if you've ever had any experience with this sort of phenomena, but it's such an amazing gift. You apparently are right on with Tipsy tonight; my friend Marsha said that she spoke with Tipsy and that she has a blockage on her left side, and she is also dehydrated. Tipsy says she's not happy about this whole tubing business; however, Marsha explained to her that it's necessary for her well-being."

Jason let out a muffled sigh; was this for real? Had Keating put someone up to this?

"Okay, here we go," he said, sliding the tube up the left nostril of the horse's nose. Janice closed her eyes and began a series of short, loud breaths. Jason turned, worried that she was going to faint, but then came the chanting. "Hmmmmmmmm, waaaaa, waaaaa, hmmmmmmmm." Jason closed his eyes; this was more than he could bear. He could feel the resistance in the tube, letting him know where it was in the esophagus as he guided it toward the stomach. He then proceeded to administer the medication, while the chanting continued. "Waaaaaaa, waaaaaaaa, hmmmmmmmm, hmmmmm."

"Okay...." He turned, hoping that his expression didn't reveal the urge to burst out in uncontrolled laughter.

Jason explained that the medication should begin to work over the next several hours, but if the mare's pain increased, then Janice needed to contact him.

"I think it's important to perform a rectal exam to evaluate her GI tract. I want to make sure an impaction is the only issue we're dealing with here." Jason began to reach for his rectal exam gloves and lubricant.

Janet interjected, "Oh, I'll need to tell Marsha about the rectal examination and see how she feels about it, or more importantly, how Tipsy feels about it." Janice turned and walked away. "Marsha, it's Janice. Yes, sorry it's so late, but the vet wants to...."

Jason stood dumbfounded, watching her walk away. Clearly he was in some parallel universe of hell. His body

111

and mind were hitting the wall; he was done. He marched back to the truck and crawled into the cab, waiting for the pet psychic's decision. He looked at his watch: 1:07 A.M. He leaned his head back and closed his eyes. "I have clearly angered the gods...."

Minutes later, Jason jumped at Janice's knock on the truck window.

"Dr. Davies? I just hung up with Marsha and she says Tipsy is depressed with the move and all. She wants to know if rectal palpation is really necessary tonight." Jason took a deep breath and said, "Well, we can wait on the palpation and see how she responds to the fluids and medication."

He climbed out of the truck. "This woman is a hot mess," he mumbled, trying to quickly gather his equipment. But as he placed the last few items in the truck, Janice approached.

"My friend Marsha wanted me to thank you for taking care of Tipsy. We both really appreciate it. She also wanted me to tell you something personal, if it's alright."

"Sure, what's that?"

"I'm not exactly sure if I'm remembering this right, but she wanted me to tell you that 'Jasper' likes carrots and that if you start giving him carrots periodically, he will stop pooping in your house."

Jason's jaw dropped, unsure if he'd heard her correctly. How did Marsha know about Jasper? As he climbed into the truck, he felt goose bumps on his arms.

He was unsettled by what he had just heard. Surely it was nothing more than a clever parlor trick. Everyone in this town knew who Jasper was, didn't they?

Jason pulled into his driveway and shut off the engine. He sat staring out at the night sky; the stars were brilliant and expansive across the backdrop of darkness. He hadn't remembered seeing the stars in Fort Collins, at least not like this. His cell phone beeped with a voice mail; he hadn't remembered hearing his phone ring earlier. Hopefully it wasn't another emergency; he needed sleep. It was from Keating. "Jason, I meant to let you know that I volunteered us, well, rather, you, I guess, for the livestock auction over in Waynoka tomorrow. Sorry for the short notice, but you shouldn't have any problem. Get over there by 7:00 A.M. and ask to talk to Peggy in the office. She'll make the introductions and show you what needs to be done. Okay then, have a good evening, and good luck tomorrow."

Chapter 19

The alarm blasted Jason from his sleep. He panicked and bolted out of bed; had he overslept? What time did Keating say he needed to be at the sale barn? He looked at his watch: 6:45 A.M. He wouldn't have time to shave or shower this morning. He quickly threw on some clothes and headed for his truck. "These are the days I miss a Starbucks drive-thru," he thought to himself.

He made the drive to Waynoka down County Road 14 in record time. The parking lot was filled with trucks and trailers, making it difficult to find a place to park. He watched the slow procession of vehicles, as well as animals making their way into the stockyards.

"It's going to be a long day," he mumbled, climbing out of the truck.

He followed a group of cowboys into the office. His eyes scanned the desks behind the counter, looking for a woman matching Peggy's description. He quietly maneuvered his way through the crowded office and found her seated at her desk. She introduced herself politely, but the ringing phone and piles of papers on her desk told him she would be all business. She quickly led him through a maze of small offices, waving at several men they passed who were staring at papers on their desks, and then finally dumped Jason at a small back door.

"Here's a list of everything you need. Supplies are in a

small cabinet down aisle 13. There should be ear tags, back tags, tattoo ink, and anything else you might need." She handed him a small notebook, instructing him to maintain an accurate count of all animals entering throughout the day. "The vet office behind the auction arena should have your supplies, but let me know if you need anything else. If you have questions, just ask any of the guys in the pens. Good luck." She smiled and disappeared.

The smell of manure, hay, and diesel fuel consumed his olfactory senses as he made his way down the wet and slimy alleys. This was too much, and he felt clueless about the entire event. He had no idea how to handle the responsibilities of a livestock auction. He would call Keating and tell him he just couldn't do this. Still exhausted from the night before, no shower, no shave, and clearly in need of some coffee, Jason returned to his truck to hide for a few minutes, hoping to clear his thoughts and temper his anxiety.

"Fake it until you make it," he mumbled to himself; words of wisdom his father had interjected at critical and infrequent father-son moments.

He took a deep breath, got back out of the truck, and headed for the pens: rows and rows of goats, cows, and hogs. He remembered that the hogs required back tags before they could be sent into the sale ring. As he climbed into the pen of sleeping sows, he remembered Peggy's cautionary words: "Don't turn your back on them, not even for a second."

He reached out gently, placing a tag on an unsuspecting sow in the corner. In a flash, the animal was awake, screaming and lunging forward at him. Jason turned and ran, only to be tripped up by another hog in front of him. Tumbling face first into the greasy, muddy manure on the pen floor, he scrambled to regain his footing, but not before the animals began squealing hysterically. He wiped the mud from his face with the corner of his shirt. "I guess showering would have been a waste," he thought to himself.

The hogs milled around the pen, waiting for another chance to attack, as Jason contemplated his next move. One tag on one hog; at this rate, it would take all morning. Once he was safe outside the pen, his fear turned to embarrassment, and he quickly scanned the aisleway, looking for anyone witnessing the incident.

At the far end of the aisle was an elderly man walking with a cane; he shuffled from pen to pen, apparently unaware of the hog tag catastrophe.

"Dr. Davies, please report to the front office. Dr. Davies, please report to the front office," said Peggy's voice over the intercom.

Flustered, Jason sighed, realizing the hogs and the tags would have to wait. He headed down the aisle toward the office, quickly passing the man with the cane. "Doc, don't you worry about them pigs. They are bound to get us all at some point or another...."

"Thanks, but a little embarrassing, I guess...."

The man lifted his cane. "Ahhh, just keep moving. That's life; it's filled with embarrassment, but just keep moving. That's all you need to do and you'll be fine."

Jason hurried to the office, where Peggy had a new task for him. "Dr. Davies, there are 35 heifers requiring Bangs vaccinations up at the chutes for you; here's the paperwork." Peggy handed him a stack of papers as she spun around to answer the ringing phone.

Jason made his way to the small cabinet on aisle 13, gathering the supplies he needed. He scurried down the back side of the pens to a little rusted tin shed. He had only ever Bangs vaccinated one cow in vet school, with a half dozen other students. His confidence wasn't high that the 8-minute vet school crash course would be of much use to him now. "Fake it until you make it," he heard the voice in his head again. "Shut up," he mumbled to himself.

Jason had no idea how to operate the hydraulic chute, and several calls for help to the yard foreman had gone unanswered. He finally looked at the cattle owner. "You know how to run this chute?"

"Uh, well, yes, I suppose; doesn't look too different than the one we have down at the ranch." The man set the head gate for the first cow to enter the chute. Jason grabbed the tags and tattoo ink, readying himself for the first animal. Out of the corner of his eye, he noticed the man staring at him.

"Don't know, but are you sure them there's the tags

117

you want?"

"What do you mean?" Jason was confused.

"Well, it seems to me that the Bangs tags are orange, not silver. Those you got in your hands are silver, not orange."

Of course; how could he have forgotten! His heart beat faster as he realized the seriousness of the accident just averted. He could only imagine the paperwork nightmare he would have had to endure from the authorities, not to mention the humiliation of having to explain his mistake.

They began moving the cattle through, as Jason struggled with the tattooing, vaccinating, and tagging each animal. The green tattoo ink made a quick mess that he feared would be permanent. He helped the owner load the cattle and then watched as the truck pulled away. "Job well done," he thought. "Well, at least done...."

As Jason made his way through the pens, he remembered that he hadn't yet found the vet office. A tall, lanky cowboy walked by. "Excuse me, I'm the on-duty veterinarian today, and I wondered if you could tell me where the vet's office is?"

"That office is underneath the sale ring over on the north side of the building." The man pointed over the rows of pens while spitting a large brown liquid wad that landed at Jason's feet. "You need me to show you how to get there?"

"No, I'm sure I can find it just fine; thank you." Jason approached the north side of the building but saw no indication of anything resembling a veterinarian's office. "That cowboy must have been wrong; there isn't an office over...." He paused as his eye caught a glimpse of a small crumbling sidewalk covered by a maze of overgrown weeds leading to a small metal door. As he turned the knob, the door creaked with the sound of grinding metal. The room contained no windows; Jason ran his hand along the wall, feeling for the light switch. In the dim light he could see the decrepit remains of ancient lab equipment, assorted dust-covered bottles of medication, and a small 1950s-style refrigerator that sputtered and whirred as if on its last leg. He wondered how many veterinarians had sat in this metal folding chair as the auctioneer's voice warbled above.

"Dr. Davies. The veterinarian, Dr. Davies, please report back to the chute," a woman's voice bellowed over the loudspeaker.

Jason sighed; he was hungry and hadn't had time to pack a lunch. The sky was darkening and the smell of rain filled the air. Although the covered chute offered him some protection from the imminent precipitation, the cattle would soon be soaked and covered in mud. He quickly hurried back to his truck to retrieve his old vet school coveralls, hoping they would offer some protection.

"Doc," yelled the tall, heavyset man positioned at the chute's hydraulic controls. "We got 147 of the raunchiest bitches you ever seen! These heifers need to be preg' checked and mouthed, and then we can sort 'em." Jason stepped nervously into the chute to inspect the first animal.

"Now don't you worry, Doc. If any of 'em start heading for ya, we'll cover ya."

Jason found the reassurance only mildly comforting. The cows were wound up, electrified, as the rain began to the fall on the tin metal roof, pausing only for a brief moment before unleashing its wrath. The cows pushed and slammed into the chute with an angry fury. They wanted no part of any of this. Jason stepped gingerly behind each one to palpate for a pregnancy, as they slung their manure-covered tails at him. He quickly ran out of clean areas on his coveralls to wipe his manure-covered eyes and face. His arm began to ache, and he hoped they were near the end.

"Doc, keep 'em rollin', we ain't even halfway yet!" The rain rallied as the cows vocalized their discontent. Jason wondered whether it could rain so hard that the tin roof would collapse. The cacophony of rain on the metal roof drowned out the angry noise of the cattle and the whining hydraulics of the chute. One after another, the animals made their way through, and with each one, his arm throbbed, aching in weakness. "Doc, doin' good, only about 30 of them nasty bitches left!"

Jason regained his energy, pushing ahead as the rain turned to hail. The temperature dropped by the minute, turning the rain to marble ice rocks. Jason cringed, imagining the hood of his pickup bombarded with hail.

Finally, the last cow left the chute with a signature sling of mud and manure across his face.

He ran to the truck and found a large plastic bag crammed underneath the seat for just such an emergency. He removed his coveralls and placed them in the bag. He turned and offered a quick nod to the cowboys who were now running for cover, then scrambled into his truck.

He looked at his watch, wondering what time the sale would end. It was only 4:30 P.M. He sighed deeply, wondering if there might be anything edible in the glove box. A package of peanut butter crackers, a small bag of almonds, and an orange that had seen better days were his only consolation, but at that moment it was a feast.

The hail finally subsided and the rain began a slow decline. He listened intently for his phone, hoping he hadn't missed something important. When he returned to the office under the sale barn, the last few pens of cows were being sold.

After finishing the last few health papers and saying a quick goodbye to Peggy in the main office, he returned to the clinic. He looked at his watch: 6:30 P.M. Wet and exhausted, he felt chilled to the bone. All he wanted to do was go back to his hole in the barn and crawl into bed, and that's exactly what he did.

Chapter 20

August was slipping by without any words of encouragement on Jason's departure. After several lengthy conversations with the Veterinary Service Corps regarding his contested placement through the Veterinary Service Act, he had finally resolved himself to the fact that Birdie would be his home for the duration. "Dr. Davies, would you like a copy of the Veterinary Services contract that YOU signed with YOUR signature?" the woman on the phone curtly demanded.

As each day and week passed, he felt increasingly more isolated. Tommy would send a random text message or inappropriate picture of some sunbather on the beach from time to time, or a video of the latest arthroscopic surgery he'd assisted with at work, but no news about prospects of Jason's escape.

And despite his desire and hope to hear from Becca, there was nothing. Well, nothing except one small box. It arrived one afternoon, addressed to Jason at the clinic. He found it on his desk; seeing the postmark from Colorado, he deduced it was from Becca. He opened it, hoping it contained some surprise of resolution and renewal. He mistook the nondescript box as a gift, but instead it contained cold resentment. She had filled it with gifts of jewelry and other sentimental items he'd given to her, and one small silver ring dug deep into his fragile emotional state. He'd given it to her on their trip to Rocky Mountain National Park when they camped at Bear Lake to celebrate two years together. He rolled the ring in his hands as he read the inscription: "As you wish." It had been a line from her favorite movie, *The Princess Bride.* He could feel his chest tightening as he gently placed the ring back into the box. No note, nothing; just the symbols of their love cast aside and shipped across country. What a callous bitch.

He quickly settled into an after-work routine of frequenting the post office, grocery store, and then home to his apartment. As he left the office one Wednesday afternoon, he was exhausted and homesick for his pre-Birdie life. He swung by the post office as usual, secretly hoping that a package from home might be waiting.

The post office appeared empty except for an older man at the far end, slowly sorting through a large stack of mail. Finding nothing in his mailbox, Jason returned to his truck. As he sat staring out the windshield, he was startled by a tap on the driver's window. Glaring at him was the man he had noticed inside: a short-statured fellow dressed in deerskin pants and a fringed coat. He looked a great deal like pictures of Buffalo Bill Cody.

"Hello?" Jason said hesitantly, slowly rolled the window partially down.

"You the new veterinarian in town?" the odd man asked.

"Uh, yes, sir."

"Well, I thought it would be appropriate to introduce myself to you. The name is William Cody. Most folks in these parts know me as Bill Cody."

"Like Buffalo Bill?"

"So you've heard of me?"

Confused, Jason hesitated....

"Don't worry, son, I'm not that crazy. Yes, Buffalo Bill was my great uncle." Cody smirked beneath his mustache. "Say, I wanted to invite you and your wife over for dinner some evening to the house."

"Oh, I appreciate that, but I...Umm...I'm not married...."

"What! Not hitched? A good lookin' fella like yourself? Well, we need to rectify that situation, yes sir, I'm tellin' you. Well, listen here now, I have an idea, you see, because I have a b-e-a-u-t-i-f-u-l daughter. She is a fine young gal, yes sir, fine daughter, a father couldn't ask for a better one. We for sure need to make a meeting with you two young kids and make an acquaintance, for sure."

"Oh...Well...I surely do appreciate the offer and consideration or...but...you see...I...," Jason stammered, feeling his cheeks flushing red with embarrassment.

"Don't think anything of it; it would be my pleasure. I'll give her a call as soon as I get back to the ranch."

"No, really, I...."

"Hush now, she needs to get out more anyway; always got her nose in a book all the time." Cody handed Jason a card, saying, "Now here, yes sir, my address is on here, and directions. Now tomorrow night around 6:30 P.M., dinner at my place, and you can meet Miss Cindy Lou."

"Your daughter?"

"Yes sir, Miss Cindy Lou, just about the sweetest girl you'll ever lay eyes on, for sure."

Jason could feel his stomach begin to clench. Skipping the grocery store tonight wouldn't be a bad plan; his appetite was suddenly gone.

###

At the clinic the next morning, Jason searched to find a good reason to politely excuse himself from the impending catastrophe awaiting him that evening. He anxiously examined the call schedule, secretly hoping he was on for the night, but Keating had requested the next two evenings for some reason.

"Damn," he mumbled under his breath.

"What's wrong?" Keating asked from behind him.

"Oh, uh, nothing."

"Not to worry, Doc, I'm covering call the next two nights, so you're a free man.

A free...single...*eligible* man," Keating said with a wink. Jason froze; how did Keating know? This town was so small, and very well-wired when it came to gossip.

"Bill already called me this morning to make sure I let you off early. Not to worry, she won't hurt you too bad."

Keating gently slapped Jason on the back as he exited the room.

Later that afternoon, Jason sat at his desk trying to make sense of the inventory list while watching the clock tick closer to the hour. He heard Keating's truck arrive and Keating quickly made his way into the office. "Is he still here?" Keating's voice bellowed. "Well, I'll be.... Jason! You need to get the hell out of here! Dammit all if Bill hasn't already called me four times today to make sure you're coming, so go! Oh...and Bill has an extensive liquor cabinet, so after the third or fourth drink, she'll be looking better and better...," Keating chuckled teasingly. Jason slowly gathered his things, not sure what he had gotten himself into for the evening.

A hot shower and change of clothes did nothing to refresh his spirits. The idea of an evening with Wild Bill Cody and his matronly daughter made him wonder if listening to his grandmother's requests for him to enter the priesthood would have been a better plan.

"Please, Lord, get me through this evening," he whispered, ringing the doorbell. The door opened suddenly and Cody grabbed him by the shoulders and pulled him inside.

"Well, welcome, Dr. Davies, welcome, yes sir, to the ranch here, yes sir, welcome! Now, hang on here one little second, and I'll get Cindy Lou. CINDY LOU!!! You found the place okay? CINDY LOU!!! Cindy Lou, Darlin', I need you down here, so I may properly introduce you to Dr.

Davies here."

Jason nervously scanned the spacious entry. The domed ceiling had been painted to mirror a lofty blue sky complete with billowy, white clouds. A massive antler chandelier hung overhead and the stone fireplace that prominently climbed the wall gave him the impression he'd wandered into a remote castle on the prairie.

"Miss Cindy Lou will join us most directly; she has been lookin' forward to meetin' the most eligible bachelor in Birdie! She's just darlin', I'm tellin' you, yes sir, just darlin'...."

"Sorry to keep you waiting." A woman's voice came from the top of the grand antique staircase.

Looking up, Jason froze in disbelief as Cindy Lou slowly and confidently made her way down the staircase. She wasn't at all what he had imagined.

"Daddy, you ought not to tell untruths," Cindy Lou said with a smile. "Good evening, Dr. Davies. I'm Cindy Lou, and it is truly a pleasure to meet you."

"Good, good evening," Jason stammered, awestruck with the beautiful woman standing before him. His brain was struggling to keep up as the pictures in his head weren't computing.

"I've heard many good things about you since your arrival in Birdie."

"Yes, well, thank you." Suddenly bashful, Jason looked down at his feet.

"This town is much in need, and everyone is delighted

to have you here." Her dark brown eyes transfixed on Jason. "Now Daddy, did you offer Dr. Davies anything to drink?"

"Very true, darlin', very true. Well, let's go and find something, shall we?" Jason followed them into a capacious room filled with various oversized leather chairs and sofas. At one end of the room stood a large billiard table and two smaller poker tables. The opposite end of the room displayed a massive saloon-style bar, complete with largest mirror Jason had ever seen. Each barstool was a uniquely different and ornate leather saddle.

"Saddle up!" Cody declared, extending a hand toward the barstools.

"So Daddy tells me you're keeping busy at the clinic? How do you like our little town?"

Attempting to navigate the saddle without embarrassing himself, Jason managed to say, "Well, it's not exactly what I planned on after vet school, but it all seems to be growing on me, I suppose...."

"Keating takes time," Cody replied, without looking up from his bartending. "I've known him damn near all my life, and he's still growing on me!"

"I can see that," Cindy Lou replied. "Birdie has a way of pulling you back...."

"Here we go, yes sir, some nice refreshing beverages for you both," said Cody, handing them each a glass.

"Thank you, Daddy."

"Thank you." Jason caught himself staring at Cindy Lou and turned his glance downward.

"My pleasure, yes sir." Cody took a sip. "Mmmm, mmmm, that sure is tart, but gooood.... Now a toast to you two kids," laughed Cody. "A toast to your health and a long stay in Birdie. May you find someone special and settle down...."

Cindy Lou glared intently at her father after his remark.

Cody set his glass down. "Excuse me, but I need to check in on Mavis and see how dinner is coming." He disappeared behind the swinging saloon doors.

"I apologize for my father, and his rude tactics. He worries about me, that's all. It's his protective nature, especially since Momma died."

"Oh, I'm so sorry...."

"Oh, well, thank you, but she's been gone since I was ten. He worries no matter how old I am, or where I live."

"So you don't live in Birdie?"

"No, I live in Tulsa now."

"How long have you lived there?"

She smiled, taking a sip of her drink. "Well, aren't you just full of questions? The truth is, it's a long story; one that we should save for another time. Let's just say I have a wandering spirit.... But, more importantly, I want to hear about how you landed in Birdie; I mean, of all places."

He set down his glass and paused. "Now that is long story...."

Just then, the doors to the kitchen burst open as Cody hurriedly made his way across the room.

"Okay, y'all, come...and...get it," exclaimed Cody. "Oh now, let me refresh that drink, yes sir," he said, grabbing Jason's glass. "Okay now, I'll take care of this, you two head in there 'fore Mavis gets to hollerin'."

They proceeded through another doorway, into a long rectangular hall with a ceiling that seemed to extend upward three stories. Twelve large windows extending floor to ceiling defined the space. A massive dining table displayed an array of dishes and decorations fitting of a large celebration; surely all this pomp and circumstance wasn't just for him. As they were seated, Cody reappeared with their drinks.

"Alright, yes sir, here we are," he said, handing Jason his glass. Just then a small, round woman flew through the kitchen door carrying a large silver platter of fried chicken. Her stocky build, round face, and jet black hair pulled tightly back, combined with her dour glare and pursed lips, communicated an all-business persona.

Setting the platter in the middle of the table, she glared at them. "Now get to eatin', so's I can get to watchin' my television program at 8." She turned and trudged back through the kitchen door.

Stories of Cody and the family history of Buffalo Bill adventures consumed the dinner conversation as Mavis begrudgingly returned periodically, refilling bowls of food and empty water glasses. The food deliciously satisfied

Jason's homesick soul; he hadn't eaten anything homemade since his arrival in Birdie. Mavis made quick work of clearing dinner, followed by a sparkling assortment of various desserts.

Jason was overwhelmed. "This has been such a wonderful evening, and this fantastic food...thank you."

"You are most welcome, Dr. Davies, and thank you for coming to dinner this evening; it's truly been an honor." Cody lifted his glass toward Jason.

"Daddy, forgive me for interrupting, but I wondered if I could show Dr. Davies the house before it gets too late."

"Well, absolutely, absolutely! I think that is a most wonderful idea, Sweetheart. Why don't you two go take the tour and I will make sure Mavis is fine," he replied, staggering toward the kitchen.

Jason followed Cindy Lou quietly down the main hallway and then up the large staircase to the second floor. "You'll have to forgive Daddy; he gets so excited when company comes by."

"Oh, no, it's great." Jason fumbled with what to say; he couldn't take his eyes off of her. His mind scrambled for something intelligent or witty, but all he could think about was how beautiful she was.

Chapter 21

Jason gazed at the countless paintings and statues that lined the hallways in Cody's house. Cindy Lou narrated the tour. "These are mostly Daddy's rooms at this end of the house; his personal office, his bedroom here, and then...."

They walked by a closed door, and Jason reached for the doorknob just as Cindy Lou turned around. "Wait! We shouldn't go in there!" she exclaimed.

Jason jumped back, alarmed. "Oh, sorry, I'm so sorry, I didn't mean to...."

"It's okay. It's just...well, that's Momma's room, and no one, not even Daddy, has been in there since she passed. Daddy keeps it closed off, and I haven't been in there since I was ten." She turned and continued down the hallway as Jason followed. She stopped and turned. "Sorry, I didn't mean to startle you."

His face reddened with embarrassment. "No, I apologize; I had no right to...."

"You didn't know. It's our hang-up, not yours. Please now, let me show you the pool."

He followed her down the back staircase to a beautifully ornate and colossal indoor pool.

"This is incredible. Your father must really enjoy swimming."

She laughed softly. "Well, that's the funny part, he

doesn't swim!"

They made their way through the remainder of the house before returning to the living room as the gong of the grandfather clock signaled the late hour. They found Cody nodding off on the sofa, stirring as they approached, and quickly jumping to attention.

"Is it really already 11 o'clock? I apologize! I've overstayed my welcome." Jason turned to leave. "Thank you both for such a wonderful evening."

"Well, yes sir, you are most welcome, but don't feel like you need to rush off and such. We sure do thank you for taking the time to stop by and we hope you come back soon," Cody replied as he stood to shake Jason's hand.

Jason turned to Cindy. "It was a pleasure meeting you."

"A pleasure meeting you as well, Dr. Davies," she replied with a smile.

He reached to shake her hand but she wrapped her arms around him for a brief hug. "I'll walk you out." Outside, he was disappointed how quickly the evening had come to an end.

"Please forgive my Daddy and his stories, he can get a little carried away at times."

"No, no, it was great, the stories are great. I learned so much; I had no idea."

"Neither did I...I had no idea that I could hear them so many times in a lifetime."

"So are they all true?"

"I think most of them are, except where Daddy embellishes at times...or when his mind slips a gear once in a while."

"I wish we'd had more time to talk," Jason said, stopping at his truck.

"I know...we will...the town loves you, so unless you run away in the middle of the night, then we'll cross paths again."

"No, I think Birdie is stuck with me."

"Right...Actually, I think it's more like you are stuck with Birdie," she replied with a wink.

"No, I like it here."

She laughed. "Don't start tellin' stories, doctor. Word is you are looking to jump town shortly."

He wondered how she knew. She saw the question in his eyes. "Oh please, there isn't a whole lot that doesn't get noticed, gossiped, or misconstrued in this one-horse town," she replied.

"No, really, I had a rough start, but everyone's been great and things are starting to improve."

She smiled. "We'll see.... Go home, you have work in the morning."

"Good night." He opened the truck door.

"Good night," she said as she turned back toward the house.

He closed the door and tried to start the truck, but as he turned the key in the ignition, nothing happened. Cindy Lou stopped mid-stride, turning back to him with a smile as he again tried to start the truck. She turned again, but this time headed toward the large row of garage doors on the far side of the house. One of the doors began to open as she approached. Pulling her car slowly next to his truck, she laughed, "Get in. I'll take you home."

"But wait, you're her!" Jason stammered.

"Her, who?"

"The girl I saw on the square when I first got here, you're her!"

Cindy Lou's smile grew. "Well, maybe...."

Embarrassed, Jason gathered his things and climbed into the black BMW. Cindy Lou slammed the accelerator and Jason's body compressed into the seat; the car impressed him with how well it purred down the dark two-lane highway.

"Cindy, please forgive...."

"Actually, call me Catherine," she interrupted.

"Oh, I'm sorry...."

"It's just that Daddy likes to call me Cindy Lou after my mother. Her name was Cynthia Louise, but after she passed he began calling me her nickname, Cindy Lou."

"So, please forgive me, but where exactly does your father get the idea...."

"The idea that he's the descendant of Buffalo Bill Cody? Well he is a Cody; William F. Cody is a great uncle. The truth is, Daddy is a dreamer, always sharing crazy family stories, so this is part of who he is, but his other life is, or was, banking. You know the bank in town,

135

Oklahoma National? He actually started that bank when my parents first moved to Birdie."

"Oklahoma National? Isn't that a pretty big bank? I mean, I see ads for them all over the place."

"Very good, doctor, you do pay attention. Yes, they're owned by a larger bank now; he sold his interest and stock after my mother passed away, and he hasn't stepped foot into the bank for years. He didn't want to leave the house for the longest time, and when he finally did, it was always in character as Buffalo Bill, more often than not. I didn't understand it at the time. As I got older I realized he did it to survive. It's his security, his way of coping with her loss."

"So he isn't in banking at all now?"

"Well, Daddy is actually pretty good at investing, and in his younger days he invested quite a little bit in oil exploration down around Birdie. As luck would have it, there is lots of it here. He also invested in some development out in Nevada."

"Nevada? What's in Nevada that's worth investing in? I'm mean, except Vegas...."

She turned and smiled. "He decided to invest in some partnerships there that became lucrative over the years."

Jason smirked, wondering just how lucrative it must be to invest on the ground floors of Las Vegas skyscrapers. He stared out into the darkness as the shadowy landscape sped by.

"So then...?"

"Yes...Daddy's loaded. Don't let the deerskin and fringe fool ya." She slowed the car and turned into the drive.

How did she know where he lived? His look of astonishment again made her chuckle. "Oh, please, don't look so surprised; this town is wired. Everyone knows everything."

He had so many questions to ask, and he didn't want the evening to end, but he knew he must let her go.

He climbed slowly out of the car. He wanted to say something profound, magical, but his mind went blank.

"Nice meeting you, Doc. Will I get to see you again sometime?" She smiled, staring at him.

"I think if I play my cards right, it could happen. Look me up next time you're in town; I mean, it doesn't look like I'm leaving any time soon."

"I don't know, Doc; word on the street is that you're pretty resourceful...." She winked as she put the car into gear. "It was nice meeting you; take care."

"It was nice to meet you, too; thank you." He watched as the taillights of the BMW quickly disappeared.

He stood frozen in the darkness, listening to the sound of the fine German engine motor off into the distance. What had just happened? Was he dreaming? How did his life take such a magical turn in an evening? And how the hell was he going to get his truck back?

Chapter 22

On Friday morning, Jason woke to a knock at the door. Daylight had just peeked through the blinds as he stumbled to the door. When he opened the door, he saw two men backing out of the driveway. The passenger waved and yelled, "It's all fixed, Doc! Take care now!" As Jason's blurred vision began to clear, he recognized his untrustworthy truck sitting back in the driveway. Jason didn't know what to think, but he realized that his morning just gotten a whole lot less complicated.

"Dr. Davies?" Shelly asked from the doorway. "There's a phone call waiting for you; it's Wilson Gibbons." Jason just stared blankly at her.

"Oh, I thought you would have met Wilson by now; he's the mayor of Birdie. He didn't say what he wanted, only to speak with you directly."

Jason picked up the phone. "Good afternoon, this is Jason Davies."

"Dr. Davies, we have not had the supreme pleasure of meeting directly as of yet, and for that I do sincerely apologize. I have heard nothing but the warmest compliments and the sincerest appreciation for your willingness to save our fine little animals. Furthermore, I would be honored if you might consider stopping by the house this evening to share in our humble hospitality in belated celebration of your selfless care for this community."

Jason was speechless, caught off guard by the invitation. "Thank you for your kind words, but I...."

"I know you may think it's an imposition, but it surely is not. We would be delighted to have you as our guest of honor this evening. Truly, I cannot take no for an answer and still be able to look myself in the mirror in the morning. Can we expect you about 6:30 P.M., then?"

"Well, I...."

"Perfect! It will truly be a pleasure to meet you. See you tonight!"

The phone line was silent. What had just happened? He'd agreed to dinner?

"Dr. Davies? You okay?" Shelly reappeared from around the corner.

"Yes, but somehow I agreed to eating dinner at the mayor's house tonight."

Shelly attempted to suppress her laughter.

"What? What? Tell me," he demanded.

"Oh, nothing, you'll have a grand time, I'm sure!"

"What aren't you telling me about all this?"

She paused. "Well, Mayor Gibbons is a talker."

"Not too surprising after this call; I'm not sure he even took a breath during the entire conversation."

"Mayor Gibbons has been mayor since I can

remember, and his daddy was mayor before that. Anyways, no one pays him much mind, until he does something stupid, like several years ago he wanted to allow this fella from Tulsa to open up a topless donut shop in town, Debbie Duz Donuts. Told everyone it would put us on the map. He was in on the deal and they were going to franchise them all over the country.

The mayor also likes the Civil War; and when I say 'likes' I mean he loves it. He coordinates all these guys dressing up in the outfits and reenacting battles and whatever. Lastly, the mayor is a huge John Wayne fan. I haven't ever seen it, but my Uncle Ron says that Wilson owns just about anything with The Duke's picture on it. The only reason I tell you this is to make sure you're planning on spending some time over there."

Jason sat back in his chair and cringed. What had he not even really agreed to? He dreaded the thought of making small talk the entire night.

"You'll have fun, don't worry. At least you'll get some good food."

"What do you mean?"

"The mayor's wife is a fabulous cook. She wins all kinds of awards around here for her baking and everything. I heard she's even been to New York a few times and gone to some pretty fancy cooking schools."

The thought of a warm, home-cooked meal did seem tempting, and reaching out to the mayor might have its advantages at some point, right? Hell, maybe he might even be presented with the key to the city.

He finished the last two appointments of the day and hurried back to the barn for a quick shower. The shower presented certain challenges; water pressure seemed to vary from day to day. If you had it, it was going to be a good day. As he pulled the shower curtain back and stepped out, he was confronted with Jasper's hind end. The donkey was taking his time, delightedly drinking from the toilet.

"Jasper! You sorry jackass! Get out!" He grabbed a towel and began beating the belligerent animal. Jasper, unalarmed, took his time before finally making his way back out the doorway. He thought about the carrots sitting in his fridge, but he didn't have the time to deal with the stupid donkey. Jason threw the towel on the monstrous dirty laundry pile, which reminded him that another weekend trip to the laundromat was in order. As he left he decided to stop and buy a bottle of wine.

Shelly had given him directions to the mayor's house just off the main courthouse square, downtown. The expansive Victorian with its ornate spires reaching high above the third story sprawled across an entire block of the historic neighborhood. The driveway wound through a canopy of mature trees and a manicured lawn. He pulled beneath the porte-cochere and turned off the truck. He took a deep breath and stepped out into the cool night air.

Before he'd made it up the stairs, Wilson burst out through the front door. "Dr. Davies, truly a pleasure, truly a pleasure! Thank you for honoring us with your presences this evening in our humble abode."

"Well...thank...."

"Oh, please now, why are we standing out here in the chill, come right in, right in." Wilson held the door, ushering him through the doorway.

"Now, what may I offer you to drink? I have some ice cold sweet tea, or lemonade?"

Jason, remembering he was holding the bottle of wine, said, "I brought this if you would like."

The mayor's face paused with a look of concern. "Well thank you for that thought, Dr. Davies, but we do not imbibe in the alcoholic realm. No, made it a strict philosophy of our faith in the good Lord Jesus Christ, and as good Baptist Christians we must decline; I do appreciate your kindness. Now how about some sweet tea or ice cold lemonade?"

Jason felt the awkwardness of his mistake; Shelly sure as hell had forgotten to mention that part. He tucked the bottle next to a chair, hoping to remember it later.

"Oh, the good doctor is here," exclaimed a voice from the other room. A woman in her early fifties entered the room, racing toward Jason with arms outstretched.

"Ohhhhhh, so good to meet the famous Dr. Davies, and thank you for coming. I'm Jocelyn; now did Wilson offer you anything to drink? Wilson, you did offer the doctor something to drink?"

"Dear, now we were just getting to that, and I think he

decided on some sweet tea, isn't that right, Dr. Davies?"

Jason's head was swimming, but he smiled and nodded to Wilson.

"Well, we have just heard the most wonderful things about you, Dr. Davies. I am just so sorry that we haven't been introduced until now."

Taking a sip of the tea, Jason replied, "Well, I'm sure we would have run into each other at the clinic sometime, I mean when you brought in your pets."

Wilson and Jocelyn paused with an air of consternation. "Well, actually, Dr. Davies, we do not have any pets."

"No, Doc, we just never seemed to have enough time with everything else going on," said Wilson. "Oh, we thought about getting a rabbit for Jessica once, but do you know how much care one of those little buggers requires? The feeding, the cleaning, so much to do there, just more than what we thought we could handle."

A young woman appeared on the staircase.

"Oh, wonderful! Jessica, you are just in time to meet Dr. Davies!" Wilson motioned for her to come down.

"It's a pleasure to meet you." Jason gently shook her hand.

"Jessica is a senior at Oklahoma State."

"Oh, that's fantastic; what are you studying?"

"Animal sciences." She smiled shyly at him.

"Yes, Jessica has a real interest in the veterinary end of things, actually." Jocelyn busily adjusted the napkins on the table. "She's always had affection for the animals."

Jason suppressed his confusion.

"Oh, I think I just heard the oven; dinner is almost ready." Jocelyn disappeared through the swinging kitchen door.

Wilson refilled Jason's glass. "You know, Jessica is off this next week and then again at Christmas. It might sure be nice to have her spend some time with you at the clinic. You know, might give her an idea of what it's like to be a veterinarian, and all."

Jessica's face lit up as Jason forced a smile. "Uhhh sure, that would be great; whenever she wants to come by, just let me know."

Dinner delivered in a grand manner; at least Shelly had been right about that. The food was a colorful array of everything imaginable that could be fried or pickled. Jason didn't realize how hungry he actually was. The platters of various dishes made the rounds, and Jason helped himself to second servings. As the ladies began to clear the plates, Jason stood to offer assistance. But Wilson waved him to sit down, continuing his breathless discussion of politics, the economy, and his hobbies.

"Now, Dr. Davies, Jason, if I may be so bold, are you familiar with the reenactments of the Civil War? Have you ever seen that performed on the main theatre of the battlefield?"

"No sir, I don't believe so, but it sounds fascinating...."

"Well, young man, let me tell you something; it is

truly one of the most amazing things you will ever witness, I mean other than being born again to our savior Lord Jesus Christ, but let me tell you, there is nothing more amazing than seeing the Battle of Middle Boggy Depot or Honey Springs played out before your eyes. Absolutely the most life-changing event."

"Wow, it does sound quite interesting." Jason could feel the tiredness settling in and his contact lenses drying on his eyes.

"Well, I thought you might agree, and so I would like to ask, and I would be honored if you would attend a reenactment tomorrow over at Dexter's Crossing."

"Oh, I appreciate the offer, but I just don't think I could, with work and all...."

"Ohhhh, goodness, I knew you were a hard worker, so committed to your work; I took the liberty of clearing your Saturday schedule with Dr. Keating over at the veterinary clinic. I tell you he was downright delighted to hear you were interested in taking part in a living piece of history!"

"I'm sure he was," thought Jason. "I'm sure he was...."

"You will fit right in, trust me. Heck, some of these folks don't even know how to shoot a gun! I think it would truly be a missed opportunity if you didn't come. Now tell me, what are your hobbies, your interests? Surely, there is more to Dr. Davies than saving lives of animals all day! Do you play golf, maybe a hunter? No, saving lives and taking them doesn't make much sense for a veterinarian, ha ha! Well, before you say anything more, let me have you contemplate this: Historical reenactments like what I am describing here are exactly what a young man should be involved with. I mean to tell you, nothin' better for the soul than being outside, clean air, exercise, and well, you get the idea. I just really feel you would benefit, truly I do." Wilson paced the room as he spoke, his arms flailing wildly. Jason could feel the intensity behind the mayor's words. It was clear; he loved playing Civil War soldier. "So I propose, and it would truly be a huge honor, if you would consider attending one our reenactments."

The ladies returned with colorful, delicious-looking dessert trays, and Wilson finally came up for air.

"Dr. Davies, you mustn't get away without having a look at my John Wayne memorabilia collection. Truly exquisite if I do say so myself, but I just know you will enjoy it." Although the hour was late, Jason followed Wilson down the long back hallway. They descended a narrow stairwell into a large, open, low-ceilinged basement. The room was a museum dedicated to "The Duke," with various display cases calling the visitor for attention. Pictures, posters, plates, and more filled every square inch of the room. Jason especially enjoyed the thirty-plus lunchboxes lined along the back wall. In a far corner was what appeared to be a life-size replica of John Wayne himself dressed in his western attire. All kidding aside, this was something special; the mayor's collection amazed him.

"So, what do you think?" Wilson asked anxiously.

"This is pretty cool," Jason stammered. "I had no idea his face was on this much stuff."

Wilson chuckled as if he knew more to the joke. "Well, the truth is, I have a warehouse across town filled with even more stuff. I just can't get it all in here."

"You should open up a museum to display all of this; I mean, this is truly something."

"Well, thank you, I sure think so. It's a labor of love."

As they returned to the main floor, Jason noticed Wilson's monologue starting to slow, and he saw his opportunity to thank his guests for their hospitality and say his goodbyes. The hour had grown late, and his eyes were screaming.

Shaking hands on the front porch, Wilson placed his hand on Jason's shoulder. "So, I'll pick you up bright and early in the morning, say around 5:30 A.M., okay? Oh, and is it okay if Jessica comes by Monday morning to help out at the clinic?"

"Absolutely, she is always more than welcome to visit and help out." He heard the words coming from his own mouth, but he hoped Keating would have the same enthusiasm. He climbed into the truck and waved goodbye. His head throbbed from the stimulus overload; at this point, he had signed on to babysit the daughter, play dress-up Army guy, and managed to forget the bottle of wine....

Chapter 23

Saturday morning came early, shrouded in the cold darkness of the hour. It was the first morning that Jason could no longer ignore the lack of heat in the barn apartment; the truth was, the apartment didn't have any. As he showered, he hoped to make a trip to the hardware store before it closed for the day. He hoped that a little space heater would improve his apartment morale.

He heard the sound of a truck pull into the drive. He glanced at his watch; the mayor was prompt. Grabbing his jacket, he had no idea what to expect, but he hoped that they weren't using live ammo....

The drive to Dexter's Crossing was a confusing, dark escapade, leaving Jason unsure as to their geographic locale. It was way too early, and Jason realized that he hadn't had any coffee before leaving. Wilson didn't stop talking during the drive, and Jason's occasional nod and "uh huh" seemed to be enough to keep Wilson going, telling one story after another.

They pulled off the blacktop onto a narrow, heavily wooded dirt road. Minutes later the road opened up into a large field. A man waved them toward a makeshift parking area where hundreds of people were already gathering. Jason had no idea this many people would show up to play war.

Wilson guided him through the crowds of costumed

revelers to two large tents at the far end of the field. Wilson searched through a hanging rack of jackets, pulling several off for review.

"Here, try this on," he said, handing one to Jason. "There are some changing rooms over there; try the pants on, and I'll go find you some boots. What size do you wear?"

"Size 12, I guess," he replied, annoyed he had ever agreed to this. His gut told him that this wasn't a good idea, but it was too late to back out now.

Wilson returned, grinning from ear to ear. "Here, I found these cavalry boots that should fit you. You ready for this? Oh, it's going to be grand, grand I tell you. Really, it's one of the better reenactments, down to the smallest details that keep it all as historically accurate as possible. We can grab some coffee before we have to go find our opening positions."

Coffee? Had Wilson mentioned coffee? Maybe things weren't going to be so dire after all.

Jason followed Wilson to a large blue tent, where a menagerie of costumed attendees sat talking. He followed Wilson through the line of coffee and donuts, and then to a large table where several men gathered in lively conversation.

"I'm telling you, Art, there is no way that the boys over in Greenville are using rubber bullets! No way! I don't care if you have it from a reliable source or not; it just ain't true!" A stocky, mustached man bounced at the end of the table in excitement.

"Men, I'd like to introduce you to our newest soldier, Dr. Jason Davies!" Wilson interrupted in his egocentric fashion. The men at the table looked up and nodded. "Welcome, Sir, welcome I say. Truly a pleasure to a have a new recruit to the ranks," replied the mustached man.

"Have a seat here, Jason." Wilson pushed his way to the center of the table and nodded at a tall, lanky man sitting quietly eating, who moved aside. "What are you men deeply conversing about over here?"

"Well, Art here is convinced, through 'reliable' sources, that the boys over in Greenville have been using rubber bullets. You ever been hit with one of them? I sure as hell have, and I'll tell you what: Take one of them in the crotch, and you won't sit for a week! They used them over in Perkinsville back during that battle of Moss Creek, and I tell you, I haven't been right since...."

"Well, surely these boys here today aren't using that kind of thing, right?" Wilson questioned through a mouthful of donut.

"Art here seems to think that's the case, and I tell ya, I ain't about to get my crotch shot off again!"

Jason's donut felt stuck in his throat. What was this talk about being shot? Bullets, rubber or not, didn't sound healthy....

"Well, boys, keep your jewels covered, and good luck! See you on the battlefield," Wilson shouted as he motioned for Jason to follow him. He led Jason down a creek embankment to a small grove of sycamores. Several others had gathered and were looking over maps of the battlefield. Wilson pulled his own map out of his back pocket and began pointing out objects and locations near where they stood.

"Now, in about 15 minutes, all hell is going to break loose as we follow the General over that embankment and down the hill to the river. Things to keep in mind are: Don't retreat unless commanded to, don't get shot, and watch out for horses. The rest should be a piece of cake, but stick close and I'll look out for you."

What?! Jason felt a streak of anxiety. Don't get shot? Watch out for horses? What had he gotten himself into? He tried to remember the previous night at Wilson's, thinking, "I should have asked more questions...."

Jason nodded, still unsure of what to expect. He wished he was stuck at the laundromat with the small Korean owner who only nodded and smiled as he slid the quarters into the washers and dryers.

Moments later, two men on a flatbed trailer started making announcements. The energy in the crowd began to intensify, reminding Jason of a U2 concert one summer when the crowd was so massive that it seemed to take on a life of its own. He remembered being terrified for a fleeting second as to what would happen if all hell broke loose; he felt that same way now.

He followed Wilson to a spot in the trees and waited, his palms beginning to sweat. What was he so nervous about? Grown men dressed up in costumes, ready to race down a hill, across a river, shooting fake guns at each other. It was no different than when he was 10 years old playing war in the backyard.

In the far distance he heard the sounds of a bugle horn, a pause, and then the blood-curdling whoops and hollering of crazed baby boomers ready to shed blood. Jason had a flash of panic; this wasn't real, right? What horror his ancestors must have endured when trapped on these battlefields 150 years ago.

Confusion and mayhem were instantaneous as Jason followed Wilson out of their hiding spot, quickly moving through the trees. Cannon blasts shook the air, adding to the melee of shouting men and women, gunfire, and panicked horses. Hundreds of figures landscaped the vast hillside as smoke quickly filled the air, restricting their vision to the larger battlefield. Jason couldn't see anything at this point, only adding to the chaos as he struggled to keep up with Wilson. He slipped as he ran down the hill and scrambled to regain his footing. A young boy was on the ground crying; his father grabbed his arm and pulled him out of the way of trampling boots and hooves. Down the hill, Jason heard screaming to his left. He stopped. Should he try to help, or was this just part of the experience? How did anyone think this was a good idea? His heart raced and the smoke burned his throat. Where was Wilson? Turning to his right and back to his left, he realized that Wilson was nowhere to be found. He must be up ahead. Jason continued on down the hillside, following two men in front of him to the bank of the river.

As they approached the river, the smoke settled even lower and Jason struggled to keep up with the two men directly in front of him. He turned around, but smoke was all he could see. He heard the sound of people and animals moving across the river behind him, their shouts and cries intensifying. Where were all these people coming from? "Damn!" He continued to push forward, hoping to catch a glimpse of Wilson up ahead. The bank of the river dropped sharply and its rocky, slick texture caused several people to slide and stumble to the river's edge. Quickly but carefully trying to make his way down the slope, Jason stumbled in the deep mud before grabbing a tree and regaining his footing. He crossed the shallow, rapid current and then started his way up the embankment on the other side. Scrambling for his footing, he dug his hands into the dark black soil, hoping to gain his balance. Nearing the top, he heard shouting. When he looked up, he faced a flash of horse hooves coming down the embankment on top of him, and then darkness.

His eyes opened. His vision blurred; he could see the outline of shadowy figures standing over him, and then everything went dark again. His senses slowly circled back to a conscious state, as Jason struggled to make sense of his world. What had happened? Who were these people standing over him? Why did they all look concerned? He wanted to move, but his body resisted.

"Doc? Doc? It's okay, it's us. You're gonna be alright," said a woman standing over him. Jason's eyes began to focus, recognizing Wilson.

"Dr. Davies, just relax. Don't try to get up just yet; we got a doctor coming to take a look at you. Just lay back and relax." Wilson placed a gentle hand on Jason's shoulder.

"No, I'm fine." Jason resisted, but his head felt like someone had struck him with a baseball bat. A man offered him a small tin cup.

"No, Ed, remember what they told us at the paramedic training over there to Summersville. Patients should never be administered any oral liquids; I mean, what if the boy has a concussion or somethin'," cried one of the older men standing over Jason, still dressed in his military attire.

"Ahh, put a sock in it. A little sip of something sure as hell ain't going to send him over the edge. Here son, have a sip." The man placed the cup to Jason's lips; the cool water felt good on his throat.

Moments later Jason tried to stand and the crowd gasped. Wilson lent his hand as Jason slowly rose to his feet. "Doc, you sure you're alright? You took quite a lob to the noggin and all, and I'd surely think we should head for the hospital and have you checked out."

"No, no, I'm alright, nothing a little ibuprofen can't cure." Jason felt like vomiting.

With Wilson's help, the two made their way back to the truck. Jason tried to rest on the drive home, closing his eyes in hopes that the wave of nausea would somehow magically disappear. Wilson finally pulled up in front of the barn; Jason thanked him and slowly made his way inside. He hoped Jasper might take pity on him today, with no special surprises. He cautiously peered into the apartment and smelled nothing except the unwavering mustiness now mixed with a recently purchased air freshener. What, no large and steamy pile of crap from Jasper? Word travelled fast in a small town, and maybe the damn donkey was giving him a break after what had happened today. Jason collapsed on the bed, hoping for a miraculous reprieve from his life. As he drifted off to sleep, he wondered, "What did I do to deserve this?"

Chapter 24

Sunday had been a much-needed day of recovery; however, it didn't seem to be nearly enough, and Monday arrived too quickly. As Jason made his way into the office on Monday morning, every step he took made his head throb and scream for relief. He tried to avoid turning his head too quickly, fearing that a wave of nausea would erupt from within. Ibuprofen had helped dull the pain from the battlefield fiasco, but his fuzzy brain would need to be in control this morning.

As he climbed out of his truck, a large SUV pulled in behind him and Jessica jumped out. Jason turned with a gasp, realizing he had totally forgotten about his agreement with the Mayor. He watched Jessica gently remove herself from the passenger side of the vehicle; her outfit appeared more suited for a day of shopping than a day of slopping. The expensive-looking knee-high leather riding boots, snow-white jacket, and designer jeans would be a recipe for disaster. What should he do? She closed the truck door and paused, looking at her hair in the side mirror. She then removed her lip gloss from her purse and proceeded with a slow, gentle application across both lips. Jason stood staring in disbelief; this wasn't actually happening, right? She replaced the lip gloss in her purse and brushed her jacket before finally waving goodbye to her mother.

"Good morning Dr. Davies, I hope it's still okay for me to ride along with you today."

"Uhh, sure it is, um, I was just getting a few things ready, but if you want to put your stuff in the truck, we should be going here shortly." Jason walked into the clinic, scratching his head. Had he missed something in the conversation on Friday night? He returned with his bag and climbed into the truck, watching as Jessica carefully made her way to the passenger-side door. She gingerly lifted the door handle and paused; she sniffed the air and wrinkled her nose. Jason stifled a laugh; the truck smelled of manure and horses. She looked at the worn seat covers and brushed the seat with her hand before climbing in. This was going to be a long day.

They drove in silence; with each minute that passed, the silence became increasingly more awkward. "So tell me why you're interested in becoming a veterinarian?"

"Well, Daddy says that I should always pursue the dreams that I love, and well, I love animals; it just made sense that I should be a veterinarian."

If Jason had a quarter for every time someone told him they wanted to become a veterinarian, he'd have a lot of quarters. "So do you have any questions before we arrive at our first appointment?"

She thought for a moment, "Well, I wondered when we will be stopping for lunch?"

This was going to be a very long day....

The first call was an examination of three horses for

health certificates. Jason demonstrated the basic steps of the physical exam, but when he handed Jessica the stethoscope, she dangled it like a snake preparing to strike. Later, after handing her the rectal thermometer, he caught her attempting to place it in a horse's mouth. She touched everything with an air of exaggerated concern, as if it might break at any second.

Their second call of the day was to Oscar Bullen's hog farm; Jason knew that this visit had the makings of a perfect storm.

Oscar's farm was second only to the major corporations that raised swine. For a one-man operation, Oscar had it all figured out...except today. For some reason a pen of adolescent pigs were in ill-thrift and not growing like the rest. Jason wondered if there could be a genetic connection with the sow, but he thought it might shed some light on the situation to examine them individually.

Jason suited up for the event with his coveralls and muck boots. He turned to Jessica with a questioning look. "I have an extra pair of coveralls in the truck if you like?"

"Oh, I appreciate that, but I'll be fine." She smiled, adjusting her pant legs and nervously looking around the unkempt farm.

They followed Oscar past an array of dilapidated structures to the pen of juvenile pigs. As Jason slowly crawled over the panels, the animals stirred with anxiousness, crowding and racing to the opposite corner of the pen. He turned to see Jessica fluffing her hair as she stood contentedly on the other side of the panels. He motioned with a wave of his hand for her to follow. She carefully climbed the rusted and manure-stained panels, her face grimacing in disgust. Making his way through the pen, Jason noted that all the animals appeared thin and their coats looked dull and greasy. He grabbed a pig by its back leg; it turned, lashing and squealing. Jason turned around to see Jessica scrambling over the panel fencing.

"Oscar, we need you over at the west barn," boomed a voice on Oscar's radio.

"I'll be right back." Oscar gave Jessica a questioning glance as he passed by.

Jason continued his examination, when suddenly he heard squealing and the sound of animals on the move. Jessica looked up from her cell phone just in time to scream as 10 boar males barreled down the aisleway where she stood. She dropped her phone and reached for the gate as the first two boars knocked her down in their passing. She tried to regain her footing, only to be knocked to the ground again by the next four. The slinging mud pelted not only her jacket and boots but also her perfectly styled makeup and hair.

Jason dropped the pig, raced to the gate, and helped Jessica to her feet as the last boars passed by. Her face and hair were splattered with mud and feces. He reached for a towel in his back pocket, but it wasn't there. "Let's get you back to the truck and let you get cleaned up." Jason helped her slowly make her way back down the alley to the truck.

He could see her eyes begin to well with tears. Jason felt responsible and worried that her folks would be livid when they heard what had happened. He should have never agreed to this, but did he really have a choice?

Returning to the truck, Jason offered Jessica some water and a towel. He quickly realized that cleanup of her clothing would be a lost cause with water alone; manure and mud would require the aid of a dry cleaner.

Jason dug through the glove box, searching for any snacks that might provide some consolation. "Why don't you wait here and rest while I finish up, and then we can head back. Do you like peanut butter crackers?" He sheepishly handed her a small package of crackers. Her white coat was now a light shade of brown, and her hair was matted and disheveled. "Thank you," she said as she reached for the crackers and sat down in the front seat of the truck.

As he walked backed to the barn he felt sick. She could have been hurt, and he was responsible. He took a deep breath and climbed back in the pen of squealing bacon.

During the return trip to the clinic, they remained quiet and awkward. Jocelyn's SUV was waiting in the parking lot when they arrived. Jessica, holding back tears, thanked him and quickly climbed out of the truck.

Jason watched the SUV disappear, wondering why he wasn't smarter. He should have known this was going to be a disaster the minute he saw her outfit; why hadn't he said something? It was a good thing he was getting out of this town.

Storm clouds formed, and the skies appeared to be taunting the Oklahoma landscape with afternoon showers. Jason packed up early and headed for the apartment. Exhausted, he dropped onto the bed, closing his eyes.

He awoke to the sound of his phone ringing. "Dr. Davies, it's Wilson Gibbons here. Just wanted to check in and see how you're feeling after Saturday?"

"Oh, as good as can be expected, I suppose; nothing a little pain management can't control." Jason tried to sound upbeat, but the attempt just made him feel worse.

"Well, please take care of yourself, and if there's anything I can do please let me know."

"Well, thank you, but I should be fine. Oh, Wilson, I hope Jessica is okay. I really felt just awful about everything."

"Oh Doc, don't worry. She's fine; nothing a good dry cleaning and a bath won't fix."

Chapter 25

Jason was checking over his appointments for Tuesday afternoon.

"May I help you with something?" asked Mary, startling him as she came around the corner. "Oh, I'm sorry, Jason, I didn't mean to scare you." She put her hand on his arm.

"Oh, no, I was just checking to see what we had this afternoon. What's this Halstead Ranch?"

She smiled, sitting down at her desk. "It's one of the oldest ranches around these parts; a lot of history there. The Halstead family still runs it, and I think John is hoping you might enjoy traveling out there with him. I blocked you both out the rest of the day, but if you have something else you need to do, just...."

"No, that sounds like it might be interesting."

Keating appeared in the doorway. "You ready? We need to get going."

"Uh, yes sir, just let me grab my hat." Jason hurriedly gathered his things.

"You boys be careful and have fun," Mary said, glancing at Keating with quiet concern.

"Hmmph," grumbled Keating, as Jason followed briskly behind him toward the truck. He tossed Jason the keys. "You drive."

Keating was in a mood today, making Jason all the

more nervous about the next several hours.

They drove in silence, Jason now familiar with how quiet his boss could be, with only an occasional finger point from Keating indicating the next turn. They finally turned off paved road, and the roads seemed to only worsen as they drove. The rugged terrain forced Jason to slow the truck as Keating's annoying glance became apparent. Keating removed his pipe, filling it with a sweet-smelling licorice tobacco that Jason's senses recalled from childhood. His father had smoked a pipe, and for a moment, the smell made Jason homesick.

"You test many bulls at the school?" Keating asked, lighting his pipe.

"Well, we had a rotation testing bulls up on some ranches," he answered, nervous that Keating would be unimpressed.

"Hmmph," Keating grunted as he puffed on his pipe. "Well, we need to test these bulls and I want to get it done before dark."

Jason continued to navigate the rough road, hoping this wouldn't turn into an event where Keating lost his temper; Jason could feel the pit forming in his stomach.

When they pulled onto the ranch, Jason could see a stand of houses and barns off on the horizon. As they approached, he marveled how well-maintained all the buildings appeared. After they parked, Jason followed Keating out of the truck and through the door of a small bungalow.

Inside, several large wooden desks were scattered throughout a large open room, with phones ringing and people milling about. Keating barked at Jason, "We need to check in with Tyson, let him know we're here, and then they should have the bulls waiting for us at the chute." He walked briskly down a small hallway, with Jason following close behind.

A tall, broad, rugged-looking man was sitting at a desk, but upon seeing Keating he rose and shook his hand. "Welcome, Doc! I see you brought help this time!" Tyson extended his hand toward Jason. "Well, if you gentlemen are ready to get started, I'll take you back to the corrals."

Jason and Keating followed Tyson. After a short drive, they arrived at the corrals. Jason was in awe of the complexity and size of the operation. He'd learned in veterinary school about serpentine walkways and ramps for handling cattle, but he had never seen these components implemented until now.

"Pretty impressive, isn't it?" commented Keating as they gathered their equipment.

"Absolutely; I've never seen anything like it."

"Well, it definitely makes the work a whole lot more tolerable," Tyson remarked, adjusting his hat. "We made some changes about three or four years ago, and I tell you, we can damn near double the number of cows through here in half the time, and with next to no injuries for cowboys or the cows."

Cowboys were scattered throughout the chutes. Once

the whistle blew, the bulls began making their way quietly through the series of gates and corridors without hesitation.

The afternoon sun high overhead quickly began its journey over the western horizon. Time didn't seem to matter here; the work would be done when it was done, and there was no watch or clock to say otherwise. With the efficiency of the facility and the expertise of the cowboys helping them, Jason and Keating were able to evaluate the bulls quickly and proficiently. As the last bull exited, Jason gave a sigh of relief, knowing Keating would at least be tolerable during the drive back to town.

"You boys have time for a drink?"

"Thanks Ty, but we had better get back to town before it gets dark. Okay if we take a rain check?"

"Doc, you don't need a rain check to drink with us; you're welcome anytime."

"I'll drive," Keating grunted as he loaded the last of the equipment. The road back out of the ranch was rockier than Jason had remembered, but Keating was also driving faster than Jason had on the way in. Jason stared out the window while his mind drifted to the day and how much he enjoyed the freedom of being out, unconstrained, working in nature, not tied to a desk or making idle chat at the water cooler waiting for the workday to end.

An odor snapped him from his daydream; it smelled like burning rubber. Keating pulled to a stop and they both got out to investigate. Their inspection revealed the shredded remnants of one of the rear tires. Keating quietly surveyed the situation. "I thought it felt a little funny.... Say, do you know how to change a tire?"

"Sure," Jason replied, eager to assist his boss with the tire change.

"Good, real good, you should find everything you need in the back there." Keating patted Jason on the shoulder and returned to the driver's seat. Jason hurried to unbolt the spare and set to work placing the jack, expecting Keating's return at any moment. The minutes ticked by while he worked, and as he finally began tightening the lug nuts on the spare, he again smelled tobacco. Peering around the side of the truck, he saw Keating still seated comfortably in the truck, quietly lighting his pipe. In disbelief, Jason could feel his own internal burning taking place; who did this son-of-a-bitch think he was? No wonder no one wanted to work for this jerk, especially when he treated you like an indentured servant.

Jason climbed back into the truck and Keating turned to him with a smile. "Good work, and you made good time with it all." Jason nodded, staring straight ahead. He wasn't in the mood. Keating removed the pipe from his mouth and said, "Oh, tomorrow let's have you take that tire by the garage and see if they can get a new one put back on that rim ASAP." Jason's face turned red as he glared out the window. He needed to find a liquor store.

Chapter 26

The town of Birdie has three claims to fame: the world's second-largest ball of twine, the home of the Stearnberry Swather, and the oldest, largest rodeo in the state of Oklahoma. The six-day Birdie Remuda Roundup and Rodeo is a red-neck version of Woodstock. The end of each September is the pinnacle of Birdie's social calendar and cause for school, city government, and bank closures. Dresses and hats are made specifically for the rodeo, and crops are planted earlier in the season to avoid any potential harvest conflict with the rodeo. Very few babies are ever born around the time of the rodeo. Birdie's rodeo is host to celebrities local and national in nature; Elvis's tour bus stopped one year to find barbeque for "The King" himself.

The Birdie Remuda Roundup and Rodeo is also a point of local and regional recognition, including the veterinarian who presides over the welfare of the animals during the week-long event. Throughout the years, veterinarians have been chosen through legislative hobnobbing at the capital in Oklahoma City and the Governor's office. But for the past 18 years, Dr. Keating has been the event's sole veterinarian.

Even as the heat of August rolled on, Jason couldn't believe Birdie's transformation as the townspeople diligently began decorating for the upcoming event.

Overnight, the courthouse square became the centerpiece of small-town USA. The old men playing checkers and the young, raucous skateboarders were replaced with patriotic banners and colorful flower displays. Where had the former downtown inhabitants gone? Jason chuckled, envisioning all of them boarding a bus together, headed out of town on hiatus until the festivities had ended. It was if Hollywood would be arriving soon to film a movie, and the whole town was pulling out all the stops. Even the ladies at the hat shop appeared more dressy than usual, with exceptionally eye-catchingly obnoxious fedoras.

Returning to the clinic late one afternoon with Shelly, Jason was surprised to see a brand-new vet truck parked in front of the clinic. "I don't believe it!" he exclaimed.

"What?" Shelly caught sight of what Jason had seen. "Ohhh," she stammered, finally laying eyes on the glistening new silver pickup, complete with vet box, parked at the front door of the clinic.

"I never thought he would actually do it! I mean, I hoped he might, but he didn't even mention that he had been thinking about it.... He finally bought me a vet truck!"

Shelly looked confused. Jason scrambled out of the truck to inspect the new vehicle. As he prepared to enter the clinic, he took a deep breath to collect himself; there was nothing Keating hated more than sophomoric behavior.

He could hear the sound of laughter coming from the

office as he entered. He found Keating seated at his own desk, and a tall, stylishly dressed man was seated on the corner of his desk. The man wore blue jeans with a sharp crease running perfectly down the front and a vibrantly colored starched shirt. A pair of custom-made deerskin boots completed his look, and the smile that emanated from behind his perfectly manicured mustache and goatee made Jason wonder if the man had just stopped in on his way to a photo shoot.

"Well, hello there, friend." The man stood and extended a perfectly manicured and bejeweled hand to Jason. The man's grip took Jason by surprise; he could feel the intentional crushing of his fingers. Whoever this guy was, he took a great deal of pride in and concern for his appearance. And by his handshake, Jason already had a bad feeling about him.

"The name's Otter, Otter Laverteen; pleasure to meet you, Doc."

"Jason," interjected Keating, "Let me introduce you to Dr. Othello Laverteen. Dr. Laverteen is a recent graduate of Mississippi State Veterinary School. His family's been ranching these parts for 100 years...."

"135 to be exact," interrupted Otter.

"Yes, well...Dr. Laverteen has kindly dropped by to inform us of his return to the area, and it sounds like he'll be providing us with some much-needed competition."

"Well, no, uh, I just sincerely wanted to introduce myself to Dr. Davies here and offer my services, and see

169

how I might help you gentlemen. That's it, pure and simple." Otter smiled and winked.

Keating stood, extending his hand. "Dr. Laverteen, thank you for taking the time to stop by. If the young Dr. Davies or I may be of assistance to you, please do not hesitate to call on us."

Otter turned to leave and paused. "Dr. Keating, by the way, I was thinkin' if you aren't interested in vettin' that little rodeo this year, I'd sure be keen and willin' to take that trouble off your hands."

Keating smiled again, staring directly at Otter. "No, it's no trouble at all, and this year, the good Dr. Davies will be taking over the care of the animals."

Otter's smile disappeared momentarily as he turned to Jason. "I see. Well, you two take care, now. I'll be seein' ya." Otter was gone in an instant, but Jason stood there and smirked as he heard the truck's engine turn over with a throttled low roar. But then his momentary triumph dissolved when he realized the truck's true owner; he turned to Keating and remarked, "I take it you didn't buy a new vet truck?" Keating sat back down at his desk and began sorting through a stack of mail. "Nope."

Chapter 27

Ever since the dinner at Cody's, Jason had hoped for another encounter with Catherine somewhere along the way. He longed for a casual, accidental rendezvous in the grocery produce section or a chance meeting in line at the post office. But no luck so far. Jason had also noticed Cody's absence around Birdie.

After work one Tuesday evening, Jason passed The Dinner Bell, a little café on the edge of town, and noticed Cody's truck parked in front. Jason decided to stop in, where he found Cody sitting alone in a booth.

"Well, hey there, young man!" Cody jumped from his seat. "Please have a seat, yes sir, have a seat!"

"Well, I don't want to interrupt your dinner...."

"Oh, goodness no, just havin' a little bite before I headed back to the ranch."

Jason sat down. "So let me guess, Mavis' night off?"

"What? Oh yes, somethin' like that, I guess. Truth is, I think she's gone this whole week. Somethin' 'bout flyin' off to Miami to meet some Cuban fella she met online. I don't quite understand, but then I'm not sure I want to either; I think I had just as soon keep it that way...." He smiled and winked as he took another bite of his meal.

The waitress brought Jason a menu. "I wanted to thank you for returning my truck. You sure didn't have to do that. What a surprise to have it back at the house the next morning, running perfectly. Thank you. I've been meaning to run by the house to pay you for the battery."

"You are welcome, no trouble at all. No sir, no sir, your money is no good for that.... Just promise me you'll come back by the house again soon when Cindy Lou is back this way. Maybe take her out for ice cream; she'd like that."

"You can count on it."

Minutes later, the waitress returned to take Jason's order. His mind raced, wanting to ask about Catherine, but he sat quietly, waiting for Cody to speak. Finally, he couldn't take it anymore. He blurted out, "So Cindy Lou didn't want to eat out tonight?"

Cody smiled. "Well, two things: Number one, she doesn't consider this place worthy of eating out; actually, she doesn't consider this place at all. Number two, she's back in Tulsa this week for work."

"What does she do there?"

"She didn't mention it the other night? She's an attorney in a firm there. Well actually now, she's a partner that handles a lot of corporate dealings. She has one of those big high-powered firms that saves the corporate world one conference room at a time."

The waitress returned with Jason's food, which looked surprisingly appetizing.

"Yes, that girl doesn't ever know when to slow down. Ever since her mother passed, she seems to always be racing somewhere, although in the last year or so she seems to come around a fair bit more, which is just fine with me.... She works too hard and I keep hoping she'll find some other enjoyment in her life. Life is too short to be working all the time."

"Do you think she'll move back?"

"Oh, I don't know. I guess I'd like to think so, but her life is complicated at times. I want her to be here because she wants to be, not because I need a babysitter. Oh, I know she worries about me, but I worry over her more; she's all I've got."

Jason stared out the window, lost in thought. The more he learned about her, the more intrigued he was by Cody's daughter.

"The truth is, I suppose there isn't a dang-blasted thing I can do about it, but a father's job is to protect his family, and I guess I'm not sure I did that in my time here on earth.... Successful in some other ventures, yes, but protecting my girls isn't something I did very well at all...." Cody's voice cracked and trailed off as he blew his nose in his napkin.

The waitress returned, and before Jason could think to grab the check, the bill was paid.

"Cody, wait. Please let me get this tonight!" Jason protested.

Cody waved his hand, brushing Jason off. "Aww, no sir, the pleasure was all mine. Enjoyed getting to chat to with you, Dr. Davies. Not many nights I have anyone to break bread with; I should be thanking you."

As they slowly made their way out of the restaurant, Cody paused. "Now don't be a stranger; you're welcome anytime, yes sir, and the billiards are always on, so stop in...."

"When's Cath... uh, Cindy Lou returning?"

"Tough to know with her, but she did mention possibly this weekend. What is today?"

"It's Tuesday."

"Right...Tuesday, so that means she might be in Friday afternoon, unless court runs late, and then, Saturday morning I suppose."

"Thanks again for everything," said Jason.

"You are welcome, yes sir, but why don't you stop by tomorrow evening, I've got a little poker game running on Wednesday nights and the boys would be glad to meet you."

"Thank you, that sounds great."

Jason hadn't realized how tired he actually was. When he got back to the barn, he collapsed into the chair in the corner. It was more comfortable than he'd remembered. "Funny," he thought, as he quickly nodded off, "I haven't even sat in this chair since I bought it, hoping that Becca was going to arrive...."

He suddenly jumped from the chair as his phone rang. "Hello?"

"Jason? What the hell? Did I wake you up?"

"Tommy? Hey, how are you?" Jason quickly tried to pull himself out of his catnap daze.

"Good, buddy, real good, but the question is, how are YOU, living out there in the middle of N-O-W-H-E-R-E?"

"Well, it's not actually nowhere; it's just a little town in Oklahoma...."

"Listen, buddy, whatever. Anywhere in Oklahoma is basically nowhere. Oh, and what's going on with Becca? She called me the other night, pissed as hell about what a son-of-a-bitch you are. I tried to tell her it was the stress of that crap-hole town and all, and that you didn't mean any of it, right?"

"Any of what? To be honest, I'm not sure what she's talking about; I haven't even talked to her in forever at this point.... It's complicated."

"Brother, of course it's complicated, that's why you don't ever get strung too tight; it's better to love 'em and leave 'em, I always say! Hey, listen, I gotta run, we're cutting a colic on that horse that ran the Derby at Santa Anita last week. Did you hear about him? Amazing...amazing, buddy we gotta get you out here; California is incredible, and the women...."

"Well, I...."

"Okay, so the truth is, one of the other interns is leaving, getting married; it means there's a spot for you! You're gonna love it! Do you remember Travis?"

"Travis? Sure...." Jason struggled to get a word in.

"Travis and I have a three-bedroom place a block from the beach! A block! Enough said, right? Right? Hey, gotta run, but what do you say; you in? I told Dr. Evanson it would be a no brainer for you, but he wanted me to call."

"Wow, really? It all sounds too good!"

"It is, brother, it is, and we'll have soooo much fun! Cuttin' colics, girls, beach, girls...."

"I know; it's just that I have that Veterinary Service Act contract, and...."

"Hell, Evanson's attorney made quick work of that, so it not's going to be a problem, trust me. We just go down behind the racetrack a couple of times a month and vaccinate a few stray dogs and we're good. No worries! Just get your gear packed and get the hell out here; you have 3 weeks. Hey, gotta' run, this horse is comin' in...."

"Wait, but...." The line went dead. Jason sat back down in the chair; it didn't seem quite as comfortable now.

Chapter 28

Jason overslept the next morning. As he raced to his truck, he noticed a strange figure wandering around the front yard of Pauline's house. The man was tall and lanky, with a long mop of greasy brown hair, and he hadn't seen a razor in months. The stranger's outfit gave Jason pause; his Scooby Doo flannel pajamas were two sizes too small. Jason moved cautiously, not knowing the man's intentions — or his state of mind, considering his current attire.

Slowly approaching, Jason quietly asked, "May I help you with something?"

The man turned, blankly staring at Jason, before returning to wandering across the yard. Jason, now even more confused by the man's lack of concern over trespassing, said, "Is there something you lost?"

The man ignored Jason's question, then finally grunted. "Oooohh," he mumbled, "Lookin' for my butts."

"Your what?"

"Oooohh, lost my butts, lookin' for my butts."

Jason feared the man might have escaped from somewhere that requires ID and has large fences, but he thought better of asking. He slowly approached the man, and as he got close he smelled cigarette smoke.

"Butts, you lost cigarette butts?"

"Yeah, butts, lost my butts."

Jason found himself looking through the bushes.

"How did you lose them here? This is Pauline's house."

"Yeah."

"Well, then how did you lose them outside of Pauline's house?"

"Threw 'um."

"You threw them over here into her bushes?"

"Yeah, threw 'um out the window last night," he said, pointing a finger toward the window.

Jason stopped. This guy was related to Pauline? How was it that if he lived with Pauline this was the first time Jason had run into him?

"Do you live with Pauline"?

"Yeah."

Jason knew very little about Pauline, but he knew that her husband was deceased and that she had no children. He'd heard that Pauline had a brother, reportedly the Albert Einstein of Birdie. The brother had apparently made a claim in his youth about cracking into the Kremlin, collecting launch codes and other sensitive data from the Russians in the early 1980s. In the weeks that followed the Russian hack job, unmarked SUVs began driving around town. Shortly afterward, Pauline's brother failed to come home one day. The family filed a missing persons report. Local reporters covered the story, and a hotshot reporter from Tulsa even showed up, bragging that his investigation would get to the bottom of the missing boy and the mysterious SUVs. But in the end, nothing. It was as if Pauline's brother had vanished off the face of the earth. Pauline and her mother struggled with the disappearance and for years continued to post missing person signs and hoped he would be found. His father blamed technology, believing that the "new-fangled computers" were the root of all evil and the reason for his son's disappearance.

Seven years later, Pauline's brother was found sitting at the bus station in Birdie. When the station agent asked who he was or if he needed assistance, the man only replied, "Not sure."

Pauline's family threatened to sue; the difficulty was identifying whom to sue. The brother claimed to have no recollection of the past seven years, other than "working with computers." When interviewed by the local authorities and newspaper and asked about his whereabouts and activities during his absence, his response had been the same: "Working with computers."

Nothing else ever came of it, and Pauline's brother never left the house after that. His nickname around town became "Boo," after the reclusive character in Harper Lee's *To Kill a Mockingbird*. Although Pauline's family was happy to have "Boo" back, only a portion of him had truly returned.

Jason stood staring at the disheveled figure before him; how had this happened? This was something he'd only seen in the movies; this didn't happen in real life. So this was Boo.

"My sister doesn't care for my smokes, so my butts go out the window to avoid unpleasant conversations."

Shocked that this man could actually speak, Jason replied, "So you toss the cigarettes out here, and she doesn't find them?"

"Uh huh, keeps the butts safe for later; only problem is sometimes it rains before I can get them picked up."

"So then you just leave them...."

"Ohhh, nooo." He turned to stare at Jason with a wild-eyed gaze. "No, I still get them, but I have to dry them out a skosh first, is all."

"I see." Jason cringed with disgust at the thought of smoking mildewing cigarettes. "My name's Jason, by the way."

Boo turned back to Jason with his wild gaze. "Okay," he said, before once again returning to his work.

Jason stood watching Boo for a few moments longer, realizing he was now officially and truly late for work. "Well, it was nice meeting you...."

A brief wave of Boo's hand signaled the end of the conversation. Jason walked back to his truck, still processing what had transpired.

The phone was ringing incessantly as Jason entered the clinic. Looking around with some confusion, he saw no one else. He reached for the phone. "Thank you for calling Birdie Veterinary Clinic, this is Dr. Davies."

"Well sir, hello sir," said a familiar voice. "This here is Bill Cody calling to remind you of the invitation this evening to my humble abode for a gentlemen's game of cards if you please."

"Oh, sure, yes, that's right, that's tonight," Jason stammered, trying to recall the conversation with Cody and what he had committed to. "It sounds great; now tell me what time I need to be there?"

"Well, yes sir, how about 7 o'clock sharp?"

"7 P.M. sharp, very good, see you this evening."

"Oh, yes sir, please inform Doc Keating he is more than welcome tonight as well."

"Yes, okay, I'll let him know."

As Jason hung up the phone, he noticed that Keating had come into the clinic and was now sitting at his desk. Before he could say a word, Keating interrupted. "No! The answer is no."

Jason drew a breath to make his case, but was again interrupted. "Bill and I go way back, and we two get along just fine; however, some others in this damn town are leeches always hanging off him, and they enjoy trying to take his money any chance they get. I am quite content to drink my own scotch and keep my own money in my own home. You, however, young doctor, may have to figure it out the hard way."

181

Chapter 29

On the drive to Cody's ranch, Jason's thoughts coursed through the events of the past week. Catherine topped the list; but even if he did want to get to know her better, he was leaving. Tommy's phone call had confirmed it: He was getting the hell out of here.

Mavis answered the door, much to Jason's surprise. "Good evening Mavis, but I thought...."

"Didn't work out," she said, her face sullen and disinterested. "They're all in there. Don't make a mess." She turned and disappeared down the hallway.

Jason entered to the sounds of laughter, as if he had just missed the punch line of a joke; a group of cigar-smoking gentlemen sat at the table.

"Well, hey there, Doc!" The vaguely familiar voice sent a jolt of anxiety through Jason; seated on the edge of the billiard table was Otter Laverteen. "Bill said you might be by to our little poker game, but I didn't really expect to see you. Daddy, this is the other vet I was telling you about."

A gray-haired gentleman stood and shook Jason's hand. "Pleasure to meet you, son," he said in a low Texas drawl. "Otter mentioned you were helping John over there. I hope you're enjoying your visit to Birdie."

"Well, yes, it's been very nice...."

"Yeah, Daddy, I imagine it's not as nice as California,

182

so Doc here probably isn't long in Birdie, right, Doc?" Otter slid off the table and slapped Jason on the back.

"Well, I suppose...."

"Now sir, yes sir, don't go speaking ill of our little town. Dr. Davies is much welcomed here." Cody approached, handing Jason a cocktail.

"I hope it's not too tart," he chuckled. "I always mess up the recipe."

"What do you call this?" Jason took a sip and felt his cheeks pucker.

"We call them Sooner Sours, but it probably depends on where you are. Down near Boarsdale they call them Pottawatomie Puckers, but that seems to be a mouthful to say."

Cody introduced Jason to the remaining men around the table: a partner of Cody's at the bank, the mortician, and the local tractor dealer. All of them belonged to the Birdie Rodeo Committee and had spent most of their lives in Birdie.

Jason had played poker in college, but after the first year of veterinary school he had little time to do much of anything. But he wasn't worried. It was like riding a bike; poker was poker.

The first rounds went quickly, and politeness dominated the room. But as the evening progressed, the wagers and voices increased, as did the seriousness of the game. The tractor dealer was going all in, and Jason was down to a handful of chips. Otter was on his game, leaving

Jason wondering if he'd had too much free time at the Mississippi State Veterinary School.

The conversation turned to the upcoming rodeo. "Well, it looks like another potential record breaker with the rodeo this year. That whole meltdown with the rodeo queen and committee in Adairsville put a bad taste in sponsors' mouths, and now they're scrambling to try to find advertising space with us. Best damn thing to happen for Birdie was that little queen over there opened her big mouth!" The tractor dealer grinned and leaned back in his chair.

"Well, change is good on a lot of levels, I think; Daddy and I have been discussing some more changes this year with the rodeo. I told him I wanted to offer my services as official rodeo veterinarian this year." Otter's snaky comment irritated Jason. His gut told him that Otter wasn't to be trusted. Hadn't Doc Keating already committed to the rodeo this year, like he had every year?

Cody was at the bar preparing more drinks, but he quickly interjected, "Now Otter, Doc Keating's been doing the rodeo for a great many years, and the committee hasn't really had any discussions pertaining to making any changes as of yet." Jason heard Cody grumble under his breath as he returned to the table, "Especially, with it being so close to rodeo time...."

"Bill, I appreciate your thoughts; however, Daddy and several of the members have already had discussions that if the current veterinarian resigns or the veterinarian is unable to perform his or her duties, then the committee selects a replacement."

Cody looked over his cards and smiled. "Well, I think most everyone on the board would agree that neither of those is an issue."

Otter smiled the way a villain always does at the climax of a movie, when the hero is trapped. "Bill, Doc Keating told me true as I am sitting here that he is not vetting the rodeo this year. I stopped in to see him just the other day and he told me he was passing the torch to someone else."

Cody looking questioningly at the others seated at the table and said, "Well, then what about Dr. Davies here? It seems to me that he should be allowed to perform the duties at the rodeo in John's place."

"Well, good evening everyone," Catherine said from the doorway. "How's the poker game tonight?"

Jason's heart jumped into his throat. She was more beautiful than he'd remembered; she intoxicated his senses. His mouth became dry and his stomach somersaulted as he scrambled for words.

"Hey, Cindy Lou, darlin', I didn't know you'd be coming in tonight; it's only Wednesday." Cody embraced her with a kiss.

"You boys need to open a window in here; it smells of cigars and booze." They nodded but remained silent. "Why is everyone so glum? Game not going well?" she asked.

"Oh no, Cindy Lou, we were just having a friendly discussion over some details of the rodeo," replied Cody.

"Seems that Dr. Keating will not be performing the veterinary duties this year, and the committee needs a replacement," said Otter's father.

"I see," Catherine replied. "And what have you all decided?"

"Cat, let me jump in here and tell you we are getting it all sorted. I have been kind enough to offer my services as veterinarian, and it would be my honor and privilege to represent Birdie this year." Otter rocked self-assuredly back in his chair.

Catherine glared at Otter with her dark brown eyes.

"Cindy Lou, the committee, or those here at least, were discussing it all. Otter has volunteered, or offered his services, and I have recommended Dr. Davies." Cody pointed to Jason.

She turned to Jason and her expression softened. She smiled and winked her eye. "Dr. Davies, would you also be honored and privileged to perform the veterinary duties?"

He smiled. "Absolutely, however I can help."

"Good. So how does the committee decide?"

"We were sorting that all out, but it seems to me that a vote would decide it easy enough," replied Cody.

Heads nodded around the table. "So who is missing from the committee here tonight?" Catherine scanned the men's faces.

"Well, there are seven members total and four of us here tonight. It's a quorum, but I think everyone should be in on the vote. I can call the others and we can get this figured out in the next day or two," Cody answered. The conversation seemed to make him nervous; he began pacing between the bar and table.

Jason glanced in Otter's direction and noticed the smirk growing across his face. What did he already know? Catherine also noticed. "Otter, what are you up to?" she demanded.

His questioning look of innocence only further confirmed her suspicions. "The only other time I have seen you get this excited about something was when you tried to get in my pants after the homecoming dance and I slugged you." Otter's face blushed as he looked nervously at the others in the room. "Well, uh, no I just want to help."

Otter's father gently pounded a fist on the table. "I say we take a vote with the committee and be done with it." Heads nodded in agreement.

"Well sir, yes sir, it's getting late, and I imagine it's time to call it a night," said Cody.

"Yes."

"Right."

The men all stood and thanked everyone. Otter walked over to Catherine and whispered, "I need to speak with you, privately."

She glanced at Jason with a look that asked him to

wait. Jason helped Mavis clean up while Cody spoke with someone on the phone. Cody turned as he hung up the receiver, saying, "Well sir, yes sir, the committee is set to meet next Monday."

"Okay," replied Jason, not knowing how he should feel about all of this. Why should he care? He wasn't invested in any of this, and furthermore, Tommy's phone call had opened the door to get the hell out of here. Lost in his thoughts, Jason didn't see Catherine approach.

"Hey," she said softly, looking at him.

"Hey. Nice to see you," he replied. She smelled amazing. He could feel his legs buckle over how beautiful she looked tonight.

"Don't worry about Otter, that's his typical modus operandi. He wanted to let me know he harbored no hard feelings about how we left things when I slugged him. Oh, and he asked me out this weekend...."

"Oh."

"I told him I already had plans."

"Sure, I see." Jason turned to grab several glasses from the table. Catherine gently grabbed his arm and said, "With you.... I mean, you *were* going to ask me if I had plans, right?"

"Yes," he stammered, with a smile.

"Great! Now it's late; let's hope your truck starts."

They walked slowly out into the cool night air. Looking up at the stars, he was amazed at how many filled the sky away from the dampening lights of the big cities.

"It's amazing how many stars are out tonight."

Catherine giggled. "You city boys are all the same; you think the stars only come out when you're in the country. Stick around and you may find more than just stars out here."

Jason lingered by the truck door, wanting to stay longer. As he climbed into the truck and turned the key, he prayed that it wouldn't start. But the roar of the engine told him the night was over.

Catherine smiled and touched his arm. "See you this weekend, Doc; take care of yourself."

"Looking forward to it; thanks, you too." Jason put the truck in gear as Catherine walked back up the driveway to the house. As he pulled away, he hoped she would turn back and wave. But she simply entered the house, and the porch lights turned off.

Chapter 30

Trailers and horses lined the clinic parking lot all day Friday and Saturday. Although the rodeo came to town at the same time every year, it still seemed that half the town waited until the last minute to get their horses into rodeo condition. Lame horses need to be rehabilitated, owners needed health certificates, and the list went on.

At the end of the day on Saturday, Jason breathed a sigh of relief as he closed the door on the last trailer. He wasted no time leaving work, quietly slipping out and avoiding Keating. As he headed for the apartment, he realized that in today's rush of appointments, he had almost forgotten that he had a date with Catherine — and in less than 45 minutes! He raced into the apartment and slid across the floor, landing in a wet, greasy pile of manure.

"Jasper!"

He hurriedly shoveled and cleaned up the mess. Jasper's kindness clearly hadn't lasted long, but he would have to deal with the donkey later. He quickly showered and found something clean to wear. Just as he was pulling his boots on, there was a knock at the door.

Catherine wore a short, floral print summer dress that hung loosely across her shoulders and a pair of 1950s-style custom leather boots. He was speechless, his heart racing as Catherine just stood there, innocently waiting for him.

Jason tried to speak but could only gape at her.

"Oh stop," she quipped. "You're lettin' flies in your mouth! You ready? Oh, and here." She handed him a large cotton bag. "Daddy wanted me to send this along."

Jason opened the bag and removed a plastic bag of vegetables. "Daddy planted a garden years ago with a variety of 'lifesaving veggies' he'd read about from some guru in India. He swears they are adding years to his life."

Jason smiled. "Are there any carrots in here?"

"Pretty sure there are a few, why?"

"Oh nothing, long story," he replied, as he pulled a small bundle of carrots from the bag and set them on the counter.

"Oh, and Daddy also included some medication that he says will fix just about anything."

Jason wrapped his hand around what felt like a bottle and removed the largest bottle of Jameson whiskey he'd ever seen. He shook his head in amusement.

As they walked across the driveway to leave, Jason noticed Boo rustling in the bushes.

"A friend of yours?" Catherine nodded in Boo's direction.

"Sort of, he...."

"I'm kidding! I know Boo, he's a bit of a legend around here. But I'm sure you've already heard the gossip. His name is actually Martin, but he's been Boo since I was a kid."

"Martin, really? Does he know that?"

"What, that his name is actually Martin? I would think he would, but not many people know him as Martin."

They headed out of town in Catherine's car. Jason listened to the car's engine wind through the gears. Catherine knew how to drive: confident, but not overly aggressive. "A perfect combination in a female," he thought, smirking as he looked out the window.

Jason felt like he had known Catherine forever; she seemed to be a calming force in his crazy world, and he couldn't help but be drawn to her. She had the ability to make everyone around her feel important and comfortable in her presence. But he wondered how normal she actually was; the loss of her mother, her borderline eccentric father, and her family's wealth could have easily shaped her into a rich diva princess.

"Hungry?"

"You bet."

"Good, then driving over to Franklin won't be a wasted effort; anyone taken you to Ray Ray's since you've been here?"

"Ray, what, what's? Is it a restaurant?"

"Absolutely not!" she laughed. "Definitely no, but it's a hell of a joint! The best barbeque, the best live band, and the worst service you will ever see."

Jason changed the subject, hoping to use the drive to get to know her better. "You never finished your story about how you ended up in Tulsa; I want to know more about where you've been in your travels."

She turned, raising her eyebrow. "Oh really? You mean Daddy hasn't shared all the family secrets?

"Well, he mentioned you're a lawyer."

"Yes...and what else has he told you?"

"Oh, I don't know.... Did you always want to be an attorney?"

"What? No, I guess in the end, it found me. After college and some traveling I had this altruistic belief that a law degree would help me save the world. I was convinced it would be important armor to protect Daddy and his assets from every 'friend' and 'business associate' that stopped by. The work I'm involved with now isn't really what I thought I would be doing back then, but I keep hoping my world will circle back there someday."

"Back?"

"Oh, simple, helpful, fulfilling...."

"Your work isn't fulfilling?"

"Well, it is from a financial aspect, but it's the making a change part I struggle with. I dabbled in child advocacy, helping some families in crisis, but my world right now doesn't allow a lot of time for that. No, my world is filled with meetings, contracts, and more meetings; pretty tame, and not anything like what I imagine being a veterinarian would be like."

"Right...," he groaned, staring out the window.

"Right what?"

"Everyone thinks being a veterinarian is the James Herriot version, driving along the countryside helping animals."

"Bummer...."

"What?" he asked.

"Oh nothing, I just heard my childhood explode."

"Sorry, it's just that people like to think it's always warm fuzzies working with cute animals."

"It's not?"

"You see this scar?" he asked, pointing to his hand. A five-inch scar extended lengthwise over the top of his hand. I broke my hand my second year of vet school when a horse kicked me. Four screws, and three months of physical therapy. It healed, I guess, except on cold days when the arthritis causes it to ache. It can predict the weather better than any meteorologist."

The engine revved as Catherine shifted gears and the car slowed. Jason read a large billboard: "Welcome to Franklin, population 210. Home to the 'Fighting Catfish,' 1A All-State Champs 1994."

"Impressive," he remarked sarcastically as they pulled into the packed dirt parking lot. Cars, trucks, and even a riding mower were scattered haphazardly across the lot. As they exited the car, Jason noticed two horses tied in the trees.

"C'mon, if you're nice I might even buy you a t-shirt." Catherine smiled, leading the way.

The car alarm beeped twice as they walked toward the door.

"Theft a big problem around here?" he laughed,

holding the door for her.

"Oh, stop; no, it's just habit, I guess."

Inside, people and picnic tables lined the perimeter of a massive wooden dance floor. A band was setting up its equipment at one end.

Catherine grabbed Jason's hand. "This way." His body tingled; her soft, petite fingers sent a jolt of electricity through his hand.

In the far corner, a woman stood on a chair waving excitedly. Catherine navigated their way through the waves of people.

"Hey Cat, how are you, sweetheart? It's been too long!" The woman gave Catherine a long embrace and then turned to Jason with a hearty "Hello!"

"Jason, I'd like you to meet my friend, Ginger. Ginger, this is Jason Davies; excuse me, Dr. Jason Davies."

"It's Jason; pleasure to meet you."

Ginger turned to two men seated in a nearby booth and tapped one of the men's shoulder. When the tap failed to elicit a response, she then lightly smacked him on the back of his head. He immediately turned and stood up, removing his hat. He was tall and thin with a broad, toothy smile. "Hi, I'm Justin," he said, shaking Jason's hand.

"Pleasure to meet you."

Ginger introduced them to the other man, still seated. "Troy is a friend of Justin's from work. Now, you two have a seat. I saw you two coming this way and had the gal bring us all something to drink, but where is she?" Ginger climbed back onto the chair, attempting to look over the waves of people on the dance floor.

Minutes later the waitress returned with their drinks and took their orders. Food and conversation filled the evening, with Ginger talking the night away. Jason secretly enjoyed the cramped booth, continually edging closer to Catherine. The dance floor filled as the band played on. After a while, Catherine grabbed Jason's hand, saying, "Let's dance!"

Jason had never had so much fun on a dance floor. Catherine patiently showed his two left feet the Birdie Stomp and the Western Swing. Jason paused to catch his breath as the music ended; his recurring headache from the Dexter's Crossing incident was back.

"You okay?" Catherine grabbed his hand with a look of concern.

"Yes, I'm fine, but the ibuprofen must be wearing off is all."

"Let's get out of here. Maybe we can go find that bottle of medication Daddy sent you. I'm going to run and use the ladies room and then we can split, okay?"

Jason returned to the table to wait patiently. Suddenly he felt a slap on his back.

"Well hey there, Doc, long time, no see!" Jason felt a pit in his stomach; he knew the voice behind him.

"Enjoying your evenin'?" Otter slurred his words, taking a sip of his beer.

"Yes. It's been good." Jason saw the glassy look of Otter's drunken gaze and sensed trouble. Otter's grip tightened on Jason's shoulder. Just then, Justin and Troy returned from the dance floor.

"What's going on, Otter?" Justin eyed a group of men standing behind Otter.

"Why yes Justin, thank you for asking, Jason and I were just havin' us a nice little chat about things."

"Really? Well, maybe I can help." Justin stepped closer to Jason.

"No, no...no. I'm pretty sure Jason and I will get along just fine here, none of your concern."

Justin smiled, looking over at Troy. "Well you see, Otter, it turns out it is my concern 'cause Jason is a friend of mine, so I suggest that you and your friends move along."

"Well, well, it appears that *Doc* here is making friends all over these parts. He's made short work of moving into town and making friends with everyone, including my girl!" Otter pointed his shaking finger at Jason, simultaneously spilling beer from his glass.

Justin took a step closer to Otter.

"Now, this isn't your concern, Justin, so you can just leave me the hell alone. My issue is with this jackass who thinks he can make the moves on what is rightfully mine. I need him to step outside so that we can discuss this man to man." Droplets of spit from Otter's slurred speech hit Jason in the face.

197

"Discuss what?" Catherine asked as she returned to the table.

"Oh, hey Darlin', nice to see you!" Otter turned, grabbing the edge of the booth to keep from falling. "We were just chatting here about how Doc Davies is getting to make so many friends in town these days...."

"Otter, get the hell out of here and on your way. You're drunk and stupid, or rather you're stupid and drunk," said Catherine.

Otter staggered as he turned around to his associates. "Now, hold on a friggin' second. I am just being neighborly is all. What the hell is wrong with that?"

"Oh, shove it, and take your drunken ass home." Catherine grabbed her purse from the booth.

"Now you listen here, Darlin', that's about all the lip I'm gonna take from you!" Otter fumed, grabbing her arm.

"Let me go, you son-of-a-bitch!"

Jason stepped between them. "Let her go, Otter!"

"Mind your own damn business, or I'm gonna send you back to wherever you came from, in a box!" Otter stumbled as he talked.

Jason reached out to steady him, but as he did, Otter regained his footing. "You asshole!" Otter swung his fist in Jason's direction but missed. Before Jason knew what was happening, Catherine planted her left fist into Otter's face. The blow knocked him to the floor.

Ginger screamed, "Oh my god! Is he dead?"

"I hope so...Jason, we can go now." Catherine turned

to her friends. "Ginger, Justin, Troy, it's been fun as always."

Otter groaned and his cronies helped him up and led him away.

Catherine's friends all laughed, congratulating her on a perfect punch.

Catherine winced, holding her hand. "We're going to go now. See you all soon."

Catherine handed Jason her purse as they headed for the door. "Grab my keys, you drive," she whispered to him, tears welling in her eyes. As they climbed into the car, Jason asked, "Let me see your hand."

She outstretched her injured arm and with one look he knew she had fractured her hand. "Where is the closest ER?" He helped buckle her in and started the car.

"Tulsa."

"How far is that?"

"About three hours by car, but I have another way. Can you take me to the ranch?" Catherine slowly removed her phone from her purse.

"Hello, Kenny? Hi, it's me, sorry to call so late. Yes everything is, well, yes, but I need a ride back to Tulsa. Yes, I'll explain when I see you. Okay, thank you." She hung up the phone and then slowly reached over and kissed Jason's cheek.

He turned and smiled. "What was that for?"

"For helping me back there...and for being here now...."

The BMW flew down the two-lane highway through the darkness. Twenty minutes later, they arrived at Cody's ranch. As Jason slowed the car into the long winding drive, he saw lights flashing in the distance. The lights were arranged in a large square pattern that he hadn't noticed on his previous visits.

"You don't see that every day," Jason said, amazed.

"No? You mean everyone doesn't have their very own helicopter?"

"And another thing, I didn't know you were left-handed!"

Catherine looked at him curiously. "How did you know I was?"

"Because you decked Otter with the meanest left hook I've ever seen!"

"I'm actually right-handed.... I knew that as hard as I wanted to hit him might break something, and I have court on Tuesday."

Just then, a tall, lean man crawled out of the helicopter and quickly jogged toward them. "Hey there, you sure you're okay to fly?" he asked, glancing at Catherine's hand.

"Yes, Kenny, I'm okay. Is Pearl ready to go?"

"Five minutes, Miss Catherine, and she will be. Your daddy hasn't had her out in a bit, so I wanted to prime and check a few things before we got going." Kenny nodded at Jason and returned to the helicopter.

Catherine looked at Jason and smiled as if she could

read his mind. "I didn't name her; Daddy did, after my grandmother. She loved to fly. Daddy bought the helicopter before this one not too long before my grandmother passed away. Poor Kenny, I don't know if he ever had a day off in the weeks before she passed. They flew everywhere."

Jason stared quietly at the helicopter. "How does Kenny take that much time off to fly everyone around?"

"Well, it soon became his full-time job. For years, he was in charge of growing the hay on the ranch and putting it up, and I guess technically he still does, but flying has become his rather full-time occupation. Daddy bought the helicopter, but he needed someone to fly it. Kenny had flown in the Army and National Guard, so a couple of trial runs, and he was ready to go. Kenny flies Daddy for work or whatever, but as Daddy likes being around here more and more, the helicopter just sits."

Kenny returned, telling Catherine, "Okay, she's ready when you are."

"Great," Catherine replied, still carefully holding her hand.

The whirling blades of the helicopter were disconcerting to Jason, and he worried that he wasn't up to speed on proper helicopter protocol. He opened the door for Catherine. "Thank you!" she yelled, planting a quick kiss on his cheek. He scrambled in behind her before Kenny closed and locked the back doors.

Climbing into the cockpit, Kenny turned and asked,

"You two ready?" They both nodded while Jason helped Catherine buckle in and place a headset on her head. Moments later, they lifted off the ground. Steadily climbing into the midnight air, Jason realized he hadn't left Birdie since his arrival almost three months ago; had it only been that long? A twinge of homesickness flooded him momentarily, as he turned to Catherine. She was leaned back in her seat with her eyes closed.

"Are you okay?" he asked her through the headset. She turned, eyes closed, and smiled, gently reaching for his hand. Her fingertips curled around his; his heart pounded as he leaned back and stared out into the darkness below.

Chapter 31

Kenny landed the helicopter at Tulsa General Hospital; technically, he couldn't use the designated landing pad. As he gently set the helicopter down in the adjacent grassy area, hospital staff was waiting to whisk Catherine away, leaving Jason at the doors to the ER.

Standing alone in the deserted waiting room, Jason wondered why the ER wasn't busier on a Saturday night. He paced around the empty waiting area chairs and stopped cold when he realized that Keating knew nothing about any of this. Jason needed to call him, but looking at this watch he realized that Keating wouldn't be amused with a 2:47 A.M. phone call. He decided to text Shelly instead, to at least head off any morning office confusion. He also hoped she might be able to soften the backlash from Keating. But wait...tomorrow...tomorrow was Sunday. The clinic was open for emergencies, but Dr. Palmer from Briggsdale was covering emergencies after Jason and Keating had covered for Palmer several weeks prior. Jason breathed a sigh of relief and continued his aimless wandering.

"Excuse me, Dr. Cody?" a nurse asked as she approached him. He spun around, startled and confused.

"You *are* Dr. Cody, aren't you? Catherine Cody's husband?"

"Uh, yes, that's right," he stammered, wondering

what Catherine was up to. "Just a little tired, sorry."

"Your wife would like to see you." The nurse motioned for him to follow her.

"Oh, of course, my *wife*, yes, my wife," he said, following her down two long hallways. He peered into the room, finding Catherine in a bed. She was dressed in a hospital gown and nurses bustled about the room setting up monitoring equipment and IV fluids.

"Hey...*honey*...how are you?" she asked, winking at him.

He sat down in the chair next to the bed. "The question is, how are *you*?"

"Oh, I'm fine, especially since the pain meds are starting to kick in. Will you stay while the doctor comes in? The radiologist thinks casting it should be fine, but I want your thoughts on the matter."

"Okay...but I'm not...."

She reached for his hand and gently squeezed it. They sat quietly holding hands as the doctor arrived and discussed the situation. Catherine had dislocated two fingers and sustained a hairline fracture in the bone of her middle finger.

"We should be able to reduce the fracture and stabilized the injuries without surgery. We will need to place a cast on that hand for the next 8 weeks, and I want you to spend the night, not because of the cast, but you have an interesting heart arrhythmia that makes me a little nervous. I spoke with the cardiologist and she would like you to stay overnight; if everything checks out in the morning, then you are free to go." The doctor spoke directly to Catherine and then turned to Jason. "Any questions?"

Minutes later, two orderlies arrived to transport Catherine for the placement of the cast. Jason stared out the window into the blackness of the early morning; he felt the hour of the day catching up with him; his contacts were tacky on his eyes, and his head was fuzzy. Just then, a nurse arrived wheeling a folding bed, blankets, and a pillow.

"I thought you would be more comfortable, since your wife needs to stay overnight."

Jason blushed, not sure what to say. He helped the nurse with the bed, and then she was gone again. He sat down in the chair and drifted off to sleep.

A beeping sound brought him from his sleep. Catherine, now back in her bed, had also drifted off to sleep. A nurse arrived, pushed some buttons on the IV pump, replaced the fluid bag, and left.

"You should make use of that little bed they brought you." Catherine turned, smiling at him. "It occurred to me that I never touched base with Kenny."

Jason shook his head. "Not to worry; once I realized they wanted you to stay, I had the nurses send him back to the ranch."

They each drifted in and out of sleep. Morning came with a 6:30 A.M. call from Cody. Jason raced to answer it.

"Hello?"

"Dr. Davies! Yes sir, this is Cody. How's my little Cindy Lou? Is she okay?"

"Yes sir, everyone here is taking really good care of her," he answered, his voice low and cracking.

"Well good, yes sir, real good news. Now I called Kenny to get me up there ASAP."

Jason saw Catherine motioning. "Cody, hang on." Jason placed his hand on the receiver.

"Tell him I am fine. He doesn't need to come," Catherine whispered.

"Cody?"

"Yes sir, I'm here."

"Cindy Lou says she's fine, and you don't need to trouble yourself in coming. But I can call you later, to give you an update."

"Well, yes sir, yes sir, that'd be just fine, just real fine, thank you. You just take good care of my girl, okay?"

"Yes sir, I will do that."

"Is he okay with that?" Catherine whispered.

Jason nodded, hanging up the phone.

A nurse had come in to take Catherine's blood pressure. "Breakfast should be here shortly," she told them as she left.

"Good, I'm starving," Catherine replied, just as another nurse entered with a tray of food.

The doctor arrived shortly after breakfast and released Catherine into her "husband's" care.

A sedan was waiting in front of the hospital; the driver took them downtown. Jason had never been to Tulsa before; he was impressed with how much it looked and felt like any other big city. The surprised expression on his face hinted at the thoughts flashing through his mind.

Catherine gently squeezed his arm. "You know, people from Oklahoma are not all rednecks; we drink Starbucks, and we even shop at Costco sometimes."

The sedan stopped in front of a sign that read "University Club Tower." Jason peered up at the amazingly tall structure as the driver helped Catherine from the car. The sedan pulled away, leaving the two of them standing on the sidewalk. Jason looked at Catherine, with her arm in a cast and her face no longer able to hide the pain and exhaustion.

"This is where you live?" Jason stammered.

"Very funny, did you think only New York or Chicago has skyscrapers?" she asked.

As they approached the double glass doors, Catherine pointed to her purse. "Wave my purse in front of this scanner." She indicated a small box below a camera.

The doors slid open with a beep, and they took the elevator to the twenty-ninth floor. Each floor had six residences; Catherine's faced the southwest side and had a bird's eye view of the city.

Catherine disappeared into the bedroom. "Make yourself at home, I'll be right back."

The immaculate, designer-decorated apartment

207

overwhelmed Jason's senses, with its floor-to-ceiling artwork, hardwood floors, and skyline view that even Hollywood celebrities would envy. At the far end of the room a large brick wall displayed dozens of framed pictures of various sizes. Jason stared in amazement, quickly scouring the pictorial history of Catherine's world, looking for any clues to her quiet and mysterious past. A small, simple framed picture hung in the center of all the others; he recognized the man, a much-younger Cody with his beautiful wife holding their infant daughter. Jason felt a twinge of sadness: a snapshot of happiness; this was all she had left. He turned and walked toward a wall of windows that looked out over the expansive Tulsa skyline. "How in the hell did I wind up here?"

"Did you say something?" Catherine asked as she appeared from the hallway.

"Oh, hey, no, nothing," Jason mumbled as he sat down on the oversized leather sofa.

"Sorry to keep you waiting, I wanted to change." Catherine sat down beside him. Jason smirked when he read her shirt: "Trust me – I'm a Lawyer."

"Don't laugh, Daddy bought it for me a while back, and I apparently I haven't done laundry for some time because it's the only clean shirt in there. May I get you something to drink? Eat?"

"No, but I'm the one who should be taking care of you. Don't worry about me; you need to lie down and rest."

"Oh, I'm fine for a bit, but how are you?" Catherine reached over and touched his cheek. "With all this drama, I completely forgot about your injury from the run-in with the horse. How's your head?"

"Oh, that. I'm fine. I just keep taking ibuprofen."

"Well, if you need anything stronger, they did give me some good pain pills at the hospital." She smiled at him.

"Thanks, but I'm okay."

"Alright then; don't say I didn't try." She patted his leg. "I would imagine you would like to freshen up and such."

"Why, do I smell?"

"Well, I wasn't going to say anything, but now that you mention it." She winked. "There's a shower in the guest bedroom, so help yourself. I need to figure out what I'm doing on Tuesday with court anyway."

Jason showered and then found a clean shirt and pair of jeans laid out on the bed. "Where did these come from?" he wondered. He smelled coffee brewing and returned to the kitchen. Looking him up and down, Catherine smiled and said, "Hmmm, not bad; they fit okay?"

"Great, but how...?"

"Long story." She handed him a cup and nodded for him to follow.

They returned to the couch. "So what's your story?"

Jason paused, taking a sip, "*My* story?"

"You know, brothers, sisters, parents? I realized

waking up this morning with my new 'husband' in my hospital room that I know nothing about you, well not really. I mean, you could be an axe murderer for all I know."

"Well, I'm a Virgo...," he replied sarcastically, causing Catherine to gently elbow her casted arm into his chest. "I enjoy waterskiing, long walks on the beach...."

Catherine jabbed him again. "I'm serious, Doc. My life is an open book and you know about all the characters in it, but you're the mystery man of Birdie. How the hell did you end up there? Have you always wanted to be a veterinarian?"

His sarcastic air faded. "No...Not always, I guess."

"See? Good, we're getting somewhere." She enthusiastically patted his leg.

He gazed at her coy smile. "Am I on the witness stand? Am I being interrogated?"

"Interrogated? No, at least not yet," she replied, setting her coffee down. "So continue, 'No, you have not always wanted to be a vet....'"

"Uh, no, I guess not. My family is all in construction."

Her inquisitive glance caused him to pause and ask, "What?"

"Nothing, it's just that you don't strike me as a builder." She adjusted a pillow.

"Great, where were you when I told my old man that very same thing? I had to figure it out the hard way. I worked for my father and brother for a couple of years, but let's just say, I am *not* handy with a nail gun...." He raised the palm of his right hand. "See this?" He pointed to a scar in the middle of his palm. "I accidentally crucified myself to a wall one day."

"Ouch!" She cried. "Good move on not sticking with the construction gig. So how did *not* doing construction lead you to Oklahoma?"

"Paul Newman."

She motioned for him to continue.

"Growing up, my father contracted with the National Park Service, so every summer we packed up and moved to a different park to either build or remodel lodges, cabins, administration offices, or whatever. Summer in the parks was a magnet for families: hiking, riding horses, having fun. The horses fascinated me; I mean, to take a 1000-pound animal and ask it to climb the side of a mountain with a rider on its back. When we moved back to Phoenix for a while it amazed me how many families had never ridden a horse, or even left the city limits.

The summer after the nail gun incident, my dad worked on a new visitor center in Rocky Mountain National Park in Colorado. He pulled some strings and got me hired on at a stable to help wrangle horses, taking people up into the Park on horseback. I loved it; I loved all of it, but when I went off to college I had no clue about what I wanted to do with my life. You know how sometimes things just happen, and you realize later it was meant to be? I was cleaning up one night when I came across this box of junk people had left behind. Digging through the water bottles and hats, I found a book written by Paul Newman."

"Like the actor, Paul Newman?" Catherine asked.

Jason nodded. "It looked interesting, so I tucked it under my arm and took it home."

"You stole a book from the lost and found?" she asked with a laugh.

"Well, it wasn't like anyone missed it, I guess. Paul Newman started this non-profit, 'The Hole in the Wall Gang'; it provides kids with a chance to go to camp."

She looked confused. "So...how does that lead you *here*?"

"Okay, cut to the chase; this camp was what I wanted to do, and I figured my family could build something like this for other families."

"So what happened? Why didn't you?"

"The money.... One conversation with my dad set me straight on the fact that you can't just go and build a non-profit kids' camp. He and my brother about laughed me out of the house that night, and I heard about it for weeks afterward."

"I'm sorry. It sounds like a really worthy cause; you shouldn't give up on something like that."

"I did for a while, but then I couldn't let it go."

"I don't understand how you wanting to build a kids' camp equates to becoming a veterinarian."

"Don't laugh, but I convinced myself that maybe I

could make enough money as a veterinarian, and that I could support a camp someday."

She silently gazed into his eyes. "Wow.... Quite a lot rolling around in that head of yours."

"I know; it's crazy." He shook his head, feeling embarrassed for revealing too much.

"No, it's not crazy; it actually sounds amazing."

The phone rang, startling both of them. "I'll grab it in the kitchen." She slowly stood and made her way across the room.

"Hello? Oh, hey. No, I'm fine. No, just a little misunderstanding with Otter. I know, he's always been a jackass. No, not to worry, I'm okay. Seriously, why would you come back early for this? No. I have the Kaplan thing Tuesday and it should go the week, but just stay and finish. Where do you go after, Munich? That's right, and how long there? How's everyone else doing? Good... Okay. Yes, okay...k... bye."

"Sorry." She sat back down on the couch. "It was my law partner wanting to know about this," she said, raising her arm. "Where were we?"

"*This* is where you go to rest." He stood up from the couch.

"Okay, okay, if you insist, *Doctor* Davies." She winked and grabbed his arm and kissed him. He resisted the temptation to pull her closer, fearing that he might hurt her arm. He kissed her forehead. "Let me know if you need anything."

Catherine slept the remainder of the afternoon, giving Jason time to call Keating and explain everything that had transpired. Keating's reaction to the news surprised him: "You just take care of that little gal," Keating grunted. "That family has been real good to this town; trust me, the work will still be here when you get back. Oh, and I told some gal that called here looking for you that you would be gone for a few days.... Good luck, Doc...."

"Wait, what gal?" Jason stammered with confusion.

"Oh, hang on, I think she said her name was Rebecca. She hung up pretty quick once I told her you were in Tulsa with Catherine. Not to worry, I'm sure she'll call back. Okay then, talk to you later."

Jason panicked; Becca calling and talking to Keating would spell disaster in the end. Her talents were award-worthy when it came to relationships and jealousy. Years ago, during one of the "breaks" in their relationship, Jason briefly dated an old high-school girlfriend. When Becca found out, she stalked the girl for weeks. A year later, Jason wanted to break off their relationship, and Becca tried to run him down with her car while he was out jogging. If history repeated itself; this would be a very bumpy ride. His palms began to sweat and he could feel his chest tighten. He returned to the living room, finding Catherine still sound asleep on the couch. He crept quietly back to the guest room and dialed Becca's number. The phone rang with no answer and then went to voice mail.

"Becca, hey, it's me, I wanted to talk to you; give me a

call as soon as you can."

He hung up and dialed the number again; this time, Becca answered immediately.

"Hello? Hello? Becca?" Jason couldn't hear her say anything. "Becca, it's me. I just want to explain things, about what's going on. Becca? Please say something." Suddenly, the line went dead.

He dialed her number again but this time the phone went directly to voice mail; he hung up and flopped back on the bed, staring at the ceiling. This would be a disaster, but no different than the countless other battles they had experienced throughout their relationship; an angry Becca took her time turning the screws of heartache.

He quietly made his way back to the living room and as he looked around the room, something caught his eye. A picture frame face-down on the piano appeared out of place. He turned the frame over: a picture of a happy wedding couple, smiling, surrounded by family. Stunned, he recognized the beautiful bride: Catherine.

He replaced the photo and stared out into the cityscape below, watching the people and cars moving along like tiny ants; the ants marching, marching, all for what? He wanted to look at the picture again but didn't want to at the same time. Could it really be true? Of course it was true; there were two missing pieces of her story. Why was she keeping her marriage a secret? Why hadn't she told him earlier, instead leading him on like she had? Numb and heartsick, he crept back to the guest bedroom and dropped onto the bed.

He checked his phone; three texts from Tommy: "Get your ass out here! The girls are beautiful!" "Do you have your bags packed and ready to get out of that dump? The deal is almost brokered and I'll let you know when everything is set for you to come!" The last text was a picture of two women sunbathing topless: "You're missing all the fun!" Jason sighed; a veterinary degree had done nothing to improve Tommy's maturity level.

Jason felt a kiss on his cheek. "Why did you let me sleep so long?" Catherine asked. "What time is it?"

Looking at his phone, he turned to her. "Almost 5:30 P.M.; are you hungry?"

"Sure, how about you?"

Jason nodded.

"Okay, where's my phone?" She pressed a button on the phone. "Hello, Sauri? It's Catherine. Good, you? Great, oh yes, two this evening. Oh no, he's still out of town. Okay, thank you." She hung up the phone. "I hope you like Korean." Jason's faced looked pained. "What? You *don't* like Korean?" she asked.

A smile grew across his face. "I'm kidding."

"So, you never told me why you just happen to have a change of clothes my size?" Jason asked.

"Well...you want the long version or the short

version?" she replied, positioning herself once again on the couch, wincing when she bumped her arm. "Or how about the medium version?"

"Sure," he replied, knowing sadly that he really didn't want to hear *any* version.

"The clothes belong to my husband, or rather, soon to be *ex*-husband. We've been separated for the past year; honestly, it wasn't great the year before that. There's a smattering of belongings around here that he hasn't claimed, and knowing him, he's forgotten about any of it. He spends most of his time other places, but he did even when we were together, which is a whole other story...."

Without looking up, Jason asked, "So where is he now?"

"Right now he's in Munich, but then he heads to Milan. He has a place in London and handles most of the firm's international dealings."

"He's an attorney also?"

"Yes.... We actually started a law firm three years ago and he's been traveling ever since." She gazed out the window. "Makes for a lonely marriage, to say the least. The truth is it should have never happened to begin with; we rushed into something before realizing we were both on different paths, I guess."

In reality, Jason knew exactly what she meant. Deep down, he felt the same about his relationship with Becca. He hoped to be married and have children one day, whereas Becca only wanted to be an aunt to her niece and nephews. She had once commented, "Kids are messy, and they'll clash with the Lexus."

Suddenly, someone knocked at the door. Jason jumped up.

"Dinner is served." Catherine smiled and winked at him.

Opening the door, Jason was met by a smiling teenager carrying a white plastic bag. Jason reached into his pocket, looking for money. Catherine yelled, "It's already taken care of." The teenager handed the bag to Jason, saying, "Have a good evening," then turned back down the hallway.

Jason closed the door and returned to the living room, where Catherine had set plates and dinnerware on the coffee table. "I hope this is okay, eating in here."

"No, it's great," he replied.

They ate quietly, absorbing all that had been shared. The food surprised him; he hadn't realized how hungry he actually was. His mind flashed back to the brewing firestorm in his head: "What the hell am I doing here?" He had fallen for Catherine, there was no doubt. But now learning of her marriage, albeit estranged.... He could already hear his mother's voice: "Whaaattt? She's married, Jason!" She would be halfway to confession at the first hint of any of it. Then his father would weigh in, reminding him of the dangers of a woman with baggage. "Furthermore," he would often say when he was wound tight on his soapbox lecture, "What about all the sacrifices you've made to get to where you are? You truly want to throw this all away on a girl? You're in debt up to your ears, and now you have the chance to work at one of *the* top equine practices in the country. Why isn't your ass on the next flight to California?"

"How's your food?" Catherine asked.

"Good, really good, thank you."

He caught her staring at him between bites. "I was just thinking," she said.

"About?"

"What you were saying earlier about the camp and everything."

"Oh, I know, I'm a bit of a dreamer. Just dreams...."

"No...No, I don't think it is with you. It's very real and I can tell you're driven by it."

"You can, huh?" he replied sarcastically.

"Yes, actually I can. What I failed to tell you earlier was that I majored in psychology. I'm pretty good at 'shrinking' people when I need to...."

She took another bite, then asked, "Do you believe that things happen for a reason?"

"I don't know, I guess sometimes," he replied.

"Do you know any history on Buffalo Bill Cody? I'm mean, not my daddy's pseudo-interpretation of him, but what his claim to fame was?"

Jason thought for a moment. "Buffalo scout or hunter and then Wild West performer, right?"

"Well, right, his later years were spent traveling with

the Wild West show. It was a staged performance with Annie Oakley, Native Americans, Buffalo, the whole deal. So Daddy...Well, let me back up...Have you seen the *rest* of the ranch?"

"No, I guess just the main house."

"So, when we get back we need to show you a few things." Catherine passed him the remaining bowl of noodles, grinning with anxious delight.

Chapter 32

They spent the remainder of the evening watching a movie and both drifted off to sleep. Jason woke. He looked at his phone: 1:30 A.M. Turning the television off, he sat in the silence listening to Catherine's slow, rhythmic breathing. She must have grown up so quickly after her mother's death; caring for Cody couldn't have been easy either. She had survived the storm and clearly had come out on the other side a strong, independent, beautiful....

Catherine moved, slowly opening her eyes. "What time...?"

"It's late, let's get you to bed," Jason said, slowly helping her to her feet.

She crawled into bed. As Jason pulled the sheets over her, she whispered, "Thank you."

"For what?" he replied.

"For being here," she said, and kissed him.

"Goodnight."

He returned to his spot on the couch, but he couldn't sleep for a long time.

###

He woke to the smell of coffee brewing. Rolling over, he looked at his phone: 7:30 A.M.

Catherine appeared from the kitchen with two cups.

"Good morning," she said, handing him a cup.

"Good morning."

Catherine gazed questioningly at him and then at the couch. "You didn't think to try out the guest bedroom?"

She sat down on the couch and stared at him as she took a sip of her coffee. "So what's the deal?"

"The deal? The deal with what?"

"The deal where you have an attractive girl all to yourself and you aren't making any moves on her."

He felt his cheeks light on fire. "Well, I...."

"I'm thinking maybe you don't find the girl attractive."

"What! No, that's not it at all...It's just that it's all so complicated and...."

"I know, I'm just giving you a hard time. I'm not really the most available girl currently. I actually am impressed; you have been such a gentleman through all of this."

She touched her hand to his face and kissed him. "So...What *should* we do today? I was thinking I could show you around Tulsa a bit."

"Sounds great, but are you up for it?"

"I'll be fine."

"Okay, I'll grab a shower." He found a razor and shaving cream in a bathroom drawer. It felt good to remove two days of facial hair. He took his time in the shower, soaking up the warm water.

A clean shirt and pants awaited him again on the bed. He dressed quickly, anxious to enjoy their day together.

Making his way down the hallway, he glimpsed Catherine searching through a drawer. She was already showered, dressed in business attire. She turned and headed for the desk, where she began placing documents into a leather briefcase.

His excitement suddenly turned to disappointment, with a sinking feeling that plans had changed. She stopped and looked at him apologetically. He nodded, letting her know he understood. She turned to walk away and then stopped, turning back toward him. Wrapping her free arm around his waist, she whispered, "I'm sorry...They need me at the office...I'm really sorry."

He kissed her. "Kenny's coming for you," she said, stepping back.

"Okay."

"Thank you," she said softly, looking down.

"Thank *you*," he replied. She kissed him one last time before stepping out the door. Minutes later he watched from the window as she climbed into a black sedan on the street below. He dropped to the floor, hugging a pillow and staring out at the city skyline: the world moving on, just another day.

This was best. He was getting too close to her, and he needed distance. He was leaving for California soon.

His phone rang. "Doc? It's Kenny. I'm here to pick you up, if you're ready."

"Yes sir, just tell me where I should meet you."

"Well, take the #2 elevator and press the button that's

marked, 'service floor.'"

"Service floor, got it."

Jason pulled the door closed behind him, feeling like he was forgetting something. In the elevator he scanned the panel and found the orange "service floor" button. When he pressed the button, the doors closed and the elevator began its ascent. The doors opened and he felt a rush of warm air and the intensity of the sun. It seemed as if he hadn't been outside in forever. He heard the blades of the helicopter and saw Kenny motioning from the cockpit.

Jason stared out the window as they lifted off, knowing Catherine was somewhere below. Kenny pointed out a few points of interest at first, but he must have sensed Jason's lack of interest because they flew the remainder of the trip in silence. When they landed at Cody's, Jason thanked Kenny and looked around, wondering how he would make back to the apartment.

"Doc, do you need a lift home?"

"Yes, that'd be great, if it's not too much trouble."

"No problem at all, just let me shut this critter down and my truck is parked over there."

Moments later, Jason followed Kenny to his truck and climbed in. On the drive into town Kenny asked, "Hey Doc, you taking over the rodeo for Doc Keating this year?"

"Well, yes, I guess so."

"Quite an honor, you know, to be the vet for the rodeo; folks from all over come down here. Hell, even the Governor shows up with his fancy entourage of folks," laughed Kenny as he pulled into the driveway.

"It sure sounds like it's going to be a lot of fun. Thank you again for everything."

"My pleasure, Doc; truly my pleasure, and if there is anything I can do to help, just give me call."

The apartment reeked of hot, stagnant air. The whiskey bottle on the counter caught his eye. He reached for it but then paused as he began to twist the lid. There might be no return if he began a walk down this road. He set the bottle in the cabinet and opened the refrigerator door. There wasn't much left, but he grabbed a bottle of Red Stripe beer and opened what remained of some kettle corn. He called Keating to let him know he was back and could cover emergency call.

He then listened to a message from Tommy: "Hey Brother, the countdown is on, my man! Your bags had better be packed and I sure hope to hell you haven't knocked up some redneck hillbilly chick.... Dr. Evanson says the paperwork is days away from being finalized. Apparently some know-nothing pencil pusher needs to sign off on it, but he's been on 'vacay' for the past week. Promise you, my man, as soon as I get the green light, we are getting you on a plane, pronto! Ciao, baby!"

He knew he should be excited about leaving, but the feeling was buried deep under a pile of emotional turmoil.

Dammit! Why couldn't something be easy for once? He dropped onto the bed and flipped through all three television channels. He paused on a rerun of the movie *Notting Hill* and lay back on a pillow. He didn't want to watch this. Why did everything, including Julia Roberts, suddenly remind him of Catherine? He wanted to turn the channel, but something kept him from pushing the button. It was like watching a car accident; too awful to witness, but you can't take your eyes off of it.

He polished off the beer and closed his eyes. He couldn't take it any longer; he dialed her number. *Ringing, ringing, and ringing.* "Hello."

"Catherine?"

"You've reached me while I'm away from my phone. Please leave me a message, and I will return your call. Take care." *Beep.*

"Catherine, it's Jason; just hoping you were well. I know you're busy. Have a good evening."

Minutes later, the phone rang. He answered hurriedly. "Catherine! How are you?"

There was silence on the other end and then "Hello?" Jason swallowed hard as his mouth went dry. The female voice on the other end wasn't Catherine's. "What the hell is going on?"

"Becca? Hey, how are you? Sorry, I thought you were somebody else and....."

"Oh, stop the crap, Jason, what's going on?"

Jason's mind reeled as he tried to pull himself

together.

"Who the hell is Catherine? I called your office number the other day and they told me you were in Tulsa with this bitch."

"Now hang on a minute."

"So is this how it's going to end for us?" Her tone burned his ears.

"End? You already ended it. So, what do you care what I'm doing? And besides, it's not what you think...."

"Really, Jason? What do I think? I think you've jacked up your life and mine for the sake of some career snafu, and now you're deciding to bone some backwoods hillbilly!"

"No, no, it's not like that, let me...explain."

Becca hung up. Stunned, Jason sat in the shadows of his dark, depressing room, unable to believe this was happening. He threw the phone to floor and shook his head.

Chapter 33

Jason's phone rang, waking him from a deep sleep. "What the...," he grumbled, fumbling for the light and his glasses, but he didn't answer it in time. He looked at his watch: 1:03 A.M. He listened to the voice mail: "Yes, Doc Keating or Davies, this is Ed. My mule is down and all bloated up. I'm hoping you might be able to come over and give her some Pepto or a shot of somethin'. I'm over across the creek from the Davidsons' by the old Johnson place."

Who the hell was Ed? Why didn't he have an address like normal people? The phone number was listed as "Private Caller," which Jason had learned in "these parts" was code for "I don't trust the government." So he had no way of finding Ed and his mule. Jason threw on his clothes and headed for the clinic. He hated to wake Keating, but how else was he supposed to decipher the cryptic message? Where was there a creek?

He arrived at the clinic minutes later and quickly double-checked the supplies he needed. He took off toward Main Street, still puzzled as to where exactly he was going and whether or not it was worth dragging Keating out of bed. Just then he saw the lights of the Buckaroo Mini-Mart. A lone car parked out front and the sign reading "Open *All* the Time" gave Jason an idea.

The man behind counter was watching a rerun of *I*

Love Lucy as Jason approached the counter.

"Hep," he said, keeping one eye on the television.

"Well, I'm hoping you can help me find someone's house," Jason replied.

"Sure, what's the address?" the man asked.

"Well, see, that's the trouble. I don't have an actual address," stammered Jason, noticing a flash of concern in the man's eye.

"You need directions to a place, but you don't have an address.... Damn mister, you really are lost," he said, grabbing a can of Copenhagen on the counter. With his right index finger he scooped a large wad of black tobacco, cramming it under his lower lip.

"Well, I have some landmarks, but I don't know if you might be able to help me with those. I'm looking for Ed's place...."

"Ed Guffey? Ed Holstad? Or Ed Frank? Or maybe...Ed Johnson? Which one?"

Suddenly realizing this was going to be a more involved project, Jason took a deep breath and started at the beginning. "Well, do any of these Eds live near a creek, or across the creek?"

The man stared blankly back at him. "Nope."

"Okay, uh, do any of them live near the Davidsons, or not too far from the old Johnson place?"

The man continued to stare blankly at Jason and then turned to a map on the back wall. "It's gotta be Ed Guffey, pretty sure. Yes, almost positive, that's the only one that could be near the old Johnson place, but mister, you don't want to go near the Johnson place, that place is haunted."

Jason looked up, surprised. "Haunted?"

The man's facial expression went stone cold. "Haunted for sure, mister, trust me; has been ever since the last war."

"War? Like Desert Storm?" Jason asked, confused about where all this was going.

"World War II," the man replied. "That whole family disappeared one day, and the place has been haunted ever since. Yep, betting you're lookin' for Ed Guffey. His place isn't but a few miles from here. Let me show you on the map."

"Okay, so down County Road 23H 'til you get to about here," he said, pointing to a spot midway on the road. This is where you're goin' to turn and head west."

Jason craned his neck to see the map over the counter, saying, "But, there isn't a road there."

"Well, no, but it's actually the O'Doogan road, but not on any maps. You'll turn west there and head down until you get to a fork in the road. You don't want to go right; that leads to the Johnson place, like we talked about. Go left, don't go right. Left takes you up the hill to the Guffeys'."

Jason, still confused about the mystery road, replied, "So why is this road not marked?"

"Oh, it'll be marked, just not on any map. See, this old boy, O'Doogan, wanted this road, but he apparently had some difficulty with making friends in these parts due to some other business dealings. Anyways, the city and county I guess refused to build it, so it 'officially' doesn't exist, but you and I know different." The man smiled, placing his index finger to the side of his head.

"What is so important about this road? Why did O'Doogan want the road built to begin with?" Jason asked.

"Well, see, so's that's the interesting deal here. No one really knows, and O'Doogan never said, but there was a lot of talk about why. My daddy told me it was because he had some things going on with the old man Johnson; some secret goings on there in that house.... This is all long time ago, long time.... Anyway, hope that helps you, mister."

Jason paused, digesting all the mystery and intrigue of Birdie, Oklahoma. "I appreciate your help. I need to head that way, but thank you." He shook the man's hand before heading back to the truck. He was mentally trying to remember the directions. "Go to County Road 23H, then west, then left, not right."

Minutes later he was at the County Road and turned west. The road was gravel, much like all the roads in Birdie; however, this one appeared to be better maintained than what he had come to expect on the back-country roads. It was devoid of washboards or potholes, and it almost appeared like it had recently been graded and treated to keep the dust down. "Weird, what would be different about this particular road that it would be so well-maintained?" Jason thought to himself.

A few miles later he arrived at the fork in the road. A sign pointing to the left read "Guffey" in faded green letters painted on a weathered board. The road to the right appeared not to be well-traveled, with tumbleweeds packed at the cattle guard. He stopped the truck. It was weird, but it almost looked *too* untraveled, as if someone were trying to make the property look uninhabited. He shook his head, realizing he was wasting time. He put the truck in gear and began down the road to the left.

The road was dark and wound its way through dense scrub brush. The truck's lights caught a menagerie of animals scurrying in the underbrush. When Jason finally thought he must have missed the house, he saw a small light in the distance. Getting closer, he saw several pickups parked near an old dilapidated barn. He pulled to a stop in front of the doors as several old men clamored out of the barn.

"Hello. Sorry it took a little bit to get here," he said to the four men.

"You the vet from Doc's place?" A short, round man in gray overalls asked.

"Uhh, yes, I'm Jason Davies; pleasure to meet you." He extended his hand.

The old man shook his hand, saying, "Well, suppose you best get in there. Ed's in there with her, but she's not good."

Jason grabbed his stethoscope and a pair of exam gloves before following the men through the barn doors.

Several large lights illuminated the interior of the historic structure. A tall, lanky man kneeled over the animal in the middle of the floor. He turned and stood as they entered. "Doc, thanks for coming so quick. I'm Ed Guffey. This here's my old mule; she's not been eating, and tonight, she's all bloated up and down. We got her up and moved her in here, but she's awful painful."

Jason went to work listening to the mule's heart rate and abdominal sounds. Her heart rate was elevated, but her abdominal sounds were absent; not a good combination. He lifted her upper lip, confirming his worst fear. There was a noticeable blue line forming along her gum line and the gums were tacky to the touch. He lifted her eyelid; the sclera was injected.

He knew that she needed to be put down. She was quickly reaching the end. As he started to place the rectal thermometer under her tail, Jason smelled onions and oil. He looked more closely and saw an oily discharge coming from the animal's rectum, unlike anything he had ever seen before. His facial expression must have given him away; Guffey interjected, "Not to worry, Doc, we're not marinating her just yet. We just have our own way of doing things around here, and that's supposed to help loosen her up."

Just then a crack of lightning outside made Jason jump. He looked around nervously. The men looked at each other and small grins spread across each of their faces.

"You ain't from these parts, are you, Doc?" asked one of them.

"No, why?" Jason replied.

Moments later, the sky unleashed its wrath. Jason ran back to the truck to grab supplies to try to tube the mule, but he knew it was probably a fruitless endeavor. He went to work administering fluids and medications. As he packed up his equipment, he noticed Ed begin to saddle the mule.

"Not to worry, Doc, it's just how we do it around here is all," Ed said with a smile and wink. The rain was coming down in sheets and Jason worried that he wouldn't be able to make it back into town. The men opened the barn door and led the mule out into the dark and drenched environment. Guffey climbed into the saddle, but not before extending his hand to Jason.

"Dr. Davies, thanks for coming out tonight and helping my mule. We'll take it from here," he said confidently.

Jason didn't know what to think. The algorithm of colic diagnosis and treatment did not involve saddling the patient and riding out into a lightning storm. Suddenly, the flash of lightning was so bright that Jason could see a herd of Holstein cows in the far pasture to the south. Instinctively, he ducked as thunder crashed overhead and the ground beneath him shook. He jumped into the truck, holding his breath and hoping that the safety of the rubber tires and metal surrounding him would hold true.

Through the rain-pelted windshield, he saw a man on horseback tie the mule's lead around the horn of his saddle as they took off into the darkness.

"These people are truly crazy," he thought, as he sat in wonder. Another flash of lightning and then a crack of thunder caused him to quickly start the truck. He pulled away, not wanting to witness the poor mule suffering in the rain and wind. As he made his way down the narrow, muddied road, he wondered how in the hell this had ever been a good decision. He should have stayed in construction. Maybe he should cut his losses and explain to Keating that this had all been a grave misunderstanding. California was crazy, but not this crazy.

He slowly made his way down the dark, narrow road, arriving once again at the fork in the road. He stopped the truck, looking at the road that led to the Johnson house.

"Haunted, huh? This town is a bubbling spring of weirdness," he mumbled, pressing the accelerator. The engine sputtered and stalled. The headlights dimmed as Jason scrambled to turn the ignition. The engine strained and he pumped the accelerator, but the engine wouldn't start.

"Damn!" he shouted. He had surely pissed off the gods somehow. "How the hell does it get any worse?"

He tried the truck again; nothing. Reality was setting in; he was sleeping here tonight. Not exactly optimal. He tried the ignition once more, pounding his fists on the steering wheel. "Dammit it all to hell, anyway," he moaned. The rain slowed to a sprinkle and the landscape grew increasingly darker. Slamming the truck door, he climbed out into the muggy, mosquito-cooled evening. He took a few steps and stopped. The walk to town would be a long one; the road back to Ed Guffey's had its own set of challenges. He turned slowly, looking up the dark, eerie road leading to the Johnson house. "Could be dry," he thought. "Could also be amazingly haunted," he heard the little voice in his head say. "It would be more comfortable than the truck." "Well, maybe...."

He gathered the few belongings he had with him and locked the truck. He had remembered leaving a small bag of Twizzlers under the seat and shoved them into his pocket. His fingers felt the welcome shape of a flashlight. He smiled, hoping that at least someone was looking out for him. He worried that this experience had the potential for ending up on *Dateline NBC* some evening, but as the rain began to pick up speed and the lightning lit the sky once again, he was happy with his decision, at least for now.

The house was set back into a large grove of Cyprus trees. Weeds slithered over several of the outbuildings, engulfing everything in their paths. The scene looked like a Hollywood movie stage, further adding to its already haunting aura. Clearly, no one had been here in years.

Jason climbed the wide wooden staircase leading up to the covered porch. The creaking of the dried wood planks made him jump; he turned, expecting to see a ghostly figure looming nearby. He took a deep breath, regaining his age and trying to forget what it felt like to be 9 years old, terrified in his grandparents' dungeon-like basement.

The house's windows shimmered in the darkness, foreshadowing trouble ahead as he made his way to the double set of doors. He thought about knocking but stopped himself. The idea that the door creaked open on command was only an indication that his movie imagination was getting away from him. The door was locked.

"Well," he thought, "I guess that's that." The porch would at least offer some protection from the rain.

Just then, out of the corner of his eye he caught a glimpse of a shadow around the corner of the house. Instinctively, he moved toward what he thought he had seen. Slowly peering around the corner, he saw another door. The glass had been broken in the pane just above the handle. He tried turning the handle and this time he was in luck. The door opened easily, but Jason froze. His brain scrambled for what to do next. "You can't just go in," the little voice in his head screamed. "In the movies, the mistake is always to just go in!" A flash of lightning lit the back of his eyelids, and then a sudden crash of thunder overhead made the decision for him. A sudden blast of warm, stale air hit his face as he fumbled for the flashlight. Shadows surrounded him. He scanned the room, searching for anything that was likely to harm him. "Nine years old is a tough thing to shake at moments like this," he thought.

The light from the flashlight guided him through what appeared to be a large, open family room. He was awestruck with how everything was so well-preserved. He made his way down the hallway to the kitchen and was even more astounded. The table was set for six. Dishes were stacked neatly in the glass-door cabinetry, boxes of items lined the shelves, and dinner napkins were set out as if guests were expected at any moment. What was this place? What had happened here that everything was left behind? Did he dare venture upstairs? Nothing was trying to kill him yet, so he slowly made his way toward the small staircase off the kitchen.

The second floor had its own set of surprises as he made his way down the dark hall. Pictures of various figures hung confidently on the walls as if they had been there for a hundred years and would continue to be there for a hundred more. He ventured into the master bedroom with its massive four-post bed. Opening a closet door, he was amazed to find the closet filled with various shirts and slacks. Shoes lined the floor. Ghosts weren't spooking him, but plates and pants were beginning to. He ventured on and came to a small parlor at the end of the hall. The large Victorian couch he encountered made him think of something out of the Old West. Several cigarette butts lay scattered in the ashtray on the coffee table. It was as if whoever was here never really intended to leave.

Just then, a door slammed downstairs. Jason froze. "What the hell," he thought. "There isn't anyone else here, and doors don't slam like that on their own." He listened but heard nothing more. He made his way back down the hall to investigate the noise. Yet another rule of Hollywood horror movie mistakes: "Never follow the strange sounds."

Rain pelted the windows. He searched for the door that had mysteriously closed on its own and would explain the noise he had heard earlier, but all the interior doors were open, and the exterior door he'd entered through remained closed and was locked. However, he didn't remember locking the door upon entering the house....

"Well, this gets weirder by the minute," he mumbled out loud.

Turning back through the kitchen, he noticed a small open door at the end of an eerie corridor, with steps leading downstairs. He directed the flashlight into the stairwell but saw only a landing with more stairs descending into haunting darkness. Jason cautiously stepped like a swimmer trying out the temperature of the pool, as he weighted the first step. They were sturdy and moved very little under his weight as he took them one at a time. He arrived at the first landing, attempting to see what mysteries lay farther ahead: more stairs and another landing. Finally making his way to the bottom, he felt the soft firmness of compacted dirt. The musty, damp smell reminded him of his grandparents' root cellar, where he and his cousins had taken turns daring each other to be locked into the terrifying tomb. But as the flashlight searched, he saw computers.

Computers! What would they be doing down here? Shining the light around the room, he saw an imposing wall of reflective, shiny metal: a door. He pounded on the thick piece of metal; it was definitely solid and made to withstand something, but what? What was this place, and why was it seemingly abandoned in a matter of minutes? Was somebody coming back, and did they know he was already here?

He scrambled back up the stairs, considering his chances in the truck. But with another crack of lightning outside, and then the increased pummeling of rain pelting the windows, he decided that whoever had been here would not be returning on a night like tonight. He returned to the kitchen in hopes of finding some piece of the strange museum that might still be edible.

Searching, he found plenty of provisions, but none that were edible in this century. He reached for the Twizzlers in his pocket and hoped morning would come sooner rather than later.

He made his way back upstairs to find a comfortable

spot to rest his eyes if only for a few moments. Trying each bed for comfort and creep factor, more of one and less of the other, he settled on a small double bed. He climbed on top of the bedspread and tried to close his eyes. How the hell had he gotten himself into this spot? He knew he shouldn't have dropped out of his catechism in eighth grade. God was pissed, and this was surely payback.

"HELLLLOOOO?" shouted a voice. Jason was on his feet in a split second, struggling to gain his wits. Looking frantically around the room, he was reminded of the previous night's events.

"Hello?" He scrambled out of the room and headed for the stairs.

"Doc, you *are* here!" Guffey exclaimed. "Well, good news today then for sure. Are you alright?"

"Yes, I guess so, all things considered," Jason replied.

"Well, I should say so; you only holed up in one of the downright creepiest places in the county and lived to tell about it. Well, let's git you out of here. I bet you're hungry."

Jason nodded.

"Half the town is out lookin' for ya, but once we get that settled we need to get some food in your belly," said Guffey.

"Oh, that's no problem," replied Jason. "I probably

just need to get the truck and get back to town. Doc's probably not going to be too happy with me."

"Ohhh, not to worry, I already called him and let him know we found the truck. The problem really is that it's about buried with all the rain, so's until we can get a big Cat earth mover or something in here, you and I are going to get some breakfast."

Dazed and confused, Jason ran his hand through his hair and smiled. "Okay, sounds good."

He followed Guffey out through the back door and was amazed at how much spookier the place was in the daylight. He might have thought twice about staying the night if he had seen it during the day. He followed Guffey around the corner to find the mule tied to a tree.

Smiling, Jason said, "Well, I guess I don't need to ask you how the mule is doing."

"Gosh, Doc, she done real good after you worked on her last night. Think all that really helped, I really think it did. I told Keating the same thing, and that he was darn sure the most idiotic buffoon in the county if he doesn't keep ya. He's gotten rid of plenty of others over the years, but sure seems like he has found a good egg with you. Speaking of eggs, we best be getting to breakfast."

"But how?" replied Jason.

"Well, with the mule here, of course. She'll take both of us for sure, so let me give you a leg up and let's git."

Guffey helped Jason on, then climbed into the saddle himself. "I apologize," he said. "Not going to be the most comfortable ride, but she'll get us there."

The road was a quagmire of thick, greasy clay. They arrived at the truck, which appeared to be swallowed up by the mud on the road.

"Not to worry, Doc, we'll git her out in a bit. Soon as they git that earth mover over here, won't be no problem," said Guffey.

Jason wondered how understanding Keating could or would be about all of this. He shook his head, wondering what more he was going to have to deal with today.

They traveled slowly through the mud and then climbed to higher ground amid the scrub oak, where the mule moved more freely. Jason was amazed at how well she had improved from the previous night.

Finally arriving back at Guffey's, Jason smelled bacon and eggs. Although he wasn't normally a big breakfast individual, Jason was so hungry that he figured he could make an exception for some home cooking.

A small woman stood over the stove, her gray hair pulled tight in a bun. She turned with a large smile and set a huge plate of pancakes on the table.

"Welcome! Sit! Sit, eat while they're hot," she exclaimed.

"Doc, I'd like to introduce you to my wife, Dot." Ed removed his hat.

"Pleasure to meet you," Jason replied, shaking her hand.

They sat down, and Jason's mouth began to water as

243

the plates were quickly passed around.

They ate in silence, until Ed finally spoke up. "So how *was* the night in that old haunted rat trap?"

"It had its moments," Jason said. "Not exactly what I had anticipated with getting stranded and all, but it was out of that weather I guess."

"Please, eat up, there's plenty of food here," said Dot. "Ed told me you two would be hungry *if* you returned," she said, with a wink of her eye.

"I don't know, that was a pretty scary storm last night, and that house was even scarier. What is that place all about, anyway?" asked Jason.

Ed continued on with bites of egg and bacon before he finally sat back in his chair. "Well, so's much as I know, that place was, and I guess still is, a secret of sorts. No one really knows much, and many don't want to. The place's been sittin' empty for 60 years at least."

"Wow," replied Jason.

"Did you see anything while you were there?" asked Ed.

"Well, I don't know, sort of I guess; just some things that didn't really add up."

"Like?"

"Well, it looks like whoever lived there hadn't really left yet, or didn't mean to leave. All their belongings are still there: clothes in the closet, shoes, food in the pantry, plates on the table," replied Jason. "In the basement or root cellar there was some old computer equipment, and a steel door that must be eighteen inches thick."

Ed sat quietly and only briefly glanced at Dot, but it was enough for Jason to realize that they knew more than they were willing to divulge. Thinking that maybe he had said too much, he quickly returned to the plate of pancakes.

"Well, I don't rightly know what the story is over there, but I'm glad the house let you leave," said Ed.

As they finished, the phone rang. Ed answered and spoke softly to the person on the other end of the line before thanking them and hanging up.

"Well, they got your truck back to town and the guys over at the shop are cleaning the mud out now. They said they spoke to Doc Keating and he's got it under control for a bit, so not to be worried."

Jason was relieved, realizing that Keating was going to let him live yet another day.

"Well, Dot, that was right tasty, thanks," said Ed as he grabbed his hat.

"Mrs. Guffey, thank you so much for the wonderful meal," said Jason.

"Oh, please call me Dorothy, or Dot," she replied with a smile and a hug. "Thank you so much for coming all the way out here to take such good care of that old mule."

"Well, I don't know how much good I did, but she is amazing for turning around so quickly from last night," he said.

"Well, I suppose we best get on it here if we're getting

you back to town 'fore too long," quipped Ed. Jason followed him outside, prepared to climb back onto the miraculous mule. But before he could do so, Ed said, "Let me go get the MOG and I'll be right back." His pace quickened as he headed for a large, solitary barn set back in the trees.

Moments later a thunderous sound of motor and exhaust spewed out of the large wooden doors as large tires began rolling forward. The tires were almost as tall as Jason. What he first thought was a tractor actually looked more like a truck as it got closer. It reminded him of the monster trucks that he and his brother had talked their mother into taking them to see as kids. More narrow than a pickup, it had a large flatbed on the back. It was painted bright orange and had "Little Mule" painted in big blue letters on the side.

Ed motioned for Jason to climb in, and as Jason grabbed the ladder handle, he wondered why Ed hadn't driven this vehicle earlier in the rescue. He smiled, figuring that nothing else seemed to make sense, so why would this be any different. They headed down the road once again and the truck handled the mud without incident. Finally Jason asked, "What is this thing?"

Ed smiled and replied, "Well, it's a MOG. Stands for 'Motor Great'; it means machine. It's a Mercedes Benz, if you can believe that. Yep, I think about the only Mercedes around these parts. Not exactly what folks think of when they think of fine German automobiles. This one was built back in the 1950s; the Germans used these during World War II."

Jason looked around the cab of the truck, smiling once again, reminded of Keating's old truck with its gears and levers. The ride was rough but the truck labored little as it journeyed to town.

As they arrived in town, Jason hoped he might have time to shower before going to the clinic. But before he had time to say anything to Guffey, Ed said, "I think the boys are going to meet you at your little place, so's you can change or do whatever you need to do." No sooner were the words out of his mouth, when they turned the corner in front of Jason's barn apartment to see the truck, freshly bathed, parked out front with a note attached to the windshield: "Tell Doc that we are cleaning the floor mats and will have them back to the clinic in the next day or so."

"Hey Doc, I can't thank you enough for fixin' my old mule, and I feel just awful that you ended up out there last night and all. If there's ever anything I can do to repay you, please let me know," said Guffey, extending his hand.

"Well, goodness, no, thank you for all your help getting me out of there. And please thank your wife for me; I really appreciate it. I don't know what good I really did with that mule, but she seemed to improve in spite of my help," he replied.

"You did just great Doc, just great. I sure hope you think about stickin' around these parts. Doc Keating sure needs you; hell, the whole town needs you."

Jason waved goodbye as Guffey shifted the MOG into reverse and crawled slowly from the driveway. Jason hurried inside and showered, anxious to get to the clinic.

Chapter 34

Arriving at the clinic close to noon, Jason dove into the mountain of mail and sticky notes.

"Dr. Davies, please call Aida Morales regarding her goat, Trixie."

"Dr. Davies, please contact Bobby Swenson regarding a dental float on his horse."

"Dr. Davies, Aida Morales has a question regarding her chickens."

"Dr. Davies, Carter Jackson wants to know if beer is bad for horses."

"Dr. Davies, Aida, again..., please call her...."

It had only been a few days, but somehow it felt like he had been gone for months. He placed an order for supplies and started some coffee. Returning to his desk, he heard the familiar sound of Keating's farm truck. "Why is he bringing that to work?" Jason wondered. Moments later, Keating walked through the office door.

"You really back?" Keating removed his sunglasses and his signature well-worn custom hat.

"Yes, thanks for understanding," Jason replied, nervously taking a sip of coffee.

"Everything okay with Cindy Lou?"

"Yes, well, I think so.... I mean, I haven't talked with her."

Keating said nothing and sorted through some items

on his desk, obviously stalling. Finally, he said, "Well, not to start your day off on the wrong foot, but I thought we should get it out of the way. The rodeo committee decided to give the rodeo vet position to Otter."

"I didn't think the committee was meeting until today? Hold on, what day is it?" Jason said.

"Today is Tuesday, all day…. They met Monday, and the vote came back 4 to 3."

Jason sat staring at his veterinary degree; Otter's hands were in all of this, and a jerk like him always seemed to get his way.

Keating must have sensed that he was upset. "Jason, trust me, the guy is a moron, and he will find some way of making a disaster out of it. I don't agree with his methods, but clearly that dumbass committee is going to get what they paid for with him. I was going to march down there this morning and give them a piece of my mind until I realized that their hands are tied and they are just trying to keep the peace with Otter's old man; that guy's always been a slimeball, and his progeny is no different. No, I think we just sit on this for a bit and see what shakes loose." Keating picked up his hat. "Well, I better get back to work." He left and went outside.

"What do I have to be upset about?" thought Jason. "I didn't really care one way or the other. The rodeo isn't that big of a deal, right?" He remembered the look in Catherine's eyes that night at Cody's. She'd wanted him to get that position; they both had, but for different reasons.

Jason wanted to prove himself to Birdie. Many people had welcomed him, but others saw him as an outsider, fresh out of school. Keating's lukewarm reception, his day-to-day hot and cold, left Jason wondering what to expect each day; no wonder all the assistant vets before him left sooner rather than later. In the end, this would have been a big deal; a chance to show Keating and Birdie that he did have what it took to be a great veterinarian; maybe even the chance to prove it to his parents, or even himself. This would have been the opportunity to show everyone he belonged.

Chapter 35

Trying to shake the rodeo committee's decision of rejection, Jason dug down deep to try to get through the day. Not having heard from Catherine only seemed to intensify his desire to cut his ties to this crap town and get the hell out. He smiled and made small talk with the endless barrage of clients as the parking lot continued to fill with trucks and trailers. As the early afternoon wore on, the heat and humidity worked to squelch what little energy and patience he held on to. At one point he walked away when an unwilling horse refused to load on a trailer after a half hour of coercion, smashing Jason into the side of the trailer. Jason lunged at the horse in rage, then paused, turned, and walked inside. Making a scene today with the parking lot full of Birdie gossips would definitely come back to bite him.

Mary arrived with sandwiches for everyone's lunch. Exhausted, they all ate in silence. Suddenly they heard shouts from outside and the screeching of tires. Jason followed Keating out the front door. "What the devil," shouted Keating. Outside a cloud of dust was clearing as Otter and his band of cronies climbed out of a truck. A vinyl sign covered the side of the truck: "Dr. Otter Laverteen, Official Veterinarian for the Birdie Remuda Roundup and Rodeo."

Keating was livid. "Otter, what in *the* hell do you think

you are doing, driving in here, scaring all these animals and folks?" Jason surveyed the lasting remains of Catherine's handiwork on Otter's face; the blackened eye had turned a putrid shade of purple and green, and two healing cuts on Otter's cheek reminded Jason of her. He caught himself staring at Otter, remembering that night, and wishing Catherine were here now. "And what the hell happened to your sorry-ass face? Looks like someone finally gave you a piece of what you deserve!" Keating grumbled as Otter turned to glare at the snickering bystanders.

Otter turned and strutted confidently back toward the truck. "Dr. Keating, I'm a very busy man these days and I don't have time to argue about how I drive on *official* business."

"Official business? What official business?" Keating asked.

"The committee informed me that I needed to collect the official veterinary equipment for the rodeo."

The screwed-up questioning look of downright disgust on Keating's face was priceless to witness. "*O-f-f-i-c-i-a-l* veterinary equipment? Is that so?" replied Keating.

"Yes, and do not delay; I have things to do and I don't have time to...."

Keating held up his hand and stopped Otter mid-sentence. "Stop, shut your damn mouth for two seconds. I will get your equipment, but on *one* condition," grizzled Keating.

253

Otter smirked at his sidekicks. "Yeah, what's that?"

With clients looking on, Keating walked closer to Otter and stared him straight in the face. "You don't ever come back here." Keating turned and walked back to the clinic.

"Well, Dr. Keating, last I checked, this is a free country." Otter smiled, looking around at the crowd gathering. "It hardly seems appropriate to be telling me where I can go, and threatening me...."

Keating stopped, turned, and stormed back to Otter. "Now listen here, you snot-nosed son-of-a-bitch! This town and I have put up with your spoiled sass for the past 20 some years, and I've about had a gut full of it. I don't care about who you think you are or who your daddy is. Your grandfather was the only one in that family with any sense, and you surely didn't inherit any of that. I don't need to make threats to the likes of you, because threats would include consideration, and you aren't worth considering or threatening. Now, I'm going to walk in that door and return with a key chain. I'm going to hand you that key chain, and you will return to that rolling billboard and leave, never to step foot on my property again. Do we understand each other?" Keating took his sunglasses off and stared at Otter. Otter stared at the ground, nodding in agreement.

"Uh, just what are the keys for?" asked Otter in childish embarrassment as Keating walked away. Keating paused and chuckled under his breath; turning, he said, "Otter, I guess that will be your first official task as rodeo veterinarian. Check all the damn locked doors in town until you find ones that work with the keys."

Keating turned and disappeared through the clinic door. Mary, overhearing the commotion, met Keating at the door with a small set of keys and a badge. Keating walked back to the truck and handed them to Otter. "Don't screw this up...You probably will, but don't; you don't have the intelligence to understand what it means to hold these keys in your hand, but maybe someday you will." Keating paused, then turned and walked away. "Okay, you boys be careful now...."

Otter and his friends looked confused; Otter nodded to the others as he slowly slithered into the truck and started the engine. The truck crawled out of the parking lot as Mary handed Keating his hat. "Thank you, dear." Keating placed the hat squarely back on his head and turned with a smile to a client standing next to him. "Well, good afternoon, how may I help you?"

Jason was dumbfounded; he had never seen Keating this riled up. He wondered how Keating would respond to Jason's news of leaving. He dreaded the thought, but until he got confirmation, it would be best to keep it to himself.

The cool air conditioning of the office felt refreshing after the intense humidity and the heated argument. Jason walked past Mary, busy at her desk. He stopped and asked quietly, "Just what *are* the keys for?"

"Oh, well, pretty much the keys to Birdie; one is to the main gates of the fairgrounds, another one gets you into the courthouse downtown...never did understand why John had a key for that...but the other keys unlock the other buildings by the rodeo arena. Sure hope Otter knows what he's doing...." She handed Jason a stack of Coggins forms and smiled. "Good luck."

The Coggins forms and health certificates before him seemed endless, but all of it needed to be completed as quickly as possible. Jason steadied himself for the reality that he would be here awhile.

After he had signed his name to the last remaining health certificate, he locked the clinic doors. He was listening to the radio on the drive back to the apartment when something caught his eye. He slowed down and noticed a truck parked in front of the Dairy Dee Lite. "Otter Laverteen, DVM – Official Birdie Rodeo Veterinarian," read the sign draping the hood. High school girls clad in postage-stamp-size bikinis handed out t-shirts with the likeness of Otter on them. Jason shook his head in disbelief; "That son-of-bitch has his own groupies."

Later that evening, Jason woke with a start as he felt the water hit his face. Drip...drip...drip. The sound of rain pouring on the roof only further confirmed that his disastrous accommodations included a leaking roof. Turning on the light, he investigated the source, this time the water finding a path through the light in the ceiling.

"Nothing like electricity and water," Jason grumbled. The hole directly above his bed took shape quickly as he searched frantically for a suitable water-catching solution. He tore open the kitchen drawers and his eyes caught sight of a half-eaten bag of Gummi Bear candies. Returning to the bed, he twisted and ground one of the small colored candies into the leaking hole above his bed.

The next morning, he smirked with delight when his eyes opened and focused on the red gummy dot still holding strong. He showered and dressed, then jotted a note for Pauline regarding the leaking roof.

Stepping outside, he observed his now-familiar neighbor in the bushes once again. Jason couldn't believe his eyes when Boo turned around. The shirt he wore read: "Otter Laverteen – Official Birdie Rodeo Veterinarian."

"Unbelievable!" Jason fumed. "Boo's a groupie too?"

Chapter 36

Jason shook his head in disbelief at the stack of papers that seemed to reappear on his desk each morning; the paperwork never seemed to end with this job.

Shelly peered around the corner, looking concerned. "Hey, everything okay?"

"Sure...What's up?" he replied.

"Well, it's just that there's a message for Doc here that I took yesterday from someone named Deborah with the Veterinary Services...."

"Yes?" he interrupted. "What did she say she wanted?" Jason shifted in his chair and began biting his fingernail.

"Well, they wanted to speak with Doc directly, but said something about you being transferred?" She looked confused.

Jason leaned back and felt the blood drain into his feet. "So what did you tell her?"

"I told her I didn't know what she was talking about and I thought she had you mixed up with someone else, but she stated you were being transferred to California as early as next week possibly."

Tommy had done a lot of things, but had he *actually* pulled this off? Jason was going to California to work at one of the top veterinary clinics in the country, scratch that, the world. He froze; what should he say?

"It's not true, right?"

"It's a long story." His reply drifted off.

"You okay? You don't look so good all of a sudden." She placed a hand on his shoulder. He looked up at her and could see the hurt and confused look on her face. He didn't know what to say.

"I'm fine, but can you hang on to that note for a bit, at least until I figure some things out?"

She paused and looked away. "Sure," she replied curtly and left.

He felt sick to his stomach. He stared out the window at his desk, biting his nail until it hurt and bled. What had he done?

He walked to the front desk and looked at the schedule for today. How was it empty, no appointments? Mary's handwriting on the book read, "John's CT, Oklahoma City – 9:00 A.M." The two had left early that morning, but Keating had never mentioned anything to him. Was something wrong with Keating's health?

Jason returned to his desk and sat idly staring at his diploma; not exactly the vision he anticipated when he'd received that piece of paper.

Shelly reappeared. "Doc said you're free to do whatever you need to today; he already had Doc Williams over in Creston on call for today when he scheduled his doctor's appointment." Her attitude was cold, and Jason could feel the hurt in her voice. "If there isn't anything else, then I think I'll go too." He nodded to her, but as she turned to go she added, "I know this little town isn't a lot of things, and it probably doesn't fit into the dream you have for being a great veterinarian. But the truth is, this little town IS a lot of things, a lot wonderful things, and you could be a great veterinarian here too." Tears welled in her eyes and she disappeared down the hallway. Jason sat stunned, frozen, wanting to disappear.

He grabbed his keys, locked the door, and left. Without thinking, he pulled into the Buckaroo Mini-Mart and asked the clerk for a pack of Camel 100s. He hadn't smoked since high school. He returned to the truck and lit a cigarette, turned up the radio, and sped off down the road.

He had never let a girl get to him like this. But was it just Catherine? This town was part of it now, too. He'd lived his entire childhood bounced from one community to the next, wherever his father's work took them. High school had been torture, especially in Chicago, and then Los Angeles. Kids were hurtful, even ruthless at times, directing unending taunts and insults. That wasn't even the worst of it; for Jason, the loneliness of trying to make new friends, and even relationships with girls, was humiliating. There were countless school dances, football games, and parties that had gone uninvited and unattended. His siblings hadn't fared much better; but while it had seemed to draw them closer at one point, it had now caused them to drift apart. Birdie was different. He felt something here he hadn't ever felt before: a feeling of belonging. The town welcomed him, embraced him, and appreciated him; for the first time in his life, he felt like this place could be home.

He drove with no destination in mind. He looked around and realized he wasn't sure where he was. He crossed Turkey Creek and pulled to a stop. The water looked cool and refreshing: gently making its way, in no particular hurry. He imagined what the water must feel like: to be carefree in its journey, no concerns or constraints; asking nothing, and no force to hinder its gentle ebb and flow.

Jason slowly climbed from the truck and found a shaded area beneath a massive large oak. He pulled out another cigarette, but as he placed it to his lips he paused. He tossed it into the water and watched it straighten to the flow of the current.

He suddenly realized that being "stuck" in Birdie had become a stabilizing force in his world. Then there was Catherine. How quickly he had fallen for her! She was beautiful, of course, but she was so much more. She was strong and independent—her own woman, but with an air of fragility. She had skeletons—they both did—but she was a magnet he found himself being drawn to. Was she reason enough for him to stay? And did she feel the same way about him? He couldn't be sure, and feelings of doubt flushed through him. She hadn't called, and she was married; these were two glaring reasons that California should remain his destination. He fell asleep to the gentle sounds of the creek and the rustle of the branches overhead.

He awoke to the sound of an approaching truck. He looked at his watch: 6:30 P.M. Could it really be that late in the day? He looked at the sun making its final descent, which confirmed what his watch had already told him. He didn't recognize the rugged old Toyota Land Cruiser or its driver. A tall, lean young man wearing a large, well-worn straw hat stepped out of the truck. He slowly made his way over to Jason and sat down.

"Evening," the man said, as he pushed the weathered cowboy hat back on his head.

"Hello." Jason worried he was trespassing on the cowboy's property.

"You okay? Truck not running?"

"No problem at all, just needed a moment to think, I guess, but now I'm worried I'm on your property or...."

"Oh, no, just thought maybe you needed a hand with something. I'm Kurt Clemens." He reached out his hand.

Jason shook his hand. "Hello, I'm Jason Davies, pleasure to meet you, sir."

They sat quietly, staring at the water. "Well, I don't mean to intrude on your thinkin', but if you need help with something, I'd be happy to."

Jason smiled. "I appreciate it, thank you, but I'll be

fine."

"Uh, huh...." Clemens placed his hands around a small rock and gently tossed it into the water. "You don't look it, if you don't mind me sayin'."

"Yeah, I guess not," Jason replied.

"She must really be worth it."

Kurt could see the confusion on Jason's face. "Oh shoot, it's always about a girl, 'specially when your head and heart bring you someplace like this. So, is she?"

"So is she what?" Jason asked.

"Worth it?"

"Sure feels like she is." Jason couldn't believe he was sharing his feelings with a total stranger.

"Then I guess you know the answer."

"The answer?"

"To your question. Isn't that why you're sitting all the way out here, so you can answer the question?"

Jason didn't respond. "Who is this guy?" he wondered.

"One thing I've learned living around here is that if you just listen, I mean really listen, the answer's always there. Not always the answer you're looking for, but it'll be there every time...every time. Just listen." Kurt placed a finger to his ear. They both listened as the sound of the creek filled their ears.

"Well," Kurt said, "I suppose we need to get that tire on your truck fixed before it gets too much later."

Jason looked surprised. "I have a flat?"

They walked back up the bank. As they approached Jason's truck, he could clearly see that the right rear tire was flat. He grimaced when it occurred to him that he had no spare.

"Where's your spare? Let me give you a hand with it and we'll get you back on the road here." Kurt stood with his hands on hips, waiting for Jason.

Jason ran his fingers through his hair. "I think I lost my spare about 2 years ago and never got around to replacing it...."

"Well, I suppose you'd better come along with me to the house; we can get you some supper and then get you home."

"No, that's not really...."

Kurt held up his hand. "Trust me, you don't want to walk to town."

Kurt made quick work of leaving and they headed off in a flurry of dust. For a guy who spoke and moved at a slow pace, he sure didn't drive the same way. Jason wasn't familiar with where they were and continued to scan for any hint of their location.

A short drive later, Kurt slowed the truck and turned into a long, winding dirt road. A modest-looking blue farmhouse sat back off the road, surrounded by large oak trees. The assorted playground equipment in the yard indicated that a family lived here.

As they pulled in front of the house, the screen door flew open and three young girls rushed from the door.

They were fresh from a bath, dressed in pajamas and hair still wringing wet. Kurt lifted each of them individually into his arms and they welcomed him with hugs and kisses. A long-haired brunette called from the door. "Hey, y'all are right on time, dinner's almost ready and on the table. Get in here," she said with a smile.

As they entered the house, the smell of the food immediately whet Jason's appetite. "Jason, I'd like to introduce to you my wife, Tracy." Tracy smiled and shook Jason's hand. "Pleasure to meet you, Dr. Davies. We've heard a lot of great things about you."

"Please, it's Jason, and thank you for having me here for dinner. Without your husband stopping by I think I might be walking back to town this evening."

She quickly finished setting the table as the children scrambled in behind them and stood quietly at their seats.

They held hands and bowed their heads while Kurt said the blessing. Jason felt a little out of place and uncomfortable. He tried to make sense of the day; hours ago he was buying cigarettes, and now he was sitting down to eat with strangers.

Jason looked up from the table to see the small smiling faces staring back at him. "Do you fix animals?" the youngest girl asked.

"Well...yes, I sure try to," Jason replied.

"Are you sad when they die?"

"Sarah, enough with the questions; let our guest eat." Tracy gently chided.

"Oh, it's okay. Yes it's sad, especially when they're really sick."

They ate quietly before Tracy asked, "Dr. Davies, are you settling into Birdie alright? The town has just come alive with you here."

"I am, thank you; everyone's been great."

"Well, we sure do hope you'll stay. This little town has struggled to keep vets. Doc Keating isn't always the easiest to get along with, and I know everyone would be real disappointed if we lost you, too."

Kurt ate quietly, without comment. Jason glanced at him, remembering their conversation at the creek.

After dinner, they watched the kids chase fireflies in their pajamas. Jason was amazed at how the family simply enjoyed being together, talking and laughing. No cable television. No internet. No Wii or iPods, just a family together. The rest of the world wondered why anyone would live in a town like Birdie, but Jason was starting to wonder why anyone would ever live anywhere else.

He thanked Tracy and said goodbye to the girls. As Kurt drove him home, Jason stared out into the dusk-lit landscape. The luminescent flickering of fireflies was a comforting reminder that quiet moments still existed in this all-too-crazy world. This part of the country had a simple beauty that he hadn't appreciated before now.

Kurt pulled the truck into the driveway, snapping Jason out of his introspective haze. "I'll get the tire figured out on your truck and have it back to you shortly."

"Oh, you really don't need...."

"No problem at all. Jason, it's been a pleasure meeting you, it truly has." Kurt paused, reading Jason's face, then said, "I know you must have a lot going on in your head, and it can take some time to sort it all out, but no matter what decision you make, it will be the right one if you follow this." Kurt placed a hand over his heart. "You take care of this, and the rest will all fall into place. You're too hard on yourself; you need to breathe once in a while." Kurt stared out through the windshield. "You were smart to go out there today. It's a pretty spot to collect your thoughts. Tracy and I realized that several years ago when we moved out here from LA."

Jason's surprise must have shown.

"Yes, I know, you thought we were all backcountry hillbillies out here. Southern California just got to be too much of a rat race for us. We lived in Rancho Cucamonga and I commuted about four hours every day. It was a mess; I never saw Tracy or the girls. We had our house broken into twice, once when we were home. That was it for me. We sold the house and moved out here three months later, and we've never regretted it for one second. I'm not telling you what to do, because I know each man has to make sense of his world in his own way, on his own terms. Whatever it is you decide to do, that will be the right decision."

They shook hands. "Thank you," Jason said, as he swallowed back the emotions welling up in his throat. He climbed out into the cool evening, and as Kurt's truck lights disappeared, Jason suddenly felt more alone than he ever had before.

Unlocking the door to his hole in the barn, he waited for the smell of donkey feces, but he didn't notice any. He glanced around, but still saw no signs of a donkey intrusion. Maybe the crazy pet psychic had been right about the carrots. No...couldn't be; it must be a coincidence.

He checked his phone, fearing he might have missed a call from Catherine. Nothing....

The phone suddenly vibrated in his hand.

"Hello?"

"Jason? It's Cat."

"Hey, how are you?"

"Good, but that was weird."

"What?"

"I don't think the phone even rang on my end."

"Well, let's just say I was anxious to take your call," Jason replied.

"Oh, I see. Sorry about not calling, but yesterday was a disaster, and I got home way too late."

"How's the hand?"

"Hanging in there, but really sore today. You made it back alright?" she asked quietly, sounding tired.

"Yes, all is well here...well...except for Otter's face."

"Ooohhh, is it bad?"

"Well, I mean, he didn't really have the greatest mug

to begin with, but let's just say you haven't improved it. He's got a pretty good shiner, and his nose looks like he ran into a concrete wall!"

She laughed. "Oh please, it can't be that bad, but how did you cross paths with Otter?"

"I didn't, Doc did," Jason replied.

"What?"

"Otter showed up at the clinic...." Jason explained the events of the previous day; none of it seemed to faze her.

"Nope, sounds about right for Otter. Educating him sure hasn't taken the moron out of him."

Catherine explained that the trial she was working on would take longer than expected, but that she would return to Birdie on Friday. They made plans to attend the rodeo on Friday night to witness the arrival of the Oklahoma Governor and his family. Traditionally, the Governor always rode in at the beginning of the performance, followed by various State officials in a horse-drawn wagon. As they talked, Jason could hear Catherine's voice fading.

"You're tired, go to bed."

"You're right. I just wish you were here to adjust my pillows."

Jason could feel himself blush.

"Well, finish the court deal and get back here. We can find pillows here to adjust," he chuckled.

"You are a piece of work."

"I know."

"Have you spoken with Daddy? I told him that you might like to see the rest of the ranch."

"That sounds great, but I haven't seen him since I've been back. Is everything okay?"

"I think he's fine. He always gets anxious and excited this time of year, that's all. Okay, I'm going to bed. Take care. See you in a couple of days."

"Goodnight," he whispered.

"Bye now."

Chapter 37

The morning sun streamed through the barn windows while Jason got dressed. As he headed for the door, he realized his truck was still stranded at Turkey Creek.

"Crap. How the hell am I going to get to work?" He wondered if Pauline might still be at her house, but her car was gone. He pulled the apartment door closed and paused, looking around and hoping that someone might magically stop and offer him a ride to the clinic.

The town was quiet as he quickly hustled down the streets and alleys to the clinic. He hoped Keating was in a good mood this morning, since he was definitely going to be late. Jason snuck through the front door of the clinic. The front desk was empty and he quickly scurried down the hallway to his desk. No sign of Keating, or anyone for that matter. He sat down and breathed a sigh of relief. He looked at his watch and realized he was only 15 minutes late; not bad for hoofing it across town.

"You're late!" boomed Keating's voice from the lab.

Jason shook his head, smirking; that guy never missed anything.

Jason's day at the clinic seemed to fly by. As the last client left in the afternoon, he quickly finished his paperwork, double-checking that no new sticky notes were affixed to his desk.

Just then he heard Keating's voice as he came through

the door. Keating looked like he'd had a day from hell and only nodded in Jason's direction before dropping into his desk chair.

Jason knew that he needed to talk to Keating. A lump began to grow in his throat as he started the conversation. "Dr. Keating, I need to talk with you about something...."

"Okay," Keating replied, glancing over his glasses with a look of tired indifference. Just then Mary entered.

"John, Gene Rakeman is on the phone about shipping some cows...."

"Hold that thought," Keating said to Jason as he reached for the phone. His expression completely changed as he said, "Hey Gene! How the hell are you, friend?"

"Oh, Jason?" Mary smiled at him. "Kurt Clemens and a friend dropped your truck off a little bit ago. Is everything okay? You seem to have the darndest luck with that vehicle." Mary patted Jason's shoulder as she left the room.

Jason knew that this was not going to be the right time to drop his bombshell on Keating. He grabbed his things and headed for the door.

The day had flown by with everyone getting their animals checked before the rodeo. Now that it had finally quieted down, Jason felt alone. He wanted someone to talk to: someone to confide in about his feelings toward Catherine, someone to listen to his anguish over the lingering dilemma of his impending move. He thought about calling his mother but hesitated; she would only worry and then alert his father, who in turn would lecture words of wisdom that ultimately would make Jason feel even worse.

Maybe Boo would be out when Jason got home. He realized that he had hit rock bottom when he looked forward to conversing with Boo Radley.

But he wasn't ready to go home yet. He stopped at the post office and then the grocery store. He aimlessly wandered the aisles, and when he arrived at the checkout and looked in his cart, he realized he had only three items: a box of Junior Mints, some apples, and stick of deodorant.

Driving down Main Street, Jason noticed that the town was bustling with activity. A large banner advertising the rodeo hung across the intersection. Muscle cars and vintage automobiles lined the streets, and masses of spectators crowded every inch of downtown Birdie.

Music caught Jason's ear. He turned down a side street and parked the truck.

Grabbing an apple and the box of Junior Mints, he headed toward the stage. "Big Willie and The Rascals," the banner read; Jason smiled, realizing that "Big Willie" was actually the local dentist, Dr. William Holgerson, who stood only 5 feet and 3 inches tall. From the reaction of the boisterous crowd, the Big Willie persona appeared to be working. Holgerson recognized Jason and tipped his hat.

Jason wiped the apple on his shirt and took a bite as he slowly walked through the booths and activities. He sat down on a park bench and watched a group of children running through the fountain. How carefree they were, living in the moment. No concerns for what lay ahead, and free of the pressures of an adult world.

"Enjoying yourself, Doc?"

Jason turned, startled, and snapped back to reality from his daydream. He had been so lost in thought he hadn't noticed Jameson Walker sit down next to him.

Jason had heard of Jameson but had never met him. Jameson had made some money the old-fashioned way, raising cattle and crops. He started with a few acres and over the years amassed enough real estate in the southern part of the U.S. to make Ted Turner take notice. In the 1970s, American bison had been on the brink of extinction, and many of the animals were genetically crossed with cattle. Jameson had worked with the National Park Service to coordinate a breeding program that had returned the species to a genetically pure herd in thriving numbers. He began a line of all-natural bison products that now shipped worldwide. Jason had recently heard that Jameson was now investing in wind turbines. Despite the financial success that Jameson's hard work had brought him, he sat humbly next to Jason on the park bench in a simple pair of worn overalls and a straw hat.

"Yes, sir," replied Jason. "How about you?"

"Oh yes, good time every year around here. Good place to be; no place else I'd rather be. Doc Keating keeping you busy?"

"Absolutely," replied Jason.

"Yes, I suppose so. You know, John and I go way back. He's a good man; you'll learn a lot from him, and he's sure given a lot to this community, but I know you will too. It's not right for everyone. We get a few that come, and then go, but I have a good sense about you. I think you're going to be one that sticks around."

They watched the crowds of people walking by. "Well Doc, I suppose my daughter and grandkids will be looking for me. I better track them down. Good talking with you, and thank you." Jameson stood to leave

Jason gave him a questioning look. "Thank you for what?"

Jameson smiled. "For being here."

Jason watched Jameson slowly walk away. He wondered why so many families had remained in this little town all these years. While other small-town communities seemed to be dwindling, Birdie thrived.

His phone buzzed. He rushed to grab it, hoping it was Catherine. It was Tommy. "Not dealing with that right now," he mumbled.

Jason made his way through the park, stopping to buy a bag of kettle corn and watch a clogging routine in front of the courthouse.

He sat down on a bench in front of the Yarn Barn. Buses from area towns and communities continued to invade and unload visitor after visitor, dance troupes, and high school bands. A car slowed beside him and stopped.

"Hey Doc, need a ride?"

The voice sent a jolt of electricity through Jason and his heart skipped a beat. Her eyes hidden behind large black sunglasses, Catherine's smile held him captive as he stumbled for a response.

"Hi! Sure!" He climbed into the familiar black BMW. They sat staring at each other for what seemed like forever before she reached her hand to his face and kissed him. He kissed her back, but she finally pulled away. "If we keep this up, the whole town will be talking."

"How's the hand? You aren't wearing the sling anymore?"

"Ohhhh, that thing was such a pain. After a couple of days, it went in the trash at the courthouse."

Catherine put the car in gear and pulled away from the curb. She quickly turned off the main street. "Where are we going?" Jason asked.

"Someplace other than here; this town will be nuts today." She paused and then said, "I have something I've wanted to share with you for a while, and now seems as good a time as any."

Jason looked at her nervously as they made their way through the crowded streets.

Catherine laughed at his confused expression. "Oh, please! Get your mind out of the gutter! Men!"

Jason turned and looked out the car window with a slight grin. "Guilty as charged," he thought to himself. "I didn't think you were coming back until tomorrow?"

"I just drove in now; we finished with everything

early this morning. It never fails; all the work and preparation that goes into building a case for trial, and then they decide to throw a plea offer at the last minute. So frustrating.... Oh wait, I need to make a call." She grabbed her phone from her purse. "Mavis? It's me, I need a favor...Yes, that would be lovely, something simple. Headed that way now, thank you."

After a short drive, Catherine pulled the car into the ranch and followed the road around the main house and then down a large hill. Jason couldn't believe his eyes: a valley so magnificent it rivaled any he'd seen in the national parks. Hundred-year-old oak trees guarded a small, rambling river as it made its way lazily along the valley floor. The pasture grasses rippled in a grassland ocean, the waves following a gentle breeze. Jason thought he must be dreaming; was this even Oklahoma?

Suddenly, as if out of nowhere, they rolled into what appeared to be an authentic western cow town, right there on Cody's property. How had Jason not heard about this place yet? In a town like Birdie, everyone knew everything—sometimes before it even happened. Why hadn't Cody—or anyone else—mentioned this place? Cody, of all people, seemed to talk about everything. Driving through the little town was like walking back in time. Looking around, Jason half-expected gunslingers to wander out on the street at any moment.

Catherine slowed the car to a stop at the edge of Main Street and shut off the engine. "Wow," Jason marveled.

"This is amazing. It's like a Hollywood movie set."

"I guess it certainly could be." Catherine turned and pointed. "All the buildings, or at least most of them, are actually connected. From the outside, it's a western town. But on the inside, it's a fully operational guest ranch, kids' camp, and my father's dream. I guess in some ways it's his 'Hole in the Wall' like you talked about with Paul Newman."

She opened the car door. "C'mon, I'll show you the highlights." Jason followed her into Drysdale's Dry Goods and Mercantile. Shelves were lined with an array of colorful items, from shirts to candies. Jason was confused why someone would go to all the trouble and expense for this place to just sit here.

Catherine led Jason through the photo shop, hat store, and livery. The stalls were immaculate and the tack room filled with saddles, all of it patiently waiting for guests.

"What is your father going to do with all of this?" he asked.

"Well, that's Daddy for you. He only has the idea; he has a vision, but then it gets a little fuzzy...."

Jason followed Catherine through the swinging doors of Cody's Canteen. The sound of slow country music filled his ears, and the sweet smell of fresh bread baking made Jason's mouth water.

"Are you hungry? I called ahead and had Mavis make us some dinner." Catherine winked at him, showing him to a small table at the edge of the dance floor.

He hadn't realized his hunger, but with the smells of home cooking, his stomach began to make music of its own. He scanned the room; it looked like a saloon in every Western movie he'd ever seen. No decoration or detail had been overlooked; it was almost beyond comprehension. The jukebox in the corner played song after song while he listened in wonder.

"What are you staring at?" Catherine asked.

"You." He felt her hand grab his under the table as Mavis flew through the door from the kitchen.

"Anything else for you, Miss Catherine?" Mavis asked with monotone disinterest.

Catherine looked questioningly at Jason. "No, Mavis; I think we're good, but thank you so much for coming down here and making dinner for us. Would you please tell Daddy I'll be up to see him later?"

Mavis nodded blankly to both of them and disappeared back through the swinging door.

Catherine sensed Jason's confusion. "She's fine," she said, as she waved her hand in Mavis' direction. "That woman has been caring for me since I was a child, and her mood is every bit as sour as it was when Momma died; it's just Mavis. I do think she's having man trouble, as always. She always seems to get mixed up with men who can't commit."

"Commit? Commit to what?" Jason asked, confused.

"Anything, mostly. But to a relationship, for starters. I keep telling her she needs to start dating men in her own time zone; she keeps finding men on the Internet, and all of them seem to have a dark past. The last one she connected with turned out to be a bank robber." Catherine paused, looked out the window, and turned back to Jason. "Come on, there's more to see." She grabbed his hand and led him out the swinging doors and onto the boardwalk. He held her hand tightly as they walked toward the far end of town.

She stopped at the Birdie Hotel. "This actually is a hotel, of sorts; it has ten bedrooms upstairs, all ready to go. Over there, those houses are all equipped to handle more families and each has two or three bedrooms. The back side of the mortician's shop over there is Daddy's bad taste in humor, because that's the nurse's station or mini-hospital. Lastly, there's a game room over at Black Bart's."

Jason's head was reeling from everything he'd seen. Catherine noticed that he seemed overwhelmed. "Hey, don't stress," she said. "This is supposed to be fun, relaxing...."

"Oh no, it's great! It's just that this is such an amazing place. It's a shame that it's just sitting here."

They slowly walked back toward the car. Catherine looked at her watch as they got into the BMW. "Oh! I forgot I probably need to get you back into town; you have to do whatever it is that you do for the rodeo tomorrow."

Jason smiled and turned. "I would have thought you'd heard by now."

"Heard what?"

"Well, your friend Otter...'"

"Oh, you've got to be kidding me!" She pounded the steering wheel. "Please tell me that he didn't get that damn chicken-assed rodeo committee to give him the veterinary position! Unbelievable!" She turned to him and said, "I'm sorry."

"For what?"

"You should be the veterinarian for the rodeo, not that jackass. I cannot believe he...."

"Hey, it's okay, really. I just can't believe how much he wants to do it. He's been all over town this week with t-shirts and stickers. The guy is obviously compensating for something else," Jason said with a smirk.

She turned, laughing. "Well, that's for sure! I mean, not that I know, I mean, but, oh whatever, he's struggling on many levels."

"Well, the more I thought about it I realized that not having to vet the rodeo means I can sit with you to watch the big kickoff."

At the outskirts of town, Jason could see the traffic at a standstill. "So, this is the one time of year that you'll actually have traffic jams in Birdie," Catherine growled as she slowed the car to a stop.

Jason laughed and looked at his watch. "Hey, you don't need to go all the way into town. Let me out here; my truck's not far. Plus, you need to check in with Cody. What time should we meet tomorrow?"

"It starts at 7:00 P.M., so meet me down in front of the

grandstands about quarter till, okay?"

"Absolutely." Jason gave her a quick kiss as the traffic began to move again. He opened the door and hopped out. "Thank you for tonight," he yelled as he jogged across the intersection.

"See you tomorrow." She winked at him and pulled away.

Chapter 38

A mumbling voice woke Jason. He rolled over to see what time it was: 5:30 A.M. It sounded like a male's voice. Jason slid quietly out of bed and stepped toward the door adjoining the barn. He placed his ear to the door but heard nothing. Turning the knob slowly, he gently opened the door, hoping to remain unnoticed. But as he looked up, there stood Boo Radley staring back at him. A quiet and resolved Jasper stood patiently next to him, wearing a saddle. Boo paused a moment, and then without saying a word he returned to tightening the saddle's cinch.

"Where are you two headed so bright and early?"

"Parade today.... Riding in the parade."

"The parade's today?" Jason rubbed the sleep from his eyes.

"Parade today.... Every year, this time of year is the parade," mumbled Boo.

Jason stared at Jasper in disbelief. He felt some sick satisfaction that the creature that had broken into his apartment and defecated on his floor was now unable to escape Boo Radley and the Birdie Rodeo Parade.

Jason smirked and turned back toward the doorway. "Have a good time."

He closed the door and crawled back into bed. He closed his eyes and tried to fall back to sleep, but instead he lay there with his thoughts racing, his emotions bubbling and gnawing until they finally welled up, threatening to burst from his chest. He decided to get up and head for the shower before he actually started crying.

When Jason arrived at the clinic, the parking lot appeared vacant: no trailers, no horses, no people. "Where is everyone?" he wondered. He saw a note taped on the clinic's front door that said: "We are closed. If you are absolutely sure it's an emergency, then come and find one of us. Have a nice day."

Jason, perplexed and frustrated, returned to his truck. Why hadn't he gotten the "memo" about "no work today"? He started the truck and headed back into town. Why hadn't Keating let him know? What was he supposed to do today instead?

He followed a line of cars and trucks to the town square, where people were gathering for the parade. He parked the truck near the courthouse and followed the sounds of music and activity. Main Street bustled with floats, people, horses, and vehicles. Walking through the crowd, he looked for any sign of Boo and Jasper, smiling to himself as he continued to look for anyone he knew.

"Hey, Doc!"

"Nice to see you, Dr. Davies."

"Dr. Davies, are you going to be in the parade?"

He passed Jacob's Flower Shop. Next door was Mrs.

Tombaugh's Bookstore; he had slipped into the store once or twice since his arrival in Birdie. He smiled. This street was familiar: the shops, the people. He no longer felt like an outsider.

The high school marching band led the parade, with countless floats and a seemingly endless stream of horses and riders following. Every classic car in the county made an appearance, carrying some local government representative. Jason heard the sound of raucous country music blasting from a black mustang convertible: "Save a horse, ride a cowboy!" He shook his head in disbelief. There was Otter, wearing a sequined jacket and sporting large mirrored sunglasses, smiling and waving from the back seat.

"Yee haw! Y'all come see me at the rodeo!" he screamed over the music as he threw candy to the kids scrambling on the street.

Just when Jason thought he'd seen everything, Otter upped the ante....

After the parade, Jason found his truck buried in a mass of people and animals. "Well, I guess I'm not going anywhere for a while," he mumbled, leaning against the hood of the truck. Just then something caught his eye: a glimpse of donkey ears as Jasper and Boo slowly made their way through the crowded street. Boo's expressionless gaze matched Jasper's as the two mingled in between rodeo queens and princesses. All of it was too much for Jason to contain his laughter; the two were a perfect antithesis to the energy and enthusiasm surrounding them.

He caught up to them. "Hey, guys! Any chance I can catch a ride back to the house?"

Boo stared blankly at Jason, then extended his hand. Jason grabbed ahold, swinging himself up behind Boo on Jasper's back. As they made their way through the crowd, several people shouted at Jason.

"Hey, Doc! Yer truck leave you stranded again?"

"Nice wheels, Dr. Davies!"

"Lookin' good, Doc. At least you can fix this one if it breaks down!"

Boo, unfazed by the harassment, quietly guided the donkey back to the barn.

"Boo, thank you for the lift; I really appreciate it." Jason slid off Jasper's back and headed for the apartment door.

Laundry day hadn't been high on Jason's list of priorities, especially since his last visit to the laundromat downtown, which had caused him great stress when an older woman with two teenage children had asked him out on a date. But as he stared at the behemoth pile of clothes in his living room, he suddenly realized he had nothing clean to wear for the rodeo. He decided to gather up a load and make his way back to the laundromat, hoping that his truck would be free by the time he finished. He found a kitchen trash bag and filled it with enough clothes to make a load but not so much that it would be too heavy to carry through the streets of Birdie.

As Jason walked the streets with a plastic bag slung over his shoulder, he worried that someone might give him grief for what he was doing. But everyone was so preoccupied with their own good mood that no one paid any attention to a young man walking along with a trash bag. The laundromat was empty, and after Jason battled the change machine for quarters and began his load of laundry he sat down and wondered what to do for the next hour. Just then his phone rang.

Jason didn't recognize the number. "Hello, this is Dr. Davies."

"Dr. Davies, my name is Jonathan and I believe we have an equine emergency." The older man's voice on the phone was monotone and to the point. "My employer has requested your services and would greatly appreciate your expediency if at all possible."

"Uh, yes, who is your employer? Or how do I get to the horse?" Jason struggled with his words, trying to understand the strange man on the other end of the phone.

"It would be most helpful if you were available that I could send the car for you."

Jason was speechless. Send the car? Who was this? "I would need some equipment, depending on the situation, and it would probably be better if I brought the vet truck."

"Very good, doctor. Give me your location and I will

have someone meet you and escort you to the property straightaway."

"Well, actually I'm in the middle of, well, and I don't actually have a vehicle right this minute. I guess I need a ride to the clinic, and then...."

"What is your current location? I will have the car pick you up and take you to get whatever you need."

Jason ran out the front door to see if there was an address on the laundromat. He gave the man the address, and within minutes a black Cadillac sedan pulled up to the curb. Jason looked hesitantly at his load of laundry spinning in the machine, then turned and walked toward the car. He slid into the back seat of the car as the driver turned toward him. "Where to, Dr. Davies?" The man was dressed in a blue short-sleeved button-down shirt, which was a bit more formal than the typical Birdie attire. He reminded Jason of a valet at a fancy hotel.

"Take the first right after the second stop sign to get to the clinic. I'll pick up the vet truck and then follow you, but I guess I don't even know where we're headed." Jason stared out the window. Had the mysterious Jonathan even mentioned who his employer was?

"No problem, it's not far to Oak Meadow, and Jonathan will be there to explain everything."

Jason pointed to the clinic parking lot as they approached. They pulled up to the front door. "Wait here and I'll pull the vet truck around." Jason quickly jumped out of the car and unlocked the front door of the clinic.

Moments later he pulled the truck into the front parking lot, behind the black sedan.

As they headed out of town on 3rd Street, Jason was puzzled about where they were going. The pavement of 3rd Street turned to gravel, and Jason wondered why he had never been out this direction before now. Several miles down the road, a nondescript gate opened. The road climbed a large hill and dropped down into an open meadow. Jason could see a large house and buildings at the far end. Who was this mystery client? And should he have let someone know he was out on call?

Jason slowed the truck as they entered through another automatic gate and pulled past the expansive hacienda-style ranch home. The stucco wall surrounding the house reminded him of a summer in California when his father had been constructing a visitor center in Yucca Valley. The sedan stopped in front of the barn, where a tall, older gentleman emerged and walked toward Jason's truck. Jason turned off the engine and climbed out of the truck.

"Dr. Davies," the man said, extending a hand. "My name is Jonathan. We spoke on the phone earlier. Thank you very much for coming so quickly. The horse you need to see is through here."

Jason followed Jonathan through the open doorway, into the cool shadows of the barn. Standing in the wash rack was a petite sorrel mare with blood running down its face. A young man ran a hose of water over a large gash above the horse's right eye and forehead. Jason nodded at the young man and quickly began to assess the seriousness of the wound.

"My employer is hopeful that you think it might be able to be stitched?" Jonathan asked without hesitation.

"Uh, yes, it sure looks like I could put it back together," Jason stammered, hoping that he wasn't being overly confident in his assessment. His intuition told him that there was no other option, given his surroundings and the mysterious client.

Jason set quickly to work suturing the laceration. Jonathan's phone rang and he stepped away while Jason continued.

The situation felt surreal, if not just plain weird. Jason wondered where the hell he was. Keating had never mentioned this place before. Birdie wasn't very big, and Jason had begun to take pride in knowing where most folks lived.

Jonathan returned and stood over Jason as he continued to repair the wound. "My employer would very much like to meet you when you're finished."

Jason nodded with agreement, although he wasn't sure what time it was. He didn't want to be late to meet Catherine.

Jason finally placed his last suture, then administered an injectable antibiotic before starting to clean up his instruments. "Okay, I'm just about finished here, and it all looks good. The stitches will need to come out in about 2 weeks. I can return then, if you'd like."

"That sounds most agreeable. Now, if you will follow me." Jonathan turned and headed for the house. As Jason followed, his stomach began to ache. Who was this mystery client?

They entered the house through a stucco archway with a rough-textured, heavy wooden door. Jason followed Jonathan through a series of hallways before approaching two large wood-paneled doors. Jonathan turned and spoke in a lowered voice. "As we enter, if you wouldn't mind, please take a seat in the chair next to the window. She may be on the phone when we enter, so we will wait for her to finish. If she extends her hand, please gently shake her it; however, she may not." Jonathan looked into Jason's eyes, seeking acknowledgment of his instructions. Jason nodded and swallowed nervously before following Jonathan into the room.

"Miss Claiborne? May we enter?"

Jason heard a woman's voice, obviously engaged in a heated discussion, and then the snapping of fingers. Jonathan looked at Jason and nodded for him to follow. A woman was standing behind a large mahogany desk at the far of the room. As they approached, she waved her hand to the chair next to the window. She smiled and indicated for Jason to be seated, as she appeared to be listening on the phone. She turned and looked out the window.

"No, David! That's not what I'm saying! I just don't think that's what I'm going for with all of this, and I think we need to bring the band back in after next weekend and record those tracks again. I realize things may have changed since I was back in Nashville, but I still have my finger on what people want to listen to, trust me. Okay, well, listen, I have guests here, and I need to run. Okay, let's talk tomorrow."

She hung up the phone and rushed around the desk, extending her hand toward Jason. "Dr. Davies, thank you for rushing right over to take care of Gypsy! Is she going to be okay? I mean, she's going to be fine, correct?" Her intent stare gave Jason a sudden feeling of consternation. Who was this woman, and how did she already have him feeling like a schoolboy in the principal's office?

"Well, yes, I think everything should heal fine, and she should make a full recovery...."

"Excellent! I surely don't want a scar of any sort. I mean, you can understand how that would look if it doesn't heal perfectly! Yes, thank you for putting my mind at ease that she will be as good as new before her next show."

Jason swallowed hard. He could feel his throat quickly drying, and his stomach ache was only intensifying. "Umm, yes, I explained to Jonathan that I could return in 14 days to remove the sutures, if that's what you'd like me to do...."

The phone rang and she raised her hand to Jason to pause. She reached for the phone to answer it. "Yes, David. What?! Of course I already explained that to them.

No, that wasn't part of the original agreement. Okay, hold on." She placed her hand over the receiver. "Dr. Davies, thank you again for everything. Jonathan will see you out."

As Jason turned and glanced questioningly at Jonathan, Jonathan nodded for Jason to follow him. They exited the room and Jonathan closed the doors behind them. Jonathan then extended his hand. "Dr. Davies, Miss Claiborne would like to thank you again for your expediency and professionalism. Please send the bill to this address and to my attention. Do you need an escort out of the property?"

"No, thank you, I think I remember the way back to town." Jason shook Jonathan's hand, then turned and headed back down the hallway in the direction from which they had come.

Climbing back into the vet truck, he let out a deep sigh of relief. That experience had been more stressful than his entrance interview for vet school.

Jason raced back toward town, hoping he still had enough time to get cleaned up before meeting Catherine. And speaking of clean, he realized that he had totally forgotten about the load of laundry sitting in the washing machine downtown. "Crap!" he yelled, pounding the steering wheel. "Well, no time to figure that out at this point," he mumbled to himself.

He arrived back at the apartment and flew through the door. He showered, dressed, and splashed on cologne. He was surprisingly nervous; he felt the same way he had before his first school dance in seventh grade.

Racing out the door, he froze as something caught his eye. The left front tire of the vet truck was flat. "You have got to be kidding me! What the hell! Am I cursed, or what the hell is the problem with my life?" Jason growled in anger. He was already running late; he didn't have time to deal with changing the tire right then.

From the corner of his eye he noticed Jasper's tail swishing just inside the barn. He walked around the corner of the barn and peeked through the door; Jasper appeared content and quietly eating, but still saddled. This wasn't a good idea. Maybe Pauline would give him a ride? The house looked dark but he knocked on the front door anyway. No answer.

"Crap!" he shouted. Would Pauline already be at the rodeo? Did Pauline even strike him as someone who went to rodeos? Maybe it was league night at the bowling alley....

Jason turned and walked around the corner of the house, near Boo's bedroom window. "Boo?" he called. No response.

He looked toward the road, hoping he might recognize a familiar vehicle passing by that could provide him a ride to his truck.

He looked as his watch: 6:18 P.M.

"Damn!" Jason returned to the barn and stared at the saddled, long-eared animal; Jasper continued to chew his hay seemingly without a care. In an instant, Jason untied Jasper, checked the cinch strap, and slipped his leg into the stirrup. "Jasper, this is going to make up for all the times you crapped on my floor," he whispered. Jasper pinned his ears momentarily before resolving himself to the idea of another trip, destination unknown.

Jason kept to the back streets in hopes that no one would recognize him. The town looked like a ghost town; the streets were quiet, and he passed no one. But as he approached the fairgrounds, the reason became clear. He could feel the town's energy as it cut loose for a party it had waited for all year. The illuminated grandstands glowed like a fireworks display, with each and every tree, pole, and structure drenched in thousands of lights. He could hear the voice of a rapid-mouthed rodeo announcer, and the music increased the intensity of an already rowdy, packed grandstand about to unhinge. He rode Jasper to the back side of the arena where the rodeo contestants saddled their horses, and he tied the donkey safely away from the heavy traffic of cowboys and horses.

He made his way through throngs of people, avoiding the eyes of the barking vendors selling beers and brats. He didn't see Catherine anywhere. He checked his watch again: 6:52 P.M. He worried that maybe he'd missed her; they were supposed to meet at 6:45. He felt a tap on his shoulder.

"Hey, you made it!" Catherine exclaimed and reached an arm around his waist.

"Well, I had a little hiccup with transportation. Sorry I'm late."

"You're not late; everyone's just heading in now." She led him through the entrance and into the grandstands.

He followed her to a box group of seats at the rail of the arena. "Daddy has some friends who should be along shortly; I told him to bring us some drinks."

"You have box seats to the rodeo? I only thought the rich folks could afford these."

"Oh, shut up." She gently punched his shoulder and smiled. "Remember, 'Dr. Fancy Pants,' this is Birdie."

Jason stared at Catherine, marveling at her beauty. Her hair was pulled back and braided, and it lay beautifully against her red and white gingham checked blouse. He felt like he had on his first date with Betsy Jardine in ninth grade: nervous, excited, and embarrassed, especially when his father had to drive them to the movies.

"Well, now, hey sir, yes sir, Dr. Davies, I presume, how are you, sir?" said a familiar voice. Cody and his friends had arrived, their hands full with ice-cold beers.

"Good evening sir, how are you?" Jason stood to let them pass.

"Well, most delightful this evening, thank you, and I sure am glad you could make it down tonight, yes sir," replied Cody, taking a seat next to Catherine.

As they stood for the pledge of allegiance, Jason glanced around, looking for any sign of Otter. He could see the vet box and Otter's truck through the far gate by the chutes, but no sign of the loud-mouthed moron.

The rodeo announcer came alive as rodeo queens and their courts from all over the state of Oklahoma made their grand entrances in a flash of thundering hooves, sequins, and spurs. Wagons of dignitaries followed, and the crowd cheered when the last wagon to enter, pulled by an eight-horse Percheron draft team, included the Oklahoma Governor's family. The Governor rode his horse just behind the wagon, waving to the unruly, buzzing crowd. As the Governor made his way around the far end of the arena, shouting erupted from the gate entrance. A man on a horse appeared to force his way into the arena, with several men attempting to stop him. The man on the horse began beating the men with a rope before kicking another with his boot and then spurring his anxious horse into the arena.

"That stupid, drunk, son-of-a-bitch," shouted Catherine.

"Is that Otter?" asked Jason.

"Of course.... Unbelievable, he's going to get someone killed. I should have hit him harder...and somewhere else," she growled.

Otter's horse, nervous and frantic, began to spin and weave erratically. Otter lost control and began sliding out of the saddle before catching himself. He spurred the horse hard, sending it careening across the arena at lightning speed. The Governor and the wagon were directly in front of the grandstands when Otter fell off of his horse and landed face down in the dirt. The horse continued across the arena, bucking. The excitement became too much for the Percheron team. The horses took off in uncontrollable chaos, causing the Governor's horse to reared up and throw him off. As the Governor fell from his horse, a nauseating crack sounded across the arena. Witnessing this scene and hearing the gasp from the crowd made Jason's stomach somersault.

Instantly, rodeo personnel ran in the Governor's direction. Jason grabbed the rail and was into the arena before he realized what he was doing. The Governor slowly attempted to stand, holding his leg. He turned toward his horse, still down and not moving. Several men shouted as they tried to slow the runaway wagon with the Governor's frantic family members aboard. Jason looked at the Governor's horse and quickly realized it needed sedation. He looked anxiously for Otter's truck and yelled to one of the men on horseback.

"Hey! I need that vet truck over here! Hurry!" Two men ran across the arena and returned moments later with Otter's truck. Jason breathed a sigh of relief when he opened the unlocked vet box. He madly searched for the medications he needed. "Come on! Son-of-a-bitch, where the hell did he put everything?" Jason yelled in frustration. Just then, he found the bottles he needed and feverishly drew two syringes. Returning to the down horse, he palpated for the jugular vein and jammed the plunger. He stood and motioned to a group of men who quickly brought over a large flat board sled hitched to a tractor. More men helped carefully move the horse onto the board.

"Hold him down, boys! He's going to try and get up, but don't let him move off this sled until we have him back behind the chutes!" Jason yelled. "Dan, I want you by his head there and I'll stay on his neck. The three of you fellas stay on this side here and make sure he stays on the sled." Jason saw the men nod in agreement before he motioned to the man on the tractor. The tractor groaned and lurched forward and the sled began to move. Jason glanced up into the stands and saw the crowd on its feet, motionless in frozen panic. As the tractor and sled crossed over the middle of the arena, the horse jolted in an attempt to raise itself as it threw its head up and forward.

"Hold him, boys! Don't let him off!" Jason yelled with confidence as if commanding the crew of a ship. "Gary! Grab hold of that rope around the down leg and don't let go! Dave, put your knee into his neck! We can't let him up yet!" The wide metal gates at the end of the arena swung open as they approached. Once through, Jason breathed only a slight sigh of relief. "Now wait until we have him back over behind those corrals and then we can stop. I want everyone safely away from us before we let him up, if he can get up."

Even in this panicked moment Jason understood what was at stake and the importance of damage control; with the Governor in attendance, the parking lot was filled with television trucks broadcasting live back to Oklahoma City, Tulsa, and everywhere else in between. He wanted this to end well for everyone, but especially the folks of Birdie. Jason scanned the area, looking for any signs of news cameras before making his next move.

"Okay, let's unhook the tractor and move it out of the way. I need four of you fellas on each side ready to jump in if need be here in a second. Dave, you sit tight on his neck for a few seconds more and when I give the signal, let's see if he can get up. Wait! Hold on a minute."

Jason ran back to Otter's vet truck. He opened the back door and began frantically searching for the medication he needed. "C'mon, c'mon, dammit! Where the hell did he stash it?" He lifted up a stack of folded towels and found the narcotic lock box with the key in the lock. "Thank goodness Otter is an idiot...." Jason fumbled with the syringes as he drew up the ketamine and valium, then raced back to the horse.

Several men made their way over to Jason and the others. "Sir, thank you for your help in there. My name is John Tilden; this is my horse, Freckles. Please tell me he's going to be alright."

Jason looked at the man standing over him, surrounded by his entourage, including the Governor. "Governor, are you okay?" Jason asked.

"I'll be fine. They think maybe a broken rib or two, but I want to know if my horse is going to be okay?"

"We need to see if we can get him up; I'll know more

then. If we can't get him figured out here, then we can send him to your vet up in Oklahoma City."

The Governor wiped the corner of his eye. He extended his hand to Jason. "Thank you, Dr. ...."

"Davies, Jason Davies."

"Thank you, Jason; thank you."

Jason took a deep breath and hoped for everyone's sake that the horse could and would stand. He nodded to Dave, and the cowboy slowly slid off the horse's neck. They waited and watched for what seemed like an eternity until the horse lifted his head, his front legs scrambled, and in the blink of an eye was on his feet. The cowboys rushed in to steady the horse as Jason quickly scanned the animal over, looking for any sign of injury. Freckles stood evenly on all four legs and showed no obvious signs of fractures. Jason turned to the man holding the reins of the horse and said, "Colton, make him take a few steps that way and let's see if he shows us anything." The man cautiously led the horse away as Jason watched each of the legs, looking for lameness. The horse moved off with some hesitation, but again, there were no obvious signs that bones had been broken. Jason administered another injection for longer-acting pain relief and then ordered the horse to a stall for closer observation for the remainder of the rodeo.

Out of the corner of his eye Jason saw Catherine hug the Governor, who then spoke softly to his wife standing next to him. The three children looked anxious and unsettled but otherwise unharmed from the runaway wagon. Catherine turned and walked toward Jason.

"Good work, Doc. You single-handedly saved the town tonight," she said with a smirk, gently punching his arm.

"Not a bad plan to save the Governor's horse, especially at the event of the year. Yep, the way I see it, you may get a street named after you."

"Did anyone scoop Otter out of the arena?" Jason asked Catherine, looking around the crowd of people now forming. A cameraman and reporter were with the Governor; Jason secretly hoped they wouldn't come looking for him next.

"The Sheriff found him passed out in a trailer with not one, but two underage buckle bunnies...."

He stared at her with disbelief. "What the...? Are you serious?"

"Probably a safe bet that you'll be the rodeo vet after tonight; a little job security, I suppose," she said with a smile. "Now, I think these boys have this under control, and if I were you, I'd get the hell out of here before you end up on every 10 o'clock news program between here and Apalachicola. It's time for you to buy me a beer, and possibly a funnel cake."

Jason turned to the man holding the Governor's horse and handed him a card. "My number is on here; if anything changes with this horse, call me."

"Will do, Doc, thanks." The man extended his free

hand. "We sure appreciate what you done here tonight."

"Thank you all for your help. We were a good team."

Jason felt Catherine grab his hand.

"Thank you for doing what you did tonight; John and Kate are close with Daddy, and Kate was one of my mother's dearest friends."

They returned to their seats as the rodeo got underway with the bareback riders. Jason felt the occasional hand on his shoulder as passersby showed their appreciation for his efforts. He wondered if all small towns were like this; a place where everyone took care of and looked out for their neighbors, even if they didn't always know them.

The bull riding ended the rodeo's first successful night, and the crowd slowly cleared the stands. Jason and Catherine made their way to the back side of the arena to visit the Governor's horse. All appeared to be well as Freckles ate quietly in his stall.

The Governor was all smiles. "Dr. Davies, I cannot thank you enough for all that you did tonight. I shudder to think what might have happened if you and these other wonderful folks hadn't been here. My family and I owe you a debt of thanks; if there is ever anything that I can do for you, please do not hesitate to ask."

Jason was at a loss for words. "Thank you. I'm happy I could help. Thank you for coming to our little town, Governor; it means a great deal to everyone here."

The Governor shook Jason's hand and said goodbye.

He gave Catherine a hug before his entourage quickly swallowed him back to his unmarked black Suburban.

Still holding hands, Jason and Catherine walked slowly to the parking lot.

"What are you smiling about?" Jason asked, turning to her.

"Oh, nothing."

"Seriously, what is it?"

"It's just that when you were talking with John, you referred to Birdie as 'our' town; as in, 'your' town."

"Oh, please. I did not. I said, 'this' town, not our town."

"Trust me, Doc, I'm an attorney; I know what I heard. Admit it; this town is growing on you. Truth is, after tonight you're a celebrity of magnanimous proportions. It's going to be hard to buy a gallon of milk without being recognized anymore. It's only a matter of time before Oprah or Barbara Walters comes calling...."

"Would you stop?" he laughed, nudging her shoulder. "Will I see you tomorrow?"

"I should hope so; I didn't come all the way back here with a broken hand, driving a stick shift, just to eat funnel cake by myself. Oh! Can you come to breakfast in the morning? Daddy is doing a big thing for the 4-H kids at the house in the morning. I mean, you do eat pancakes, don't you?"

"Of course, but only with chocolate chips," he replied as they stopped at her car. He turned and kissed her; he could feel her reach her arm around him.

"Hey, get a room you two," said a woman's voice. They turned and saw Ginger and Justin.

"Oh hush," Catherine replied. "You're one to talk!"

She turned back to Jason. "So, see you in the morning?"

"Of course, but, oh no, I forgot!" he exclaimed.

"Forgot what?"

"Well, I had to ride Jasper over here tonight and I left him tied on the backside...."

"You are killing me!" Catherine replied. "Well, let's go see if he's still over there."

They walked hand in hand through crowds of people continuing to exit the grandstands. Jason looked confused as he approached the spot where he had tied Jasper earlier.

"Are you sure this was where you left him?"

"Well, pretty sure...Yes, I'm sure this is where I tied him; I'm going to be in big trouble with Pauline if I lost her donkey...."

"Oh, not to worry, everyone in this town knows Jasper. He's bound to show up sooner rather than later. But I'm confused; why are you riding a donkey through town? Is that geriatric truck still giving you trouble?"

"Well, actually, it was buried in people earlier, but I'll keep my fingers crossed that it will start."

"Let me give you a ride. We can look for Jasper on the way."

They made their way through throngs of rodeo

patriots making their path homeward or to the handful of bars downtown. "Where the heck would Jasper be?" Jason wondered. Maybe he had gotten loose and returned home. They drove in silence, with Jason wishing he hadn't taken Jasper without discussing it with Pauline first. He regretted not finding a more secure spot for Jasper as the fear of Otter's compatriots taking revenge started to creep into his mind. Surely they wouldn't hurt the little donkey, would they?

"How does a donkey just disappear?" Jason groaned after they had made their way around the crowded courthouse square.

"I'm sure he's fine; it's Jasper, for goodness sake! That animal will outlive us all." Catherine turned the corner and pulled into the driveway. She put her hand on Jason's knee. "Let's check the barn, maybe he's already back."

Jason quickly followed Catherine through the barn doors. "Jasper? C'mon little fella, please tell me you're here," Jason pleaded. There was no sign of him, but Jason checked the outside pastures to be sure.

"Jason, I'll have Daddy call the Sheriff and ask him to have his guys keep their eyes open tonight. A loose donkey roaming around town isn't the most unusual thing they've encountered in Birdie, especially with the rodeo in town...." Catherine turned and kissed him. "I had a fabulously odd evening with you tonight; thank you."

Jason smiled. "Well, I'm sorry about all the drama, and thank you for your help looking...."

"Don't apologize; trust me, I know drama, and this isn't it. See you in the morning, about 8:00 A.M. at the house?" She blew him a kiss as she climbed back into her car and pulled away. His heart panged as the taillights disappeared around the corner.

Chapter 39

Jason readied himself for bed, tired and yet anxious about what had become of the carrot-eating, defecating hot mess of a donkey he had somehow lost on the streets of Birdie. He checked the barn twice before finally climbing into bed and praying that morning would bring good news.

His sleep was interrupted throughout the night when he hoped the sounds coming from the barn were Jasper returning. But several times when he ventured out to check, there were no signs of the donkey.

He awoke early, remembering the breakfast at Cody's. He made his way out to the driveway and then realized that the tire on the vet truck was still very flat. Why was his life such a disaster? His own truck was still sitting downtown, his wet laundry was still mildewing at the laundromat, and the tire on the vet truck wasn't going to fix itself.

"Shit!" How had he forgotten to pick up his truck last night? The disruption with the search for Jasper had made him totally forget about his truck, and now he had no transportation.

He removed the tire iron and positioned the jack under the truck. As he began to loosen the lug nuts on the tire, he paused, remembering the last time he had changed the tire on this truck. Had the spare even been replaced?

He stopped and looked under the rear of the truck where the spare should be, but all he saw was an empty space. He shook his head in disbelief. He threw the tire iron on the ground with frustration. He wanted to scream as he stood up and dusted himself off.

He turned and began walking toward downtown, hoping his truck would still be there, and more importantly that it would start. He looked at his watch: 8:15 A.M. Suddenly his phone rang.

"Dr. Davies? This is Mel at the rodeo, and we have a bit of a problem. With Otter in a bit of heat, we don't officially have a vet to oversee the slack for the cowboys this morning, so I've got about 250 grumpy cowboys down here that want to rope something, and if I don't get this thing started soon, it's gonna be me they're ropin'...."

Jason sighed, realizing that pancakes, chocolate chip pancakes, would not be in his future this morning. "Sure, I'll be right there...." Jason picked up his pace and finally found his truck. "I sure hope to hell you start," he grumbled. The truck whined and finally turned over as a cloud of black smoke clouded the rearview mirror. "Well, that's a new one," Jason said, shaking his head. As he made his way to the fairgrounds he called Catherine, but she didn't answer.

"Hey there, it's Jason. Hey, I'm really sorry, but they need me at the rodeo this morning for the slack. I hope I can take a rain check on the pancakes. See you tonight?"

Jason checked in with the rodeo office and the PRCA judges before heading for the hospitality tent in hopes of finding coffee and something to eat. The day dragged on for what seemed like an eternity, with an endless stream of cowboys competing for a go at the rodeo that night. Jason wondered if the day would ever end. Finally, the last steer was turned out and Jason hurried home, hoping for a quick nap before seeing Catherine later that night.

He closed the blinds, turned on the air conditioner, collapsed on his bed, and fell right to sleep.

There was a knock at the door. Or was it? With the roar and rumble of the air conditioner, Jason wasn't sure. He cracked the door, and there she stood.

"Becca? Whaaat...? Hey, what are you doing here?" he asked in utter disbelief.

"Surprise, were you expecting someone else?" she said with an air of suspicion.

"I didn't know, I didn't think...It's early...."

She stepped around him and entered the apartment. Her smile turned to a look of disgust.

"Seriously, you live here?" she asked.

"Uh, well, it's a little messy, I mean, I didn't know you were coming, and I would have spruced it up...."

"Yeah, well, it would take a bulldozer and a wrecking ball to spruce this place up. Wow, this is a joke."

Becca was here? Had he missed something? The last conversation they'd had didn't so much as hint at any attempt of a future visit. And yet, here she was. Why? It seemed a little sudden, which made Jason suspicious.

"Well, it's not that bad. I mean, it's not great, but it's a roof," Jason replied in defense. "What are you doing here? I haven't heard from you in weeks, and after our last conversations, I guess I thought we were through."

"Well, things change, I guess. I heard from Tommy that you're getting yourself out of this rat hole, so I reconsidered and decided I would come rescue you. So, you're welcome." She walked slowly around the room, absorbing the reality of his accommodations. She turned, saying, "Jason, face it, you're living in a barn. A barn! Seriously, the fact that you don't see a problem with that is a problem," she sizzled.

He hurriedly changed his shirt, hoping to get Becca out of his apartment before she took full stock of his current living conditions. "Are you hungry?" he asked, slipping on his boots.

"Sure, what did you have in mind?" she replied with an air of false sweetness that was clearly aimed at diffusing the current tension.

"I was headed to the rodeo, but we could stop somewhere first if you'd rather," he said, looking for the keys to his truck.

"Are you serious? It's hot and buggy and you want to take me to a rodeo after I flew all this way to rescue you?"

311

"Would you stop saying that? What are you rescuing me from? I'm fine."

"Are you serious? Look around, Jason! This whole place is a mess, and I'm not just talking about this dump you're living in! You need to get out of here, and fast. I think this place is rotting your brain."

Jason gave her a questioning glance.

"Never mind, I'm sure the rodeo food will be great," she said sarcastically. "May I use the bathroom? I mean, this place does have a bathroom, right?"

Jason pointed around the corner. He was trying to quickly pick up the scattered laundry on the floor when he heard Becca scream. "Ahhh!"

He turned and ran toward the kitchen. Becca was standing face to face with Jasper.

"What the hell is that?" she screamed.

"That's Jasper!" Jason smiled, stepping toward Jasper and wrapping his arms around the little donkey's neck. "Aren't you a sight for sore eyes!" Jason turned, catching the look of disgust on Becca's face.

"What the hell...?"

Jason let go of Jasper and stepped back. "Long story...," he replied, smiling. He walked toward the bathroom and turned on the light. "*This* is the door you want."

Becca disappeared into the bathroom, and Jason led Jasper into the barn, closing the door behind him.

"Where the hell have you been, old man?" Jason

asked, staring at Jasper. The saddle was still attached. Jason quickly returned it to the tack room. He glanced around the barn, looking for any other surprises. He hoped Pauline hadn't missed the donkey.

Jason returned to the apartment just as Becca was exiting the bathroom. Her steely glance and drawn lips told him the bathroom hadn't impressed her, either. "Sure could stand to use some cleaning, an air freshener, something...maybe demolition...."

"Well, I guess we should get going." Jason faked a smile, hoping to just get her out of the apartment. He grabbed his keys, then held the door for her. As he locked the door behind them, she said, "Really? Is it necessary to lock up that dump? Best thing that could happen is that it might burn down while we're gone...."

Fumbling with the lock, he wanted to say something nasty in return, but he just stared at the door. Turning away from the apartment, he said, "I'm sure we'll be able to find something to eat...."

"Right...let's go get some fried food on a stick," Becca drawled, in a poor imitation of a Southerner.

As Jason drove Becca's rental car through town, Becca quietly looked out the window at the neighborhood homes. Jason wondered what she was thinking. He realized by her body language that she clearly regretted coming to Birdie.

She asked, "Are there any newer parts to this town, I mean like newer homes? Everything seems so old. It just seems drab, like wearing the same clothes over and over again. Do these people ever leave?"

"Leave? You mean leave town?" he replied.

"Yeah, I mean, is this all they know? Do they grow up and stay and then marry the same people, kind of like inbreeding or something?"

"Becca, what in the hell are you talking about? This isn't *Deliverance*. These people are like you and me, and they're great people. They read, write, go to the movies. I've even seen some of them get *The Wall Street Journal* delivered each morning."

"Oh don't get defensive, it's just odd," she replied.

"What do you mean by that? You haven't even met anyone yet."

"Jason, you have a jackass or donkey or whatever the hell that thing is living with you in a barn. You live in a barn!"

As they arrived at the fairgrounds, Jason waved to the parking attendants.

"Good evening, Dr. Davies; nice to see you," said the gentleman who handed them a program as they entered. People and vendors were plentiful and the smells of smoked turkey legs, funnel cakes, and barbeque filled the air.

"Do you think they might have a salad, maybe some sushi? How about anything not fried or covered in grease?" Becca asked.

Jason gave her a questioning glance. "This is a rodeo,

not Rodeo Drive...."

Jason finally found a food wagon that had a grilled chicken sandwich. Becca seemed only partially interested in eating, but Jason was quickly losing interest in finding something that interested her. They gathered drinks and headed for the grandstands. As they found a seat, Jason scanned the box seats looking for Catherine.

"Is it always so hot here? And what's up with these little bugs that keep flying around?" groaned Becca.

Jason said nothing, trying to ignore Becca's questions and complaints. He should be excited that she was here. He was excited, wasn't he?

"Are these benches normally this hard?" she whined.

"Since when did you get to be this high maintenance?" Jason turned to her, rolling his eyes. "It's a rodeo."

"You keep saying that, but what does that mean? You can still be comfortable at a rodeo, right?"

Jason glanced toward the box seats again, but still no sign of Catherine, or Cody for that matter.

"Who are you looking for?" asked Becca.

"Oh... just some friends I thought would be here, but I don't see them," he replied, still distracted.

"Well, maybe they will show up and they have more comfortable seats that we can share."

"Yeah, maybe."

The rodeo queen presented the flag and everyone stood for the national anthem. Still no sign of Catherine; something must have happened. The wagon entered with its royalty for the evening. The Governor was absent this evening, and Jason breathed a sigh of relief when the wagon left uneventfully from the arena. As they watched the events in silence, Becca asked, "Have you talked to Tommy lately?"

Jason turned and looked at her again with a questioning glance. She disliked Tommy, and the fact that she was even mentioning his name meant he had called her.

"Not recently, why?" he asked innocently. "And why is Tommy calling you?"

"Because for starters, you haven't shared shit about anything with me, so I called him. He told me that Rio Vista has a position for you. I thought about it and decided I needed to try to fight for us; and that meant coming down here, you apologizing, and us leaving."

"Apologize? Apologize for what?"

"For all this! I mean, come on, wake up and see what's going on here. Don't go all 'mister holier than thou'; you're on the threshold of flushing your life away in this crap-ass little town, and not to mention the local floozie that's trying to make her moves!"

The couple in front of them turned, overhearing her comment.

"This whole thing is going to be detrimental to you, and to us, and this is your last chance to realize that."

"Really? How's that?"

"Seriously, why wouldn't you jump at the opportunity

to get the hell out of this crappy cow town?"

"Shhhh," commanded Jason as the couple in front of them turned once again in response to Becca's comment.

"I just don't understand; I thought you wanted what was best for us, for our future."

"I did...." Jason sat and stared at the rodeo clown in the arena. "The plan was California, but now...."

"But now? But now what?!"

"It's hard to explain.... This town, the people here.... I guess I just don't know if California is the best decision...."

Tears began to well in Becca's eyes. Jason stared off into the distance. He was confused and numb. He had wanted out of Birdie, at least until Becca had arrived. Her evaluation of his situation seemed to only push him in the other direction.

"You're an idiot!" she screamed. "I've sacrificed a lot for you, for us! I thought we were on the same page, but clearly we aren't. So stay; wallow in this stagnant wading pool of redneck slop. But mark my words, someday you're going to regret this decision, and I won't be around to rescue your sorry ass. Asshole!" Becca stood and started down the steps.

"Hey, Becca, c'mon...," he called as he followed her out into the midway.

She turned, pointing a finger at him. "You had better listen, and listen good. If we have any hope of continuing, then you'd better get on the next bus out of this shithole. This town may be cute to think about, but there is no way,

NO WAY, that I am even remotely interested in wrecking my life for you here."

Jason's heart sank as he looked down the midway to see Catherine staring at him. She smiled briefly upon seeing the distress in Jason's eyes. Becca caught sight of Jason's gaze.

"Who is that? Is she the bitch you've been messing around with?"

Jason was caught off-guard by Becca's comment and quickly snapped out of his daze. "What?"

Becca started toward Catherine.

"No! Wait!" Jason tore after Becca, hoping to catch her before she confronted Catherine. A group of people walked in front of him, blocking his path. Jason quickly moved around the group and caught up to Becca just as she jumped in front of Catherine.

"Who the hell are you to get involved in our personal affairs?" Becca demanded.

"Excuse me? What are you talking about?" Catherine replied, stunned by the affront.

Jason jumped in between the two women and turned to Becca. "Leave her alone. She's got nothing to do with this!"

"Oh really? I'd say she's got a whole hell of a lot to do with this!" spewed Becca.

"Hello, I'm Catherine," said Catherine in a calm tone, extending her hand to Becca.

"I don't give a damn who you are; I want you to leave

us alone." Becca glared at her.

Catherine gave a courteous smile. "I'm sorry, I didn't know I was interfering...."

"Shut up! I've about had it with this shit!"

"Becca! Enough!" shouted Jason.

Catherine interjected, "I'm sorry, but where I'm from ladies don't interrupt while others are speaking, and they're able to express themselves without mentioning fecal matter."

"Really? This, coming from the redneck princess of Hickville! Well, I've got news for you, Queenie, Jason is getting the hell out of this little hell hole and we are headed to California. So you can just keep wandering around this inbred paradise and look for some other man to sink your teeth into!"

The pain of Becca's news showed clearly on Catherine's face as she turned to Jason. He'd meant to tell her about Becca, but what was he supposed to say? What had there really been to tell? He could feel the pain in her eyes and a rush of sadness filled him. Tears began to well in both their eyes.

"Well, I do hope you will both be very happy." Catherine's voice drifted off as she turned and walked away.

"Catherine!" Jason shouted over the voice blaring through the loudspeaker.

"Dr. Davies, please report behind the chutes. Dr. Davies, they need you back behind the chutes."

Jason stared at Becca, unsure what to say. "Wait for me. I'll be right back." Without waiting for her response, he turned and raced to the chutes.

A bull was down in the chutes and wouldn't get up. He had a large amount of fluid coming from his nose and mouth. It looked like the bull had frothy bloat cooking. Jason asked, "What's this one eaten today?"

The stock contractor's help looked at each other before one man stepped forward and spoke. "Well sir, we were all out of hay, so I thrown some of the bulls the horse hay and they cleaned it up lickety-split."

"Does that hay have any alfalfa in it?" Jason looked around at the group surrounding him.

"Well, yes sir, pretty much just alfalfa."

Jason looked around, searching for anyone carrying a knife. "Anyone have a clean knife I can borrow?" Immediately, six blades flashed in front of him. He reached for one and jabbed it into the bull's flank. Immediately, a bubbling, foul-smelling mixture of gas and fluid erupted from the opening. Two of the younger bull riders turned their heads and stepped away.

"Let's get this bull up and over to the clinic. We need to place a rumen trochar to open up a port to allow the gas to come out a bit," Jason commanded with authority.

Suddenly the bull jumped to its feet and the men scattered. "Doc, we're going to need to turn the bull out. The pickup men will rope it, and then we can load from the chutes into a trailer, if that's okay with you."

"That's fine. I need to take care of some business, but I'll meet you at the clinic." Jason turned and ran back to the grandstands. Catching his breath, he scanned the crowds of people, searching for her. He couldn't let it end this way. He looked toward the box seats, but they were empty. Catherine was gone.

He turned and raced back to the midway. Would Becca be there? He hurried down through the crowds of people to where he'd left her, but there was no sign of her. He checked his watch and realized he'd been gone almost 40 minutes. He quickly made his way to the parking lot, hoping her rental car would still be there. The spot was empty. Jason sat down on the bumper of a nearby pickup and stared out into the darkened landscape. What the hell was he going to do now? He hoped Becca wouldn't be rash and leave altogether. He hoped that she'd driven to the Super 8 and was checking in. But if she were going to do that, she would have waited for him. He knew her well enough that if she was gone, then she was really gone.

Left once again without a vehicle, Jason sat staring up at the night sky. Tears again began to well up in his eyes. What the hell was he going to do? Everything...everything had collided. Tonight had created a storm he wasn't prepared for. This was really the end for him and Becca; they'd both made that clear.

He was tempted to call the sheriff's office and report a missing person, but didn't they have to actually be missing? Becca was most likely at the airport in Tulsa. He should follow her, like in the movies. Moments before she stepped onto the plane, he would arrive, says something magical, and they would live happily ever after. But he knew better. Becca hadn't given him an opportunity to make the situation right, like he usually did. When Becca had a problem, Jason was the fixer.

"Hey there, you look like a man without a horse."

"Hey, Justin; how are you?"

"I'm alright, but you don't look so good; you need a lift or something?"

"Well, maybe, where's Ginger?"

"Oh, she's 'chatty-chatty' with some of her friends, but I'm more than happy to give you a ride somewhere."

"I appreciate it, that'd be great. Hey, did you see Catherine tonight?"

"Yeah, earlier, but she got real upset about halfway through and she left."

Jason felt his shoulder blades begin to burn with the stress of the situation.

"I don't know nothin', Jason. These damn girls; they only talk to each other. They went to the ladies room, and when Ginger came back she said Cat wasn't feeling well and went home."

"Heeyy, y'all, what's going on here?" Ginger came around the corner of the pickup carrying a large drink and her bling-laden handbag. "Oooooh, you are in some hot water, Doc. Who was that cute gal on your arm tonight?" Ginger asked in her distinctive southern drawl.

"Oh Ginger, hush; this man is hurtin'. He done been left for some reason in the parking lot here, and he needs our help." Justin opened the truck door, attempting to hurry Ginger into the vehicle.

"Goodness," Ginger said, looking concerned. "Are you really hurt?"

"Oh no," replied Jason. "Just my pride, maybe."

"Darlin', get used to it. You men are constantly setting yourselves up for disaster," she said, laughing.

They climbed into the single-cab pickup, and as they headed out of the parking lot Ginger leaned over and whispered in Jason's ear, "I think Cat was upset to see you with that little gal tonight."

Jason could feel his cheeks beginning to flush. "I know, it's a big misunderstanding, and a mess.... Justin, would you mind running by the Super 8?"

"You bet, Doc. That gal of yours didn't care for your barn accommodations, huh?" chuckled Justin.

"Not exactly, she had a little run-in with one of my roommates...."

"You have other people livin' with you over there?" Ginger asked.

"No, I meant the four-legged kind. She had a little mis-introduction to Jasper.... Where is Cat now?"

"Oh, I don't know. Said she had to go. I figured she went back to Cody's, but I don't know for sure." Ginger took a sip of her huge drink. "Now, are you supposed to be marrying this girl, and she doesn't like animals?"

"What? No! I mean, I don't...."

There was no sign of Becca's rental car in the Super 8 parking lot. Jason grabbed his phone and called her but it went straight to voice mail. "Hi, you've reached Becca, leave me a message."

"Is everything okay?" Ginger nervously took another sip of her drink.

"Ohhhh, who knows; I think she's gone." Jason's voice drifted off.

"Like gone out of town, or gone for good?" Ginger asked, as Justin bumped her arm and signaled her to stop talking.

"Both."

"I'm sorry," she replied, patting his leg.

"Justin, would you mind dropping me off at the clinic?" Jason scanned the parking lot one last time.

Minutes later, they pulled to a stop in front of the clinic. A large stock trailer was already along the side of the building to unload the bull. Jason took a deep breath; this wasn't what he wanted to be doing right now, while his life seemed to be slipping away in opposite directions. He hopped out of the truck and thanked Justin and Ginger.

"You let us know if you need anything."

"Thank you.... Oh, Ginger?"

"Yes?"

"Is Catherine okay? I mean, I want to try and talk to her about all this, and...."

"Don't worry about Cat, she's going to be fine. But you need to sort out what makes sense in your world. Cat's got some things she's been hanging on to way too long, if you ask me. Maybe this is a good thing for both of you." She winked and closed the door.

The truck drove away and Jason was left staring at the taillights.

Jason sighed and stared up at the stars, wondering how everything would work out, or whether it would. It didn't seem possible that his world could be swallowed any deeper into the abyss. He turned and headed into the clinic.

After loading the bull into the chute, Jason set to work on placing a temporary, but more permanent, trochar into the rumen portion of the bull's stomach. The cowboys watched, commenting in low breaths to each other, critiquing Jason's work. He recalled one late night not long ago, stitching a horse's leg together and then stepping back to take pride in his surgical skill, especially considering what the wound had looked like to start with; the owner had smirked and said, "Nice job, real nice, but I betcha Doc Keating could have buttoned that leg a little faster."

Jason started the bull on antibiotics, advising the handlers not to feed it anything but strictly grass hay for the next week. The stock contractor was headed to west Texas and Jason advised him to see a veterinarian in the area to remove the trochar. Jason helped load the animal, and when the cowboys finally left and the clinic was quiet he staggered back to his office and collapsed into his chair.

What the hell was he going to do? He was so upside down in his head; he didn't know which end was up at this point. Didn't Keating keep a bottle of something stashed somewhere in here? He needed a drink, although it was probably best that he didn't know where Keating kept his bottle. Shelly might find him passed out on Monday morning.

He tried Becca's number again. Still no answer. This time he left a message, saying, "Becca, I don't know what happened tonight. Are you still in town? Call me."

He was familiar with Becca's dramatic ways, but this was over the top, even for her.

He locked up and walked to the parking lot, looking for his truck before realizing that it was still at his apartment.

"Damn...." What good was a truck that never started and was never around when you needed it? As he looked up at the night sky, the cool breeze felt good on his face. He needed to clear his head, and the walk back to the apartment surely wouldn't hurt.

Neighbors were still out on their front porches, talking and soaking up the relative coolness of the night air. The walk was sobering to the realities of Jason's situation. In less than a few hours he had single-handedly made an even larger disaster of his world than he ever thought possible. Maybe this was all for the best; California was his calling, and Catherine's world was complicated. But even as he walked the streets, he couldn't make himself believe his own thoughts. Truthfully, he was terrified over the thought of losing what he had started to build in Birdie: roots. California had been a promise and the cure to healing himself from his past; he had thought that California would make everything okay again. However, the truth was that nothing could heal the hurt and isolation of his past. No person, no amount of money, no job, and certainly not California. But in only a few short months, this hole-in-the-wall town had shifted the tide of his thoughts and goals.

These were the moments when he wished he could reach out to his father, for a close conversation and some sage advice. Jason had tried in the past, but the interaction was never what he had envisioned. In the end, the short, awkward conversation usually left him feeling even more confused and alone.

Pauline's house was alive with activity; laughter and music poured from the open windows. Every light in the house was on, which made Jason even more aware that Boo's room was dark, the curtains drawn. He hoped nothing was wrong. He sat down in the dusty lawn chair that had remained on his small front porch. He watched the house and listened to the laughter coming from the windows. The katydids played their musical ensemble as the humid lull of the evening settled in around him.

This place had changed, or rather it had changed him,

and Becca's arrival had made it obvious. He went inside and crawled into bed. He was exhausted, but he couldn't fall asleep.

Chapter 40

Jason woke up to the sound of rain hitting the metal barn roof. He momentarily panicked when he saw that the ceiling light was filling once again with rain water. He decided that getting up sooner rather than later was a wise decision.

He showered quickly and grabbed his phone to leave. He noticed that the message light was blinking. He hadn't been in the bathroom long, but he'd missed a call.

"Jason, I don't know what the hell you're doing in that two-bit rat hole, but unless you decide to make a change, we are through. I cannot, and will not, flush my life away for you. What are you thinking? Think about what we've been through. We've grown up together, and you need to make the right decision. Think about *us*."

At least he knew she was still alive, but it was sour consolation with his current state of affairs. Ultimately, he had a choice: Stay and risk losing Becca for good, or go and risk losing himself. What the hell he was supposed to do? His head hurt, and he needed coffee. He wanted to talk to Keating about the situation, but what would Keating say? "Jason, you've made a hell of a mess. You made your bed, and you'd better be damn comfortable sleeping it." His head was pounding. "I need coffee," he grumbled to himself. Minutes later he made his way to the only coffee house in town that didn't serve Folgers.

The young woman behind the counter acted as if she had been sampling caffeinated beverages since early that morning. Her exuberance did nothing to lift Jason's spirits. She handed Jason his scone and he found a table and sat down. He felt a hand on his shoulder. "Doc, you look sadder than a boy who lost his puppy."

Jason turned around to see Tom Harkins standing in front of him. Tom was Birdie's pseudo-celebrity. He was a Hollywood actor with small, frequent roles on television and in several Westerns over the years. He had also been involved in a variety of entrepreneurial enterprises following his acting, currently including hat making and frozen yogurt. He and a few venture capitalists had developed a chain of frozen yogurt shops coast to coast. His hat making was becoming popular, with other celebrities wanting his hats, sometimes making personal appearances to buy them. However, Birdie's residents never believed that celebrities would actually visit their town, so they assumed that some of Tom's friends just happened to look like someone famous.

"Must be girl trouble," Tom said with a grin as he sat down.

"Why do you say that?"

"Because the last time I saw someone so sad, it was 1986 and the love of my life had walked out on me. And I felt just like you look now."

"Yeah," Jason replied, taking a sip of the coffee that had been placed in front of him. "I don't know exactly what's going on, but it's the beginning of the end of something."

"Did I ever tell you that I want to write a book? Seriously, I even have a title picked out for it: 'The Cowboy's Guide to Crazy Women.' Seriously, it's going to be a hit, I'll tell you right now. I've gone on countless dates with crazy women for the past 20 years, and they just seem to get crazier and crazier, far as I can tell. I tell you, I have a technique that in twenty minutes I can figure out if a woman is compatible or crazy, simple as that."

Jason looked up from his coffee. "Well, you could have saved me a lot of heartache over the past 8 years if that's true."

"You think I'm crazy, but I'm serious. If you think about it, relationships come down to four things: God, money, politics, and family. If those things don't, and won't, match up, then kiss her good-bye." Jason didn't know what to say to that. Tom stood up. "Well, listen, I didn't mean to intrude, but it sounds like you're going through a rough time. Remember what I told you, and maybe some part of it can help with what's rollin' around in your head right now. But given a bit of time, it will come out like it's supposed to."

"You mean, it will come out all right in the end?" Jason asked.

Tom turned with a smile and said, "No, but it'll work out like it's supposed to. Take care." Tom waved to the girl behind the counter before placing his hat on his head and sauntering out the door. Jason stared out the small curtained window into the dreary Oklahoma sky, watching the rain come down and pondering Tom's words. He thought, "He's crazy; what does he know about relationships? Had Tom ever even been married?"

Jason headed to the clinic with more questions than answers. God, money, politics, and family; of course there had to be more to relationships than just those four things. Jason and Becca had always agreed on God, mostly. They both had grown up Protestant, but her family never really attended church. Each time he brought the matter up, she became defensive.

Money; they both liked it. That was something they had in common, right? Well, except Becca had a way of discovering new ways to spend it. Her parents had never been good with money, living week to week, with her father blowing whatever money he did make on beer and bets at the track. Becca had an almost obsessive-compulsive disorder about money. She wanted money, and more was always better.

Then there was politics. At least there, they could mostly agree. Becca always took a hard bend to the right with all of her views, regardless of the topic, whereas Jason seemed to find comfort in the middle ground. Politics were tolerable, as long as they didn't discuss them.

Last but not least, there was the family topic. Again, easy enough. Jason wanted children; Becca did not. She enjoyed joking that she would always make a great "auntie." Jason, on the other hand, wanted at least three kids, if not four. He always hoped that Becca's views might change as their relationship evolved. People do change, he reasoned . . . but as his father always contended, "Just not that much."

So in the end, if Tom's theory was right, his relationship with Becca had run its course, and there were no "do-overs."

The clinic parking lot was empty when Jason pulled up. He wondered where everyone was, but then he remembered it was Sunday. Sitting in his truck as the rain continued, he realized that with the drama of yesterday he'd forgotten what day it was. No one would be at the office on Sunday. He put the truck into gear, intending to return to the apartment, but then paused; what was he going to do holed up all day in the barn? He remembered he hadn't put in any charges or completed the medical record for the bull from last night. At least it might take his mind off of everything else for a bit. He entered the quiet clinic, but as he made his way down the hall toward the office, he realized the light was on. He hoped he hadn't left it on last night. He found Keating seated at his desk. Jason walked in slowly, not sure what to expect. He sat down at his desk and began digging through a stack of mail.

"Everything okay?" Keating asked, looking up from his work.

"Oh, uhhh, sure, I guess. Had a bit of a situation with

some of the rodeo stock last night...I didn't expect to find you here this morning."

"I heard about the bull. Did it go okay?" Keating replied, looking over his glasses, which had slid down on the bridge of his nose. Jason nodded and returned to the stack of mail.

They continued on in silence but Jason could feel the tension in the air that made it obvious Keating had more to say.

"Did you make it to the rodeo last night?" Jason asked, hoping that casual small talk might force the awkwardness out of the room.

"Oh, no, Mary had a honey-do list a mile long, and then I got on the tractor until after dark.... Hey, I need to discuss some recent things going on, and I guess I need to hear what you're thinking about all of it."

Jason's heart began to race. What did he expect? Of course Keating had questions; why wouldn't he?

"I got a call from a gal a while back wanting the details about you leaving and shipping off to California. To be honest, it's troubling that she was the one to tell me. I think she was confused; of course, so was I, but the first I'd heard of it was from this woman. I told her that I needed to have a conversation with you, and I'd call her the first of the week," said Keating as he removed his reading glasses and leaned back in his chair.

His eyes became fixed on Jason. He motioned with his hands. "This is when you talk."

334

Jason's faced flushed. Keating was pissed, and he knew it.

"Well, I, um, had this opportunity presented to me, umm, recently, and I guess I was considering what options, umm, I might have, and...I guess I don't know. I've been meaning to discuss it with you in person, but I wasn't sure what I should do...."

"Well, the way the lady spelled it out for me, it's a pretty much done deal. It sounds like your mind's made up. I just wish you would have had the courtesy to tell me about it before everyone else."

"Yes, sir, I completely understand, and I want to say...."

"Jason, stop. I know, I know...you're sorry, and you've enjoyed working for me, but this is a great opportunity.... I got it, don't waste your damn breath. I've heard it all before, too many damn times, to be honest with you. Do you know how many veterinarians I've had come through these doors over the years, sitting where you're sitting, and telling me the same sincere bullshit? Too damn many.... I'm not saying it isn't a great opportunity, they usually are; it's just that I'm not getting any younger, in case you hadn't noticed, and I don't want to work so damn much anymore. Somehow I thought I had a different feeling about you, different from all the others before you, that you were going to be different.... Well, I guess not; I guess I was wrong...." Keating stood up and shuffled a stack of papers on his desk. "Nonetheless, I don't want to be what holds you back, so if this is what you want to do, then so be it." Keating placed his glasses back on his head and stared at Jason. "I'd appreciate if you'd let Mary know when you'll be leaving."

Jason, staring at the floor, didn't know what to say. He wasn't sure what he wanted to do anymore, but here was Keating's blessing, of sorts. He should be packing his bags, right? He stood from his chair, wanting to say something. He wanted to tell Keating he didn't want to go, but the wheels were already in motion; it was too late. Jason turned and slowly made his way back through the reception area to check the appointment book for the morning. He still wanted to say something to Keating and went back down the hallway to the office, but the light was now off and Keating had slipped out the back door. Jason stood in the dark, looking around the room. It wasn't like he had disliked working here; California was just going to be a better fit for him, right?

He dropped into his chair and put his feet on his desk. He hadn't realized how tired he was. He leaned back and closed his eyes, hoping that a few minutes of shut-eye might magically resolve all the drama. After what felt like only a few seconds, a crack of thunder made him jump from his sleep. His eyes flashed open and for a moment he wasn't sure where he was. The room was dark and the rain continued to fall.

"Dr. Davies, are you okay?" Shelly stood by the doorway with a look of concern on her face.

"Uh, yes, sure; what time is it?" he asked, still puzzled.

"It's 12:30 P.M. I just stopped by to pick up my rain jacket and heard you snoring in here." She smirked and rolled her eyes.

"I was snoring? Wow, I must have fallen asleep, sorry...." He straightened in his chair and ran his fingers through his hair. The fogginess in his eyes cleared and he could see the hurt on Shelly's face.

"I'm sorry you don't like it here." She stared with an intensity that made Jason uncomfortable, and he turned to look out the window. "We really wanted you to like us." Tears welled in her eyes. "I guess I thought somehow you were different from the others who came to work for Doc. He's a good man, he is, I don't know where I'd be without him. He gave me a job, a career, something that gave me a purpose in this hick town, and it may be a hick town, but it's honest and it's real. I thought you were real...." She turned and walked out of the office as tears ran down her face.

Jason stood to chase after her. "Shelly, wait!" The hallway was dark but he heard the front door of the clinic slam shut.

He returned to his desk and stared at his diploma on the wall. Anger welled within him as he felt the past and present push and pull. Grabbing the framed diploma, he picked it off the wall and threw it against the cinderblock wall. The glass shattered and the frame disintegrated on the tiled floor. Tears poured down his face. He felt so alone; he couldn't remember a time when he hadn't felt this way. He wiped his face, then found a broom and swept up the remains of what he had been so proud of only months earlier. He locked the front door and walked through the rain to his truck.

He climbed into the truck and started the engine. Where the hell was he headed? He had nowhere to go. Maybe going to California made the most sense. He drove to the motel in hopes that Becca had had a change of heart; the motel clerk stated that the room had never been checked into last night. Had she just left like that? He drove aimlessly through the drenched town, not sure what he was looking for. Maybe a glimpse of a black BMW.... He took the long way through town, passing the now-familiar haunts of Birdie. The little town had begun to strangely feel like home. A place where someone could lay down roots, build a family, be successful. Didn't everyone want those things?

He thought it was strange that Catherine hadn't bothered to call him. Given everything they'd been through, to just walk away didn't seem like her style. Becca's, yes, but not Catherine's.

He made his way to the outskirts of town, passing field after flooded field. Water had been unforgiving to everyone, including the land, and the more properties he saw almost underwater made him nervous about the welfare of Catherine and Cody. He took the turnoff toward their property and saw the large covered archway leading into the ranch. The road was muddy, but not as badly affected as others had been. He pulled up in front of the main house and saw a red BMW that he didn't recognize. His stomach knotted; he already had a sense whose car it was. He made his way up the walk and rang the bell. He heard no movement inside, but then suddenly the door opened. A man stood in the doorway.

He was tall and fit, with a muscular build that immediately let Jason know he spent time during his day working out at the gym. His hair was dark brown and his skin held a vibrant bronze color of the summer sun.

"Hello, I'm Jason Davies. I was looking for Catherine or Cody," Jason stammered.

"Hello, I'm Mark, Catherine's husband. Was she expecting you?"

"Uh, well, umm, no, not really. I was, uh, just worried that the storm may have damaged some things around here, and I just wanted to stop by and make sure everything was okay."

"I think there was some water in the barns, but other than that we're doing fine. Cat and her dad ran into town, but I'll be sure and let her know that you stopped by."

"Okay...thank you." The door closed and Jason staggered in a state of shock back to his truck.

His mind fell into a clouded mess of emotion and confusion, swirling, as he quickly put the truck in gear, wanting to leave before they returned home.

Had she decided to try and work things out with him? He wouldn't blame her if she had. She was a married woman, and she should work it out if that's how it was supposed to be. However, this logic didn't help the feelings of sadness welling up inside him. He needed to get himself together; maybe it wasn't what he thought. "Mind your own mind," he repeated to himself.

Now where, now what? He considered heading to the Buckaroo Mini-Mart for a pack of cigarettes.

A second wave of the storm was brewing; the wind blew a chill he hadn't felt in Birdie until now and the temperature continued to drop. He stopped at the Buckaroo but decided to forgo the cigarettes and instead bought a package of Twizzlers and a Diet Coke. The truck struggled to start and he shook his head, wondering why he had ever been cursed with this vehicle.

He drove past the edge of town, wondering why he felt like a man without a country, a purpose, or a place. No one was missing him now; what would happen if he just disappeared? He pulled off the dirt road under a grove of large oak trees and shut the truck off. The storm seemed to charge the air around him and angry lightning lit up the sky just before a crack of thunder shook the truck. There were probably smarter places to be at a time like this. He ate the Twizzlers quickly and listened to the sad songs of Keith Whitley as the storm once again took hold. He would wait it out.... He turned up the radio and closed his eyes as the rain pounded his windshield; with the cacophony of sound at that moment he felt a momentary sense of peace. A half hour passed before the rain once again relented its hold on the saturated county. Jason opened his eyes and realized that the day was getting late and he should get back to town. He turned the key in the ignition. "Wahhhh, cliiiick, cliiiiick...." And then the truck was silent. The radio and Keith had disappeared too.

"Shit." He popped the hood and scrambled out to see if he could make sense of anything under the hood. Minutes later he realized that either the battery or something in the ignition was to blame; either way, he was walking.

He locked the truck and grabbed his Diet Coke. The jacket he'd brought would do little to keep the rain out if the storm decided to perform an encore. The road was the same slippery mess he'd experienced not long ago at Guffey's and the haunted mansion. What was it with rain and getting trucks stuck; it seemed to be a reoccurring theme. The road was quiet, but he hoped for a friendly neighbor to stop before long and offer him a ride into town.

The growling whine of a diesel pickup quickly approaching made him jump. The truck slid to a stop inches from Jason and four men scrambled from the jacked-up 4x4. "Well, well, well, what have we got here, boys? The fine little chickenshit doctor is out for an evening stroll!"

"Hey, Otter, I don't want trouble." Jason's voice

341

quivered as he realized that an entirely different storm was upon him.

"No trouble...Really? Son, the minute you moved to Birdie, you got trouble, and now I'm going to take what you owe me out on your dumbass hide!"

Jason attempted escape but the men threw him into the back seat of the truck. He struggled to breathe as the men mashed his head with their boots. The truck came to a sudden stop; the door opened as they grabbed his collar and drug him out onto the dark, cold, and muddy landscape. Where the hell was he? Jason attempted to look around but the lights of the truck blinded him. A boot caught the side of his face, tossing him facedown into the mud; he lay motionless, fearful of what was coming.

"Get up, you pansy!" Otter raged. As Jason slowly stood, Otter struck him in the face, sending him spiraling back to the ground. As he writhed in pain he could taste the dirt and blood on his lips. A kick to his stomach took his breath away and he gasped for air. The pain was nauseating and unlike anything he had ever experienced. A heel to his head and his left ear burned and he cried out in pain.

"Shut up, you moron! You had your chance to steer clear of my girl; this is payback!" Another series of kicks to the face and stomach, and then his mind went dark.

He rolled and tasted the choking coagulated dirt and blood in his mouth. Pain emanated from every point of his body. He attempted to roll over, but a wave of nausea overcame him and he vomited. He panicked, worried Otter and his clan might still be around in the darkness, waiting to take a second round. But in the stillness of the cold, wet night, the only sounds he could hear were the ringing in his ears. He lay still, not wanting to startle the vomit gods again, fearful of what he might discover with the trauma done to his body. He attempted to lift each of his legs and then his arms. His hands were responding to his requests for movement. His vision was blurry, but he tried to remember his surroundings before the attack had begun. He again rolled to his side and this time slowly lifted himself to his knees. He waited for the wave of nausea to pass before attempting to stand. As he made it to his feet, he felt dizzy and reached out into the darkness for something to steady himself. A roadside sign conveniently was only a few steps away and he lunged for it as if it were a life preserver floating in the ocean. He grabbed hold of the sign post as the nausea returned. This time he dropped to the ground and vomited. Laying there, he wanted to die. He closed his eyes as his mind fell into darkness once again.

Chapter 41

Jason opened his eyes as the first cast of sunlight hit his blood-encrusted face. He grabbed hold of the sign post and painfully pulled himself to his feet. His vision was blurry, but faintly off in the distance he saw what he thought was a farmhouse. Each step caused him excruciating pain. The waves of nausea were unrelenting, pulsing through his core. He stopped to vomit, and when he saw blood he knew he was in trouble. Would anyone find him? Who knew where he was? It was quiet, with only the sound of his throbbing head and his boots sticking to the rain-soaked mud. He didn't want to even begin to think about what his face must look like. He was scared to move his tongue for fear he might feel missing teeth.

The pain in his stomach made him nauseous again and this time he dropped to his knees and dry heaved. He had never experienced pain like this before. The farmhouse slowly came into better view. He hoped to find someone willing to help him. When he finally arrived, he realized by its dilapidated appearance that the place had been deserted for some time.

He sat down on a stump in the front yard and tears fell from his face; they stung as they raced across his open wounds. Would anyone really miss him if he didn't return? His decomposed body might make the paper in three months when authorities found him. As he sat motionless on the stump, he heard a sound through the wind and rustling leaves; the sound of tiny horse hooves on the road. He picked his head up and looked through a grove of elm trees. The image he thought he saw couldn't be; it wasn't possible. A small brown donkey slowly made its way toward him. Jason blinked, wondering if his eyes deceived him; was it really Jasper?

"Jasper! It's me! Over here, Jasper!"

Jasper paused on the road; his ears perked up when he heard Jason's voice. How the hell had the donkey found him all the way out here, wherever "here" was? Bewildered and exhausted, Jason slowly limped back to the road. Jasper pawed, showing his impatience to his weary traveler.

"Well, it's definitely you, isn't it," Jason remarked. Jason climbed on apprehensively and grabbed hold of Jasper's mane. As if the donkey knew what to do, he turned and headed back the way he had come. Jason first wondered if they were traveling in the right direction; but he soon relented, realizing that Jasper had found *him*. He closed his eyes, hoping he could hang on long enough.

The methodical clopping of Jasper's tiny feet lulled Jason into a semi-conscious bewilderment filled with pain and exhaustion. No cars passed as they made their way to town. As the outskirts of Birdie became visible, Jason felt a rush of emotion, like a lost sailor seeing the lighthouse beacon. Jasper continued his march through the back streets toward the clinic. Upon arriving, Jason slid off his mount and staggered to the front door of the clinic. He paused and turned back toward Jasper, but the little donkey had disappeared.

Jason opened the door of the clinic and staggered in, collapsing into a nearby reception room chair.

"Jason! My God, what happened?" exclaimed Mary, racing from her place behind the counter. "Shelly!"

Shelly appeared in an instant. "Let's help him into one of the exam rooms and make him lay down on the table," Mary shouted with motherly authority.

The women set to work assessing his most critical wounds. "Jason, I think we should get you to the hospital." Mary stared at the pupils of both of his eyes, looking for any signs of what could be a concussion.

"No, I'll be okay, just need a little bit to get myself cleaned up." His speech was slurred by a swollen upper lip. He asked to use the restroom and they helped him off the table and stabilized his walk down the hallway.

"I really do think you need to go the ER," Shelly whispered as he closed the door to the bathroom.

The sight of his reflection in the mirror made him nauseous again. His right eye was swollen almost completely shut, and his upper lip was split and doubled in size. He breathed a sigh of relief as he ran his swollen tongue across all his teeth.

He slowly made his way to his desk and sat down. He felt like hell. "Where do you go from here?" he wondered.

As he sorted through the mail on his desk, Shelly peeked around the corner.

"You really do need a doctor; you realize that, don't you? May I at least bring you some ice?"

"Oh, I'll survive, thank you. It's just going to take some time. Maybe a Diet Coke and some Tylenol," he mumbled through his fattened lip. He could only imagine what Keating was going to say.

Shelly returned with the drink and gently set three white capsules on his desk. His eyes thanked her without a word, then darted toward Keating's desk with a questioning look.

"Oh," she said. "I don't know exactly, but he called a while ago." She glanced at her watch. "Asked if you were in yet. He didn't sound happy," she said with an air of nervousness in her voice.

Jason heard someone come through the front door and a muffled conversation before Mary appeared in the doorway behind Shelly.

"Jason, I'm sorry to ask this of you, but we have a bit of an emergency. John was supposed to be back by now to take care of this euthanasia. Is there any chance you would feel up to seeing it? So sorry, and I tried to reach John, but I didn't get an answer on his phone." He knew that Mary wouldn't ask, given his current state, if it weren't truly an emergency.

Taking a sip of the Coke, he nodded. "Yes, I'll be right there. Is it a dog?"

"Well, not exactly.... It's a turkey...." She turned and exited.

Had he heard her correctly? "Did she say someone wants me to put their turkey to sleep?" Shelly nodded. "Well, essentially yes; you see, it's his pet turkey."

"Okay, sure, I'll be there shortly."

Jason had never euthanized a turkey. He had watched his aunt "process" chickens on the farm when he was younger, which had involved wringing their necks. This traumatic episode in his life had been even more traumatic for his fourth-grade teacher during show-and-tell the following week at school. He could still remember Mrs. Carter's face as he explained every intricate detail to the class. She had quickly tried to move on, and it wasn't until he arrived home disappointed and told his mother the details of his day, that he understood why.

When he entered the exam room, he found the turkey resting comfortably on the table. Swenson Parker was an old-school Oklahoma farmer. He had been through it all, the good, the bad, and the really bad over the past 57 years. He had been in the hatchery and turkey-raising business for the past 20 years and his birds were legendary, especially at the holidays. The Governor's mansion had him on speed dial and his birds were second to none. Swenson in his denim bib overalls stood quietly next to the bird as Jason entered. The two had never met, but Jason recognized him from seeing his familiar hatchery truck circa 1948 that he still drove through town.

"Mr. Swenson, it's a pleasure to meet you." Jason tried to smile as he closed the exam room door.

"Nice to meet you too, Doc. This here is Jambalaya; he's been my top Tom for some many years, but Doc, I just can't bring myself to killin' him. I know it's probably a little foolish, but he's almost like a pet to me and I just don't want to see him suffer anymore."

"I understand," replied Jason, knowing how difficult it must be for this old farmer to be so open and honest with his feelings.

"Well, Doc, okay then, whenever you're ready," choked Swenson.

Jason drew up the sodium pentobarbital and paused, wondering what Swenson's intentions were for the bird's remains. Swenson must have anticipated the question, because as Jason turned to ask him, Swenson interjected, "Not to worry, Doc, we ain't going to eat Jambalaya, so whatever you need to do."

Jason turned back and continued drawing up the medication. He decided to administer a few cc's of valium initially to help sedate the bird. He didn't know what to expect, and he figured that the valium would only help everyone involved. He set to work and found a large vein underneath the bird's wing. It had been a while since he'd learned the anatomy of a bird, but in the end, a vein was a vein.

The bird sedated quietly and slowly dropped its head and tucked it underneath its wing, as if in a peaceful sleep.

The sight even made Jason a little emotional; he could feel his chest tighten with sadness. Swenson gave the okay when Jason glanced in his direction, and with that, he administered the pentobarbital. Jambalaya continued on in his sleep as his breathing increasingly slowed. Jason could feel himself holding his breath as the turkey finally fully relaxed and the breathing ended. The room was quiet.

"Thank you, Doc. Damn near the most peaceful thing I ever seen. If all of them could go like that, it'd be a blessed event," Swenson almost whispered in a low, soft voice.

Jason shook Swenson's hand. "Doc, it's none of my business, but I sure hope to hell the other guy looks worse than you do." Jason tried again to smile as they exited the room. Swenson asked if he could take the turkey's remains home and bury them under a large oak in the pasture.

Jason explained that the only requirement was that the hole needed to be at least six feet deep. Swenson nodded, saying, "Not a problem. My son has a backhoe and we can get that deep without any trouble."

Jason quietly and slowly made his way back to his desk, impressed that he'd kept it together through the entire turkey euthanasia. He had barely returned to his chair when Shelly appeared around the corner.

"I didn't know you could euthanize birds like dogs and cats," she asked inquisitively.

Jason looked up at her. "Neither did I."

"What? You mean you haven't ever done that before?"

"That's why they call it 'practice,' Shelly."

"Well, I guess, but I would be so nervous doing something like that for the first time. I mean, what if something went wrong during the middle of it?"

"I don't know, I guess make it up as you go along. My dad used to always say, 'Fake it 'til you make it,' but that's what my day is usually like. Make it up as you go along."

"Well, here's something that isn't fake, or I wish maybe it was; that lady from the Veterinary Services doo-hickey called again today and wants to know when you're moving, in order to finalize the paperwork. She left a number for you. Oh, and there are some folks here to see you." Jason held the piece of paper with the phone number in his hand, marveling at how something so small possessed so much control over his future.

In the waiting room he recognized a mother and daughter from the market fair at the rodeo; the young girl was clinging to a large hand-drawn poster.

"Dr. Davies, we are so sorry to interrupt your day, but Melissa would really like to give this to you. She's been working on it since last week, and it's all she's been talking about," said the young woman.

Jason knelt down beside the girl as she opened the poster toward him, revealing the vibrant colors and drawing of a girl and her lamb.

"I don't know if you remember us, but last week you were so kind to check our lamb in at the fair. We had friends drop us off because we didn't have a trailer, and our shearing job wasn't so good. Some of the kids in

Melissa's 4-H group made fun of her lamb; you were so kind, and you told us that you were happy we were there. Melissa has battled autism since she was diagnosed five years ago, and she doesn't say very much, to anyone. After our visit with you the other day, she has slowly started to become more verbal, and especially with her lamb."

Jason could hear the woman's voice start to quiver. "For this we are so appreciative, and thankful for meeting you the other day. My husband and I truly believe it was a blessing from God; it was meant to be. We are forever in your debt. Thank you." Tears flowed down the woman's face. Melissa handed Jason the poster. He could feel tears within himself starting to well. He turned to Mary and saw tears flowing down her face.

"We hope that you will be our vet in the future," the woman said, as Melissa reached over and hugged Jason. Melissa's mother looked at Jason with surprise.

Jason didn't know what to say. He thanked them and told them goodbye. As he closed the door behind them, he turned to Mary and saw her wiping tears from her eyes. "Don't ever forget these moments; wherever you end up, always remember the good stuff."

Jason felt a pit in his stomach as he heard the clinic's back door slam.

Keating entered, not making eye contact, but his face already told the whole story. He shuffled through a stack of papers, and never raising his glance he began to talk.

"Jason, I know what I've got going here isn't what you

had in mind, and it's become apparent that you have other plans in place, I mean without any discussions with me, but that's what it is I guess. What I'm trying to say is..., What the hell happened to you?" Keating cried, finally taking notice of Jason's face.

"Oh, got into a little disagreement," Jason mumbled through his fat lip.

"A disagreement! I should say, you look like you got the shit kicked out of you.... But this is exactly what I'm talking about with you; the person I hired a few months ago isn't who is standing here now. Somehow I thought...I hoped...you would be different than all these other prima donnas graduating...I guess not...I got to thinking last night and decided that maybe the best thing for you is just to get going on to California," Keating glared stone-faced at him, looking for a response.

Jason, stunned and confused, was at a loss for words. He knew Keating was upset, but hadn't he been agreeable to Jason leaving in due time? Their conversation the day before had contained no talk of leaving so abruptly.

"Oh, well, I thought...." Stumbling with his words, he looked away from Keating's laser glare.

"Yes, well, I got to thinking and realized that today seemed as good as any. No sense in sticking around a place when you've got other places to be and all. I think it'd just be best to clear your things and go. Appreciated the help...." Keating leaned on his tightened fists on the desk.

Keating then shuffled through a few papers and abruptly walked out of the office without another word. Jason wanted to scream. He felt numb; this was the end, and not at all how he'd wanted leave.

He began collecting his personal effects off the desk. Shelly entered and placed a cardboard box in front of him. Before he could form a word of thanks, she turned and disappeared. He reached for his once cherished diploma before realizing that the broken remnants rested in the bottom of the desk drawer. Did he really want to go? Why did everything suddenly seem to be out of his control? He'd put the ball in motion, but now it seemed to be rolling down a hill uncontrollably.

Shelly and Mary stood at the back door with tears in their eyes. Keating hadn't returned, and rightly so. Jason knew Keating's disappointment, and no eloquent parting words would change anything. Tears of his own began to well as he choked with emotion. Mary reached out to hug him, saying, "I'm so sorry to see you go, you'll be missed, but I know there are great things awaiting you in California."

He couldn't speak at first, and then only a whisper. "I'm sorry." He turned as Shelly grabbed him. He could feel her tears on his shoulder.

"Good luck, Dr. Davies; we're going to miss you."

He wiped his eyes and scanned the parking lot for his truck. "What the hell...." His truck was still somewhere in the middle of nowhere. How the hell would he ever remember where he had left it? Humbled and embarrassed, he couldn't even make an honorable departure.

Chapter 42

Jason looked at the boxes containing his belongings and wondered how he would carry it all back to his apartment. Setting the boxes under the eave of the building, he decided he had no other option than to go find someone to tow his truck. He remembered the auto shop off the square. They'd fixed his truck once; maybe they would have a tow truck. The rain had let up, at least for now, and he started down the sidewalk, making his way toward the square.

He walked past a tiny white cinderblock building; he'd driven by The Elbow Room countless times, never mustering enough courage to venture inside until now. He looked at his watch; was it too early to have a drink? "3:30 P.M., close enough." The dark, smoke-filled room was a far reach from the flashy, colorful college bars of Fort Collins, Colorado. This wasn't a place to be seen by others socially, but a place to disappear from your troubles or even yourself.

He sat on a stool at the far end of the bar. He waived to the bartender and then in the direction of the draft on tap. Without a word the bartender slid a tall, icy mug in front of him. It was cold and refreshing across his lips, and within minutes he waved the bartender for another.

He felt a hand on his shoulder. "Mind if I have a sit with you?"

Jason turned with a look of surprise, suddenly connecting the voice with the face of Ed Guffey.

"Oh, sure, have a seat. Didn't expect to find anyone I knew in here." Jason glanced around nervously, wondering who else recognized him in here.

"Well, you keep forgetting this is Birdie. Everybody knows everybody, even the folks you'd like to forget you know."

Ed took a seat next to Jason and sat quietly drinking his beer. "Heard you was leaving us."

Jason smirked. It had only been a couple of days, and the word had spread like a range fire. "Well, I guess that's right."

"Don't sound so convinced."

"I guess I don't know that I am."

Ed took another sip of his beer, staring down at the condensation on his glass. "City folk are so confusing."

"What do you mean?" Jason turned with a look of surprise.

"It seems to me that if a guy wants to stay, then he stays. If he ought not want to stay, then best if he just gets on down the road, simple as that. But it sounds like it's more than just staying or leaving."

Jason could feel the effects of the beer taking hold. "I suppose. It just seems so complicated sometimes, being pulled in different directions, I don't know...." Wanting desperately to change the subject, he turned to Guffey. "Hey, what's the story with that old Johnson house?"

Guffey's face immediately took a somber tone as he stared again at his drink. "What is it you want to know?"

"Why does everything look like someone left in a hurry from that place?"

Guffey took a long sip of his drink before slowly setting it back down on the bar. "Because they did, or I guess they were forced to...."

"What do you mean?"

"We don't have too much trouble around these parts, but that particular incident was kind of a strange one. I don't know how much I really know, or how much I'm supposed to know, but either way it didn't turn out so good. Supposedly, this fella had been a high-ranking scientist in the Soviet Union. He and his family were able to escape after World War II, and the U.S. found them this place to hide out. In the end, they disappeared in the middle of the night."

"What do you mean? The whole family just disappeared?"

"Well, I was a teenager at the time, but my folks and a bunch of others went looking for them, but no trace of them, as if they disappeared into thin air, weirdest thing. That was, until about 10 years ago. Some folks out east of Summersville, which is about 40 miles south of here, had an old house tore down. There's a small creek out behind the place and when the excavator came in to move the house off, they unearthed some shallow graves. It was the scientist, wife, and a couple of kids as much as they could figure. Some U.S. Marshals and FBI agents showed up in big fancy trucks and took a bunch of samples, and what was left of the bodies. I see a government-lookin' kind of truck drive in to the house every so often, but nothing else; I imagine it will just sit there forever."

Jason sat staring at his drink in wonder. What did this poor guy know that cost him and his family his life? He could only imagine the terror they must have experienced that night sitting down to dinner, table set and glasses filled, all in an instant turned upside down. He thought of the young girl's room where he had fallen asleep. She must have been so scared that night; the thought sent chills down Jason's spine. He thought of his own family and missed his parents. This poor family had struggled through so much, and then to meet their fate on a dark night; it was almost impossible to imagine. Jason felt guilty for even thinking his own family struggles could come close to what they must have endured.

Guffey finished the remaining drops of his now empty beer. "Well, suppose I best be moseying on. Pleasure talking with ya Doc, and hope it all makes sense in the end to ya." They shook hands and Guffey placed a hand on the back of Jason's head. "Remember, listen to what's in here...and here too." Guffey placed his hand on Jason's chest. "Don't worry; you'll make the right decision in the end."

Guffey turned and started for the door when Jason remembered his truck. "Ed!" Jason jumped up and ran toward the door. "I need a favor. I wondered if you would give me a lift? Oh, and you don't happen to have a set of jumper cables?"

Jason gave Guffey a brief description of what he remembered about his truck's location. Guffey smiled and motioned for Jason to come with him. They headed down the road in silence, arriving at the truck a short time later.

Guffey set to work attaching the cables. Jason jumped into his truck and when Guffey gave the signal, he turned the key and hoped for a miracle. "Whirrrr, whirrrr.... Vroom!" Jason couldn't believe the music to his ears as the old truck rattled to life. Guffey disconnected the cables and closed the hoods of both trucks. As Jason shook Guffey's hand, he asked, "How can you be so sure, I mean, what you said earlier about making the right decision. How can you be so sure?"

Guffey smiled with a wink of his eye. "You haven't messed up so far.... Your life is a journey; there are no wrong decisions. Each twist and turn on your road is there for a reason." Guffey patted Jason on the shoulder before climbing into his truck and driving away.

Chapter 43

Jason made his way back to town. His head throbbed and his lip felt like it needed its own zip code. As he pulled into his driveway, he remembered the abandoned boxes still at the clinic, but he decided to grab them later when no one would be there. He collapsed on the bed and hoped that by some miracle this wasn't all happening. He was exhausted, but after a few minutes of trying to rest he accepted the inevitable task of packing before him.

He took a shower and found some clean clothes. He sat on the edge of the bed wondering what Catherine was doing. He twirled his phone in the palm of his hand, waffling on whether or not to try and call her. He finally dialed her number. It rang several times before he heard her voice mail message. He wanted to hang up, but maybe this would be his last chance, his only chance. "Catherine, it's Jason. I'm so sorry for how things ended up the other night, and I'd really like a chance to explain things, or at least apologize. I've sincerely appreciated my time with you, and I don't want it to end.... It just seems.... It just seems like the world is telling me that it isn't supposed to be how I hoped, or at least how I thought it should be.... I'm sorry. Take care, goodbye...." He slowly hung up the phone and dropped back on the bed. Tears rolling down his face stung the cuts, but the physical pain was no match for how much he hurt.

He pulled out his suitcase and began packing. He needed to tell Pauline he would be vacating the barn, but her car wasn't in the driveway. Come to think of it, he hadn't seen Boo around, either; he hoped there wasn't anything wrong, but what did he care if there was? Soon he would be in sunny California where all the promises of a new start would come true.

Jason stacked the few packed boxes of his possessions by the door, taking note of what else he needed for his trip. He should have the truck looked at before attempting a cross-country journey, but it started without incident moments later when he checked. He hoped it would make it just long enough for him to get to California, where he would abandon the old clunker in the California desert.

Just then his phone rang. He stumbled over boxes as he reached for it on the bed. "Catherine?"

"...I guess I have my answer...Goodbye, you asshole!" Becca's voiced snarled.

"Becca! Wait!"

"For what, so I can make an even bigger fool of myself? I called because I needed to know! I needed to know if you still love me, but I guess I already know the answer." She began to cry.

"Becca, I'm sorry, it's just...."

"What? It's just what? Spit it out! I have wasted so much of my damn life waiting, hoping that we'd be together, that it would all be worth it someday, and now this. OHHH! I am such a fool!"

"I'm sorry...I...."

"You're SORRY? That's the best you can do? After everything we've been through all these years? We've grown up together; we've done so much. We were a great team.... And you're sorry; well, so am I. I'm sorry that we didn't break up before now and I could have moved on with my life. I'm sorry that while everyone else I know is out enjoying their lives, starting a family, and building a house, I'm stuck driving around in a rental car going to some two-bit hick rodeo in some God-forsaken hole of a town!"

"Becca...."

"No, it's too late, you've made your decision; you'll regret the choice you've made. Someday you'll think of me and wish I gave even a thought about you, but when you do, know I'm smiling that you're gone, forever. So run off with that hillbilly whore and have a nice life."

"Becca, wait!"

The line went dead. He raised the phone, ready to throw it, but then paused. It was his only lifeline and he would need it for the trip. He went to the fridge and found a lonely can of Coors Light that someone had given him on a call one night. He also found a package of Ramen noodles in a drawer and made his last meal in the apartment. He turned on the television and pushed Play. The familiar appearance of Chevy Chase as "Fletch" was mildly comforting when he felt so alone. He wanted so badly to call Catherine again, but he thought better of it.

He wasn't hungry and stirred the noodles in the bowl for a while before finally dumping the food in the trash. He would leave first thing in the morning, and now all he had to do was convince himself to sleep. He slammed the beer, turned off the lights, and climbed into bed with his clothes still on.

Chapter 44

The clouds were building once again and the sky was filled with gray-black masses of swirling threat. Jason looked out the apartment window as he lay in bed. His face burned and his throat was dry and scratchy.

"Why can't I get a break with this rain?" he sighed.

The exhaustion of what was ahead of him took hold. He stayed in bed, listening to the wind blast against the barn; almost simultaneously, the rain began to fall in erratic and heavy drops.

He raced into the kitchen, grabbing pots from underneath the sink, anticipating the leaky metal roof as the sky unleashed its wrath. He paused, wondering what good it was going to do at this point. The storm was only going to get worse, and he needed to hurry if he had any hope of getting out of there today.

He dashed into the pouring rain, trying desperately to load and protect what few earthly possessions he owned. He pulled a tarp from under the seat and began covering everything in the bed of the truck. The wind blew the tarp in all directions, further adding to the madness of his day. "I can't catch a break for shit sometimes!" he cursed to the fury of rain settling down on top of him. The tarp slapping the side of the truck suddenly stopped as Boo Radley's hands grasped the end. Without a word, Boo set to work tethering a free end. Jason, stunned, followed suit and strapped the other free end. Once the tarp was in place, Jason looked up at Boo, who slowly put out a hand. "Thank you," Jason said, shaking Boo's hand. Boo stared past Jason momentarily, then turned and made his way back to the house. Getting soaked in the rain, Jason stood in awe as he felt the sadness fill his chest. "Take care," he whispered to the rain.

Drenched from head to toe, he went back into the apartment and checked the refrigerator one last time, then stood frozen. The place was a dump, but it had become home, more so than anywhere else. He closed the door behind him as he left. He scrambled across the driveway to Pauline's house to say goodbye, but again saw no sign of her car. He turned and scurried to the truck.

The wipers struggled to keep up as he made his way one last time through the deserted streets of Birdie. This was all wrong; this wasn't how it was supposed to go. But most stories never ended well, anyway; did he really expect a special town sendoff, with folks lining the streets waving goodbye?

Would he ever talk to Catherine again? Did he really care? Hours from now he would be long gone and all of this would be a bad, and hopefully distant, memory. The rain continued to hammer the truck as the pebbling sound of hail hitting the truck's roof furthered the frenzy of his already increasing anxiety. Screw it; all the more reason to buy a convertible sports car when it he made to California.

He slowed the truck and stopped at the intersection

leading to Highway 26. Should he pull over and wait it out? He could barely see beyond the hood of the truck, but what if someone came up on him from behind? Driving seemed dangerous, but so did just sitting there. He slowly pulled out onto the road, realizing that his best option would be to keep moving forward. His white knuckles gripped the steering wheel and he prayed that whatever lay ahead, he would see it in time to stop. Sudden flashing lights sent a jolt of panic through his veins; he slowed the truck, pulling alongside a drenched police officer. He recognized the sheriff's deputy from the rodeo, and the young man's shaken expression spoke volumes about what lay ahead.

"Doc! It's you! We've been trying to track you down! What the hell happened to you?" The man stared at Jason's bruised and battered face.

"It's a long story...," Jason replied, touching a hand to his cheek.

"Doc, it's a mess out here."

"Why? Wha...What's happened?"

"A semi-trailer leaving the auction carrying a full load of cattle overturned on the highway up there about a quarter mile; cows are everywhere out here on the road. Most of them are injured, and a lot of them are still wedged up in the front of the trailer. The highway patrol is here; Doc, they need you desperate up there."

Jason felt all the blood in his body settle to his feet as he slowly drove toward more flashing lights. Arriving at the overturned truck, he wasn't prepared for what he saw. The truck had rolled on its side in the median and cattle were scattered all over the road, many with multiple lacerations, broken legs, and struggling to move. As it started to hail, passing motorists who had stopped to help quickly ran to their vehicles in search of shelter.

Highway patrol officers approached as he arrived. "This is the biggest damn mess I have ever seen. What the hell do we do with these cows? Two of my officers have attempted to penetrate the trailer, but there is a mess of those animals pushed up in the front. They are literally stuck inside. We have a crew headed down from Wilco with an extraction saw to cut the lid off, but it's too damn dangerous to go in there at this point."

Jason's mind reeled. "Okay, so we need to take some fences down over here to herd the ones that can move into one of these pastures and off the road. Do any of your officers have experience euthanizing cattle with a gun?"

"Doc, you're in the heart of deer country. These boys were raised hunting, so that won't be a problem. We just want to know which ones need to be shot, so we need your advice there. Then we need to know what to do with the ones in the truck."

"Anything with visible fractures or that can't move, shoot." Jason's confident, authoritative reply surprised even himself. "Anything that's able to walk, have your officers herd them into the pasture and we can look at them later...I'm going into the trailer to see what I can do."

"Doc, we can't let you in there; it's too dangerous." The officer stepped between Jason and his view of the trailer.

Jason hesitated. He was never one to argue with a police officer. But then he heard the cries of the cattle. Jason felt a pang of horror; what were those poor creatures enduring in that mangled metal box?

"Officer, with all due respect, I don't have a choice. Those animals are suffering; I have to go in there."

The officer paused, then stepped aside. "I want an officer to follow you from outside, and if you run into trouble, at least we'll know where you are, and we can figure out how to get you out of there."

Jason ran back to his truck, looking for any supplies that might prove useful. He reached under the seat to find a headlamp; he'd camped with Becca the previous spring and purchased it to walk in the woods at night. He hoped the batteries were still good. He quickly scanned the interior of the truck, and sitting in the cup holder was the pocket knife his father had sent him last Christmas; he didn't know how useful it would be in this situation, but knives were always handy for something.

The hail had ended, but the rain continued, intent on turning the day into a complete muddied disaster. Jason ran toward the back door of the trailer and climbed into the black hole. The stifling humid heat of wet, crowded, stressed cattle made it difficult to breathe as he made his first few steps. Trying to gain his footing, he slipped, falling on the hard metal. He squelched a cry of pain from the bruised ribs, not wanting to alert the officer outside. Regaining his footing, he crept forward. The sounds of bawling cows reverberated off the metal walls. The cattle were littered throughout, many down and not moving. He saw the dark black mass furthest forward. The force of the crash had propelled most of the cattle forward on impact. They were piled on top of each other in a crushing, smothering hell.

"What in God's name am I going to do with this?" he said to himself.

"Doc, you okay in there?" said a voice from outside the trailer.

"Yes, I'm fine. It's just an awful mess."

"Doc, you be careful in there. The sergeant says to do what you need to do, but don't get yourself hurt."

The moaning of pained cows was almost unbearable and Jason felt a wave of nausea. So packed were the creatures that Jason struggled to find their heads as they kicked and struggled for freedom. Standing there, he felt helpless, longing for Keating's wisdom and confidence in a crisis. But there were only his frantic thoughts. He needed to make a decision. Reaching into his pocket, he removed the knife. Rolling it in the palm of his hand, he slowly unfolded the blade.

He slipped on a pair of latex gloves from his jacket pocket and began making his way toward the wall of cattle. Gently reaching into the first cow's rectum, he paused, hoping he was making the right decision. With a solid, swift cut, he severed the artery and bright red blood poured from the rectum. Moments later the strained and stressed muscles gently, quietly relaxed; it was done.

The second one went quietly as well; the third, and so on. As he cautiously made his way to the second level of the trailer, he heard a shout from the sergeant. "Doc, watch yourself now, that top part of the trailer is the weakest and I sure as hell don't need you hurt!" He crawled along the slick metal ramp and wasn't prepared for what he saw on the top level. Many of the cows were dismembered and torn in two, watching him helplessly. Several animals' legs had punched through the trailer's wall, leaving the animals to bleed to death while others suffocated under the weight of those piled on top of them. The feces- and blood-drenched floor caused Jason to lose his footing and he crashed into a pile of bloody carnage. He cursed, wiping his mouth with a small patch of shoulder sleeve that remained clean.

After what seemed like hours, the trailer finally grew quiet. Jason, bloody and exhausted, held back tears at what he'd done. He'd made the right decision, hadn't he? These poor beasts were no longer suffering, but he couldn't help feeling like he'd failed. He remembered one of Keating's comments early on: "Jason, you always work for the animal first; do what's right for the animal, and you'll always make the right decision." The putrid smell of feces and blood made his stomach turn. Suddenly the trailer shifted, metal groaning as the floor below him fell away.

"Dr. Davies! Dr. Davies!" Jason lay at the bottom of the trailer; his body was motionless, in a bed of twisted metal and blood. Moments later, Jason could hear shouting voices and attempted to move, but the burning pain of his leg made him cry out.

"Dr. Davies? Dr. Davies?"

"Yes, I'm here, but I think my leg is broken."

"Dr. Davies, don't move, we're sending some men in after you," the sergeant commanded.

"No, it's too dangerous; the floor isn't stable and broke loose. I'm going to make my way to the back, but don't let anyone else in here." He looked around for something to help pull himself to his feet. He grabbed a tail and pulled himself up. He felt a rush of adrenaline pulsing through him and suppressed the nausea percolating in his stomach. He stood up, but his leg crumpled beneath him, and the excruciating pain made him turn and vomit. Wiping his mouth, he groaned and began crawling over the animals toward the back of the trailer.

"Dr. Davies? You still with us?" yelled the sergeant. "Dr. Davies?"

"Yes, still here." He winced with each movement forward.

When he finally arrived at the opening of the trailer, his eyes struggled to adjust to the light. The rush of cool rain felt good against his face as he took a deep breath of fresh air. The rain continued to fall steadily, with a renewed commitment of washing everything in the county away. A group of bystanders had gathered and were staring at him, but a quick glance at his blood-soaked clothing answered their questioning looks. Jason collapsed to the ground in pain as the sergeant waved paramedics forward. They set to work assessing the extent of Jason's injuries, moving him to a gurney and placing blankets over his injured and broken body.

He was having difficulty breathing, and the paramedics quickly responded with an oxygen mask. He had severe bruising, as well as several possibly fractured ribs.

Jason frantically scanned the crowd, looking for any sign of Keating; then he saw the familiar truck. Keating jumped out, running toward the scene and pushing bystanders out of the way. Keating placed a hand on Jason's blanketed body. "You okay, son?"

Jason nodded, waiting for the verbal barrage of anger that he feared would follow.

One of the paramedics pushed forward. "We need to transport him to town, and it looks like he may have fractured his tibia."

Anger grew across Keating's face. "Well, what the hell are you boys waiting for? Get him in there!"

Keating patted Jason on the shoulder. "About the dumbest thing I've ever heard of someone doing, and now you've wrecked your plans; I sure as hell don't know what possessed you to go play hero today."

Before Jason could reply, the paramedics carried him across to the ambulance. He struggled to raise himself on the gurney. "Doc, I need to tell you something! Doc!"

Keating waved and yelled, "Get to the hospital and get that leg looked at!"

The ride to the hospital was lonely and humiliating. He'd tried to do something good; now he was injured, embarrassed, and alone.

The doctors at Birdie Community Hospital confirmed what the paramedics had suspected, a fracture of the right tibia. They also confirmed three broken ribs and a partially collapsed lung. Jason would survive, but a few days in the hospital would be his reality, and a cast would slow him down for at least six to eight weeks.

A couple of hours later, as Jason sat his hospital bed flipping through channels, the door opened. It was Keating. He was drenched and bloody, as if he had driven straight from the accident site.

Keating removed his hat and stood near the foot of the bed. "How you feeling?"

"Good; apparently I fractured my tibia, but with the cast I should be back on track in a bit." Jason scanned Keating's face, attempting to read his thoughts and preparing himself for a round of brow-beating.

"Well, that was probably one of the worst things I've

ever seen. They finally cut the top off that trailer and I don't think anyone could have imagined the disaster inside." Keating paused and turned toward the window. "You did something pretty amazing, and you relieved a lot of suffering."

Keating stood quietly, still looking out into the dark rain. "I hope you find what you're looking for out there, I really do. This job is tough no matter where you end up, but you did something pretty heroic today and I know the whole town appreciates what you've done." He turned and extended his hand. "Good luck to you in California."

Jason slowly extended his hand as emotion welled inside him. "Dr. Keating, I...I want to stay...I need to stay."

Keating appeared confused, not sure if he had heard Jason correctly. "No...No, you need to go. This is the best decision and it's what's best for you."

Jason looked down, shaking his head. "No, sir, this is where I need to be; this is where I want to be." His defiance gave him strength as he continued. "For once in my life I'm making a decision that is best for me, no one else; this is where I need to be."

Keating stared intently at Jason, his face taut in deep deliberation. "Jason, I don't think you know what the hell you want! You keep changing your damn mind every which way the wind blows; I'm sure as hell too damn old to be jerked around anymore than I already have been!" Keating's face twisted with frustration. "I know the right thing to say is 'Of course, stay,' but I was your age once, and the minute something doesn't work out with all these girls running around here, or something else, then you're gone again...."

"Dr. Keating, again, with all due respect, I've worked my ass off for you...I know I've made some mistakes. I hope you might consider giving me a second chance."

Keating turned back to the window, motionless for what seemed like an eternity.

Slowly he placed his hat back on his head and walked to the door. He stopped and turned. "Okay." With that, he was gone.

Jason watched the door close in disbelief; that was it? No warning, no threats? Keating had never been at a loss for words, but tonight his demeanor had changed. Jason watched the door a moment longer, half expecting Keating might return. He lay back on the bed and closed his eyes. He should feel exalted, but instead all he felt was pain and exhaustion. He had convinced Keating to let him to stay, and yet he felt so alone, no one to share the news with.

His nurse arrived, checking the monitors next to his bed. "Dr. Davies, on a scale of 1 to 10, what would you say your pain level is right now?"

"I guess somewhere around a 7." He looked down at his leg and wondered how it would ever be right again.

She handed him a small cup with two oval pills. "These will help your pain and let you sleep."

He took the medication and watched the nurse check the machines before she left him alone once again in the stillness of the sterile hospital room. He turned down the light near his bed and stared out the window into the dark, wet night. Why did he always feel so alone? Did anyone other than Keating even know he was here? He should call his parents, but why? They were thousands of miles away; his father would be off in some remote location working, and although his mother would be concerned, she surely wouldn't drop everything and come to his rescue. His head started to spit and sputter as he felt the medication take hold.

Chapter 45

The room was quiet when Jason opened his eyes. The morning sunlight had broken through the rain's hold. He looked around the room, hoping it had all been a bad dream. Then he looked down at the cast on his leg and reality waved its Welcome flag. He breathed a deep sigh, wondering what he would do lying in this bed all day; it hadn't even been twenty-four hours yet and his skin was crawling. The nurse brought in a colorless tray of eggs and fruit; he nodded and attempted a smile.

He stirred the small congealed yellow mash of eggs on his plate, lost in thought. "I wonder when I'm going to get the hell out of here...."

Just then the door flew open with a blast. "Weeeelllll hellllooo there!" Cody stormed into the room. "Well sir, yes sir, it's truly a blessing that you are okay after your ordeal and all, yes sir it is," said Cody in his characteristic drawl.

"How did you know I was here?"

Cody smirked with a wink. "Yes sir, not many who don't at this point; this is Birdie, after all."

Jason smiled and nodded, realizing the foolishness of his question.

Cody glanced at Jason's leg. "Mercy, quite a mess. I heard about last night out there, and you saving the day, yes sir. The town's sure blessed to have you caring for it, and I sure hope my friend Keating sees that too!" Cody's boots echoed on the tile floor as he paced in front of the bed.

"Sir, there's a chair over there if you'd like to sit for a bit."

"Yes, sir, why don't I just do that, have a seat for a minute or two as I say hello." Cody wrestled the chair from the corner and dragged it alongside the bed.

"Yes sir, quite a little scrape here for you and your plans for California. Not to worry, though; California will still be there when you're healed...."

Jason wondered how Cody knew of his California plans. Then he remembered, this was Birdie....

Cody winked with a smile. "Ohhh, I think California is a fine idea, really do, really do.... This little town isn't the right fit for everyone; it's best you follow your dream. No hard feelings and such, but just the way the world works. The biggest thing is to keep moving, and don't ever stop moving."

Cody's voice drifted off as he stared out the window into the sunny blue sky; he paused, lost in thought. "When I lost my wife it broke my heart. Alone with a little daughter, I was lost and felt maybe like you do right now. Those feelings will eat you up if you let them, and truth is they almost did me; if it hadn't been for my Cindy Lou, well, I'd be dead."

Cody stared down at his hands. "That little girl is all grown up now and figuring out her own world these days.

Oh, I've tried getting her to move back to Birdie, but it's not the right fit for her either, and she needs to follow her dreams. No parent wants to be getting in the way of their children's dreams, no sir, no sir." Cody turned and looked at Jason's questioning face. "I'm sorry, I'd hoped the two of you would hit it off, I really wanted you to, that's for sure. After the rodeo I guess she headed back to Tulsa to try and mend fences; I really don't know...."

Cody's words sent a jolt of pain up Jason's leg, landing in his chest. He glanced down at the cold eggs sitting on the table, his stomach tossing and turning in misery. Surely it couldn't be true. "When...When did you speak with her last?"

"She called me up after the rodeo and tried to explain all this finagling to me, but the truth is I surely didn't want to hear it. No, never much cared for that fella, no sir, but I guess if that's what she needs to do, then I will support her decision. Oh, I'm sorry, but now you leaving for California won't be conflicted, I mean any more than it already is...."

"Cody, I'm staying," Jason said, trying to get a word in between Cody's breaths. Cody's voice froze, his face puzzled by Jason's statement.

"Well sir, this is most unexpected, delightfully unexpected!" A smile grew across his face as he jumped out of his chair. "Why, may I ask, the sudden change of heart and fortune for this little community of ours, if I may be so bold as to inquire?"

"I need to be here. I need this town." Jason looked

down at his hands as he continued. "The truth is, I hoped things might work out better with Catherine, but I realized this is even bigger than that. I need to stay for me."

Cody looked down as he toyed with his hat in his hands. "I understand, son, I know that feeling and it's a feeling that I am grateful you listened to. Not everyone does, but making a difficult decision like this takes a special person to realize what's important to them, to you, I mean. Proud of you." He patted Jason's arm with his hat. "Yes sir, I should be going now, but sure am glad we talked. I look forward to seeing you soon."

Jason leaned back on the pillow but his head and heart writhed in pain. Would he really be able to make a life for himself in Birdie without Catherine? He was a big talker, but did he really believe it himself? "Fake it 'til you make it...," Jason whispered.

"Dr. Davies? I need to check your blood pressure, will that be okay?" The nurse entered quietly, immediately noticing Jason's sadness.

"Yes, that would be fine, thank you." Jason tried to covertly wipe the tears from his face.

"On a scale of 1 to 10, what is your pain right now?"

His leg felt better than it had the night before, but as he looked into the nurse's eyes he visualized the number: 12.

Chapter 46

Thursday came and went with countless hours of television. Time seemed to crawl with each lonely hour that passed. Jason thought, hoped, a visitor or two might stop in and see him, but the day passed quietly with no sign of Keating, or anyone for that matter. He had second thoughts about his passionate stand the day before. His convictions had seemed more powerful on Tuesday night than they felt at this moment. He would be released tomorrow, but he was unsure who would help him. He was fairly useless to himself and a burden to anyone else who might offer to break him out of this joint; but no one seemed interested in claiming the young, broken veterinarian.

Late in the afternoon the hospital floor had grown quiet. There was a knock on the door. Jason turned, waiting for Keating to enter, but he couldn't believe his eyes.

"Well, hey there, stranger." Catherine shyly stood at the door. "Aren't you going to invite a girl in?"

Jason smiled and Catherine moved toward him, throwing her arms around him and gently kissing his cheek.

"What? How did you...?" he stuttered.

"Daddy called. I wanted to get here sooner, but I

needed to transfer my court case. Kenny picked me up and flew me back." She smiled nervously. "What are you staring at?"

"How have you been?" he asked, almost whispering.

"Oh, please, you know, miserable; downright miserable. I haven't stopped thinking about you."

"You're all I think about too...I'm so sorry...."

She gently put her hand on his mouth. "Not now. We'll talk later when we're back at the ranch."

"Wait, what? What do you mean?"

"Well, your mother is such a sweetie...."

"You talked with my mother?"

"So, it turns out there's this new-fangled thing called a telephone, and I called your folks with it. Apparently you've never invited them out to Birdie before, and after hearing about your accident, I decided to give them a little ring. Kenny is picking them up at the airport as we speak...."

"Seriously?"

"Your mother and I have a plan. It's a great plan, and it involves you saying goodbye to that apartment in the barn. I mean, let's face it, that barn isn't the place for you, especially in your current state. Trust me, if you were my client, I would have to strongly advise you against staying in that infested hole. It's my turn to take care of you; don't you remember how well you cared for me with my broken hand?" She bent down and gently kissed his cheek.

"The way I see it, you need care. You need lots of it,

but first we need to talk. I want you stay at the big house with Daddy and me."

He turned with a look of objection, but Catherine continued. "Look, I know we have things to sort out, a lot of things to sort out, but right now I'm a woman who wants to take care of you, so don't mess with me."

"I need to tell you something. About leaving the barn...I...."

Catherine once again put her finger to his lips and nodded. "I know."

"But...How?" He looked at her questioningly.

She smiled. "Haven't you figured out by now, between my father and this town, nothing happens without everyone knowing everything?"

The nurse entered and held the door open. Jason couldn't believe his eyes. "Mom...Dad?"

His mother hugged him. "We're sorry to hear what happened; your father and I are just sick that we haven't made it out for a visit until now, and under these circumstances."

"I...I just can't believe that you're here." A flash of graduation day scrambled his brain; how he'd so longed for them to surprise him then.

His mother held court for the next couple of hours, with unending stories of his childhood adventures and the antics of his nieces and nephews. Catherine whispered in his ear, "You're an uncle?"

The time flew by before his mother finally came up for

air, having temporarily exhausted all of her stories.

"Well, we should let you rest, and your father needs to make some calls. We'll be back in the morning."

His otherwise quiet father placed a hand on Jason's shoulder. "Rest up, son; see you in the morning."

After they left, Catherine sat down on the bed and gently took Jason's hand. "Well, it looks like it's just you and me. First off, I want to apologize for how I left things. It truly wasn't my intention to just disappear, without any explanation."

"I tried to call you...."

"I know. I'm sorry...."

"I so badly wanted you to call."

"I'm sorry, it's just that after that whole mess at the rodeo it made me think that you needed to figure things out, and I was only complicating things; I mean, aside from the fact that Mark decided to show up out of the blue that night, too. It was all like the perfect storm...I should have ended it with him before he basically moved to Europe, but I didn't want to give up on it at that point. I still had this idealistic piece of me that wanted to persevere and right the listing ship." She paused and stared out the window. "He came back here after he heard about me breaking my hand, mostly because Daddy made him feel guilty, and he's pretty keen on Daddy's money, so he hustled back to tell me how much he wanted to work things out. But the truth is, there was nothing left to work out, and it was just a matter of being done with it, or so I thought. Mark has never played fair in his life; I guess that's why he's a great attorney."

"So where does that leave us?" Jason took her hand.

"I'm not sure. My life needs to get untangled, and so does yours it sounds like; I guess I never asked how things are with Becca, that's her name, right? I mean, is she interested in coming here, or...?"

"No, nothing good came out of her visit, and if anything it clinched the fact that our relationship is permanently derailed."

"I'm sorry," Catherine replied, pulling her hand away and standing up. "I truly never meant to complicate your world...."

"You didn't.... This, I mean with Becca, has been a long-brewing mess for too many years. It seemed easier to stay in the dysfunction because it was comfortable, but you made me realize, and this town has made me realize, what I want, and no longer am I living someone else's dream."

She laughed. "You mean your dream is to live in Birdie?"

He smiled. "For now, yes, and maybe forever. But even recently when I realized I might never see you again, Birdie still felt like home to me, and that was enough to try and convince Dr. Keating to let me stay on at the clinic."

Catherine smiled and again sat down next to him on the bed. Her expression changed as she became more serious. "Here's how I think we need to work this. We need to take our time. I'm crazy about you, but I'm also still a married, soon-to-be-divorced, woman. You need time to grieve the loss of the last how many years of your life with Becca, and that's okay. We aren't going anywhere, especially after you swore to Keating about wanting to stay.... The way I see it, you're sticking to this town for damn near ever."

"So where do we go from here?" He picked at the edge of his cast.

"Well...good question; I guess one day at a time." She bent down and kissed him.

Chapter 47

The following morning, Catherine wheeled Jason out of Birdie Community Hospital. The warm sun blinded his senses but it felt great to be outside.

When they arrived at the main house on the ranch, Jason struggled to make his way up the walkway with his newly commissioned crutches. "Hurry up, slow poke." Catherine opened the front door, waiting for him. The smell of food sparked Jason's waning appetite; he'd been unaware until now just how hungry he actually was after suffering through hospital fare. As they entered, Jason recognized his pathetic belongings neatly stacked by the doorway. Most of it appeared undamaged from the rain; he smiled, remembering Boo's help with the tarp.

"That is the sorriest lookin' lot of stuff I have ever seen," Catherine laughed, motioning Jason to follow her down the wide, long hallway. The serpentine hallway turned this way and that in a snake-like fashion. On the walls as they passed were large oil paintings beautifully displayed in antique-looking frames. "These all must be originals," he thought. The hallway branched out into other smaller hallways leading to various parts of the house. The end of the main hallway opened into a small living area with two small leather couches centered around a large stone fireplace. Catherine opened the farthest door into a large bedroom.

"This will be your new home-away-from whatever you were living in over at Pauline's.... I'll show you where the fresh towels are, and then let you settle in." Jason started to express his concern about intruding into Cody's home, but Catherine quickly raised her hand and continued with her instructions.

"Now, I'm pretty sure the doctor would be very impressed if you actually took it easy for a while, so I'll get in touch with the physical therapist and see what we can and can't do for the foreseeable future."

Jason turned with a questioning glance. "What do you mean, we?"

"Well, I guess I failed to mention that part. I've recently become unemployed, and I'm considering setting out my shingle here in Birdie." She winked and a large smile spread across her face.

"But I don't understand?"

"When Mark and I finalize everything, our joint assets will be divided. I told him I would sell him my portion of the firm. I'm keeping the apartment, at least for now, but I decided it was time to be back here."

"Kinda like in the movies, where the city girl comes back to her roots?" Jason smiled while trying to sit down onto the couch.

"<u>Kinda</u> like." She threw a pillow in his direction.

"Now, doctor's orders, I need you in bed, napping for a bit, and I'll make some calls for you." She shuttled him to his room, gave him a kiss, and told him to get some rest.

He lay down on the bed, sinking into the soft, pillowy down of a feather comforter. He had never slept on a bed this soft. He looked up at the ceiling. There was no water dripping from the light. No smell of bull feces or the kicking of a horse on the other side of the wall. He wouldn't miss the Jasper surprises in his room, but he would miss the little donkey that had saved him more than once in recent weeks. Yes, he would miss his hole in the barn...well...maybe just for a little while....

Epilogue

"Okay, thank you. I'm stopping for a second at Cody's ranch and will be back for my 1:30 appointment at the clinic; thank you, Mary." Jason hung up the phone and climbed out of the truck. The sound of power saws and hammering filled the air.

"Jason, over here!" shouted a man's voice above the roar of a massive crane. Jason turned and made his way past a cement truck as men hurriedly poured a large patio and sidewalk.

"Dad, this is looking great." Jason smiled, looking at the work taking place before him. Jason's father stepped down from the crane's ladder.

"Yes, it's coming together a little faster than I had scheduled for this week, but the weather this spring has been mild enough to let all this concrete come in earlier than expected."

"This thing is going to be huge!" Jason stared in amazement at the size of the massive log timbers being set into place.

"I think it's coming together like you all thought it would; Cody was just down here and seemed pleased. If this weather and schedule continue then there's no reason why you won't be open by your deadline this summer."

"Dad, I can't thank you enough for taking this project on, especially with such short notice." They both turned and walked toward the construction trailer parked near the saloon.

"Well, Cody is a hard man to say no to, and your mother is enjoying spending time with Catherine."

"Speaking of Catherine, have you seen her today?" Jason asked, looking around.

"She stopped by earlier when Cody was here, but she said she had court this afternoon in Birdie."

"Okay, keep up the good work; I need to head back to work, but are we all still on for dinner later?"

"I guess so, but your mother runs that part of my world; I'm sure that's still the plan." Jason's father climbed the steps toward the trailer. "See you later."

Jason waved goodbye and hustled back to the vet truck. He didn't want to be late, especially if Keating was there. His hour lunches recently with Catherine were taxing Keating's patience....

The afternoon raced by as Jason, with Shelly at his side, made quick work of two colt castrations and a round of puppy litter vaccinations. Driving back to the ranch, his mind wandered to thoughts of how much had transpired in the previous months following his injuries and the horrible cattle trailer incident.

His physical wounds had healed with the help of steady therapy and Catherine's encouragement. The emotional wounds from Becca had stopped bleeding, although he was realistic about the fact that there would forever be a scar, however large or small. He thought of her on occasion and hoped she would find her own happiness.

He smiled when he thought of how professional Catherine was in the tiny Birdie courthouse. The Birdie Gazette had publicized her first court case as if Clarence Darrow himself had returned to the small town. She was having a ball with being herself and finally returning to a way of life she'd longed for in a community that loved her.

Jason pulled through the main gate and immediately headed to what was now referred to as "The Camp" or more correctly "Scout's Rest Camp," named after Buffalo Bill's ranch that had served as his safe haven. And in homage to the family, this too would be a safe, happy place for ill children and their families to come and rest. Jason planned to keep his "day job" at least for the foreseeable future, but this place was tangible proof of his dream finally coming true.

"Well, hey there, 'James Herriot.' I didn't think you were ever showing up." Catherine jumped down from the construction trailer and walked toward him.

"How was your day in court, 'Judge Judy'?" he bantered back, grabbing her waist and pulling her close. He turned and looked around at the amount of work that had been done since his visit earlier. "They are really getting this together quickly."

"Your father doesn't mess around when it comes to building; he's about the only person I've found that can keep up with Daddy. What do you think about those families whose applications I emailed you? Are we ready to open this place and really do this?"

Jason smiled and kissed her forehead. "Absolutely; that is, if you are? This whole thing's a dream; I still can't believe it's really happening."

"Well, even in a little hick town like Birdie, dreams can come true...." She stepped back and jingled her car keys in her hand. "We'd better get to dinner or Daddy is going to start his story telling, and I don't want your parents to have to endure that."

Jason followed her back to the house, lost in thought about how amazing his time in Birdie was turning out, after its disastrous beginnings. He didn't have any regrets about California. Tommy was still Tommy, hoping Jason would change his mind one of these days, and occasionally texting him a photo of a scantily clad female on the beach.

A few weeks later, four large vans pulled in through the main gates and headed toward The Camp as Jason stood hand-in-hand with Catherine to welcome the first families. His stomach tossed and turned and he still wondered how all of this was even possible.

"Don't be nervous," Catherine whispered in his ear, squeezing his hand.

"Can't help it." He turned and smiled. "I really hope this works...."

She turned and kissed his cheek. "It already has."

About the Author

Growing up, Dr. Suit enjoyed countless back country trails on horseback throughout Arizona with his father and brother. Upon graduation from Arizona State University with a Bachelors of Science in Outdoor Recreation and Tourism, Dr. Suit worked on dude ranches in both Arizona and Colorado prior to entry in to the veterinary program at Colorado State University. Dr. enjoys combining his love of the outdoors and back country with equine veterinary practice. He is in equine private practice in Loveland, Colorado, but cares for clients and their horses throughout Fort Collins, Estes Park, and the Northern Front Range of Colorado.

Dr. Suit is an equine veterinarian in Loveland, Colorado. He graduated from Arizona State University with a Bachelor's of Science in Outdoor Recreation and Tourism. Upon graduation he worked on dude ranches in both Arizona and Colorado prior to entry into the veterinary program at Colorado State University in Fort Collins. He and his beautiful wife, Kyla, keep very busy raising three incredibly talented children.

29

Made in the USA
San Bernardino, CA
22 April 2016